GONE FOR GOOD

Also by Joanna Schaffhausen:

The Vanishing Season

No Mercy

All the Best Lies

GONE FOR GOOD

Joanna Schaffhausen

MINOTAUR BOOKS
NEW YORK

First published in the United States by Minotaur Books, an imprint of St. Martin's Publishing Group

www.minotaurbooks.com

Designed by Gabriel Guma

The Library of Congress Cataloging-in-Publication Data is available upon request.

ISBN 978-1-250-26460-2 (hardcover)

ISBN 978-1-250-26461-9 (ebook)

Our books may be purchased in bulk for promotional, educational, or business use. Please contact your local bookseller or the Macmillan Corporate and Premium Sales Department at 1-800-221-7945, extension 5442, or by email at MacmillanSpecialMarkets@macmillan.com.

First Edition: 2021

10 9 8 7 6 5 4 3 2 1

For Ethan

It is a universal invariant that every writer starts out terrible. You need that one person who looks past the awful prose and clunky dialogue and sees the story to root you onward. For me, that one person was Ethan Cusick. His early enthusiasm for my teenage ramblings is the reason this book exists, and his optimistic, generous spirit remains a force for good.

GONE FOR GOOD

PROLOGUE

....

GRACE NOTES

Journal Entry #441

Do you remember the moment you realized you were going to die? I was five years old, lying in my princess bed with its canopy and pink dust ruffles. My mother had sent me there after I put her expensive brassiere on Louie, our beagle. I might've gotten away with it, but I also used the Polaroid camera to take a picture of him and showed it to our mailman. "You think I'm the butt of all your jokes," Mama hollered at me. "You'll be sorry one day when I'm gone."

I already knew about dead people since Mama's mother died of a heart attack when I was three. I understood she'd been on earth walking around like the rest of us, and then poof, she died and wasn't coming back. I hadn't considered it would happen to Mama and Daddy—or that if it happened to them, it would happen one day to me, too. I remember holding out my fleshy little hand and staring at it until my vision blurred. I was going to die. Worms would eat me. I imagined my skin melting away until I thought I could see my skeleton poking out underneath. I screamed so loud that Mama came running, and after that, I slept in her and Daddy's bed for a week.

The truth is, I still look at my hand when I lie in bed at night and contemplate my death. I think the rest of us Grave Diggers have similarly morbid fascinations, whether they'd admit to it or not. We take on dead cases, gone cold so long that most others have forgotten about them or given up. We tell ourselves that we're chasing other people's deaths. We solve a case, and we feel like we got a win over the ultimate Man in Black. Maybe, though, we wonder who will be there to remember us when our time comes.

....

I'm writing this in front of a wall full of dead women. They were different in life—unique hairstyles, varying skin colors, different kinds of jobs—but they all look the same now. They are dead on the floor of their own homes, tied up like Christmas chickens. The intricate interlacing of the rope and knots reminds me of *shibari* or *kinbaku,* the Japanese ritual binding that can be a form of torture or erotic pleasure, depending on how you employ it. The man who bound these seven women surely meant to torture them. The police reports on their deaths emphasize that he suffocated them slowly, loosening the ties periodically to revive them before choking the life out of them completely.

Their eyes are all closed in the crime scene photographs. I presume that's how they were found. I believe they shut their lids against the horror of what was happening to them, and also to deny him the pleasure of watching the light go out from their eyes. I've read up enough on his kind by now to know that they seek out that moment of transition. A beating heart and racing pulse, the shuddering breath that dies in the chest—these guys get off on that moment. So, I understand why the women closed their eyes while he stood over them, tightening the ropes. But when I look at their pictures, I wish I could see what they saw. They are the only ones who know his true face.

He's older now, like the rest of us. He went underground twenty-one years ago after Victim Number Seven, which likely makes him anywhere between forty and sixty-five years of age. Many experts say he must be dead, but not me. I've been walking the streets he walked, looking in the same windows. Sometimes I think I catch a glimpse of his reflection in the glass, at least what I imagine he must look like. I bet he's got the same wall of photographs that I have, but his are kept private where no one else can see. His newspaper clippings must be yellowed and fragile, so old that they look like ancient history. He surely believes he got away with it. But I've checked the weather reports for all seven murders, and now I know where to find him.

I've been working on this case for months, writing up all my notes, recording conversations, visiting the crime scenes. Last week, I went on TV and practically dared him to come after me. I lay awake all night afterward, thinking every creak on the stairs could be him. Those other women never saw him coming. When the storm rolled in off the lake and cut our power for five hours, I took a kitchen knife and hid in my bathtub with it. But it was then I realized how to get him, and so I can't chicken out now.

People are going to think I'm doing this for the glory or the credit, and I'll admit a nice, fat book deal would be sweet, but mostly, I'm thinking about that moment when he gets the cuffs slapped on him and dragged out in front of everyone. I want him to see it was me who found him. Me, an ordinary woman living in Belmont Cragin, working at a grocery store. Just the kind of woman he killed and presumed he'd get away with it forever. Because right now, he's a faceless spook, a ghost story, and the women he killed get known only by the way he murdered them. You can google them to see it's true. No one remembers that Shauna Atkins played Maria her senior year in *West Side Story,* or that Lauren Gardner wanted to be a foster mom. They are permanent victims now, the way he made them. So, I'm chasing him because they can't. Because maybe when he gets his life taken away, they can get a little bit of theirs back.

I get shivers when I think about it. Literal goose bumps on my arms. He's going to feel so small, so helpless and powerless. I imagine his perp walk in front of the cameras and I can almost see his fa—

CHAPTER ONE

············

D ETECTIVE ANNALISA VEGA HAD SWORN OFF DATING WHEN THE THIRD GUY IN A ROW ENDED THE EVENING BY ASKING TO SEE HER HANDCUFFS. Or maybe her stomach had turned during the last homicide she'd worked, in which the ex-husband blew out a glass door with a double-barreled shotgun, hunted down his terrified wife, and executed her as she cowered next to the bed they'd once slept in together. Hard to make upbeat chitchat over apps and cosmos after viewing the remains of a relationship like that.

This guy is different, Sassy had assured her when she'd arranged the setup. *I know him from church, which he attends with his mother. But don't worry—he doesn't live with her.* Lured out from her reclusive lair by this ringing endorsement, Annalisa now regarded her date across the narrow two-person table and tried again to sell herself on his numerous good points. Todd Weatherby, tax attorney, had a full head of dark hair, nice teeth, no food on his tie, and he'd selected a lovely Wicker Park restaurant for their first date. Italian, with cloth napkins and a real candle flickering on the table. Her mother would be over the moon for him.

Annalisa wasn't sure if this last point was for or against Todd Weatherby. Her mother, who had been positively apoplectic when Annalisa had up and married a cop at the tender age of twenty-one, now reminded her constantly that "the clock is ticking" since she had turned thirty.

"Annalisa is a pretty name," Todd said gamely. "Is it Spanish?"

"Portuguese." Her great-grandfather's grandfather had emigrated to New Bedford in Massachusetts in the mid-1800s when the city boomed thanks to a thriving whaling industry. Family lore said Great Grandpapa Vega had once worked alongside Herman Melville, but Annalisa suspected this was just a fish story. Whatever the case, her own great-grandfather had jumped ship and moved west to Chicago to cash in on the surge of construction after the Great Fire. The Vegas hadn't budged in the hundred years since, living and dying within the city limits like the place had a wall around its borders.

"Todd is a nice name," she offered. "Is it, um . . . English?"

"Maybe? I'm named after my uncle. He runs a button-manufacturing plant in New Jersey. Did you know buttons date back to almost 3000 BC? Their earliest known use was in Indonesia, back when they were made from shells. But later . . ."

She repressed a yawn and drifted away inside her head. Maybe next time she could ask Sassy to recommend a good movie or a talented masseuse. *I should just accept my destiny and adopt a cat,* she thought. *Or maybe two.* They could keep each other company while she was at work. Todd was still talking, and she forced herself to focus on his words. He had his wine glass in the air as if to make a toast. Obligingly, she lifted hers as well. "To us," he said. "We are fated to be together always."

"Uh . . . what?" She held her glass back.

"Us," he repeated, looking chagrined as he motioned between them. "You know—death and taxes. We're inescapable!" He grinned at his own joke about their respective careers, and her smile became frozen in place. "Get it?" he prodded.

"Oh, I got it."

He cleared his throat. "Are you interested in the dessert menu?"

Decision time. Ticktock. He looked at her with hopeful eyes. She knew she could do a lot worse, but she didn't want a lackluster relationship just to say she had one. She wanted her parents' marriage, soul mates for forty-four years and counting. George and Maria still held hands under the dinner table. Meanwhile, Annalisa went on these going-nowhere dates, making talk so small she needed a microscope to parse it. Her ideal dessert at this point was a pint of Ben & Jerry's, alone, curled up on her couch with a Netflix backlog. "I—" In her purse, her work phone started to chirp, and she pulled it out for a look. Dispatch had sent a text asking her to call in, Code 10-54. *A body.* "Oh," she said with what she hoped sounded like regret, "I'm sorry, I've got to go. It's work."

"Work? Even at this hour?"

She was already gathering her things. "Homicide doesn't punch a time card," she declared, maybe too cheerfully.

Todd deflated in his chair, unable to argue with this truism. "Death," he said glumly, taking up his glass again. "It's inescapable."

....

Annalisa phoned in from her nondescript gray Civic, ready to point it wherever the dispatch captain directed her. He gave her an address in Belmont Cragin, which would be a relatively straight shot west, only about five and a half miles, but with city traffic it would take her close to half an hour. "Okay, I'm rolling," she said as she started the engine.

"Be advised it's Code 3."

"Code 3?" She never had to run the lights and sirens since making detective. The victims were always dead and getting colder by the time she arrived. Ten minutes either way didn't make a difference.

"Patrol is wigged. I guess it's a bad one."

She flipped on her light and mentally adjusted the drive time down to fifteen minutes. The trip down North Ave was pure Chicago—a wide boulevard flanked by a crowded mix of residential and commercial buildings. They passed in a blur tonight as she wove in and around slower traffic. What the hell could have the responding units so spooked they asked for a Code 3? Even your average beat cop had seen an eyeful after one year on the job.

She reached Belmont Cragin and slowed her pace as she cut over into the residential territory. Originally founded in the 1800s by a single saloon, the neighborhood principally housed the men and women who worked at the myriad businesses built up in Belmont Central. Violent crime was relatively unusual. Annalisa didn't get many calls here, period, let alone anything that required a Code 3. She knew she'd hit the right street when she saw the swirling lights of four separate black-and-white units. Curious neighboring residents had turned on their lights and emerged from their homes, flocking in the street such that Annalisa had to slow down and nudge her car through the crowd. "It's the friggin' event of the season here," she muttered as she gave up finding a parking space and abandoned her vehicle next to an older Chevy Lumina with three parking tickets on the windshield.

She frowned when she saw two uniformed officers come out of the front door, talking animatedly to one another as they jogged down the steps. A third guy headed inside as they came out—high traffic at what should be a protected scene. Aware she was arriving in a pencil skirt, a tight, arterial blood-red top, and stacked heels, Annalisa paused to shrug into a Chicago PD windbreaker despite the mild May temperature outside. She took a pair of gloves and booties from the boxes on her passenger seat and went to find the responding officer who'd called it in. He stood at the edge of the walkway near the neatly trimmed bushes, looking just as green. She noted a fine sheen of perspiration on his upper lip.

"You're the RO?" she asked.

"Yes, ma'am. Marc Reyes. I responded to a call asking for a welfare check at this address. The female resident—a woman by the name of Grace Harper—had not been reachable for several days and missed her most recent shift at work. I arrived at twenty twenty-five and found the front door locked. I went around to the back and saw the door to the kitchen had a panel smashed out of the window. I was able to reach in to open the door and immediately I smelled a strong odor of decomp inside the house. I followed the scent upstairs and found the female victim nonresponsive on her bedroom floor." He checked her reaction. "Obviously deceased. That's when I called it in."

"And then who else did you call?" she asked as she snapped on the gloves.

"Ma'am?"

She nodded toward the house. "You could be selling tickets out here, Reyes. There's unis crawling all over the scene, and as a result, the gawkers are lined up like we're putting on a World Series parade."

He had the grace to look embarrassed. "The DB, she's . . . well, a wild one. Freaky. I've never seen anything like it before. That's some real sick shit in there—if you'll pardon my language. I guess I got kinda shook up about it, being out here alone with her. I called my buddy Dickerson, and then he called his boys. . . ." He trailed off, apparently aware how weak the excuses sounded. "They know not to touch anything."

She could already see they weren't wearing protective booties. God only knew what they'd trailed in and out of the house. "I don't care if they have an edict from the pope. They're getting the hell out of my crime scene. No one except the ME goes in or out from now on, you hear me?"

His gaze slid over her shoulder. "Even him?"

"Hey, Vega, wait up," called a familiar male voice. She closed her eyes in resignation but did not turn around. The grape vine had told her that her ex-husband was back in town, back on the job, and now literally on her back as he braced himself on her shoulder to slip a bootie over his shoe.

"Carelli." Making Nick Carelli's acquaintance again over a dead body seemed like a fitting metaphor. Her commander, Zimmer, had asked her when Nick transferred back from Florida if Annalisa would have a problem working with him. Annalisa was the greenest detective on the squad, the newbie. Nick had almost ten years under his belt. She knew if she blinked which one of them Zimmer would choose to keep. *The split was amicable,* she had said to Zimmer. *It's ancient history.* This last part was true enough. She and Nick had married when she was twenty-one and divorced before she turned twenty-three in a union that was, in hindsight, dead on arrival.

Her ex-husband leaned heavily on her shoulder as he slipped a bootie over the second expensive leather shoe. He still had a full head of dark hair, she noted with clinical detachment, and that same damn twinkle in his eye.

"Dispatch called you, too?" she asked him.

"I was already in the neighborhood."

"Sure. There's a high school down that way, and it is prom season. I suppose her parents wanted her home by curfew, hmm?"

He flashed a smile, genuinely amused as they started up the walkway. "Hey, what happened? The last I heard, you wanted to be a lawyer."

The legal bills on top of regular bills meant it had taken her seven years to complete a typical four-year college degree, and by the time she'd finished, the last place she'd wanted to go was law school. She spent two years temping in offices, bored out of her mind. A recruitment poster on the L one day showed a pair of proud uniformed cops, one male, one female. It read: *Protection. Honor. Compassion. These are our family values.* Annalisa cared about keeping the city safe, but it was the word *family* that got her to call the number on the poster.

"Yeah?" she said to Nick. "The last I heard, you'd moved back to Florida." Her brothers liked to think they'd chased him out of town, his tail between his legs.

"What can I say? I missed the hot dogs."

"You couldn't have found work in another district?"

"Maybe I missed you, too."

She rolled her eyes. "You didn't miss me much when we were married, Carelli. It's a little late to start now."

He held open the gate for her and eyed her cleavage as she walked past. "I see I wasn't the only one out on the town this evening."

She yanked her windbreaker closed. "Let's try to focus on work right now, shall we?"

"You're the one who brought up dating." He extended a gallant arm toward the front steps. "After you."

She climbed ahead of him and stopped on the small front porch to survey the scene while Nick poked his head inside. "Party's over, fellas," he hollered. "Everyone out. Now." Three more uniformed officers, two male and one female, trailed out like naughty schoolchildren. Annalisa noted the stoop was well-kept, free of the dirt, sand, and salt that tended to accumulate over a Chicago winter. Grace Harper's place had flower boxes filled with pansies and a decorative star affixed to the siding. Annalisa touched it with one gloved finger before following Nick inside the house.

She coughed when the smell hit her.

"Yeah, she's a ripe one," said Nick, making a disgusted face from his place by the windows in the front room. He inspected them for signs of tampering.

Annalisa looked around at the sparse but tasteful decor—warm beige walls, a couple of framed prints that you could find at any big-box store. The fireplace contained an iron candelabra with large white candles in it that appeared to have never been lit. The overstuffed pillows on the sofa were plump and precisely placed, no dents. Annalisa ran a finger along the top of the mantel and her glove came away clean.

"The body must be upstairs," Nick said, heading for the staircase.

She nodded, not keen to follow him. The woman who had kept a house this pristine would be humiliated to find herself decaying on the floor, her fluids leaking everywhere. Annalisa went to the back of the house, to the kitchen, where she found the broken window pane that Reyes had mentioned. Glass shards lay all over the floor but the room was otherwise undisturbed. No dishes in the sink. No photos on the fridge. Annalisa sometimes used an imagined crime scene as motivation to tidy her own apartment. *Anyone investigating your murder would think your place had been ransacked for heroin,* she'd tell herself as she forced herself to put away the pile of laundry on her bed and pick up the landslide of junk mail from her kitchen floor. Looking around now, she realized it hardly mattered. Dead was dead, no matter how clean your house was. She was careful to hug the walls in case the forensics team could find footprints on Grace Harper's otherwise squeaky-clean floor. Resigned for what lay ahead, Annalisa went to the stairs.

Nick appeared like a prowler from the shadowed hallway at the top of the staircase. "Jesus." She grabbed her chest and stepped backward. "You scared the crap out of me."

"You've got to see this," he replied, a fevered glint in his eye. She followed him down the narrow hall to the bedroom, their feet creaking the warped wooden floor. For once, she was happy to have him take the lead. The bedroom door was old like the rest of the house, continually falling closed, and Nick pushed it open with the flat of his hand.

Annalisa halted the instant she saw the body. The female victim, presumably Grace Harper, was an average-sized Caucasian female with a tangle of dark hair. She lay nude and facedown, her hands bound behind her back and yoked to her feet and neck in a complicated series of slip knots. Her pale flesh was discolored around the neck, and the ligature around her throat suggested this was the cause of death. Annalisa breathed through her mouth and tried to ignore the creeping dread winding its way up her spine like a summer vine.

"It gets weirder," Nick told her grimly.

She nodded to show she'd heard him, but she was unable to stop staring at the body. He had to tug her elbow to get her to move. They walked next door to another room, this one set up as an office. She could see a desk and chair. Nick walked into the room and turned so he faced the wall abutted by the desk, so Annalisa mirrored his posture. "Oh, my God," she breathed when she saw the wall of photos. Dead women, all of them strangled by ropes. The one in the center could have been taken from the room next door. It showed a dark-haired woman facedown, her hands and feet bound together. The only difference was the red scarf around her neck. Annalisa gulped in air and stared wide-eyed at the picture, come to life right out of her dreams. Twenty years dissolved around her. She felt dizzy, sick.

"It's like a murder shrine," Nick breathed in fasciation. "And some-one went to a lot of trouble to stage a rerun. Look at that one—it's the same number of knots, same position of the body."

"He's back." Annalisa swallowed twice in quick succession to bring back her voice. "We're going to have to tell her son."

"Her son? I thought the vic lived here alone."

She reached out and stroked the picture of the other dead woman. It took all her power not to rip the photo down and hold it to her chest. "Not Grace Harper's son. Hers."

CHAPTER TWO

....

H ER SON?" NICK ASKED AS ANNALISA STROKED THE PHOTO OF THE OTHER VICTIM. "You know that woman?"

There was a time when she couldn't have imagined a future without Katie Duffy in it. Now her corpse was tacked up on a dead woman's wall—a dead woman who could have been her twin sister, from the looks of it.

"I knew her, yes. Her son Colin and I, we . . . we went to school together." It was the barest truth she could tell. She'd been careful to keep Colin a secret from Nick during their brief marriage. She'd kept Colin from everyone. In her memories, he was always hers.

"This is some supremely freaky shit," Nick said, rolling his shoulders like he couldn't get loose. "We find our victim dead on her bedroom floor, tied up like a Christmas roast, and she's got pictures hanging up like she was alive to take photos of the event. It's like she was working her own murder."

"In a way, maybe she was." Annalisa's gaze roamed over the wall.

"What are you talking about?"

"You're saying you don't recognize this?" She regarded him with surprise. "This whole wall is covered in information from the Lovelorn Killer case. Katherine Duffy was the last known victim." She pointed at another picture at the top right that showed a similarly macabre corpse, bound in intricate fashion and laid out on the floor. "That one looks like Lisa Sheffield. And there's Denise Marklund." Grace Harper had tacked up all seven victims, along with a map showing the locations of the crimes and a police artist's sketch of the possible suspect—a non-descript white man with a broad forehead and thin mouth. The picture had circulated for years without generating a single lead. The killer, if it was even him, wouldn't resemble the sketch anymore.

"Oh, right, yeah. The Lovelorn Killer. I remember that guy. He's the one who wrote letters to the papers afterward about how much he loved his victims. He was so sorry he had to kill them." He scanned the row of victims. "What a crock."

She looked at him, confused by his detachment. Then she remembered he was a first-generation cop who had been born in Jacksonville, Florida. He hadn't grown up with this case in his house, an unwanted guest who moved in one night and then stayed for twenty years. Annalisa's father was on the job for thirty years, and he once had a room just like this. She felt a fresh pang at the thought of Pops. She would have to tell him, too. "He killed seven women over a period of a few years in the late '90s. Then he dropped out of sight around Y2K. He murdered Katie Duffy on Halloween night and then nothing since. I think most people thought he was dead or locked up somewhere."

Nick glanced back toward the other room. "Yeah? Well, it looks like he got hungry again. Either that, or he's got a gifted understudy. You realize this is a goddamn powder keg we're sitting on, right? The whole city's going to go boom." He rubbed his hands together, maybe nervous, maybe excited by the prospect. Annalisa flinched. She had been caught in the explosion once before, her whole world imploded. Katie's murder had been horrible on its own, never mind everything that had followed. Annalisa had known that her father worked on murder cases sometimes, but she had not understood then how one death could blow a hole through an entire neighborhood.

They went back to survey Grace Harper, careful not to get too close before the scene could be processed and documented. Annalisa saw the same meticulous character in the bedroom that she'd noted downstairs: a brass bed, neatly made, one nightstand that had a lamp, a clock radio, and a single mystery novel bookmarked halfway through, all precisely placed with no traces of dust. She drifted to the dresser, which displayed a series of different silver music boxes. All of them sat open but noiseless, like a row of clams gaping for a feed. Annalisa's skin felt tight and itchy, looking at them. "He opened all these music boxes," she murmured to Nick. "I think he made her listen to them while he was strangling her." There was no way a woman as persnickety as Grace Harper would leave her collection sitting open like that.

She turned and saw Nick crouching by the bed. "I think he must've sat here to do it. See how there's a slight dent in the bedspread? And that rope looks like it probably stretches six feet or so. He sat back in comfort to watch her struggling on the floor." Nick rose and looked to the door. "Where the hell is the medical examiner already? We need to get the scene processed now. This guy has at least a couple of days' lead on us already."

"The ME's office is running late. What else is new?" Bogged down by short staffing and an upsurge in opioid-related deaths in addition to the ubiquitous South- and West-Side gang violence, the Cook County Medical Examiner faced a large backlog of investigations, many of which were incomplete. Annalisa looked again at Grace Harper and the ligature marks all over her body. She suspected Grace would jump the line once the ME got a look at her.

She moved to check the bedroom window. There was a fire escape outside, but the window looked locked and undisturbed. The tidy bed said their victim hadn't been surprised in her sleep, but the extended torture suggested the killer knew he could be alone with Grace Harper for many hours without being interrupted.

"No photos on display, only one bedroom in the place. Seems like our vic was pretty isolated." He picked up the novel, opened it, and put it back down. "You said that other woman had a son?"

Colin. He'd been the sun in Annalisa's sky once, the first boy to notice she was a girl in a family full of brothers. They'd been inseparable her whole junior year, right up until his mother died. She remembered him on the day of Katie's funeral, sitting on a ratty lawn chair on the front porch and watching the rain gush down from the overflowing gutters. No delicate teardrop mist for Katie Duffy. It was an ugly rain, like someone took a hunting knife to the belly of a cloud. The rest of the mourners had crowded into the house, the street jammed with cars, many of them black-and-whites. Katie had been a cop's wife once, her husband, Owen, partnered up with Pops, and her death brought out the whole family.

Annalisa's eyes had been raw from crying that day, but Colin had stared straight ahead, no emotion evident on his face. His pale wrists and ankles had poked out from his dark suit. "I brought you a coffee." She'd held out a paper cup that was steaming in the cold November air.

"I don't want coffee."

Inside the crowded house, the adults drank it by the potful, like it had magically restorative powers. She'd tried some for herself and it was dark and bitter, sour on her tongue. She'd drank it down anyway and felt it bubbling, lavalike, in the pit of her stomach. "I'm so sorry about your mom." She'd wanted him to hold out his arms like he usually did, inviting her into his lap, but he didn't even look at her.

"I don't like all this rain on her."

Back at the cemetery, Annalisa's heels had sunk into the soft earth, and she had a flash of terror that she would slip all the way down to the coffins underground. Later she'd scrubbed the dirt off in the bathroom sink, sobbing as she'd washed away the dark smears of mud that once were human flesh. "It'll stop soon," she told him on the porch. "Rain this bad, it doesn't last long. We could go inside. To your room." They'd had many stolen moments in his twin bed, frantic couplings under an open window while their families laughed outside at a backyard barbecue.

"You think I want that now?" His hands had balled into fists so tight that she'd taken a step back. "You think I want her looking down and seeing that, today?"

She'd wanted to go somewhere, anywhere with him. Alone, they could talk freely. He would see how devastated she was. She'd known Katie her whole life, grown up eating snacks in her kitchen and turning cartwheels in her backyard. Katie had taught her how to paint her nails without the polish getting everywhere and taken the blame when Annalisa's bike got stolen from the front yard. Before the murder, the worst thing she could've imagined was making Katie or one of the other parents angry with her, especially Pops. Annalisa's father was a man's cop, big and strong, always cautioning his kids about the dangers out there, and that's exactly how it had felt to Annalisa—the danger was out there, someplace amorphous and far away from their tree-lined blocks. The muggings and beatings and killings were part of some comic book world her father played in before coming back home to them. Not anymore. The entire police force had crowded in the shingled house, bringing their fear with them. They spoke among themselves in low, tense voices and hushed whispers. Annalisa didn't have to hear their conversations to realize they had no answers.

"Colin Duffy moved away after she died," she told Nick, shaking off the memory. "Never came home again." Years of tamped-down anger kept the bitterness from her voice.

Nick looked pointedly at the corpse on the floor. "Would you?"

Reyes's voice called up to them from the front door. "Detectives? I've got a woman out here who says she's a friend of the victim. Says she's the one who called it in. You want to talk to her?"

Annalisa and Nick regarded each other in a silent standoff. The initial witness statement on a case like this was a big get, a major "in" on a case that would probably get taken away from them when the chief of Ds saw what was at stake. "It's a woman?" Nick said, looking Annalisa up and down grudgingly. "You should take it. I'll stay with this one."

Annalisa let out the breath she'd been holding and headed for the stairs. Technically, Nick outranked her, but he'd never been one to play power games. The night they'd met at the bar, he'd lent her his leather jacket in the fickle October air with no expectations of what she'd do for him in return. She went outside the Harper house and saw the crowd had thickened to three rows deep, and two news vans had arrived on the scene. Still no coroner. Setting her jaw, Annalisa sought out Reyes and asked him to point to their witness. He indicated a zaftig woman with red hair and mascara runs on her face. She was clutching the hand of a tall bearded man standing next to her. "That's her. Gives her name as Molly Lipinski."

Annalisa crossed over to where the woman stood by the yellow tape. "Ms. Lipinski?"

"Yes." Molly dabbed at her face with a fistful of tissues.

"I'm Detective Annalisa Vega. I understand you're the one who made the initial 911 call to this address?"

"That's right. I hadn't heard from Grace in two days, and that's just not like her. When I called over at the Foodsmart, they said she hadn't shown up for work yesterday, and that's when I knew something bad must've happened. Grace hasn't missed a day of work in eight years."

"I see. Do you mind if we talk over here?" Annalisa saw the bright lights of the roving reporter coming toward them.

"Is she— Is she okay?" Hope quavered in her voice.

"Please come this way." Annalisa held up the tape so Molly could walk under it. The man with her tried to follow. "I'm sorry, you are?"

"Travis Hefner."

"Travis is my boyfriend. We were supposed to go out to the movies tonight, but I just couldn't stop thinking about Grace. No one got back to me after I made that 911 call. So Travis drove me over here to check on her, and that's when we found all this."

Annalisa nodded. She couldn't imagine the boyfriend would be of any value, but she let him follow them to the side of the house, out of sight behind some parked cars and an overgrown hedge. "When was the last time you spoke to Grace?"

"Wednesday night. We chatted online." Molly was tearing up again. "Please, tell me what happened to her."

"We're not entirely sure yet," Annalisa replied gently. "How do you know Grace Harper?"

"We met online in the Grave Diggers group, but we're real-person friends too. We'd go to dinner and coffee and stuff like that."

"The Grave Diggers group?"

"We're like . . . amateur sleuths, I guess you could call it. Just a bunch of people interested in old crimes that haven't been solved. We chat online and go over the clues and try to find new leads. Our group got some attention a couple of years ago when we helped find that boy's body down in North Carolina. The one who got taken by the school janitor?"

Annalisa made some notes about this, but she felt they were getting off track. "Does Ms. Harper have a law enforcement background?"

Molly let out a laugh through her tears. "Gracie? Oh, no, she is an assistant manager over at the Foodsmart. She just grew up watching a lot of *Law & Order, Forensic Files,* kind of like all of us. We're just nosy, you know? We like to ask questions. You read about these unsolved cases and it's like a loose thread dangling in front of you. You can't help but start pulling on it."

"What thread were you all tugging on lately?"

Travis made a noise in the back of his throat that sounded like disapproval. Molly shot him a warning look. "We're working on more than a dozen cases as always. But Grace wanted to tackle the Lovelorn Killer investigation. Do you know it?"

A frisson went through Annalisa but she kept her voice steady. "I've heard of it."

"The cops have been saying he's probably dead or in prison somewhere, but we thought maybe he went underground because he almost got caught."

Annalisa dropped her pen from the notebook and peered hard into Molly's tearstained face. "What makes you think that?"

She swallowed visibly. "Well, Katherine Duffy's murder—she was the last victim, you know. Number seven? Her death always seemed odd compared to the others. The other women's husbands or partners were away at the time of their attacks, but Owen Duffy was right down the street when Katie got killed. She'd been out at a Halloween party and came home early because she'd started feeling sick. The killer would've had to have been waiting there for her—like, hanging out in her bushes, right?" She gave a small shudder and shot a look at the nearby hedge. Travis started rubbing her shoulders.

"So, he waited for her," Annalisa replied. "Why did this matter?" As far as Annalisa knew, this was part of the Killer's established pattern, to stalk his victims before murdering them. The letters he sent to the press after their deaths showed he knew them intimately.

"How did he know she'd be home by herself? Maybe he was watching the house and saw the opportunity, I don't know. But Katherine's husband, Owen, came home from the party to check on her just an hour or so after she'd left. What if the killer heard the car pull up and had to run out of there? A close call like that, especially with a cop, it might have spooked him. That's why he quit."

"Sure, maybe."

"We got to talking about what kind of guy he probably was."

"Who is 'we'?"

"The Grave Diggers," Molly said with a trace of impatience. "The local ones meet for dinner once a month to talk about cases and chat online in between. Let's see, there's me, Grace, Barnes, Oliver Benton. Oh, and Travis tags along too, sometimes, but he mostly just plays games on his phone because he thinks we're nuts."

"Have you seen the pictures of this guy's victims?" Travis interjected. "They're completely hinky."

Molly laid a hand on his arm to shush him. "Anyway, Grace has a theory about the killer. She thought wherever he was, he was probably stewing about not getting attention. 'Cause the killings were only part of his deal. He wrote those letters to the press afterward. He knew the victims' addresses, right? He could've mailed the letters personally, but that wasn't the point. He wanted everyone to see them."

This struck Annalisa as a decent insight. "Sure, he wanted the press to put them on TV and in the papers."

"Right. But when he had to stop killing, the headlines went away. No more Mr. Big Shot Killer on the front page every week. So, Gracie thought—why not give him what he's craving? Make him feel important again. She called up all the papers and TV stations and pitched them the idea, how they could do a piece on our group and how we're still hunting him. Her idea was that maybe he'd see the story and make contact with the press again."

"I see. Did anyone do a story?"

Molly cast an anxious glance to the house, where the ME was at last making his way up the front walk. "Channel Seven did a feature last week. Gracie got interviewed and told them all about the Grave Diggers. She even said she had a new theory she was working on about the killer, one the cops hadn't explored."

"What was that?"

"She didn't tell me. She said she wanted to do some more research, and she would share it at our next dinner. Why? Did she figure something out? Is that why you're all here? Please tell me what's going on."

Annalisa couldn't give the woman any answers, not yet. They didn't even have an official ruling of death from the ME. But she couldn't send

Molly off without a strong word of caution. "We're going to ask you to sit tight for a little bit while we gather more information. In the meantime, I strongly suggest that you and your friends refrain from saying anything online or to the press about the Lovelorn Killer."

Molly sniffed hard. "You think Grace was right. That he could find out what we're doing and make contact."

"Ms. Lipinski, this man operates with a bunch of ropes. If you've looked at the pictures, you know what he does with them. Trust me when I tell you he's not someone you want to make contact with."

She thought of Grace Harper on the bedroom floor, her eyes shut and her mouth gasping for air that would never come. *We liked to imagine what kind of guy he was,* Molly had said. Grace now knew the answer. Maybe that's why he'd come back, to show off for one of his greatest admirers. How he must have puffed up to see her wall of devotion to him.

You wanted me so bad?

Here I am.

CHAPTER THREE

....

GRACE NOTES

Journal Entry #417

THE FIRST TIME I NOTICED THE LOVELORN KILLER WAS THE DAY HE DISAP-
PEARED. No one knew at the time that Katherine Duffy would be his
last victim. The newspapers—they were still a thing back then—they
ran a picture of her alongside the other women that he killed, and I
couldn't stop staring at their faces. They were everywhere. They watched
us while riding the L. They looked out from the glass pane of metal
newsstands. They sat on my mother's round kitchen table next to her
tea and peanut buttered toast. I was twenty-one back then, but when I
saw these women, I felt they could be me. Average looks. Shoulder-length
dark hair, parted in the middle. Living in ordinary homes in nice neighborhoods.

I went to the library and started reading everything I could about
them, including the letters he sent them after their deaths. The lovelorn letter for Josephine had arrived at the *Sun-Times* before anyone
found her body, so it took another year and a second woman's death
for anyone to connect the letter with Josephine's murder. The intern
who found it had showed it to her boss who'd told her to get rid of it,
but she'd stuck it in a drawer and kept it anyway. When the second one
came in the following year, for Denise Marklund, the *Sun-Times* turned
both of them over to the police. Of course, they also ran them. You can
read the text online now and see pictures of the actual letters. They're
hand-printed in nondescript black ink on ordinary white paper, not

fancy stationery. If written to a woman by her lover, it would be sweet. Instead, they showed how long the killer stalked the women before he strangled them to death. He knew where they worked, the color car they drove, and whether they had curtains on their windows. These ladies walked around with an invisible noose around their necks for days, maybe weeks, and never even knew it. This guy was thorough. Check out the letter he wrote to Denise Marklund:

> My dearest one,
>
> When I woke this morning, I thought immediately of you and wished I could turn to see you lying there, your legs drawn up, arms folded protectively over your chest. Your messy hair spreads over your cheek, wild and free, not like the severe ponytail you wear for the rest of the world. The first time I saw you, I noticed your adorable habit of tucking that stray bit of hair behind your left ear—that one curl that refuses to behave, no matter how buttoned-up you are. If we were together now, I'd undo those buttons with my teeth, let your hair go wild across the pillow.
>
> I was hesitant at first to make a move. You smiled at me that day, but then I've seen you smile at everyone. So I waited and observed you. I saw how you looked up, expectant, when someone new came in. I knew then you were waiting for the sign, for someone to set you free from that clunky computer and plastic nametag. You changed your hair—oh, those new red highlights!—and you put on that gold nail polish. It's like you knew I keep a gold coin in my pocket at all times, just for luck.
>
> We are lucky, my darling, to have found each other. We are kismet. We are destiny. We are stars who orbit each other, visible only as distant light to those on earth.
>
> —Mr. Lovelorn

I read all the letters. I read the news stories and the false leads and the mounting frustration as the killer took one victim, then another, then another, and the police could do nothing to stop him. But then a curious thing happened—the Lovelorn Killer stopped himself. He murdered Katherine Duffy on Halloween night and subsequently vanished into the ether. Law enforcement says he's probably locked up for some other crime, and they just don't know it's him because he left no traceable DNA at the murder scenes. Or maybe he's dead. With each passing year, the Lovelorn Killer recedes into history and people shrug at the mention of his name. Looks like he's gone for good.

Last fall, I started doing something a little crazy, even by Grave Digger standards. I went to the victim's houses. It started when Josephine Harvey's home came up for sale, and I went to the open house. I stood in one of her closets and wondered if he'd stood in that exact same spot, waiting for her with his ropes. I got this idea that I could walk his steps back in time and maybe find him there, the place where he'd vanished twenty years ago. I went to Denise Marklund's place in Irving Park and saw the same lace curtains hanging in the front window. I went to Lisa Sheffield's and saw all the bushes around the house had been torn out and replaced with flat grass—nowhere to hide.

On Halloween, I went to Katherine Duffy's neighborhood in Norwood Park. There were shrieking kids and grinning jack-o'-lanterns and empty candy wrappers stuck to the street. The lights were on in her old house and I saw a blond woman with black-cat ears dancing around inside. I moved closer to the hedges so I could watch her without being seen. Had he been surprised how easy it was to spy like this? I swear I could almost feel him there with me. Hear his excited breathing.

I've now walked everywhere the Lovelorn Killer has been, and while I did not find him, I feel he's out there, still alive. I think the cops just don't see him because he blends right in. Twenty years ago, I looked at the photos of his victims and was struck by how much they looked like me. Now I know his secret: he looks like me too. He might be my neighbor. Or yours. And he's been watching and waiting all this time for someone to figure it out.

CHAPTER FOUR

··············

ANNALISA STRODE INTO THE STATION WITH A SINGLE MISSION: TO GET A CUP OF COFFEE INTO HER SYSTEM BEFORE SHE HAD TO BRIEF THE COMMANDER ON THE HARPER CASE. Her plan fell apart when she spied Harry O'Hara camped in front of the coffee pot, hiding a laugh behind a mug that read OFFICIAL BADASS. O'Hara was forty-six and just divorced from his third wife. Rumor had it he was already auditioning for number four. "Something funny, O'Hara?" she asked as his titter became a full-blown guffaw. Behind her, O'Hara's regular partner, Sam Gunderson, started to chuckle, too. O'Hara began a cheerful whistle of "Here Comes the Bride" as Nick materialized behind her. That's when Annalisa noticed a cheap white veil adorning her chair. Someone had also put a bouquet of gas station flowers on her desk.

"Heard you two got hitched," O'Hara said in a singsong voice. "Guess old Nicky Boy wanted a second go-round on your carousel, huh, Vega?"

"Cute," Annalisa said as she picked up the flowers and dumped them into the nearest basket. "So original, too." She forced O'Hara aside and poured herself a cup of coffee that had to be four hours old at this point. It tasted like it had been brewed in a pothole. "Whatever your issues are, O'Hara, please cancel my subscription, okay?"

"Just wishing our new happy couple all the best. I bet we have some fried rice in the fridge we could throw if you're interested."

"Hey, what's your problem, man?" Nick lunged in O'Hara's direction.

"Can't take a joke, Carelli? You got to protect the little woman now?"

Nick looked like he might actually take a swing. Annalisa yanked him back by the tail of his sport coat. "Knock it off, Carelli."

"Me? You're mad at me?"

Zimmer appeared from her office across the room and called out to them sharply. "Vega, Carelli. In my office now."

"Uh-oh. Honeymoon's over," O'Hara said. "Again."

Nick glowered at him and followed Annalisa as she threaded her way through the bullpen. "If you'd let me deck him once, this would all be over," he muttered to her as they walked.

"No, it would just make me into some big button they could push whenever they wanted to make you go cuckoo."

Zimmer, who was waiting for them in the doorway, squinted at the guys still enjoying their joke across the room. "Do we have some sort of problem here?"

Nick glanced back and opened his mouth, ready to snitch. "No," Annalisa said, heading him off. "No problem."

"Good. Get inside."

Commander Lynn Zimmer had earned the nickname the Hammer back in her patrol days, and Annalisa always thought there must be some story about her coldcocking a perp with a Craftsman titanium, but she knew better than to ask Zimmer herself. Instead, she'd asked Pops a few years ago, as he had helped train Zimmer, and he'd laughed so hard his belly shook the table. "No, not that she wouldn't have taken a swing with whatever tools were handy. You can see a scar on her chin if you get real close, where she cut herself on a chain-link fence chasing down an armed robbery suspect. Leapt down on him like a puma, she did. Bled all over his clothes in the process. But no, she became the Hammer after work, down at the bar. She could drink a sumo wrestler under the table if given the opportunity, and he'd wake up hurting like his head was in a sling the next day while the Hammer would wolf down a plate of eggs and bacon at Smitty's Diner and then do back-to-back shifts."

Usually Zimmer conducted herself with quick, precise movements, the hallmark of a woman who had to accomplish twice as much as the men to earn her stripes. Her high cheekbones and slim form echoed her

Maasai ancestry, and Annalisa would choose no other to lead her in battle. Zimmer took her seat behind the desk and motioned for her detectives to avail themselves of the other chairs. She scanned the printout of the Channel Seven news story that Annalisa had already forwarded to her about the Grave Diggers.

"Let me see if I have this straight: You're saying our victim, Grace Harper, was a member of this amateur murder group trying to crack the Lovelorn Killer case, and she ended up bound and garroted the way the victims were in the 1990s. And thanks to this little feature last week, everyone watching the evening news knew she was working on the case."

"Yes, those are the facts as we have ascertained them so far." Annalisa glanced at Nick, who had crushed his paper cup into a ball in his fist. His left leg started to bounce.

"Look at the pose, Commander. It's like a carbon copy of the ones hanging over her desk. Whoever this guy is, he's got the playbook down pat."

Zimmer tossed the printout down on her desk. "There have been dozens of media profiles on the Lovelorn Killer case over the years, with much bigger muscle behind them than Channel Seven. I don't see how a bunch of computer geeks got him to surface when nobody else has. You think the FBI has given up on this guy? You think the Staties have? Hell, we've got open files on Duffy, Sheffield, and Lyons. Detectives Reynolds and Brown are technically still assigned to the case."

"Yeah, and when's the last time they actually worked it?" Nick asked.

"There hasn't been any need to work it," Zimmer snapped at him. She picked up the printout again, like maybe it had new answers. "This guy's been underground for more than two decades. He was already a spook story by the time I came up. You said the victim lived alone?"

"Alone, yes," Annalisa confirmed.

"No boyfriend? Girlfriend? Normally the victims had a family."

"Molly Lipinski says no. There's an aunt living in upstate New York somewhere. Molly thinks maybe Binghamton, but she doesn't know the woman's name."

"Makes no damn sense. On the face of it, it's more likely that someone knew her creepy hobby and murdered her with it than the Lovelorn

Killer pops up after twenty years to off some Nancy Drew with a house full of old pictures."

Yes, but who? Annalisa wanted to ask. The woman's spartan house showed no sign of human connection. She worked at a grocery store, not a bank or a brothel or someplace that would give cause for others to target her. A search of the bedroom and bathroom showed no signs that Grace Harper had a drug problem that might have put her in contact with the seedier side of Garfield Park.

Zimmer chewed her lip and looked out the window at the brightening sky. The city would be awake soon, ready for the morning headlines. The press could only be held at bay for so long. If this were the work of the Lovelorn Killer, the *Sun-Times* might be getting the biggest tip of all when his love letter arrived. "We're going to have to play it both ways," Zimmer said at length. "You two get a power nap and then work the local angle. Grace Harper looks clean at first glance, but odds are she pissed off some ordinary schmo who decided to ape the pictures hanging in her home. Talk to the neighbors. Look at her finances. Everyone's got a secret or two, and I want to know what's hidden in Grace Harper's underwear drawer by the end of the day. Meanwhile, I'll have Reynolds and Brown put together the highlights from the Lovelorn Killer file."

"We're keeping the case?" Nick asked, leaning forward in surprise.

"For now, yeah, we run with it on our own. I'll loop in the Feds when it looks like they need looping."

Annalisa looked at the news printout lying on the desk. She didn't state the obvious, that one national story would be all it would take for the Feds to loop themselves in.

....

Outside, the damp early morning air had a chill, promising a colder spring day ahead. May in Chicago had a schizoid quality to it, lurching daily between cold and wet and scorching hot before settling in for the long, humid summer that put a shimmer on the lake and a sizzle on the sidewalks. Annalisa hunched inside her windbreaker as Nick fell into step beside her. "Want my coat?"

She eyed him sideways, him and his omnipresent leather jacket. She wondered if it was the same one she'd taken from him ten years ago, or if he'd lost that one in the game somewhere along the way. "Pass, thank you."

"How about coffee and an egg sandwich, then?" He nodded to the pancake house across the way. "My treat."

Nick always offered to treat. Beers, jackets, rides downtown—he'd give you a diamond tiara if he had it. She'd thought he was the most generous man she'd ever met until she'd realized he never took anything in return. No debts for Nick Carelli, not even a temporary one. He gave and gave until he was sure he had provided you with whatever you wanted, and then he moved on to charming the next one down the line.

"Come on," he said when he saw her hesitating. "You've got to eat."

"Fine. Make mine with bacon."

He gave her a grin, the one that showed the dimple on his left side. "I remember."

At 5 A.M., Alicia's Pancake House catered to the shift workers like themselves, cops and nurses, pharmacy techs and warehouse employees, people who kept the world spinning for the rest of the nine-to-fivers. The coffee-bean-and-sugar aroma made her abused stomach give a feeble rumble, and Annalisa took a red vinyl booth by the window. The waitress slapped down plastic menus on the table and poured them coffee without being asked. Nick ordered the breakfast sandwiches for both of them as Annalisa took in the decor with tired eyes. The squat brick building had survived untouched over a dozen construction booms happening around it. The long Formica breakfast bar with its stainless steel–rimmed stools and little ceramic sugar bowls remained unchanged from the last time the Lovelorn Killer dominated headlines. She saw people checking their phones and wondered if they'd read about Grace Harper's murder, if it would seem important yet. It had taken a year last time, until the second dark-haired woman turned up dead on the floor in an otherwise undisturbed house, for the panic to set in.

"Gut-feeling time," Nick said as he blew on his steaming cup of coffee. "Is it him or not?"

She chuffed. "You make it sound so casual. You weren't here the last time, Carelli. You don't know how it was."

"So, then tell me how it was."

"Let me put it this way: some poor guy in a clown suit on his way to work a kid's birthday party got pulled over and strip-searched on the side of the road by a couple of patrol cops."

"Clown suit?"

"You know, like John Wayne Gacy, our last serial killer. It took decades after Gacy for clowns to be funny again, and then bam, they were persona non grata just by association. People were wigged."

The third murder came faster, followed quickly by a fourth. Even then, Annalisa had felt it only at a distance. Her father hadn't worked the Lovelorn case at all at first, merely followed the news and gossip like the rest of them. Her mother fretted more, tightening Annalisa's curfew. That had been the most painful part for Annalisa. She had been fifteen back then, in love to the point of ruin. When she'd thought at all about the future, she'd imagined exotic cocktails, her own credit card, and a bright red car she could keep out as late as she'd wanted. Adults, she was sure, had all the fun.

"He kept killing and no one could seem to stop it. Women started dying their hair blond because all the victims had dark hair. Gun ownership shot up twenty-five percent. Even the animal shelters ran out of big dogs."

Nick winked at her as the waitress delivered their food. "I bet you'd look cute as a blonde."

"The fact that you can make jokes shows how much you don't know," she replied with mild exasperation. He was still dangerously attractive, she could admit that now, with his sweep of dark hair, gray eyes, and Roman nose. The two-day stubble and sleepy eyes made him seem like he'd just rolled out of someone's bed—which, most days, she presumed he probably had. She'd loved him, but she was never enough. The priest at their wedding had admonished them to "fill each other's cup first," but Nick's cup turned out to have a hole in the bottom.

"I think it almost doesn't matter if it's a copycat," she said. "Whoever did that to Grace Harper is a dangerous human being. When this story breaks, women are going to be terrified again, especially if they live alone."

He looked up at her. "Don't you live alone?"

"Yeah, but I have a gun and I know how to use it. I gotta tell you, though, I sometimes wonder if I was murdered, how long it would take for anyone to find the body."

He snorted. "Ten hours, tops. If you failed to answer one of Maria's calls, she'd have the cavalry out quicker than you can say, 'Hi-ho, Silver.'"

"Not true." She took out her personal cell and held it up for proof. "I have five unanswered texts from my mom right now." Six was the magic number, so she'd better be answering soon or her mother would start raising hell.

"Tell her you're having coffee with me. She'll call in the National Guard." She grinned because he was probably right, and he ducked his head. "I have a confession to make."

"Oh?"

"I heard your handle when the call went out earlier tonight. Well, I guess it was yesterday night, now. I showed up because I wanted to work a case with you."

She drew back, skeptical. "You did?"

"Sure. You've got a rep, Vega. On the job only a year and you've closed more than three dozen cases so far."

Just three homicides, she thought but did not say. Those cases still usually went to the big boys. "You. You wanted to work a case with me."

"We were always good together. You have to admit that."

"I admit nothing outside the presence of my lawyer." It was humor, but also a barb. By the end, their lawyers had done all the talking.

"I saw you at the scene and I saw your face in Zimmer's office. You're thinking the same thing I am about this case."

"Which is?"

He gestured as if to give her the floor. "You tell me."

God help her, she still wanted to impress him. "Zimmer was floating the theory that Grace Harper ticked off someone personal, and this someone used the Lovelorn Killer's MO to kill Harper, maybe as an extra special ef-you."

He nodded. "That's right."

"I don't think so," she said, and he raised his eyebrows at her. She ticked her reasoning off on her fingers. "This guy broke and entered, while a personal connection probably would've used that to come through the front door. This murder had a high degree of difficulty—executed with extra points from the Russian judge. A hothead perp would use a gun or maybe a knife. He wouldn't be able to subdue a healthy adult woman and tie her up like a human pretzel without some practice. Finally, aside from the body fluids, that scene looked neat as a pin. Maybe we get some DNA or fibers but there was certainly nothing obvious. An inexperienced killer likely panics once the corpse starts getting cold."

He'd started nodding halfway through her speech. "This guy's no rookie," he agreed. "Either he's some Lovelorn Killer–obsessed freak who's been planning his debut for a long time or . . ."

She regarded him over the rim of her coffee cup. "Or he's the real deal."

CHAPTER FIVE

············

MAYBE IT WAS THE IMAGE OF GRACE HARPER'S TIED-UP CORPSE SMOKING IN THE BACK OF HER BRAIN, OR MAYBE IT WAS THE TIDAL PULL OF OLD MEMORIES THE CASE DREDGED UP, BUT ANNALISA DID NOT GO TO HER SOLITARY CONDO AS USUAL. Instead she pointed her car toward Norwood Park, the place she always thought of as home no matter where her mail got sent. Technically still part of Chicago, Norwood Park had a semi-suburban feel, with many single-family homes and tree-lined streets. The law said Chicago's cops had to live within the city limits, and many of them had settled here, including George Vega and his wife, Maria, for the past forty years. Generations lived and died within the confines of this one neighborhood. Most of Annalisa's high school class still lived within a few streets of the homes they grew up in, sending their kids to the same schools they had attended.

Annalisa used her key and pressed her shoulder to the sticky backdoor, willing it not to make too much noise with her shove since the hour was still early. It burst open as usual, sending her stumbling into the kitchen. A gruff voice from the semidarkness called out to her. "I got more grace than that, and I'm the one who had the brain surgery."

"Pops," Annalisa said with affection and surprise to find him up this early. "What are you doing sitting here with the lights off?"

"I know where the table is, and the chair, because they ain't moved a foot since the day I brought them in here. Why am I gonna pay extra for the lights?"

"Same old Pops." She kissed his cheek and hugged an arm around his shoulder. He winced but tried to hide it. Suspicious now, she went to the wall and flicked on the switch, revealing a nasty bruise on the side of his face. "Oh, Pops."

"It's nothing. Don't you worry about it."

She reached out, but he ducked awkwardly from her touch. "What happened?"

"I took a little tumble, that's all. Nothing serious."

Annalisa's gaze darted around the kitchen floor as if seeking out the perpetrator. She and her brothers had stripped the house of all area rugs and loose cords when George had been diagnosed with Parkinson's disease six years ago, but his shuffling gait still made him vulnerable to falls. "Was it the damned cat again?"

"It wasn't the cat," he replied in a soothing voice that told her it was the cat. "Mitzi's a good girl who loves her papa. Can I help it if she likes to be near me? Unlike some ungrateful children who haven't been to Sunday dinner in almost a month now."

"I had work." She took an apple from the fruit bowl and bit into it, trying not to make her study of him too obvious. The tremor in his hand looked no better to her eyes, despite his new medications. "You know how it goes."

He grunted. "Don't try to tell me about the job. Me and the badge, we go way back. Is that why you're here? You got hold of a bad one?"

She halted her chewing. "How did you guess?"

"You and me, we go way back, too." His smile was twitchy, uncontrolled. She saw he hadn't been shaved in several days and wondered about the aide she and her brother Tony had coordinated to come assist with his care. "Tell me about it," he commanded.

She knew she shouldn't. "Where's Mom?"

"Sleeping, like the rest of the world. Spill it."

She took a deep breath. "It's a homicide over in Belmont Cragin. A woman murdered in her own home."

"Boyfriend?"

"Not this time, I don't think." She hesitated. "The victim was tied up, her neck, hands, and feet bound together in a series of slip knots. Ritual fashion."

His tremor ceased. "Raped?"

"Can't say for sure yet. She was naked, though. Not gagged or blind-folded." The killer had wanted to hear her gasping for breath, wanted to watch the growing terror in her eyes when the air didn't come.

Pops sat back in his chair, head bobbing slightly as he absorbed the news. "So, he's back," he said with grim determination, like he'd been waiting this whole time. Annalisa didn't pretend to misunderstand him.

"We don't know that. Could be a copycat."

He made a face like his stomach turned. "You think one city would hold two of them? No, he's been waiting, bi-biding his time. Guess that old itch got too strong. Maybe he wanted to remind us he's still here, like a thumb in the eye." His eyes were weepy, a side effect of the most recent medication. "You gotta tell me everything."

"Pops. We don't even know anything yet."

"Dammit!" He banged the table and she jumped. "Th-they took this case away from us, the ones who knew it best. These were our streets, our people dying. A bunch of stuffed suits flew in to tell us crap we al-ready knew, like how he has trouble relating to women and he gets off on the fun of watching them die. He doesn't really love them like the letters say. It's the opposite. He hates them and how small they make him feel. You . . . you think we didn't suss that out for ourselves when we saw the bodies? They sum up by telling us he probably set fires as a kid and wet the bed when he was a teenager. Like that's supposed to help us round up a suspect. Sure, right, we'll just go door-to-door, ask-ing people, 'Did you piss the bed in high school?'"

His face turned red, the bruise almost black. His tremor increased and he had a string of drool hanging from the corner of his mouth. Annalisa handed him a napkin, and he swiped at his face clumsily. "I know you wanted this case," she said. "I know how bad you needed it after Katie died."

"No one wants this case, you understand me? No one. If this guy is who I think he is . . . you'll know soon enough what I'm talking about. Tell me more about the victim."

Annalisa figured she could divulge as much as would be in the papers. "Her name is Grace Harper. Age forty-three, worked in a grocery store. She lived alone as far as we know."

Pops lurched forward in his seat with a wheeze. "Grace Harper? Little bitty thing about yea high? All wrapped up in her computer?"

"Yeah, that's her."

He let out a curse under his breath and crossed himself with an unsteady hand. "That sonofabitch."

"Pops. Did you know her?" It seemed impossible. Pops barely left the house these days, and he hated computers. He shook his head, but she didn't believe him. "If you knew her, you have to tell me. Now."

He stretched his fingers toward the fruit bowl in the middle of the table, touched the gleaming skin of an apple. "Sh-sh-she came to see me," he admitted in a gruff voice. "Six, maybe seven weeks ago. Waited until your mother went out shopping and then rang our doorbell like some Jehovah's Witness."

"What did she want?" Annalisa could already guess the answer.

His chin rose up. "Same as you, asking me about the Lovelorn case."

"I didn't ask you about the case."

"Oh, the hell with that. You don't come around home for a month, and then suddenly this case gets hot and here you are at my table, asking me questions."

"You had recent contact with a homicide victim, Pops. Don't put this on me. What did you tell her?"

"I told her no good would come from mucking around. I told her to take up bird-watching or stamp collecting, or some other decent hobby. I said she should leave any investigating to the professionals because— Ah, Christ." He balled his hands into fists and his eyes grew wet. When he spoke again, his voice was low and hoarse. "I said she could get hurt."

Annalisa bowed her head and sat with the weight of that statement for a long moment. "What questions did she ask you?"

Pops took his time with an answer. "She wanted the timeline of the Halloween party the night Katie died. She wanted to know if we'd seen anyone hanging around in the neighborhood beforehand, if there were signs up for the party that he might've seen. She asked—she asked if it was true that the guy used Katie's own scarf to choke her."

"I see." Annalisa revised her initial visualization of Grace Harper showing up at the door and Pops angrily shooing her away. The two had obviously spoken at length. "And did you answer her?"

"I'll tell you exactly what I told her, okay? I said it's been twenty years now. I'm an old man who can barely get myself to the can without help. I don't have any answers." He paused. His mouth tightened, then twitched. "I never did."

Her head swimming, Annalisa left Pops to his breakfast. She flopped onto her old twin bed and lay atop the covers. Her desk now held her mother's sewing things, and the posters of boy bands had been replaced with family photos, but otherwise the room was unchanged. She tried not to notice the widening crack on the ceiling or think about the loose tread she'd found on the stairs. Her father restricted his movements to the downstairs, but her mother, battling arthritis, was a fall risk herself. She could ask Tony to fix it, therefore putting off the hard conversation about their parents and this house yet another month. Or two, or ten. In her more honest moments, she could admit that they were all waiting for disaster to force their hand, but she wasn't going to be the first one to mention the possibility of selling. Tony could do it. He was in real estate. Or Alex. He was the favorite.

She rolled over and looked at the family portrait on the wall, the one taken when her oldest brother, Vincent, was in high school. Vincent moved the farthest of all of them, to Naperville, where he lived with his wife and three kids, two boys and a daughter. Vinny tried to claim he still lived in Chicago, and they busted his chops about it all the time. *If your zip code doesn't start with 606, you don't live in Chicago.* He'd already been gone a couple of years when Katie Duffy died. Tony, too, was living on campus at DePaul at the time, although he'd stopped by with a few buddies for the neighborhood Halloween party. He hadn't stayed, though. Not that night and not later, when Pops got sidelined from the one case he was desperate to work. Not when Owen Duffy keeled over from a heart attack while shoveling snow, and then Colin had to leave town in the middle of his senior year. In their collective grief, none of them had noticed at first when Alex began trying to drink himself into oblivion. They could have lost him too.

She turned around the other way, facing the pale green wall. Her phone said it was coming up on seven, and she'd arranged to meet with Nick at nine back at Grace Harper's house. If she was going to sleep, it had to be now. Instead she went to her contacts and hit the smiling blond face labeled *Sassy*—her longtime best friend and Alex's wife. Sassy picked up immediately.

"Sorry, did I wake you?" Annalisa asked. "I know it's early."

"I have a preschooler and a baby," Sassy replied. "I've been up from dawn and am already covered in Cheerios, dog hair, and little magnet letters."

"You're magnetic now?"

"No, I'm lying on the couch. We're playing the 'Mommy has an operation' game because at least I can do that horizontally. I presume you're calling to tell me about how fabulous the date was last night."

Annalisa shut her eyes. She'd forgotten all about Todd the tax attorney. She forced a note of cheer into her voice. "He was nice, just like you said."

"Oh, poo," Sassy replied, clearly holding back her more favored word because there were small children present. "Nice is the kiss of death. What didn't you like about this one?"

"He was fine. Listen—"

"Okay, so I know Todd's not the most exciting guy, but he's cute and steady and funny if you get to know him. You are going to have to become less picky, Anna, or you're going to end up being one of those ladies who dies in her sleep and gets eaten by her cats."

She revised her plan to get a cat. "Listen, I wanted to ask you about Colin. Do you have a phone number for him?" Sassy was Colin's second cousin. It had been he who gave her the unusual nickname, back when he was two years old and couldn't say the name of his newborn cousin Cecelia.

"Colin? I don't, but my mom might. Last I heard he was in Kuala Lumpur or somewhere like that, writing for *Rich Boys* magazine or whoever's paying him now." The baby wailed. When she spoke again, her voice had a noticeable bounce in it. "What do you want with Colin? Please don't tell me you're still pining. We've been over this a hundred times. You can't live your life wondering about the one who got away."

"He didn't 'get away.' He ran away."

Her family had offered to take Colin in after his mother's murder and father's heart attack, but he'd refused. He went to stay with an older cousin on his father's side in the middle of nowhere, Ohio.

"Honey, it's been twenty years. Maybe it's time to let go of the Colin fantasy, huh?"

"You are one to talk," Annalisa retorted lightly. Sassy and Alex had dated in high school and into college, only to break up when Alex temporarily went off the rails due to his drinking. Annalisa gave a lot of credit to Sassy for helping Alex, even if it meant rebuffing him for a couple of years while he got his act together.

"Seriously. He's got a website if you just want to do some snooping. His email is there too, I'm sure, if you really want to make direct contact."

Annalisa had snooped often over the years, drinking in the gorgeous travel photos he had on his site. The brilliant green of a bamboo forest in Japan. The breathtaking Zhangye Danxia geoformation in Gansu, China, its patterned rock like a layer cake drawn by M. C. Escher. A pair of cheetahs frolicking at the Okavango Delta in Botswana. She paged through each stunning photo, holding her breath in anticipation of seeing Salar de Uyuni in Bolivia, a giant salt flat that acted as an enormous natural mirror. Salar de Uyuni was the place they had planned to go together, back when they'd daydreamed over *National Geographic* magazines in the school library, their heads pressed close against one another and their fingers laced together under the table. Salar de Uyuni looked like something from a Dalí painting, a vast white landscape where the earth reflected the sky. It seemed impossible to Annalisa that such strange beauty existed on the same planet as her boring neighborhood, with its standard oak trees and chipped concrete sidewalks.

If Colin had made it to Salar de Uyuni, he had not posted a picture. Her favorite was a panoramic shot of the cliffs of Ireland. Someone else must have taken this photo because Colin himself was in it, a solitary figure dressed entirely in black with his back to the camera. She'd spent too many hours studying the familiar curve of his shoulders and tracing his image on her screen. A hundred times, her finger hovered over the

SEND EMAIL link, but she'd never even gotten as far as composing one in her head. Colin had left, had kept on leaving, as far as she could tell from his pictures. She'd stayed right where he'd left her, and he knew how to get in contact if he wished. Instead, Colin Duffy had not come home for twenty years. He hadn't even sent a postcard.

"No, I don't want to email him. It— It's not personal." She cleared her throat as she tried to sell the lie. "It's related to work."

"Work?" Sassy liked to joke about her "mom brain," but the truth was, she'd graduated top of their class and missed exactly nothing. "You have news about Aunt Katie?" The city may have forgotten the murders, but the family never did.

"No," Annalisa answered honestly. There were no new leads on the Katherine Duffy case. So far, it remained just as cold as it had been twenty hours ago. "Nothing yet."

Sassy went quiet, no doubt parsing the *yet*. She knew better than to press for answers that Annalisa couldn't give her. "I'll get you the number," she said finally. "But I don't know if he'll talk."

CHAPTER SIX

....

A SHARP BUZZING, LIKE A SAW, WOKE ANNALISA FROM A DEAD SLEEP. She gasped as the dream fell away—a terrifying miasma of ropes and blood and an unknown man's footsteps following behind her—leaving only her pounding heart and sweaty brow. Groping blindly for the source of the noise, her fingers closed around her cell phone, which had slipped under her pillow as she slept. A terse text from Nick: *It's out.* He also sent a link to a big black headline in the *Sun-Times*. GRUESOME DEATH RECALLS OLD MURDERS: HAS THE LOVELORN KILLER RETURNED?

It was inevitable. Meet you at the Harper place at 9, Annalisa texted back. She ducked into the avocado green bathroom, the one she'd had to share with three brothers, to wash her face and comb her hair. She'd had maybe two hours of sleep and was counting on a continual drip of caffeine to get her through the long day ahead. She smiled into the clean, fluffy white towel as she dried the water from her chin. They didn't have much money growing up, but her mother never skimped on the towels. The bathroom was the only room in the house with a lock on it, so Annalisa lingered out of habit in the place that guaranteed her privacy.

She clicked the link that Nick had sent. Details of the Lovelorn Killer were always available to anyone who cared to look, even if most people hadn't cared as much as Grace Harper. Annalisa recalled them easily once she started paging through the old news stories on her phone. The first one to die was Josephine Harvey in December 1992, only it took some time for anyone to notice because of all the snow. A giant blizzard had swirled over the Midwest for two straight days, with Chicago taking the knockout blow. Accounting for drifts, some areas got buried under four feet of solid white stuff before the storm churned over to Canada. The airports closed. Mayor Daley declared an emergency, and only essential personnel like medics and plow drivers and cops were supposed to be on the road. Josephine Harvey was far from essential. She worked in a rental-car agency out by O'Hare. Josephine's husband was a drug-company sales rep, and the storm had trapped him out of town.

When he got worried because he couldn't reach her, her husband raised the help of the building manager to enter the apartment, where he found Josephine's decomposing body. The series of ropes convinced the investigators it was a sex thing. The apparatus in her bedside drawer—fur-lined handcuffs and an array of vibrators—cemented their image of young Josephine as some kinky slut who'd enticed the wrong man. They turned up an ex-boyfriend who had a history of slapping women around and took turns leaning on him and her husband, asking them intimate questions and probing their perversions. Annalisa wondered how many man-hours got wasted in those early months, but she knew the cops had simply been playing the odds. A murder that close, one where the killer sat back to watch his victim die, that had to be personal, right?

Annalisa stared at the smiling picture of Josephine that her family had provided after the murder. Josie, as they called her, had been dressed in a green sweater for an early Christmas party the week before she'd died. The camera captured the light dancing in her dark eyes and her affection for the photographer—one of her parents? Her husband? Either way, it was a better memory than the true last pictures ever taken of Josephine Harvey. Annalisa's stomach clenched at the thought of having to view the crime scene photos, and she shoved her phone deep into her pocket as she left the bathroom.

"Wait, you're leaving so soon?" Her mother's plaintive voice stopped her as Annalisa tried to bounce down the stairs and out of the kitchen. "You just got here."

"I have work, Ma."

"But it's Saturday."

Saturday meant that Grace Harper's neighbors would likely be home.

She felt the tug of the scene across town, a persistent hum in her veins. Each hour she was away was another hour that separated her from the killer. "The bad guys don't punch a clock," she said, stopping to kiss her mother's sagging cheek.

Maria grabbed her around the upper arms, her grip surprisingly strong. "You at least need to eat. I'll make breakfast."

"I ate, I swear. Where's Pops?"

"He's sleeping," she said, and Annalisa cast a worried glance at the den, which had been converted into a makeshift bedroom. Her mother shook her lightly. "I'll make you a sandwich, then, for the road. I have leftover meatloaf."

She went to the refrigerator before Annalisa could form a protest. Food was love, in Ma's world, and she'd be glad to take some for the road, even if the sandwich itself ended up in the garbage. She didn't need it baking in her car half the day. "Ma, how's the new medication working out?"

"Good," her mother said, like always.

Annalisa bit her lip and looked toward the den. "He said he took a fall."

"On the steps, while I was at the grocery store. I told him to wait for me to bring in the mail, but he sees the truck go by and he just can't wait. He rushes out there like Ed McMahon sent us a check."

"What about the aide who was coming to help?"

Her mother's lips thinned and she slapped a piece of bread on the counter. "We—we dismissed her."

"Ma!"

"She was fresh, telling me how to organize my kitchen."

Annalisa eyed the coffee maker, the toaster, the jars of flour and sugar and pasta all sitting on the counter. Clean dishes piled up in the drying rack. "Part of her job was to help you tidy up."

"I am perfectly tidy," her mother declared fiercely. "Who says I'm not? You think just because a few ants get in, I'm not fit to clean my own house?"

Annalisa blew out a frustrated breath that stirred her bangs. "I don't think that. I'm just trying to help."

Her mother wrapped the sandwich in tinfoil and shoved it at her. "You want to help? Come by and keep your father company. Watch the game with him."

Prick, prick of the guilt, hot under her skin. Annalisa took the sandwich and mumbled at the floor. "I will. I promise. Love you, Ma."

She pushed open the door and nearly collided with her brother Alex on the back steps. He grinned when he saw her and pulled her in for a strong hug that lifted her off her feet. "Hey, what are you doing here?" he asked as he set her down. "We never see you now that you're a big shot detective."

"Just leaving, actually."

"Aw, really?"

"Spare me the guilt trip. Ma already laid it on with a trowel. Why are you here?"

"I want to borrow Pops's chainsaw. That last storm we had took down a birch tree in our backyard."

"Yeah, well, can you check the back stairs while you're at it? There's a tread loose and I'm worried about Ma."

He squinted up at the house, tilting his head in a boyish gesture as he ran a nervous hand over his stomach. "Pops fell outside last week. Nearly split his head open on the concrete."

"I heard. Why didn't you call me?"

"I wasn't here. His old partner, Rod Brewster from down the street, picked him up, and he told me it wasn't the first time. Ma called him last month when Pops fell trying to get off the toilet."

"We can't let them go on like this. It isn't safe."

He shot her an amused glance. "You gonna give Pops his marching orders?"

Her phone buzzed, a text from Nick: *At Harper house. Where R U?*

Alex looked down at her phone as well. "Duty calls?" His usual booming baritone came out high and uncertain. Her job always made him nervous. Not the job, exactly, but the fact that she wore the badge and he didn't. Pops had hoped Alex would be the one to follow in his footsteps. The second DUI had made that impossible. So instead of a cop, he'd become a middle school math teacher, the class clown now with a captive audience five days per week. "It's perfect for me," he'd told Annalisa the day he'd gotten the job. "The math never gets harder than algebra, and my fart jokes are killer."

"Got to run," she said, giving him a squeeze. "Kiss the girls for me."

"Come over sometime and kiss 'em yourself." He stopped her with a hand on her chest when she moved to leave. "Anna, this case, whatever it is . . . be careful, okay?"

Their eyes met, and she saw concern there but also a hint of something darker, an understanding maybe, that most civilians didn't have. She wondered if he'd seen the news yet or if just the idea of murder took him back to the one that had exploded all their lives. The victim paid the ultimate price, but no one involved ever walked away clean.

....

When she reached Seneca Avenue, she had to slow to a crawl to accommodate double-parked news vans, the forensics truck, and flocks of curious neighbors clogging the street. *At least they won't be hard to find for an interview,* she thought to herself as she felt the eyes of several dozen people follow her down the block. She hung her shield around her neck and stepped out of the car and into a throng of eager reporters, most of whom she knew because they had performed this dance before. "Detective Vega, Grace Harper was working on the Love-lorn Killer case. Do you think this was connected to her death?" the woman from Channel Five shouted at her.

"Was Grace Harper writing a book about the killer?" another reporter shouted from the back.

The on-air reporters covering the crime beat in Chicago were mostly women—thin, leggy, and aggressive because they had to be. They wore false eyelashes and heavy makeup that did little to conceal the hunger in their eyes at the scent of the big story. They had her surrounded on the sidewalk. She couldn't move without literally stepping on their peep-toe shoes.

"Is it true that the victim was found tied up with ropes?" Marsha, the Fox reporter with the big hair and French manicure, wanted to know.

Channel Seven's blonde smelled blood, too. "Did Grace Harper find a new lead in the Lovelorn Killer case? Could the other Grave Diggers be in danger?"

Annalisa held up her hands. "All I can confirm for you is what our office said this morning—the resident of this house, Grace Harper, is deceased, and her death is being investigated as a homicide." She tried to move but they blocked her, quick as a bouncer down on Clark Street.

"But is this the work of the Lovelorn Killer, resurfaced after all these years?"

"We're exploring all options at the moment."

"So, it could be him."

She backpedaled. "I didn't say that."

"The city has a right to know."

"Detective Vega." From the back came a male voice, this one almost apathetic. She glanced back and saw Bob Roberts from the *Tribune*. Bob, with his thinning hair and jowly chin, had been pounding the city beat since the Lovelorn Killer's early days. He clearly wasn't excited just yet. "What can you tell me about a domestic call to this address last month?"

Annalisa blinked. "What?"

He made a point to check his notebook. "There was a 911 call from this address on April 13th just past nine o'clock."

"I have no comment on that right now," she replied, hoping that her face didn't give away the fact that this 911 call was news to her.

"All right, all right. The show is over, folks. Move along back over there to your designated area." Nick appeared and started breaking up the group by physically nudging them aside.

Marsha put a hand on her hip. "Watch it, Carelli. We're not a bunch of zoo animals you can shove in a cage."

He didn't stop walking her backward, away from the front of the Harper house. "See that yellow tape? You stay on the other side of it."

When he returned to the spot where Annalisa stood, she shot him a glare. "Thanks, but I can handle a few reporters on my own," she muttered as they walked to the door.

He looked amused. "Yeah, you were handling them, all right. They had you up against the fence down there."

"This is my case, remember? My scene. You're backing up me."

"That's what I thought I was doing," he said, annoyed now.

"No, what you did was signal to the press that you're in charge of this investigation."

He halted at the front steps. "You want me to go back down and make a statement? Tell them that Detective Annalisa Vega is large and in charge? That her piece is the biggest one around?" He grabbed for the shield around her neck and pretended to spit shine it. "Just let me make it all pretty for you, ma'am."

"Stop it," she hissed, yanking back her badge. "You're the one who wanted to work with me, remember?"

"Yeah, I forgot how much joy you took in busting my balls."

"Ha. Your balls were never in the house long enough for me to bother with."

His jaw dropped slightly. "Yeah, okay." He nodded to himself, looking off to the horizon behind her. "I suppose I earned that." He glanced at her face. "Sorry?"

She thought about asking him to spell out exactly what he was sorry for, but that would probably be an example of ball busting. Zimmer would no doubt be watching the pair of them, assessing whether they could work together, and there was no question which one would lose if the answer came back negative. She swallowed back her anger and gave a tight nod. "Let's go in."

The fetid air hit her in the face, but the stench was less pronounced than the previous night due to the removal of the body. They paused inside the doorway to put on fresh gloves and booties, which lay in open boxes on the floor as a reminder for everyone not to contaminate the scene. Crime scene techs worked in every room of the house, printing and photographing. Annalisa and Nick proceeded directly upstairs. "I checked out the Grave Diggers online," he said as they walked. "It's a closed group. Membership requires approval of an admin. Grace Harper is listed as one of them. The others are Molly Lipinski and a guy named Christopher Colburn."

"We're going to need to get a full list of membership." She remembered the reporter's question about whether the other people and the group could be in danger. "It's possible they may need protection."

"Or an alibi."

She halted to look at him. "What do you mean?"

He shrugged a single shoulder. "If she was writing some big book, maybe one of the others killed her and took the manuscript."

"Hell of a frame-up job, then."

"Hey, they've admitted to studying this guy's motives and patterns. I'm not saying they did it. I'm saying let's keep all our options open for the moment."

"Fair enough."

They entered the office-cum-murder room, which was just as disturbing in the daylight. "Do you notice anything missing?" Nick asked her as Annalisa inspected the wall of photos, news clippings, maps, and notes.

"Yeah," Annalisa replied without having to look. She'd noticed the night before. "Her computer. She's supposed to be in this online sleuth group and writing a book, so where's her computer?"

Nick peeked under the desk. "There's a power cord here. Looks like maybe she had a laptop. We'll have to do a complete inventory of the house to make sure it isn't hidden somewhere, but maybe we get lucky and the killer took it with him. Could be we can track it."

Annalisa made a humming noise of agreement as she studied Grace Harper's handiwork on the Lovelorn Killer case. Electronic tracking often made their job much easier. GPS. Find my phone. You could track practically anything these days with a chip in it if the device was powered on. A fellow cop liked to tell the story of how his daughter, a college student at Northwestern, had her laptop stolen from the library when she got up to use the bathroom. She didn't even call the police. She had simply activated a tracker and found the guy who'd snatched it at a café two blocks away, sipping a grande latte and watching porn in the corner. Somehow, Annalisa did not think this killer would be as stupid, but they would follow every potential lead.

She leaned in for a better look at a news headline Grace had tacked up near Katie Duffy's picture. No Longer a Hurricane, Judy Still Packs a Punch, it read. Annalisa had forgotten about the storm until she saw the name. Hurricane Judy had smacked Cuba hard and then hit the lower USA full-on as a category-three storm. By the time Judy reached the Midwest, it didn't merit a hurricane rating, but the powerful storm still caused tons of rain and wind damage. Two people were killed by flying tree branches. The weather had cleared just in time for Halloween, the night of the party. The night Katie Duffy was murdered.

Annalisa shifted to look at the photos and notes on Josephine Harvey's murder, because that one had also taken place near a big storm. Sure enough, she found another news clipping about the weather. POWERFUL BLIZZARD POUNDS MIDWEST. Scanning the rest of the wall, she uncovered two more—a tornado in southern Illinois, far removed by geography from any of the murders, but proximal to Lisa Sheffield's murder in terms of date, and another snowstorm, this one not as dramatic as the 1992 blizzard, but still responsible for almost a foot of snow two days before the death of Denise Marklund.

She recalled her encounter with Alex and his quest to borrow their father's chainsaw. *That last storm we had took down a birch tree in our back-yard,* he'd said. Six days ago, they'd had a rash of thunderstorms and howling winds. Annalisa had lain in bed, gripping the edge of her mattress and feeling the walls shake. The storm seemed to be trying to peel back her roof like the lid on a can of sardines. She recalled Grace's music boxes lined up so carefully on the dresser in the bedroom. Had they trembled in the storm? Fallen to the ground? Grace's notes suggested that she'd been trying to make some connection between the weather and the murders, but Annalisa couldn't see what it might be. Extreme weather events were not unusual in Chicago, where the city's warm air often battled with the cold lake for control of the skies.

Nick poked his head back in the room. "I've checked all the drawers and cabinets in the place. No sign of the computer."

"Maybe Molly or one of the other Grave Diggers knows the make and model."

"Let's ask them. Oh, and we've got company next door, by the way."

Intrigued, Annalisa followed him to Grace's bedroom. Ed Brown, one of the detectives currently assigned to the Lovelorn Killer case, stood near the bed, watching as a crime scene tech in full coveralls, gloves, and goggles swabbed the hardwood floor. He greeted them with a grim expression. "Vega, Carelli. Sorry about crashing your party without calling first, but Zimmer wants that report from us ASAP."

"No problem," Annalisa replied as she eased into the room. Brown had been on the job fifteen years and had a reputation for serious, careful work. He had the skin color to match his name, closely cropped hair, and a prominent forehead, but what always stood out to Annalisa was his suit. He had several of them, all in the same gunmetal gray, which he wore with a collared white shirt and red-striped tie. "It's about respect," he'd said to her when she'd asked one day about his formal attire.

"Sure," she'd replied. "You want people to take you serious when you're questioning them."

"No. It's about respect for them." He'd pointed at the face of a man shot dead on the concrete. "You wouldn't show up in blue jeans and a T-shirt at a funeral, now, would you?"

Annalisa had made sure to dress better after that—no jeans or T-shirts, not even on weekends. "What's going on?" she asked him now, nodding at the tech on the floor.

Brown rubbed his chin as if weighing whether to answer. "Back in the original case, investigators made the decision to hold some stuff back. One thing they didn't mention was that the guy must've jerked off at the scene."

Her heart leapt to her throat. "There's DNA?"

"No," Brown replied scornfully. He eyed the tech, who was now analyzing the cotton swab he'd rubbed on the floor. "This guy's too careful for that. He cleaned up after himself with bleach—probably with those single-use wipes you can get in any store. Destroyed any biological evidence."

"Then how do you know he was . . ." Nick made a hand motion that Annalisa found entirely unnecessary.

"Position on the bed where he watched them. The size and distance of the bleach residue on the floor. The profilers agreed it would make sense with his pattern. Super control freak, this guy. The way I figure it, this is the fastest way to know if we're dealing with the same sick creature—find out if he used the bleach."

Annalisa could almost picture him there where Grace Harper's bed-spread lay dented. The music boxes would be playing. Grace, writhing, gasping for air. Annalisa shook her head to clear it. *Don't be him,* she thought as the tech watched the swab turn blue. *Maybe there's a boy-friend we don't know about. A scary neighbor.*

"Well?" Brown asked.

They all watched as the tech held up the tube. "It's bleach."

CHAPTER SEVEN

....

GRACE NOTES

Journal Entry #421

MY HIGH SCHOOL ENGLISH TEACHER, MRS. FRUM, WOULD BE SHOCKED TO KNOW I'M WRITING THIS BOOK. I wish the old bat were still alive so I could tell her. *Poorly argued,* she wrote on my essays. *Conclusions not supported.* She gave me C-pluses and said the work was plain average, but she added the plus as a reminder that I was supposed to be "working up to my potential." I guess it's fair, wondering why a C student has the chops to write a book like this. The thing with me is, I can always tell when people are up to no good. The Grave Diggers all come with different skills. Molly can get anyone to talk. Barnes is great with computers and military stuff. Oliver knows the law. Me, I can spot a perp before he's even made a move. The guy on the L train who keeps dropping stuff so he can bend over and look up the girl's skirt—I see him like he's got a spotlight shining down on his sweaty, pig-like head the minute he first takes out that pen. The kid out on the street with a can of spray paint in the back of his baggy pants, looking for a wall to tag? I see him, too. Mostly, I see the shoplifters who come into my store with their puffy jackets, giant reusable totes, or a gaggle of small children in tow. Once, I stopped a woman who had three packs of C batteries shoved down the back of her kid's diaper. Technically, Bill's supposed to be the one watching for the shoplifters, and he does get his share when he isn't on a smoke break or chatting up Yolanda over in produce. But I get plenty, too. I spot them right away when they come through the doors, and it's not what you're thinking—they're all shapes and colors, different ages. It's not like they're all poor, either. Some of them just do it for the thrill, or because they can. Well, that's why I stop them. Because I can. I'll tell you the secret if you really want to know. They look for the cameras. Most shoppers come in with their eyes looking for a cart or scanning the sale merchandise. The thieves? They look up in the corners for the camera angles.

Molly put up a new case for the Grave Diggers this week, before I could figure out how to say something to her about the Lovelorn case. It's okay. I mean, it's been more than twenty years now, so what's another few days at this point? Plus, I think Molly knew Oliver needed the distraction with his wife starting chemo again, so she found us a good one. Janeesa Bryant, age nineteen, left her job at the gas station mini-mart one summer night and never made it home. This was six years ago, and she hasn't come home yet. What makes this case so interesting is that there's video from the mini-mart security camera. You can watch her selling people their scratch tickets, soda, and cigarettes all night long. Then she closes up shop and locks up—all with the camera still running. A second camera picks her up outside. She's wearing jeans, a white T-shirt, and a poofy ponytail. There's a bounce in her step even though it's one in the morning and she's been on her feet all day. She walks toward the right side of the screen, where the small parking lot is for employees and customers, and disappears from view. Later, when her mother reported her missing, the cops found her car still parked in the lot. A check of the cameras from the liquor store next door showed they had a view of the gas station parking lot, and you can watch this online too. It shows people coming and going, but Janeesa's little blue car just sits there until it's the only one left. Whoever took her, they grabbed her in the exact twenty yards of space with no cameras watching. Coincidence? I don't think so.

The cops didn't think so either. They liked her boyfriend for the crime, a young do-nothing named Hector Sanchez. He and Janeesa argued a lot. She'd started classes at the junior college, training to be a dental assistant. Maybe he didn't like her showing up his lack of ambition. Maybe he didn't like her having other priorities. I made a comment to the group about how it's true what Gloria Steinem said: a woman needs a man like a fish needs a bicycle. Chris of course asked me if I was a lesbian, but Barnes agreed with me. He said, "There's a reason we always say 'look at the boyfriend' when a woman turns up dead or missing. I don't think I'd want to date men either." If you look at the tape, you can see Janeesa was maybe coming to that conclusion herself. Hector and his posse dropped by the store around ten for candy and smokes. He didn't want to pay, and Janeesa called him on it. They had a shoving match, with her yelling at him and pushing him toward the door. He left with his snacks, his money safe in his wallet, but you can see on her face that she's had enough. That fight would've been the beginning of the end, I think, if Janeesa ever made it back to her little Kia in the parking lot.

The cops leaned on Hector hard. He swore he didn't do it, and his buddies backed him up. Investigators couldn't shake his alibi, and with no body, no blood, no proof even that she'd been harmed, there wasn't much left they could do. Molly's skeptical that they gave it their all. She wrote: "I bet if she was named Cindy or Lisa, if she had blond hair and blue eyes, they would've looked harder for her. I bet if she'd been working in Glencoe instead of K-Town, the whole city would've turned upside down." Janeesa's mom worked as an assistant manager of a Burger King. The one TV interview we found with her, she's plainspoken but dignified. Also terrified for her daughter. She said Janeesa planned to enroll in university that fall—more proof that she was moving on from Hector. Her mother cried just as much as anyone else we've seen in that situation, and the salt in everyone's tears is exactly the same.

When I watched that video of Janeesa on her last night, I saw something else: At about 8:30, there's a small line formed at the counter. A skinny guy in long shorts is paying for three Red Bulls. A woman in a tank top standing behind him picks up a candy bar from the rack, puts it back, then picks it up again. She's waiting to pay for a quart of milk. The third guy in line is heavy, older with a ring of thin white hair around his big round head. He's wearing a bomber jacket despite the summer heat, and he's not looking at the merchandise. He's watching Janeesa. Except for this one moment when he looks right up at the camera.

I froze the video so he was looking into the screen, and I was looking back at him. Yup, he was checking out the cameras. He knew right where to look, too. The guy eventually paid cash for a bag of chips off the front rack and slipped out the door into the night. I played with the video until I got the best angle on him, and I took a screenshot. I posted it to the whole group with a message: "We have to ID this guy."

Because that dude? He was up to no good. I can tell.

CHAPTER EIGHT

············

Annalisa worked one end of the block while Nick took the other. The hardest part was taking notes fast enough to keep up with the eager neighbors, each jostling the other for a turn to be interviewed. "She was nice enough," said Louisa Vann, the woman next door, reporting on Grace Harper. She bounced a baby on her hip, a chubby-cheeked girl with dark curls and eyes like a lemur. "She never complained to us, even when this one started howling at five in the morning or our two boys got into her backyard. But she wasn't quite friendly, either. Never came to our barbecues or anything."

"She worked at a supermarket too," one of the men grumbled. "Probably could've gotten us a good deal on the meat."

"Dad, stop it," replied a teenager with a messy topknot and barely-there shorts. "She died. Someone murdered her. It's not about steak right now."

"Just because you've gone vegan doesn't mean the rest of us—"

"What about visitors?" Annalisa interrupted him. "Did you see anyone go into or out of Grace Harper's house?"

A few people shook their heads. "She didn't seem like she had family," one woman offered.

"There was one guy," Louisa Vann said, unhooking the baby's vice grip on her boob. Annalisa winced inwardly in sympathy. "I saw him once or twice, maybe last winter? Then he showed up a few weeks ago, and Grace didn't want to let him in. He made a scene about it, and the cops showed up."

"Where was I?" her husband wanted to know.

She rolled her eyes at him. "Down in the basement with your video games, like usual."

"Can you describe this man?" Annalisa asked.

"Mmm, he was real big, with round shoulders. He had a bushy beard, like the hipsters wear. Down to here." She indicated her chest, and the baby went in for another grab. "It was kind of reddish blond–colored."

"Age?"

"Maybe late twenties? I don't know. I only saw him from a distance. I went out on my porch to see what all the hollering was about and he scared me so bad I went right back in."

"What was he yelling?"

"'You won't get away with this! It's mine!' Something like that. He was pounding on her door real good."

"Did you see what kind of car he was driving?"

She shook her head. "Sorry, no. We get a ton of cars on this street now, on account of those traffic apps routing people off the main road. We're even thinking of moving, it's got so bad in the afternoons."

Annalisa asked Louisa and then the others, one by one, if they had seen anything else suspicious in the days leading up to Grace's murder. One man said he'd found his garbage cans turned upside down. Another woman reported a package had been stolen from her mailbox. "What was in it?" Annalisa asked, prepared to follow up.

"Cooking spices. Turmeric, lime leaves, chili paste . . ."

Annalisa stopped writing. "Anyone else?"

A middle-aged man in a Blackhawks jersey shuffled forward, his gaze downcast. "I almost don't want to mention this. It's probably nothing."

"Please, tell me."

"We live on the back side of the Harper place, across the alley from her." The man looked around at his neighbors and cleared his throat. "My boys, they're six and eight. Good kids. Active. They're always climbing the furniture, so my wife, she sends them outside. Go climb a tree, she tells them. So they did. We've got a big old oak in the back-yard. Then one night last week, I heard them in their bedroom, giggling like they were up to something. I went in to see what was up, and they showed me a pair of women's panties. They said they found them in the tree."

"Did you keep them?" Annalisa asked quickly.

He scowled. "No, I didn't keep them. I'm not a pervert."

"What did they look like?"

Twin red spots appeared on his cheeks. "They were pink with little purple stars on 'em," he said, and some of the group tittered.

Annalisa wrote it down and put her notebook away. "I'm going to need you to show me that tree."

The man, whose name was Terry Guzman, led her around the block to the houses that sat behind the Harper place. His yard had a high fence, suitable for containing rambunctious boys, and a pair of old trees at the back overlooking a two-car garage. Each tree was probably a hundred years old and perfect for climbing. Annalisa grabbed a limb and lifted herself up. She ducked and eased around the leafy branches until she arrived at a solid V in the middle of the tree. A couple of months ago, she would have been easily spotted, perched among the naked branches, but spring hit like a bomb in early May, spraying the whole region in vibrant green. The tree made a perfect blind. No one could see her sitting there unless they stood directly by the trunk. She pulled down the nearest branch to peek out, her skin going cold when she saw the view. Straight ahead at eye level sat Grace Harper's bedroom window.

....

When Nick found her back inside the house, she had a handful of lingerie in one hand and was digging through Grace Harper's drawer for more. "Uh, are you looking for inspiration?" he asked, cocking an eyebrow at her. "Because I always liked you in red."

"Look at these," she said, showing him a pair of cotton blue underwear with purple stars and a pink pair with blue stars. "Don't they look like a set to you?"

"Sure, maybe. Why?"

She told him about the bizarre finding in the neighbor's tree and how the underpants had stars on them. "You can see right into her bedroom from out there."

Nick went to the window to see for himself. "Okay, but if he had a pair of her underwear, either he lifted them from a laundromat somewhere—"

"Or he'd been inside before." She fisted the underwear. "I checked. There's a washer and dryer in the basement."

"Good find," he said, turning from the window. "You did better than I did. The neighbors down that end mostly wanted to rat each other out for noise complaints and some fight about a parking spot. None of them really knew Grace Harper."

"Seems like she kept to herself."

"In real life, yeah. But we know she was active online. I called up our friend Molly Lipinski and got the names of the other local Grave Diggers in the group. I figure we can start with them. I ran them through the system and sent you a copy of the results. All of them look clean so far."

"Thanks." Annalisa pulled out her work phone and checked her email. Several names looked familiar. Jared Barnes, Molly, Oliver Benton. She stopped scrolling when she reached Christopher Colburn, age thirty-five, with a photo of his driver's license. He had a big bushy beard like the hipsters wear. He was listed as six foot three, 250 pounds, someone who could make a ruckus if he started pounding on a door. She held up her phone to show Nick. "I think we start with him."

CHAPTER NINE

·············

I SAY WE GO HIT HIM NOW," NICK SAID AS THEY LEFT THE HOUSE. A pair of black-and-whites held back the reporters. "The fact that her computer is missing makes it even more important that we track down all the nuts in this fruitcake. I figure we've got time to talk to Chris Colburn before the 4 P.M. chat."

"Chat," she repeated, amused at his description of the all-hands meeting scheduled at Chicago PD headquarters that afternoon. "You say that like there won't be a throng of FBI agents in attendance."

"Is that what you call a group of Fibbies? A throng? I always thought it was called a snooze."

He gallantly held the front door open for her, and she grinned in spite of herself. "You'd better watch it, Carelli. Talk like that will get you thrown right off this case."

The day had brightened, and he pulled out a pair of sunglasses. "If the bleach that Brown found on the floor up there means the Love-lorn Killer is back in business, we're both getting thrown off this case, pronto, unless we can find an angle of our own by four o'clock."

She thought of her father, shut in his den, with the TV on but nobody watching. "Let's go."

He jangled his keys in his pocket. "I can drive."

She had her own keys. "Yeah? So can I."

"It's a waste of gas to take both cars. Where's your sense of responsibility to Mother Earth, Vega?"

"I meant that I could drive both of us."

"Oh," he said, as though this possibility had just revealed itself like a shiny clue. "Sure."

Nick had driven them most everywhere in their brief courtship and marriage. Back then it was a black BMW M coupe, its arch like a cat. He'd juice the throttle at stoplights just to feel the body shiver with the engine's power. Pops had been suspicious right away. *How'd he afford a car like that on a cop's salary?* But Annalisa was hooked by the force of the engine, roaring them forward with such certainty. She'd had one life envisioned for herself, and when it had vanished, she hadn't conjured a replacement. Nick knew all the streets like he carried a map in his head—back-alley shortcuts, sweeping drives along the lake, straight shots right out of town—and she'd been happy to go along for the ride. Only later did she realize he knew all the directions because he never picked any one of them for very long.

They climbed in her Civic and Annalisa started the reliable if unexciting engine. She asked for Colburn's address, and he named a place in Wicker Park. "Not too far from our old apartment," he added with a sideways glance at her.

"I'm not sure it rose to the standard of an apartment. A hovel, maybe." Their walk-up, four-room flat backed up to the local L, which came rattling through every twenty minutes. It had rickety stairs, a window that wouldn't open, and a shower that had only two temperatures: freezing cold or blazing hot. He'd lived there first, and she'd moved in with him after their quickie marriage. She had sloughed off the peeling paint and given the whole thing a fresh coat, bought new curtains and throw pillows, and put rubber bands around the cabinet knobs so that the doors didn't fly open and send their wedding china crashing to the floor every time a train lumbered past. She'd spit shined the place as much as she could muster and invited her parents to dinner, hopeful and eager to impress upon them that she was a fully functioning adult now. She had been so concerned they might spot the water damage in the ceiling or the rust at the base of the stove that she didn't see the real telltale sign of disaster until it was too late: Nick had failed to show.

"Yeah, it wasn't the Ritz," he conceded. "But we had some good times there, didn't we?"

She couldn't read his expression behind the sunglasses. More than once, she wondered why he had married her. He'd chased a hundred women and loved them all for fifteen minutes at a time. How had he looked at her and ever thought she'd be enough?

He leaned back in his seat as she drove. "So, tell me about this vic you know. Katherine Duffy. She was the last known victim, yeah?"

"She was the wife of my dad's partner Owen Duffy. He and my dad came up together, rode a car for a couple years in the '80s around the time I was born. They hit it off right away, I guess. Family men from the area with the same dark sense of humor. They even bought houses on the same block. My dad worked his way up and became a sergeant, then a detective, but Duffy got tired of the grind. He went into computer repair just as everyone started buying them by the truckload and made a killing—which was a good thing, because he dropped dead shoveling snow the winter after Katie got killed." She shook her head, disbelieving even after all this time. "He was a big guy, strong as an ox."

"Happens that way with couples sometimes. Were they married long?"

"Twenty years."

"Happy?"

"God, I don't know. I would've said yes at the time, but I was a kid. You don't think about parents having interior lives. They're just robots there to ruin your life. I will say I wished a million times that Katie was my mom."

He gave a wry grin. "You were emotionally cheating on Maria? Nice."

"Hey, I was a teenage girl and she was my mother. We were obligated to get on each other's nerves. My mom nagged me about chores and homework, while also criticizing my clothes, my hair, my eyebrows, my shoes, my posture. . . ."

"I get the picture."

"Mom was always proper and conservative—cardigans and knit pants, penny loafers and pumps on Sunday. But Katie had style. She wore high heels with jeans, Jackie O glasses. Her nails were so pretty they looked fake, and she always painted them some wild color. 'Hooker red,' Owen used to say, and she'd just laugh and sass him back. 'What're you looking so close at the hookers for?' She had a handbag to match every outfit. I think she might have wanted to be a designer. Sometimes I'd see her sketching women in different outfits."

"Did she work outside the home at all? Someplace the Lovelorn Killer might've run into her?"

"She did the usual mom stuff. PTA, church committees. I think she took a painting class once at the local community college."

Nick looked out the window at the passing scenery, his expression inscrutable. "Pretty bold move, targeting a cop's wife. Even an ex-cop."

They'd had four in total on the block back then, counting Pops. Rod Brewster, his other ex-partner, was still on the job. The Lovelorn Killer had crept right to the heart of the lion's den.

"Did you see her that night?" he asked.

"Yes. I was at the Halloween party." So many bodies in the house that it was sweltering like summer, despite the October air. The O'Briens had the biggest place around, and people poured out of it, into a backyard lit by twinkling lights and glowing jack-o'-lanterns, covered with hanging spiders. There were dishes of candy corn and bat-shaped cookies, peeled bananas dolled up with candy googly eyes to look like ghosts. Someone had strapped fairy wings to the Kennedys' shaggy black dog, who had wandered the party mooching for food. "Katie Duffy dressed up as a fortune teller. She wore a bunch of crazy scarves, a long flowy skirt, and a curly black wig. For a while, she was reading people's palms on the swing on the back porch."

"Did she do yours?"

Annalisa smiled, remembering. "Yes."

"What did she say?" he asked, glancing at her hands on the wheel.

You will have a great love. "None of your business."

He sat back, wriggling awkwardly in his seat. His knees bumped up against the dash. "She can't have been much of a fortune teller," he remarked. "Or she would've seen it coming."

For a split second, she thought he meant their marriage and divorce. "No one did," she said, although that wasn't quite true. The grown-ups had been all wound up about the Lovelorn Killer, fretting about the dangers of trick-or-treat even as the kids got an extra charge out of it. There was a special kind of subversion to dressing up that year. Fake blood and trick knives took on a heightened danger with a real monster roaming somewhere in the vicinity. She and Pops had a blowout over her skin-tight, skimpy-skirted devil's costume. *Asking for trouble,* he'd told her, like some killer would pick her just because of a seductive outfit.

Colin had sure appreciated it, had let his hand creep under the sequined skirt every time Pops's eyes went elsewhere at the party. *All for me,* he'd murmured into her neck. She'd let him do it, thrilling to his touch, high on her newfound power to make him want her this much. Pops, wearing old-timey black-and-white prison garb, drank his beer straight from the bottle and glared at her across the room. Her performance was as much for him as for Colin. *How do you like me now?*

"Is Katie why you picked homicide over law school?" Nick asked. "Unfinished business?"

"No. I never expected to work this case." She'd figured like the rest of them, that the guy was probably dead. "If anything, Katie Duffy's death blew a hole through my illusions. Pops, he was invincible to us kids. We didn't think anything bad would happen as long as he was around. Now I can see how scared he must have been. He knew the truth, even if we didn't."

"Then why?"

I wanted to have a family again. She didn't dare say that to him, this man who had pledged to be her family but had instead tomcatted his way up and down Milwaukee Avenue. Pops always called the men he served with his "brothers," and to Annalisa, the sound in the kitchen when they'd bellied up to Ma's table was much the same as big Vega family dinners of yore. Laughing, taunting, the scrape of forks against the plate and then hugs and hearty slaps on the back on the way out. "Alex told me I couldn't hack it, being a cop," Annalisa said aloud. "I decided to show him up. It's not too hard if you ignore the idiots. There are some good guys, but also a bunch of swinging dicks."

"And you decided yours would be the biggest in the room."

"Nah." She smiled. "Turns out, if you're busy swinging it, someone can come along and whack it off."

"Youch." He sucked in a breath and clutched the armrest for show, but he was grinning. "You're cold, Vega. Ice-cold."

She laughed, a genuine one. She could dish it out and Nick would take it. This part of their marriage had always worked well. He would tease her, but he didn't fight her. Or fight for her, as it had turned out. "What about you?" she said, realizing she'd never asked. Her dad was a cop, her neighbors were cops. Back then, she'd figured it was part of the male DNA. "I assume you discovered the allure of the badge bunnies and never looked back."

Nick cracked his knuckles, a habit that used to drive her crazy. "Nah. I realized early on that death isn't at the end, waiting for us at some finish line. Death is everywhere, all the time. It's on the ballfield and at the supermarket and hiding under the bed at night, just like we feared when we were little kids. Hell, it's probably riding right here in the car with us, waiting for any opportunity—a truck to slam into us out of nowhere."

She checked the mirrors. "Thanks for that cheery thought."

"Yeah, well. I decided if death was going to stalk me, I'd stalk it right back." He nodded to himself, as if reaffirming his decision. "I look it right in the face. It's not a fair fight. Death wins in the end and always will. I'm just trying to even the odds a little."

CHAPTER TEN

············

GRACE NOTES

Journal Entry #423

For book purposes, I've started carrying a digital recorder to our Grave Digger meetings. I didn't tell the others because I want the conversation to seem natural, but really, the recordings are for them. I want to make sure I give them credit in the book for any contributions they make to the Lovelorn case. Tonight, we mostly stuck to Janeesa's disappearance. We met at the pub near Barnes's place, which meant that Chris was in rare form because we were accommodating someone other than him. He ordered a beer and made the server bring it unopened, cracking the top himself, like he was some feudal king whose food might be poisoned. After he sent back his burger not once but twice, he might've been right to check the food for toxins or nails and at least a gob of spit. We were supposed to be talking about Janeesa's case, but Chris just replayed his glory days from when he founded Grave Diggers. He yammered on about how the cops dragged a dead guy out of the Harbor wearing a Reilley family reunion T-shirt. "It had been almost ten years since they found him, and no one had ID'ed this guy," he told us, like we hadn't already heard this story a hundred times. "But I looked at that shirt and knew it had to be the key to cracking the case. A Day-Glo shamrock? The family name right on it? How many Reilleys could there be? Turns out, a motherfuckin' ton, but I used the genealogy sites and tracked them one by one."

I give Chris all due kudos for the big "get." He's right that the cops probably weren't ever going to identify this guy on their own, and when it turned out the dead guy wasn't even a Reilley, but a boyfriend who just happened to get a leftover shirt, Chris gets even more credit. He emailed and called every member of that family who attended the reunion and asked them the whereabouts of their shirts. After ten years, the accidental drowning victim got a name, thanks to Chris. Yahoo. Can we move on now, please? I think we have a chance to do more than put a name on a dead guy. I think we could unmask a serial killer. I just need a way to get the group on board, and they're still preoccupied with Janeesa's case.

Molly talked to her uncle, the one who is a retired sergeant from the Chicago PD, about Janeesa's disappearance. She said he's pretty convinced Hector the boyfriend did it and just no one can prove it. We've all seen these cases, and as much as we like to rag on the cops sometimes for not following up, usually when they like a guy, they're not wrong. What are we always saying when a woman disappears? It's got to be the boyfriend, right? It's always the boyfriend.

Molly's boyfriend, Travis, harrumphed at this, and we had a good laugh. #NotAllBoyfriends, right? Molly says Travis hates coming to our meetings because of the gory talk, but I think he secretly hangs on every word. Anyway, Molly's idea is to track down Jimmy Gomez, the buddy who was Hector's alibi the night Janeesa went missing. "Maybe they're not so tight anymore," she said. "He might be singing a different tune."

I disagreed and said it was Bomber Jacket Guy from the video. That creeper set off every one of my alarm bells.

"That's great, but we have no way to tell who he is," Chris told me. He had sorted the container of sugar packets so every color was together and all the edges lined up. I swear, he's wound so tight you could bounce a quarter off him.

I said I wanted to go down to the mini-mart to check it out for myself. Watching true-crime shows has taught me the value of walking the scene. Chris made fun of me. "What do you think you're going to find after six years? Do you think Bomber Jacket Guy is just hanging around the parking lot, maybe with a chunk of her hair?"

But Barnes backed me up, and he actually is an ex-MP so he knows what he's talking about. Chris likes to brag that he got the highest score possible on the police entrance exam, but he figured his intelligence would be wasted just walking the beat so he didn't take the job. He went into IT instead, because it takes a genius to drive around suburbia and show housewives how to plug in their PCs. "The bomber guy may not be waiting right at the mini-mart," Barnes said. "But he might be in the immediate area. One thing I noticed in watching the videos is that he doesn't show up in the shots of the parking lot where Janeesa's car was. It's possible he left his car at the pump while he went inside, but it's also possible he came on foot, meaning he could live nearby."

Oliver was quiet most of the night, and I saw he hadn't eaten much of his fish and chips. I asked if he was okay, and he said he was hanging in there. "All this talk about who took her, it's important. But I can't stop thinking about that poor girl, out there somewhere, with no way to get home. We know she's certainly dead, but without proof, everyone's still got that little bit of doubt. How cruel is that for her mama, having to wake up every morning wondering where her baby's at?"

His eyes got wet. Oliver always feels the victims deeply, sometimes shaming the rest of us who maybe look at these cases more like a puzzle. These days, Oliver's grief is right up near the surface. He'd sounded upbeat at our last meeting, saying his wife, Sandra, is getting this great new experimental drug. But I got to thinking later, if she's got a new drug, that means the last drug failed. Sandra's been fighting her cancer more than two years at this point, so I don't know how many more drugs there are left to try.

"What would you like us to do to find her?" Chris asked him. "Go beat the bushes with sticks? The cops searched Hector's and Jimmy's homes. They looked in the nearest fields and parks."

"I realize that," Oliver said with authority, like he was reprimanding an uppity student. He'd taught history for forty years, and he could still take us to school any time he wanted with just a pointed look. "But it was twenty-four hours before the cops even started to look for Janeesa, and longer than that before they located Hector and Jimmy for questioning. They said they'd been out driving, no place in particular. I'm wondering if they might have crossed state lines with her."

"So, we should check for Jane Does in surrounding areas," Barnes said with admiration. "Excellent idea."

When the meeting broke up, I walked to the L with Barnes as usual. We live at opposite ends of the city, but our journey begins from the same subway stop. I always like this opportunity to talk to him alone, away from Chris especially. Tonight, I told him about my plan for the Grave Diggers to resurrect the Lovelorn Killer investigation. Chris took a whack at it years ago and came up empty, so he'd moved it into the "graveyard" section of our caseload before I even came on board. But I've been poking around in there lately, and I see a few possibilities we could explore. I don't think this guy is dead like the cops say. I think he went underground like BTK in Kansas. I've been studying that case too, and I see some parallels with the ropes and suffocation of the victims. Barnes didn't try to shout me down like Chris would have. He seemed intrigued—interested enough to wait around in the freezing cold air while I explained it to him.

"BTK reported his own murders," I said. "He wrote letters to the media like the Lovelorn Killer. His main thing was killing, yeah, but he also wanted to be famous for it. That's what ultimately got him to crawl back out of his hole—people had stopped talking about him. But the cops used his enormous ego against him and got him to send them chapters of his autobiography, which they then traced back to Dennis Rader at his church computer. I think the Lovelorn Killer must be feeling that same urge. He could've written those letters to the victim's address, or to their families—you know, to rub salt in the wound. Instead, he wrote them to the *Sun-Times* for maximal attention."

Barnes pushed his glasses up his nose, the way he does when he's thinking hard about something, so I know he was taking me seriously. "You think the mass hysteria and the giant headlines were just as exciting for him as the murders," he said. Barnes can always take my ideas and say them in way less words than I use.

I'm sure there are still cops assigned to this case, but they aren't looking for him. No one writes articles about this guy anymore. He's probably sitting in his mommy's basement, stewing about how she's still the boss of him, getting by on his memories of the good old days when he held the whole city at attention. Only the thing is, those days are really old now.

I want to make some headlines of my own. Give him a taste, only make the story about the Grave Diggers and how we're going to find him. He's not the lead. We are. I'll bet he gets furious when he sees the news, and maybe that's enough for him to send up a flare.

Barnes listened to me the whole time without interrupting to shout his own opinions over mine, unlike some people. He has these pretty eyes that are hard to describe, green with flecks of yellow that make him look like he's lit from the inside. I forget sometimes that he's the only one of us who's actually seen a dead body, over in Iraq. He doesn't lord it over us the way Chris would if he were the decorated Army vet. "It could work," he said. "Maybe. You'd have to find an angle that would interest the news enough to do a story."

There's one part Barnes warned me about. He shook his head at me. I couldn't tell whether he was pissed or impressed. "You know Chris isn't going to like this," he said. "He marked the case as closed."

My boss works at the Foodsmart, and his name is David, not Chris. On the Grave Diggers, we're supposed to be equals. "Except it's not closed," I told Barnes. This guy tortured seven women to death and never had to answer for it. He's out there, breathing the same air as you and me, eating nice food, and walking all over this city, wherever he pleases. Meanwhile, the women are underground, right where he wanted them all along. I wonder if the cops have ever thought to stake out the cemeteries where the victims were buried. This guy is just the type to come around and admire his handiwork. Hell, he probably brings flowers. *So sorry I had to kill you.*

I don't want to make trouble for Barnes, so I told him he doesn't have to help me work the case. If he doesn't want to risk Chris coming down on him for going behind his back, I totally understand. I can work alone for now.

Barnes didn't need to think about it. "No," he said immediately. "I'm in."

CHAPTER ELEVEN

....

DESPITE HER ROUGH PERSONAL HISTORY WITH IT, WICKER PARK REMAINED ONE OF ANNALISA'S FAVORITE AREAS OF THE CITY, THANKS PARTLY TO ITS BOOMING RESTAURANT BUSINESS. Whatever you were hungry for, whether it was fine dining with starched napkins or a grungy bar with greasy burgers, you could find it in Wicker Park. She loved the Middle Eastern food at Sultan's Market, fresh sushi at Enso, carnitas tacos at Big Star, and a big steaming bowl of ramen at Furious Spoon. When she did venture out on a rare date, she often suggested drinks at the Robey hotel. The art deco–style Coyote Building gave sweeping views of the city that guaranteed that the evening would rate at least a 9/10, even if the guy turned out to be a total zero.

"Chris Colburn has a nicer place than we did," Nick remarked as they rolled up in front of his building.

"Sewer rats have a nicer place than we did," she replied.

Colburn lived on the third floor of a six-story redbrick building, erected some decades ago when developers still cared about style. The facade had gray brick inlays that formed an arch over the main door, and gold flourishes flanked the front windows all the way up. They hit the buzzer for Colburn's apartment and identified themselves as Chicago PD. Moments later, he opened the front door and filled the whole frame with his considerable size. He had the appearance of someone who had not slept in some time, with the brier-like beard, lank hair, and bags under his eyes. "Figured you would get here eventually," he said. "Come on up."

They followed him up three flights of steep stairs and into a bare but tidy front room. It held a leather sofa, a giant widescreen TV that was on but muted, a rack of DVDs that went nearly to the ceiling, and most notably to Annalisa, a gun closet in the corner. From her vantage point, she could make out at least two handguns and three long-range semiautomatic rifles. Alarm bells clanged in her brain, and she had to stop herself from reflexively touching her own weapon in reassurance. Colburn caught her looking and deepened his frown. "Hey, those are all legal. I can show you the papers if you want."

Grace Harper had been strangled, not shot. "Not necessary at this time," she answered mildly. "As long as you're not armed for this conversation."

"Why would I need to be?"

"I guess you know why we're here." Nick walked to the window to study the view from above.

"Yeah, I've seen the news. What a horror show." He nodded at the TV. She followed his gaze and drew up short when she saw her own face there, dodging questions from reporters in front of the Harper house. The crawl across the bottom screen said LOVELORN KILLER CLAIMS POSSIBLE NEW VICTIM. "Grace wanted to draw him out," Colburn continued. "I guess it worked."

His tone was curiously flat, neither satisfied nor concerned, but he looked like he hadn't slept in three days. Annalisa glanced into the dining room, which Colburn seemed to use as an office. He had a desk with two separate computer monitors, a printer, a captain's chair, and, like Grace Harper, a wall full of dead people. She took a couple of steps closer, trying to see if it was the Lovelorn Killer case, but she didn't recognize any of the victims. "We heard the Grave Diggers group was working on the case," she said, turning to face Colburn again.

"They were, yeah. I told them it was a bad idea."

"Why?" Nick asked, a hand on his hip. He wasn't above advertising his own piece.

Colburn scratched the back of his neck, then rubbed his stomach, stalling for time as he worked out an answer. "The Grave Diggers do the most good on cases where the cops haven't investigated thoroughly, whether that's due to lack of interest or lack of resources. The Lovelorn Killer had every LEO in the state focused on him at one point. The FBI still has an open file. There are plenty of amateur groups that have taken a whack at it too. Just seemed to be well-trodden ground."

"Still," Nick persisted. "Think of the headlines if you cracked it. You'd be famous. The mayor would name a bridge or a street after you. Hell, they'd probably ask you down to Quantico to give lectures."

"Grace was the one who chased headlines, not me."

"Oh yeah? What did you chase?" Annalisa asked.

His jaw tightened. "The truth."

She had to hold back her laugh, but in that instant, she got him. He fancied himself a rogue, TV-style detective bound by duty to uphold a noble cause. He might have been mucking around with the Grave Diggers, but he didn't view these amateurs as his peers. He was as big a civilian snob as any of the lifers who sat around Pops's kitchen, telling war stories. "What was your relationship like with Grace Harper?"

"Pretty good, at first. She was smart, observant."

"Were you close?" Annalisa moved nearer to him, trying to study his hands without being too obvious about it. The ME hadn't reported yet whether Grace had struggled with her attacker, but either way, it was a physically involved murder, and the killer could well have abrasions or cuts from the effort. Colburn's hands looked clean, although he'd bitten his nails down to the quick.

"We chatted a lot online. She was an insomniac like me, so we'd be up in the middle of the night together. We'd watch the same true-crime show and try to guess the outcome."

Nick tilted his head. "Kind of like a date."

"What? No. No, it wasn't like that." The strength of his denial told Annalisa he had wanted to start something with Grace, but it hadn't worked out. Maybe she'd rebuffed his overtures.

"Why not?" she asked. "You were single, right? She was single. Both of you were professionals around the same age, and obviously you had a lot in common." Grace was forty-three, and his driver's license listed

Colburn at thirty-five. Their quick computer check on his background told them that he drove a van for the Tech Squad, doing ad hoc computer repair and consulting in Chicagoland.

Colburn looked to Nick. "Look, I don't want to speak ill of the dead. I just didn't see her like that."

"Hey, I feel you," Nick replied. "If the chemistry isn't there, you can't force it."

"Exactly." Colburn extended his hands in relief at Nick's understanding. "She was nice and all. Just not my type."

"You ever been to her house?" Annalisa asked, and Colburn dropped his arms in defeat.

"If you came all the way over here, you know I have."

"Suppose you tell us about it."

He looked at the TV, which was replaying footage of the night before, showing the coroner's van taking away Grace's body. "A couple of months ago, there was going to be this TV special on famous unsolved crimes throughout history—Jack the Ripper, the D. B. Cooper case, the Gardner Museum heist. I asked Grace if maybe she wanted to come over and watch it."

Nick's eyebrows lifted. "In person?"

"Sure, why not. Sometimes I get sick of looking at the computer screen so long. Eye strain, you know?" He tried to play it cool, like this invitation to Grace was no big deal, but Annalisa saw his ears had turned red. He cleared his throat. "So, she came over, we had some pizza, and watched the show. I showed her my collection." He jerked a nod to the rack of folders he had sitting on a table next to his desk in the would-be dining room.

"Your collection?"

"I have some rare items related to unsolved crimes. Original photographs from the scene. Memorabilia from the families. You never know what might turn out to be useful in the investigation. You can check it out if you want—I've got it all catalogued and preserved." He seemed eager to show it off, so they followed him to his stash. "Like, look here." He took a folder and opened it to reveal a handwritten letter on yellow legal paper, carefully smoothed out and sealed in a plastic bag. "This is a letter written by Henry Lee Lucas to his cousin during the years he was killing people. You can see the crazy right there on the page."

"Do you have anything pertaining to the Lovelorn Killer?" Annalisa asked, and Colburn's lips thinned in menace.

"I did," he said as he replaced the Lucas letter. "Until she stole them from me."

"She? You mean Grace Harper?"

"I bought her dinner, opened up my home to her, and while I'm in the can, she takes my Lovelorn Killer file and stuffs it in her bag. I didn't even know she wanted to work on the case."

"What did she take?" Nick asked, making notes.

"I had copies of the original police reports from three of the victims. Copies of the autopsy photos of Denise Marklund, and a bunch of candids from the Halloween party Katherine Duffy was at the night she died. Not to mention my notes from the case when I looked into it six years ago. I'd have given her copies of this stuff if she asked, but she just stole it."

"So, you went to get it back?" This explained what he'd been doing at Grace's house, pounding on her door.

"Damn right I did, once I realized it was missing. Molly let it slip that the rest of them were looking into the case even though I'd marked it inactive on our site. When I went to confront Grace about the stolen files, she had the balls to call the cops on me, when she's the one who's the thief!" A thought occurred to him. "Hey, can I get it back now? Did you find the stuff in her house?"

"You never got it back?" Nick asked him.

He shook his head. "The officer who showed up told me I could file an official complaint against her, and they'd investigate if I wanted. I didn't get the feeling it would be a real priority for him, though. Plus . . ."

"What?" Annalisa asked when he didn't continue.

He shrugged, seeming almost embarrassed. "The Grave Diggers was my group first. My idea. But the guys, they were all following what she said, looking into the Lovelorn case. If I went after her with the cops . . ."

"You could lose everyone for good," Annalisa continued.

He looked at the floor. "She should've listened to me," he murmured, shuffling his feet. "She should've left it alone." He went to the couch and sank down on it, turning his puffy eyes to the television. "It's got to be him, right? Grace got too close and he decided to shut her up permanently."

"We heard she had a new theory about the case," Annalisa said. "Any idea what it was?"

He shook his head vaguely, still watching the news footage. "We weren't exactly on speaking terms these past few weeks."

"Any idea who she might have told?"

"The others, maybe." He glanced up. "If anyone, probably Barnes. She's always trying to impress him."

Nick's cell phone rang, and he took it out onto the tiny metal balcony that overlooked the alleyway. Annalisa tried not to think about the fact that she was now alone in the room with a brick wall–sized man and his army of guns. She shifted so that she was between Colburn and the door. "When you did look into the Lovelorn Killer investigation," she said, one eye on Nick and one eye on her suspect, "what was your read on the guy?"

"Huh?" He didn't seem to register the question, as fixated as he was on the TV. She found this curious, that he would have actual cops in his house who were working the Lovelorn Killer case, especially with a victim Colburn knew personally, and yet he seemed to prefer the canned version on the screen to the live action in his living room. Nick beckoned her out to the balcony, so she excused herself to join him.

"Zimmer's calling us back in. The all-hands meeting has been moved up now that the press has gone bananas." He nodded inside toward Colburn, who hadn't moved from his sofa. "What do you make of him?"

"There's something he's not telling us."

"What do you think it is?"

"I don't know. If she stole his stuff, that explains why he went after her. The part I'm having trouble with is where he didn't want the Grave Diggers investigating the Lovelorn Killer case. It's a major unsolved investigation right in his backyard. Seems like he should want to be all over it."

"He says the cops had it covered."

She snorted a laugh. "This guy thinks he's as good as a cop. He's not ceding ground to the men and women in blue out of any kind of respect."

"So then what?"

She tapped her pen against her notebook and considered. "When you used to come home late with some bullshit story about working an extra shift, and I'd catch you with your undershirt inside out, you'd just spin your story harder. You said you had to change unis because some drunk puked on you."

"Hey, that actually happened."

"Once, maybe." She sighed. "I'm not pissed at you, Nick. It's way too late for that. I'm just saying, if anyone understands a liar . . ."

He grimaced and clutched at his ribs. "Ouch, you're shooting to kill today, aren't you?"

"Are we done with this guy, or what?"

Nick put his phone away and leaned out over the balcony. "I always liked these old buildings. Look at that scrollwork in the trim over the window. You don't see that kind of stuff in Jacksonville."

"Nick . . ."

"I was ashamed," he said, without turning around.

She froze, wondering if she'd imagined the admission.

"I knew it was shitty, what I was doing to you." He gave her a rueful shrug. "I wanted you to like me anyway."

She folded her arms. "At least you're honest about it now."

"Maybe I'm a changed man."

She no longer traded on maybes. "So, Colburn in there, what's he ashamed of?" It was a rhetorical question for the moment since neither of them had an answer. She pondered the possibilities as they walked back inside. He could be ashamed that Grace got the best of him, that she walked in past his heavy artillery and waltzed out with part of his prized collection. He might also be ashamed that she was leaching the group from him. He clearly wanted to project strength, authority, and superior intelligence. A man like that, he would most fear . . . weakness. She decided to try to riff on that idea before they let him go. He was dazed, sleepless. Maybe he'd give up something useful.

She crossed to where he sat and got right in his personal space, standing over him. "Level with us, Mr. Colburn," she said. "You didn't want the Grave Diggers taking on the Lovelorn Killer case because you'd tried to solve it once and failed. You didn't want to admit you'd come up empty."

The gambit got his attention. He snapped his head away from the TV. "Okay, I didn't solve it," he said. "Last I checked, neither had you." He pointed, and sure enough, there she was again on the screen, looking lost in front of a sea of microphones. He took in the news footage hungrily, as though he hadn't seen it on a constant loop. "You realize he's probably watching you right now. He followed all the media attention."

His words made the hair on her arms stand up. She stood her ground and kept pushing him. "Maybe he is. Maybe he'll make a move, and we'll be the ones to take him down."

"If you find those notes that Grace took from me, you'll see I did contribute to the case. I found a woman in Skokie who'd been getting hang-up calls during the night. This was before the first murder, before everyone had caller ID. She thought it was her ex-husband trying to scare her into giving up the house. Then one night, she came home from work and found a noose hanging in her kitchen."

He swung his head up to look her right in the eyes. She held his gaze. "What happened?"

"She called the cops, which is how I found the report. They discovered a footprint in the garden by the back door. The woman still thought it was her ex because there was no sign of a break-in and he knew where she hid the spare key. But the footprint was a size twelve, and her ex-husband took a ten."

"You think it was the Lovelorn Killer, is that it?"

"I don't know who it was for sure, but fourteen months later, Josephine Harvey came home to find a guy waiting in her bedroom with a handful of ropes."

"We'll look into it," she said, preparing to leave. "Thanks for your time."

"There's more," he called out. "If you care to hear it."

She turned around again. Nick paused at the door. Colburn stood up from the couch, demonstrating once more his considerable height. "I tracked the woman down and asked her about the incident. She's still blaming her ex-husband. Seems he eventually got arrested for slashing her tires and spray painting the C-word on the side of her car. But I walked around that neighborhood, and all the other neighborhoods where the women got killed. There's a sameness to them. They're quiet but not so quiet that a stranger stands out right away. They have lots of trees and bushes—good for cover. Kids ride their bikes, people barbecue on the weekends. See, the profilers who detailed this guy always went on about how much he hates women, but I think he hates the whole package. People move to these areas because they think they're safe, yeah? Well, he's going to take all that away."

Annalisa risked a glance at Nick to see how he was taking this, and he looked as intrigued as she felt. Colburn had obviously given this some thought. "It sounds like you had good insight into the case," she said. "That makes it even more surprising that you shut it down for the Grave Diggers."

He balled one hand into a fist and looked away. Whatever the problem was, she'd hit on it. Nick could feel it too because he stepped back into the room. "Look, man, if you can help get this guy . . ."

"I can't," he snapped. "There, I said it. Are you happy now?"

"Mr. Colburn," Annalisa began, trying to soothe him. "I—"

"I'd been working the case about a month, talking to different people. The Grave Diggers had kicked around some ideas before, but I thought this noose-in-the-kitchen story was a new angle. If he'd broken into one home like this, maybe there were more. But before I could assemble a full report, we got busy at work. I came home late one night and found a noose hanging over my door."

"What did it look like? Do you still have it?" Annalisa asked quickly.

"I don't think you're hearing me. This guy, whoever he is, he never went away. He's been watching the whole time." There it was: His shame. His fear. "Grace should've listened to me when I told her to leave this case. Maybe the others will have the sense to give up now, too."

"Mr. Colburn, if we could bring you down to the station for a formal interview—"

"I can't help you," he said, waving them to the door. "I'm not sure anybody can."

CHAPTER TWELVE

....

MOST INVESTIGATIONS, ANNALISA KNEW, STARTED SMALL. They might have a single detective working the scene, looking for a lone detail that would break the case open. If the victim was dead in the living room, why was there a broken coffee cup in the bathroom? The lifers, the ones who thrived in this role, had a particular combination of patience and tenacity. They were nosy nudges, the kind who would see a loose thread and pull on it till the whole thing unraveled. They would go back to the scene to crawl around on the floor, comb through high school yearbooks and cell phone records, and ask you the same question two dozen times, just to check that your answers matched. After a year or two or ten, the perp might think he'd gotten away with it, until one day, he'd be enjoying a drink at the bar or loading his kids into the minivan, when a detective would come walking out of the past, having DNA tested a single human hair—a mere two-thousandths of an inch wide, but strong enough to send a guy to prison for life. The Lovelorn case had a thousand dangling threads, but so far, the cops hadn't yanked on the right one.

As she took her paper coffee cup into the windowless briefing room, Annalisa faced a crush of humanity. The room held double its usual capacity, men and women squeezed shoulder to shoulder, the whole place buzzing like a hive. Nick waved her over to where he stood with the rest of his usual crew from day shift. "Saved you a chunk of wall," he said as she wedged herself into the narrow opening between his body and the cream-colored paint. They hadn't been this close since they had shared a bed together.

"I guess no one is complaining about being called in on a Saturday," she observed as she looked around at the animated discussion. At the front of the room, she saw Zimmer, the police commissioner, head of state troopers, and a man and woman in matching dark gray suits that had to be FBI. "I see we even have the mayor here," she remarked behind her coffee cup.

"The governor's on via conference call. I'm expecting them to whip out a crystal ball and loop in J. Edgar Hoover at any moment now."

She giggled, laughter escaping her like air from a pressure valve. Unfortunately, the sound attracted Ike Johansson's attention, and he turned around to look at them and their two inches of personal space. "Well now, isn't this cozy? The ball and chain, together again. I hear you're working nights together now—hope it's not too long and hard for you."

"Funny, that's just what I said to your mom last night," Nick replied.

Ike gave a dark laugh and poked Nick in the belly. "My mom's been dead since '94. I guess that makes you a necrophiliac."

He turned around again, chuckling over his victory, and Nick muttered a bunch of choice curse words under his breath. Annalisa arched an eyebrow at him. "I don't know what you're complaining about. If you're into dead people, then I'm the corpse in that little scenario."

"He's a troglodyte."

"Go with that as an insult next time," she advised. "Ike can't spell it so he won't be able to look it up."

Eventually, the meeting got underway with the police chief serving as the emcee even if he didn't have much to contribute directly to the conversation. What he did admit out loud for the first time was that it appeared as though the Lovelorn Killer had resurfaced. A hush fell over the whole room as he said the words. Annalisa noticed a broad-shouldered man in his fifties with a buzz cut and wire-rimmed glasses standing off to the side. She stared hard at his angular face, sifting through her memory banks until his identity clicked into place. He was Don Harrigan, the detective who had worked Katherine Duffy's murder. He rocked up and down on the balls of his feet as though eager to be called off the bench. *Let him wait,* Annalisa thought. This was the guy who'd sidelined Pops, given him scraps of the case he'd hungered to solve. And for what? Don Harrigan had moved on from Chicago PD years ago with Katie's death still unsolved.

They sat through a recap of the current status of the case from Reynolds and Brown. Annalisa noted that they withheld the bleach detail again, stating only that Grace Harper's murder had the unique signature of the Lovelorn Killer. They had alerted the media to be on the lookout for a letter.

"Maybe he's given that up," called out a voice from across the room. Annalisa couldn't see his face. "They never found one for the last victim, right?"

Don Harrigan came to attention and they passed him the mic. "That's correct as far as we know," he said. "We have not found a letter connected with Katherine Duffy's murder. The folks at both the *Tribune* and the *Sun-Times* turned their mailrooms upside down looking for it, but it's always possible it went missing before ever reaching them. Mail gets lost all the time."

Annalisa thought of Chris Colburn and his gruesome collection of murder memorabilia. Maybe someone in the mail delivery chain had spotted the last letter, guessed what it was, and taken it as a souvenir. Harrigan had some souvenirs of his own to display. Annalisa flinched as he put up a slide showing Katie bound and dead on the floor of her home. Annalisa, Colin, and her brothers had built forts in that den, roasted marshmallows at the fireplace, and chased each other around the green sofa that was just visible in the corner of the photo. She had to force herself to pay attention to Harrigan's highlights of the case.

"We know this guy stalked his victims for days, maybe even weeks, so you can bet Katherine Duffy was not a random choice. Her husband, Owen Duffy, did ten years on the job. The neighborhood had four other officers living on those two blocks alone, squad cars often parked right on the street. Katie fit the profile of the other victims, as much as there was one. Female aged twenty-five to forty-five, dark hair, living in a nice neighborhood. But we'd been after this guy for years without any success, so I'm sure he got a special charge out of tiptoeing past a bunch of cops to commit his heinous crimes right in their own backyard. It was the ultimate ef-you. What he may or may not have known, depending on how closely he watched her, was a tidbit we kept private at the time: Katie was eight weeks pregnant."

Annalisa audibly gasped, but she wasn't the only one. Colin had been an only child and, at sixteen, had seemed likely to stay that way. She had shared her brothers with him, the pack of them running in and out of each other's houses. Bike races down the big hill. Packing sandwiches to bring to the community pool in the summer, where they took turns dunking each other in the chlorine until suppertime. Only her brothers grew up one by one, escaping childhood into their own lives, leaving just Annalisa and Colin alone together at the end. By the time he took her hand and led her behind the soaring oak in his backyard, it felt like she'd been preparing her whole life to kiss him. She wondered if he had known that his mother was pregnant; if so, he had never breathed a word.

Harrigan walked through the parts of the case they all knew by now. Katie had been at the neighborhood Halloween party but then suddenly felt ill, so she had gone home early. With the news of the pregnancy, this development made more sense. Her husband, Owen, and son, Colin, stayed behind. A couple of hours later, around eleven thirty, Owen went to check on his wife and found her dead on the living room floor. Her costume was laid out beside her, except for the scarves, several of which the killer had incorporated into his bindings. The red one encircled Katie's neck, and this festive party prop, in the end, was what killed her—choking her until she could not breathe.

Annalisa discreetly averted her gaze from the gruesome photos. Katie had taken her to buy her first bra because Ma refused to do it. She'd given her makeup tips and shown her how to change a tire. *You don't want to be caught out waiting for some guy to do it,* she'd said. *Then they'll think you owe them.*

She swallowed back the lump in her throat as Harrigan gave way to the FBI profilers. They, too, had little information to impart that hadn't been covered by the voracious news stories back in the day. The offender was probably a white male, aged twenty to thirty-five at the time of the initial attacks, so add twenty-odd years to that estimate now. He's educated; the letters he sent reveal an erudite vocabulary. He picked confident women in residential neighborhoods and studied their habits, which meant he was comfortable in the environs. He blended in. His familiarity with diverse areas in and around Chicago suggested that he was from the area and also that he might travel for his job. A regional salesman, perhaps. Someone who could be charming when he chose to be. The complex knots in the bindings might mean he was a sailor or military man, or just someone really into Boy Scouts.

Annalisa thought of Grace Harper and her weather reports. None of the briefings had mentioned anything related to this angle, so Annalisa raised her hand at question time. "Has there been any link to the weather?"

Brown fielded the response with a slight frown. "What type of link?"

"I don't know," Annalisa replied honestly. "Some of the deaths were preceded by large storms. I wondered if that could be triggering him somehow."

The men looked at each other and then back at her. "He hates the women," Brown said finally. "Not the rain."

When the meeting broke up, Zimmer called Annalisa and Nick over for a private consultation. "What was that issue about the weather?" she asked, curious.

"Grace Harper was tracking the weather reports around the time of each murder. I don't know why."

"Well, stay on it."

Annalisa glanced at Nick, and his face showed he shared her surprise. "We're keeping the case?"

Zimmer looked over to where Harrigan, Brown, and the chief were deep in conversation with the Fibbies. She jerked her head to the side, indicating that Annalisa and Nick follow her out into the corridor. Once there, she trained her intense brown eyes right on Annalisa. "I remember how bad your father wanted the Duffy case," she began, and Annalisa opened her mouth to defend Pops. Zimmer held up her hands to ward off the protest. "Harrigan was right—he was too close to it. He and Duffy rode together, and he had a long-standing social relationship with the victim. I'm sure you must've known her pretty well yourself."

Annalisa looked away. "I was just a kid."

"A cop's kid," Zimmer replied.

Annalisa wasn't sure how much this mattered. Adults were inter-changeable in her world back then. Now she could view Katie with an adult lens, with a cop's view, as Zimmer would put it. Katie had taken such pleasure in putting together an outfit, coordinating with playful accessories and funky shoes. The killer had left her naked, her clothes laid out where she could watch them while she died. Like Grace Harper had been forced to listen to her music boxes as he'd choked her. It wasn't enough to take the women's lives. He wanted to humiliate them in the most personal way while doing it. "The neighborhood back then subscribed to the whole 'it takes a village' theory. We all knew Katie Duffy. I knew if I got out of line, Katie or some other parent would report it back to Pops." With Katie gone, the chain broke down. People retreated inside their homes and kept their doors locked and curtains closed.

"A neighborhood with eyes like that made her a high-risk victim," Zimmer said. "An ef-you to the cops, like Harrigan was saying."

"If Katie was picked to highlight the cops' incompetence, then Grace Harper had to be a statement victim as well," Nick replied. "He knew she was working his case."

Zimmer nodded. "We don't know where this asshole is, but we have a good idea of where he has been lately—close to Grace Harper. I want you two to keep working the victim. Somehow, she crossed paths with this guy, and we need to find out where. I want to know everything about her and this Grave Diggers group she was in. You turn that neighborhood upside down. If there was a refrigerator repairman out recently, I want to know about it." She glanced down the hall to where the men in suits stalked off together, making plans of their own. "The Washington contingent brings fresh eyes and more resources, which we sorely need. But they don't live here like we do. Go shake all the trees you can, and just be careful with what falls out. If this guy was watching Grace Harper, he's damn sure going to be watching us. Report anything you find first to me."

....

Zimmer's words stayed with Annalisa through the rest of the day spent logging witness statements and drafting a list of new people to interview. It was dark by the time she drove Nick back to his car, which sat two doors down from Grace Harper's house. The media vans had vanished; the crowds had dissipated. The street was draped in shadow and silence. She cut the engine but Nick seemed in no hurry to leave her car. He sat with his head back against the seat, his eyes closed, but she felt a tense energy radiating off of him.

"Have you told him yet?" he asked without opening his eyes.

"Told who?"

"Him. The son. Colin, I think you said his name was." He finally looked at her, his eyes dark in the low light. "You never mentioned his name to me before."

Silence stretched between them, and her tongue grew thick in her mouth. "It was a long time ago," she said finally.

He gave a dark chuckle. "You were twenty when I met you, Vega. Your entire life was modern history back then. I know we weren't together long, but you might have brought it up somewhere in there that your boyfriend's mom got murdered by the Lovelorn Killer."

"I never said he was my boyfriend."

He looked her over. "Please. Have some respect for my professional capabilities, at least."

She felt her face grow hot. They were trained to listen for all the things that people didn't say. "Okay, so we dated." Lame words, in which he could probably hear the lie. Or maybe he was like her family who'd smiled condescendingly and tut-tutted about the cuteness of puppy love. Notes exchanged on lined school paper. Phone calls under the covers at night, when Colin's was the only voice she heard. They'd had plans, so many plans. They would both apply to the University of Chicago. He would go for English, or maybe journalism, and she would be prelaw. They would marry after graduation and take a year off to explore the world. He could write from anywhere. Annalisa still had the notes he'd given her, funny stories he made up to amuse them during endless boring classes in hot June schoolrooms. Her favorite was one about how Mrs. Hill the geometry teacher had been a poodle in another life, which explained her odd sniffing habit and the jar of dry biscuits on her desk.

She kept the notes in a shoebox along with other mementos—a ticket stub from the first movie they'd seen together, a plastic spider ring he'd given her at Halloween. Included in the set was a color picture taken at a Fourth of July barbecue, back when people printed out pictures to hold in their hands rather than confining them forever to a tiny screen. Annalisa had held this particular photo a lot. It showed her and Colin at a picnic table with juicy slices of watermelon in front of them. They were young and dewy from the summer heat, her ponytail a mess, Colin's strong, tanned arm across her shoulders. Ten minutes before the photo was taken, they'd been having frantic sex up in his twin bed on top of the rocket ship comforter. Ma had sent them in to chop the watermelon, but instead they'd crept upstairs to fool around. She could still recall the feel of her shorts sliding down her bare legs, of Colin's naked weight on her body. They'd been intimate before, but this was the first time he'd actually made her come. Her head was hard against the board, the window open so she couldn't make any noise as the pleasure coiled tighter, tighter, until the fireworks went off behind her eyes.

"We loved each other," she said to Nick. The grownups thought they had been playing around, rehearsing for some greater love in the future, but Annalisa knew it was impossible even then. Her heart couldn't hold any more.

Nick let his head fall back, his gaze drifting to the shard of moon just visible through the car's sunroof. "I think I saw that," he said eventually, his voice wondering. "Back then. I think maybe I fooled myself into thinking it was for me."

Annalisa clenched her hands in her lap. He broke up their marriage, not her. "Why do you think Zimmer wants us to report only to her?" she asked, pointedly changing the subject.

He sat up. "You and me, we're new to this story. Our hands are clean."

"What do you mean, our hands are clean?" She rested hers on the steering wheel.

"There's one theory about the Lovelorn case that didn't get mentioned today. Another kind of person besides a sales guy or deliveryman, someone who patrols the neighborhoods. Someone who could access lots of information on the victims without any trouble at all."

She gripped the wheel. "You mean a cop."

He pointed a finger at her. *Bingo.* "I don't know about you, but I am dead on my feet. I gotta get some rest if we're doing this all again tomorrow. Let's say eight o'clock?"

"Eight it is."

He got out but leaned in through the open door. Grace Harper's house loomed completely deserted in the background, the front yard cordoned off with yellow tape. He patted the roof of her car. "Drive home safe, okay?"

She watched him get into his vehicle and then pointed her car west, toward home. She reached over and turned the radio on for company, for a human voice in the dark. As she idled at a red light, Tom Petty sang plaintively how waiting is the hardest part. The song finished and the female host came on, full of cheer. "For you sports fans out there, the Cubs clobbered the Cardinals tonight, ten to one. They'll go for the sweep tomorrow, but we'd better hope they get the game in early. There's a storm rolling in."

CHAPTER THIRTEEN

....

NORMALLY, ANNALISA LIKED LIVING ALONE, AFTER SPENDING HER YOUTH TRIP-
PING OVER HER BROTHERS' HOCKEY SKATES IN THE HALLWAY AND WAITING
HALF AN HOUR FOR HER TURN IN THE BATHROOM. She had been lucky enough
to snag her ground floor condo when it came on the market during the
downturn a few years ago. Her upstairs neighbors, a young couple who'd
moved to the outer suburbs after they had spawned a couple of kids, had
their unit up for sale at a price Annalisa could never afford now.

She had lived in the same spot in Avondale for four years, but she
still felt a pride of ownership every time she arrived home. The two
1920s brick buildings sitting side by side had an identical outward appearance, each with three flats that had been fully renovated. Annalisa's
garden-level apartment had its own front entrance, a stunning exposed
yellow brick wall in the living area, and a tricked-out chef's kitchen that
was completely wasted on her. She dragged herself over the threshold
and unloaded her jacket, holster, and tote bag full of reading on the
nearest flat surface.

Pops hadn't viewed her treasured oasis with the same appreciation. He
had visited just once, before his Parkinson's worsened. He had inspected
her substantial front lock with a nod but scoweled at the gorgeous front
windows. "Why don't they have bars?"

"Because this is my home, not a prison."

"I don't like the idea of you sitting here alone on your sofa in front of the big open windows like that. Anyone could be out there watching."

Annalisa had been unable to resist needling him. "Who says I'm always alone?"

At his glower, she had given him an affectionate squeeze. "Trust me, Pops, I'm not doing anything interesting enough in here that anyone would want to watch."

Pops had been even more put out by the best feature of the place, in Annalisa's opinion: a shared green space in the back of the units, tucked between the brick buildings and the alley. It had deck chairs and a grill and even a pair of shady trees, but her favorite part was the three large planters, each overflowing with flowers in the summer, maintained by Amy Yakamoto in the unit next door. Annalisa's lone contribution to the garden was a large green ceramic frog, its wide mouth fixed in a cheery smile. Made by Annalisa's grandmother, Filmore the Frog had sat on the Vega family stoop since before Anna was born, and Ma had gifted it to her when she got her new place. Her brothers were still openly bitter.

"No bars back here either," Pops had said of her portal to the back-yard oasis. "And look at this big window. Perfect for peeping."

Annalisa had refused to cow to his fear. "I know, right? There's a squirrel who won't leave me alone."

Now, in her first return home since the discovery of Grace Harper's body, Annalisa walked to the windows and stared out into the black night. She could see only her own reflection, which appeared haggard and pale after nearly two days on her feet. She went to the kitchen and took out a frozen package of macaroni and cheese to stick in the micro-wave. While it zapped her food, she opened her refrigerator and contemplated the array of wine bottles lined up in the door. Red or white with Lean Cuisine? She compromised on a rosé and poured herself exactly one glass. Her mother would die if she could see her daughter eating like this, right out of a cardboard box, standing at the kitchen counter next to a stack of junk mail. No matter what had happened during the day, Maria set her table with stoneware and cloth napkins every night.

Annalisa's personal cell phone buzzed on the counter, and she turned it over to read the text. It was Sassy. *I've got the number you asked for. Are you really sure you want to do this?*

Annalisa texted back. *Yes, give it to me.*

She waited, phone in hand, as the little dots went back and forth for some time, indicating that Sassy was either composing a novel-length response or writing and deleting her reply repeatedly. Annalisa rolled her eyes and picked up her wine glass for another long sip as she waited for Sassy's response to come through. This was their sworn duty to one another, she knew. She had been the one to pull Sassy into the alcove at the church right before her wedding to Alex. *You don't have to do this, you know,* she had whispered to Sassy at the time. *You, me, this big white dress—we can call a cab and get the hell out of here right now. Everyone in there will just have to suck it up and deal.*

Sassy had given her a dazzling, peaceful smile. *No, sweetie, thank you. I'm good. It took so long to get here, which you know better than anyone. But this is it. This is finally our happy ending.*

Back in high school, she and Sassy had joked about having a double wedding one day. Sassy and Alex, Annalisa and Colin. Happy endings all around. Finally, Sassy's text came through: *It's thoughtful of you to want to be the one to tell him, but you should ask yourself how much he wants to know. He left on purpose. He hasn't come back. Unless you can tell him that you caught the guy, I don't know how much there is to say.*

Annalisa's throat ached, full of one-sided conversations she'd never spoken aloud. Part of her was afraid when she made contact with Colin, the years of stored-up emotion would come rushing out. *It's my job,* she wrote back. *I didn't choose this.* She drained the rest of her wine, her gaze trained on the phone. Nothing from Sassy for a long time. Then the dots. Colin's number came through on the screen. Then more dots. Pausing, erasing. Silence. Finally: *I love you.*

Now that she had what she wanted, Annalisa tried to talk herself up before placing the call. She paced with her phone for a few minutes before retrieving the wine bottle and pouring another half glass. Growing up, their parents made alcohol seem like witty, boisterous fun as they had mixed cocktails by the basement bar and then laughed the night away playing cards or sitting in the wicker chairs in the backyard, listening to music. The Duffys and the Vegas had their own clubhouse, no kids allowed. That last Halloween night, Colin had sneaked out a bottle of rum from his parents' stash, and Annalisa had been terrified he'd get caught with it. But his mother had been too busy scoffing at Colin's choice of costume to notice anything he'd smuggled inside it.

"David Bowie?" she'd said, taking in his red leather pants, punk rocker mullet, and the signature lightning bolt drawn across his face. Colin had been very into "Rebel, Rebel" at the time.

"What's wrong with it?" His chin had lifted in defiance. Annalisa had hung back against the kitchen wall, trying to blend into the fruit design on the wallpaper.

Katie had had her fortune teller's garb on, her exotic eye makeup and flowing scarves. "His 1973 show at the Hammersmith Odeon," she'd told her son. "You can look it up because they were making a movie of the tour. Bowie owned that stage, strutting and gyrating and practically setting himself on fire to hold that crowd's attention. He was weird and wonderful, and then all of a sudden, there he was, saying it's over, this was the last show. You can actually hear the hearts breaking, everyone's but his. He knew Ziggy was done, and it was time to become someone else, no matter how much Ziggy was loved. He just walked away." She'd made a magician's poof gesture with her hands. "When you can kill off part of yourself so that the rest can get better—then you'll know."

"Know what?" Colin had asked, still skeptical.

She'd tugged his leotard and snapped it back. "How to carry off this costume, for one thing. It's not in the wigs and makeup, my boy. It's the attitude."

Annalisa shook off the memory, drank down her wine, and looked again at her phone. Colin had done it. He had walked away. She had to see if she could summon the words to make him come back. She swallowed twice and tapped the phone number with her finger, closing her eyes as it rang through.

"Hello?"

She startled and nearly fumbled the phone. Her mouth had gone completely dry. "Colin. Hi. It's—it's me."

"Anna?"

"Yes," she managed, sinking into her couch for support. "Annalisa Vega."

"As if there's another one," he replied with a low chuckle. "Wow. I can't believe it's you."

"I hope I'm not interrupting anything."

"Just my sleep," he said. "It's 4 A.M. here."

"Sorry." She cringed inwardly at her Luddite mistake. "Where are you?"

"Budapest. I'm taking in the thermal baths. They're full of minerals and supposed to have restorative powers."

"And do they?"

"I'll let you know after I do a pub tour tomorrow on only four hours of sleep."

"Could be fun," she ventured.

"Probably less fun if you have to take notes and pictures for a 2,500-word magazine piece. The concept is cool. They're 'ruin pubs'—ancient buildings converted by a ragtag conglomeration of anarchists, artists' collectives, squatters, and hipsters. You'd probably love the place."

She felt a jab of annoyance. How the hell would he know what she loved anymore? "Colin . . ."

"I heard you got married," he said abruptly.

She didn't reply right away, just listened to him breathing. "Yes. For about ten minutes."

"I didn't get an invitation."

"I wouldn't have known where to send one."

"Yeah, I suppose so," he said after a beat. Was that actual regret in his voice, or did she just want to hear it? "Sorry it didn't work out."

He could have someone lying in the bed next to him, she realized with a start. She'd asked Sassy once, years ago, what his status was. She'd thought enough time had passed by then that she could sell her interest as casual, but Sassy gave her a pitying look that meant she hadn't pulled it off. *He doesn't talk to us about that stuff,* she'd replied, *but I can't imagine he's too serious with anyone. He's never in the same place long enough to form attachments.*

"Colin, I'm calling in an official capacity."

"Oh?" Caution crept into his tone. "You're a cop now, right? Not a lawyer."

So, he did remember something about their plans. She took a deep breath. "Yeah, that's right. The other night, I got called to the scene of a murder. A woman had been killed in her own home."

"That's terrible." He sounded robotic, remote, like she'd told him about a bomb going off half a world away.

"There were pictures and notes tacked up on the wall. It turns out she was part of an amateur sleuths group that has solved some cold cases, and this woman, Grace Harper, decided to try her hand at the Lovelorn case. She petitioned the media to do a story to try to draw him out."

"I see. And you're thinking it might have worked."

Colin was always quick. "It's possible. She was murdered in the same fashion as the original victims. The FBI is here looking into it."

"And what about you?" His voice was high and tight. "Are you looking into it too?"

"Yes." She stroked the couch pillow absently. "Grace Harper's case. Not—not your mom's."

"If they're related, then it's all the same."

"If they're related, it means he's come out of hiding for the first time in twenty years. It's a whole new chance to catch him."

"Sure," he said, plainly unconvinced. "Maybe this time."

She plucked at a bit of fluff and looked to a framed photo of her family and his that she kept on the bookshelf. They crowded together in the Vegas' lush summer yard, wearing red, white, and blue for the Fourth of July holiday. Happier days, when everyone was still young. Pops had hair on his head and arms strong enough to hoist Alex on his shoulders, years away from getting sick. Katie Duffy had a girly ponytail and a gingham crop top that made her look youthful and carefree. Annalisa calculated that she was older now than Katie had been the day the photo was taken, math that never seemed possible no matter how many times she refigured it. "It's probable that the FBI will want to talk to you." He was the last Duffy standing, the only direct link they had to Katie from those pictures.

Colin faltered at the prospect. "I— What would I have to say?"

"I don't know. What do you remember?"

He didn't answer for a long time, and she felt the weight of all the intervening years. "Everything."

She let out an involuntary sob and covered her mouth with her hand.

"I'll—I'll book a flight right now." She heard him scrambling, knocking something to the floor. He started tapping on computer keys.

"Okay, great. Sassy will be so glad to see you," she said, recovering as she wiped at her eyes with her sleeve.

The typing stopped. "And what about you?"

She shook her head, denying him even though he couldn't see it. "Just let me know when you get here."

She ended the call and tossed her phone far away from her on the couch, as though it had become radioactive. She was shaking and wrapped her arms around her middle. Outside, the wind swelled up and rattled the windows. Annalisa grabbed an afghan from the back of the couch and curled up under it, pulling it even over the top of her head. Unbidden, her mind whirled through old memories, fast and jerky like the reel running out at the end of an old movie. Climbing trees with Alex and Tony. Colin's rum-soaked kiss on Halloween night. Katie lying out in the backyard with shiny sunglasses hiding her face. Pops and Alex screaming at each other in the driveway at the party because Alex showed up drunk.

A crack of thunder woke her up, her heart already thudding from her dreams. She sat bolt upright, the blanket sliding from her head. The lights had gone off, and she could see nothing in the dark. She'd hated the dark, ever since that Halloween. Even now, she slept with a light on in the bathroom. Her heart in her throat, she felt her way across the room and pulled back the curtain, revealing nothing but a black hole outside. No ambient light at all. The whole block must be out, she realized. A flash of lightning turned the room bright white for a split second just as her cell phone buzzed.

She tried to find it in the dark and realized it was her work phone, not her personal one. It reverberated as she tracked the sound to her jacket. *Please not another murder,* she thought as she yanked it free. She did not recognize the number.

"This is Vega."

There was a long, eerie pause. "Annalisa," said a whispery voice on the other end.

"Yes. Who is this?"

Nothing. Her temper piqued.

"Who am I speaking to?"

"You're really pretty. I just wanted to tell you that."

"Thanks," she said flatly. "Now tell me who you are."

"You already know me," he said, and the hairs on her arms stood up. "You just can't see me yet. Tell me—are you afraid of the dark?"

Wait, he could see her? A gust of wind shook the trees outside and rattled her bones. "What the hell is this? Some kind of joke?" She stumbled to the window and pressed her face against the glass. "If you're on my property . . ."

"No, it's too soon to visit," he said. "We've only just met." And then he was gone.

CHAPTER FOURTEEN

....

GRACE NOTES

Journal Entry #427

IF YOU WATCH A LOT OF TRUE-CRIME SHOWS, YOU START TO NOTICE A SAMENESS TO THEM. The murders take place in towns where "this kind of thing never happens," and I always shake my head at these people who are trotted out by the producers to demonstrate the innocence lost. What I can't understand is, how is anyone innocent anymore? The first time they tracked down one of these guys and hauled him out of his hole, only to find a nebbish of a man instead of the monster they'd been expecting, maybe then you could understand the initial surprise. But now? BTK had a wife and kids in his suburban home and a shack full of murder props outside in the back. Gary Ridgway was just average-sized, and he wore thick glasses, peering at the hookers on the street like a granny ordering soup in a restaurant. John Wayne Gacy had a heart condition that excused him from gym class at school, but somehow, he found the strength to murder more than thirty people. Cripes, if you told me today that old Mrs. Saunders on the corner had a bunch of bodies buried in her backyard, I wouldn't be that shocked. You never know about people.

Molly came over today so I could show her my progress. She didn't like the photos of the victims on the wall. "It seems like something he would do," she told me. "Displaying them like that."

If he had, he would need someplace completely private to do it, like BTK with his shed. You wouldn't want to risk any family member or hapless landlord stumbling in to see the evidence. "He didn't take trophies," I reminded Molly. Or, if he did, the cops kept a tight lid on it.

Molly brought up an interesting idea as she looked at the newspaper clippings I tacked up. "Maybe he didn't need to," she said. "Maybe that's part of why he sent those letters to the press, to get them to make trophies for him." That would mean he's been subsisting on yellow, faded paper for years now. Sure, the news throws him a bone every so often, but the Lovelorn Killer doesn't make the serial killer hit parade because he's never been caught. You need that happy ending when the monster's true face is revealed. If he wants to be famous, he has to be caught. What a torture that must be for him. Probably ties him up like those knots he loves so much.

"That's how we force him out," I said to Molly. "We get him back in the news, give him a taste of that old high."

Molly turned around so she didn't see the dead people. I forget sometimes how it must look to other people. "But there's nothing new to report on," she said.

That's why I keep all the pictures and reports tacked up on the wall. There's something in there. I just can't see it yet.

I can see him, though. He's older now, less nimble, but just as ordinary as he ever was. He has thinning hair and a jowly face, aging like the rest of us who've grown up alongside him. I see him driving around the old neighborhoods where he made his kills, watching for the women in particular. I wonder if it's harder to find them now that we're all inside, yoked to our screens. Sure, he could go to a beach or a park where lots of people gather, but that's not his scene. He's at home on a street just like mine, with trees and families and delivery trucks. He's probably been among us this whole time, laughing to himself about how stupid we are not to recognize him. He must be feeling pretty damn smug right about now. If he can just keep a lid on his urges, if he can just keep his mouth shut a little longer, he will have gotten away with it. But there's the rub. The longer he waits, the farther he fades into history. Into eternal anonymity.

Because that's the thing with these men: they could be anyone, but they're mostly nobodies. Nobody important, anyway, because no one knows their secrets. They live in the same houses and eat the same food and wear the same skin as other humans, passing by us on the street like whistling past a graveyard. Only in the end when they finally come out into the light do we blink at them in a horrible kind of recognition: Oh, it's you. You were right here all along.

CHAPTER FIFTEEN

....

ANNALISA WAITED OUT THE REMAINING HOURS OF THE NIGHT ON HER COUCH WITH HER GUN AND HER CELL PHONE IN EASY REACH. She kept hearing Chris Colburn say how he'd come home to find a noose over his door and his warnings about how the killer still tracked the case. By dawn, her nerves were so frayed that it was just as well her phone hadn't rung again—she'd probably have shot it. She held her breath leaving her house, half expecting to see a dangling rope, but she found nothing but the birds chirping down at her from the trees.

Sunday morning in Chicago meant church traffic, cars streaming out of the various parking lots, pedestrians dressed in their worship-service finery. Annalisa remembered with a shudder how Ma had forced her into some frilly frock and spit shined her face as she'd hustled her into St. Thecla's for morning mass along with her brothers. Tony usually dozed off, Vincent doodled cartoons in the edge of the bulletin, while Annalisa and Alex had elbowed each other for space in the hard wooden pew. Today, the bright colors on the women's spring dresses clashed with the stormy sky overhead. The rain had stopped in the early morning, but the thick clouds churned, gathering strength for another round.

At the station, she found Nick unshaven and already into his second cup of coffee. "Couldn't sleep, so I figured I'd be more useful here than watching infomercials on my couch," he said.

She nodded at the paper printouts on the desk in front of him. "Find anything?"

"I ran Jared Barnes through the computer. He's forty-six and a local lad, born and raised in Cicero, now makes his home on the Near South Side. He signed up with the army out of high school and worked as an MP before being honorably discharged eight years later. Clean record. The only other mention is a traffic accident fifteen years ago. I don't know the details. I figure he can fill us in when we talk to him."

"Ex-military, huh?"

"Yeah, I noticed that too. Bet he knows his way around a knot." He got up and snaked his suit jacket from the back of his chair. "You ready to roll?"

Annalisa glanced at Zimmer's office and saw her on the phone in deep conversation. She'd run her hands through her short dark hair so often it now stood on end, and Annalisa spotted a bottle of antacid medication sitting on the desk. The last thing she wanted was to make more problems for her boss. "Something weird happened last night," she said to Nick. "I don't know whether to tell the commander or not." Her late-night call seemed strange but less frightening in the cold light of day.

Nick sat on the edge of the desk and gave her his full attention. "You can start by telling me."

She recapped the brief conversation with her anonymous caller, and it sounded outlandish when she said it out loud. Men didn't call her pretty, for one thing. She had strong, angular features and didn't bother with fancy hair or makeup. She dressed like the guys around her, in suits and shoes meant for walking the pavement all day. She'd deliberately adopted body language that said *don't mess with me,* and so the men who got past this barrier, the men who desired her, wanted her because of her steel core. Nick had shucked her jeans and yanked her T-shirt off that first night like he was a man dying of thirst, his open mouth hungry on her skin.

Her caller, whoever he was, didn't know her at all. "Then he hung up," she said to Nick as she finished the story.

"He," Nick repeated. "You're sure it was a male?"

"I'd say ninety-five percent sure." She made her voice low and raspy. "He was talking like this, so it was hard to tell."

"Did you trace the number?"

"This morning. It's a burner phone."

Nick looked troubled and Annalisa's anxiety bubbled up again. She'd been hoping he would say it was a stupid prank, nothing to worry about. "We tell her," he said, turning around to look at Zimmer. "We tell her right now."

Zimmer also did nothing to reassure Annalisa's fears when she heard the story. "You say he called your work number?" she asked, taking careful notes.

Annalisa and Nick stood next to each other in front of her desk, like kids called to the principal's office. Annalisa made sure to get her story straight. "Yes, but I gave out at least three dozen copies of my card yesterday alone when we canvassed Grace Harper's neighborhood. I've given out hundreds of them since I got the phone last year."

"Did the voice seem familiar, like it might've been somebody you talked to yesterday?"

Annalisa searched her memory and shook her head. "No, but like I said, he was trying to disguise it. I was on television . . . anyone could've seen me."

"That's what I'm afraid of. Give me the number. I'll see if we can find out anything about the phone and where it might've been purchased."

Annalisa had it memorized by now, but she hesitated before reciting the numbers. "You really think it could be him?"

Zimmer regarded her with serious eyes. "It's a long shot at best. Probably he's just your garden-variety creeper, but either way, he's messing with one of my people, and I plan to put a stop to it. I've been on the job twenty-nine years now, and I haven't lost anyone yet. If it's all the same to you, I'd like to keep that record going. So if this guy calls back, try to record it. Then call me immediately. I don't care what time of day or night it is."

"Call me too," Nick was quick to add.

Both women looked at him. He spread his hands in self-defense.

"What? I can't be concerned about my partner?"

"I can handle myself," Annalisa told him. "I've had the exact same training as you, remember?"

Nick ducked his head in acknowledgment of this, but then he

touched the photo of Grace Harper that lay on Zimmer's desk. "Yeah, but I don't look like the victims."

....

If the Near South Side were a person, it'd be a squinty old gentleman in a suit and bow tie, sitting on the porch in a creaky rocking chair, saying, "Boy, I've seen some things." Over the past century, the neighborhood by Museum Campus had been a blue-collar residential zone, a slum, a warehouse district, and a hotbed of railway action. It had re-gentrified throughout the 1990s thanks to a housing boom that included Jared Barnes's nondescript but well-kept brick apartment building. There was an intercom system outside the glass front doors, and Nick and Annalisa used it to let him know they'd arrived. "Come on up," he said, buzzing them inside. Annalisa saw signs for both a gym room and a pool, and she felt a pang of longing for the easy access to these amenities. They reached the third floor and knocked on the door marked 323, which opened right away to reveal a man sitting in a wheelchair.

"Detectives," he said, rolling back to admit them. "Jared Barnes. Please come in."

Annalisa looked at Nick to see if he'd previously picked up on Barnes's disability, but his slight shake of the head told her he had not. "Mr. Barnes," she said, "thanks for seeing us."

"Please just call me Barnes. Everyone does." He looked like ex-military, with his close-cropped hair, toned arms, and collared polo-style shirt. "I have coffee on if you'd like some," he said as he pushed himself toward the kitchen.

"No, thanks," said Nick. "Any more of the stuff, and my blood will run brown."

"I hear that," Barnes said as he helped himself to a cup. "Did you know back in the Army, they ran tests on us to determine the exact amount of caffeine consumption required to achieve peak performance? Made us take these capsules and do all kinds of reaction-time tests."

"Oh, yeah?" Nick sounded intrigued. "What'd they find out?"

Barnes smiled broadly. "Well, now, that's classified." He gestured at the living room. "Please make yourselves comfortable."

Annalisa and Nick sat side by side on a cheap, futon-style couch.

Like Chris Colburn, Jared Barnes had a large-screen TV and an exten-sive computer setup at the desk in the corner. Unlike Chris Colburn or Grace Harper, Barnes didn't display his macabre hobby on his walls. Instead, he'd hung a canvas painting of a stylized American flag with a soldier in silhouette and a framed Ansel Adams picture print showing a black-and-white forest, full of skinny ghostlike trees.

"I'm still in shock over Grace's death," he said, shaking his head. "And what they're saying on the news, that it's the Lovelorn Killer . . . is that true?"

"The media is focusing on that angle, but we're investigating all possibilities right now," Annalisa replied. "How long had you known Grace?"

"Let's see. I joined the Grave Diggers shortly before she did, so that would have been about three years ago."

"What attracted you to the group?"

"I'm online all day now. I do medical transcription from home, and, not to brag, but I can type a hundred fifty words a minute, so I can knock out my work in a few hours and then have the rest of the day free. I ran across a little news story a few years ago about Chris Colburn and the group's efforts to locate a girl who went missing in Rhode Is-land back in 1986. I thought with my training and background, I could be of some help."

"You mean your service as an MP," Nick said.

"That's right. There are a number of us vets in the group, from all over the place. Ex-cops, too. Most are civilians, through and through, but that doesn't mean they can't make valuable contributions to the investigations."

"What about Chris Colburn?" Annalisa asked.

Barnes blinked at her. "You haven't talked to him?"

"We have, but we're interested in your opinion of him."

"Chris is . . . intense. He's extremely committed to the mission of the group, but he can be territorial about the cases."

"Like the Lovelorn case?"

Barnes's mouth thinned out and he put his coffee cup aside. "Espe-cially that one. He didn't want us investigating, but Grace was deter-mined to take it on."

"What did you think?"

He tented his fingers together as he considered his words. "I thought it could be an exciting challenge. It's higher profile than anything the group has attempted before—a bigger puzzle, if you want to think of it that way."

"How did Chris react when he found out Grace wanted to pursue the case?"

"He went off on her. Threatened to shut down the whole group. She said we didn't need him and could just start another site with a different name. He'd be all by himself with no group to lead."

"I can't imagine that went over well," Annalisa replied.

"It was a huge mess for all of us, especially because most of us didn't want to choose sides. It was like we were the kids and Mom and Dad were fighting." He paused. "And, well, like any family fight . . . things can get personal."

"What do you mean?" Nick asked.

Barnes looked almost coy. Annalisa repressed a beleaguered sigh at the prospect of dealing with another would-be Sherlock Holmes eager for his time in the sun. Whatever this guy knew, he was going to make them work for it. "Oh, I assume you know about Chris already, but it was news to us."

Annalisa gritted her teeth. "What news?"

"About his application to join the Chicago Police Department. He was always bragging to us about how he got a perfect score on the entrance exam, like he was some investigative super genius. But Molly has an uncle on the job, and she finally asked him about Chris and his perfect score. It turns out he aced the written test, all right—but he flunked the psych evaluation." There was a triumphant gleam in his eye. "Perfect on paper, but he couldn't hack it in the real world."

Annalisa made a note. There were myriad reasons to fail the psych screening, so they would need to follow up for additional insight. "Did Molly tell Grace this news?"

"Oh, yeah, and she told Chris, too. I kind of don't blame her, the way he'd been acting like he was the only one who got a vote in determining the cases we took on. Like he had some divine knowledge."

"How did Chris react?"

"He had his usual temper tantrum. He locked Grace out of the forums and accused her of stealing his stuff. Molly had to use her admin power to override him and let Grace back in."

"What was your relationship like with Grace?" Nick asked. Annalisa recalled Chris's assessment: if Grace told anyone her theory, it would be Barnes.

"I liked her. She got the group to start meeting near public transportation so that I could join them, and she was fearless about calling out bad behavior. One time, we were walking to the L together, and this guy ahead of us tossed his lit cigarette into the grass on the common. He was a big dude, over six feet and two hundred pounds at least. She snatched up that butt and chased him down to give him hell about it. I think he was genuinely remorseful by the time she got done."

"Did you see her socially?"

He looked from one to the other, incredulous. "You mean like a date?"

"Like whatever you Grave Diggers do when you're not solving crimes," Nick said.

He wrinkled his brow. "She came over here to work a couple of times. Once, we went to a screening of *Psycho* together, but we paid for our own tickets. I liked her well enough, but not in that way."

"She told Channel Seven that she had a new theory about the Lovelorn case," Annalisa said. "Any idea what it was?"

He cocked his head, curious. "You mean you didn't find her notes?"

"Her computer is missing."

"A MacBook Air. She took it everywhere with her. I believe she also kept a journal on it." He leaned forward in his seat. "You mean the killer took it? She really was on to him?"

"I don't know," answered Nick. "You tell us."

"I didn't think it would work, her idea about calling him out. Who's to say he's even still around here to see the news story? The cops thought he was dead." He shot them an accusatory look, as if miffed by how wrong they'd been. "If this guy thinks we know his identity, he could come for all of us."

"We have no reason to think that's the case," Annalisa replied, soothing him. "But it would help if you could tell us everything you know about what Grace was working on before her death."

He sucked on his top lip. "I can show you," he agreed eventually, and he turned the chair around so that he could wheel it up to the desk. He moved the mouse to wake up the computer and clicked around until he found a file marked *Lovelorn Killer*. He called up what appeared to be a scan of an old news clipping from the *Sun-Times*. The headline read: MY NIGHTMARE TRYST WITH THE LOVELORN KILLER. "Chris found this a few years ago, but he never followed up on it."

Annalisa leaned in to read the short article. A woman named Lora Fitz, who had worked as a waitress at O'Malley's Bar, claimed the Lovelorn Killer had come into the bar about a month before Katie Duffy's murder. He'd ordered a few pints and sweet-talked her into sex in his truck outside after the bar closed. "He called himself Ace," she said. "He was nice and polite, flirting with me but not dirty about it the way some of them get. But then when we were alone, he changed. He started slapping me around and he tied my hands behind my back with rope."

"I know O'Malley's," Annalisa murmured. Pops had liked to drink there. All the cops on the block did.

"Did you get to this part here?" Nick asked her, pointing at the lower half of the screen.

Anna continued reading. Lora said she'd fled the truck and not seen or heard from Ace since. "But a couple of weeks after that, I was walking home after work by Myrtle Street, behind the Duffy house. I saw this guy in the yard, standing in the shadows near the house in the middle of the night. He wasn't doing nothing, just standing there, but I got the creeps and crossed to the other side of the street. Only then is when I saw it—Ace's red truck parked down the block. When I heard later about the lady who got killed, I knew it had to be him."

Annalisa straightened up. "That's quite a story."

"Chris didn't believe it, and I guess the cops didn't either. It's surprising what people will make up about famous cases. We've had people join Grave Diggers who claim to be surviving victims of Son of Sam or Ted Bundy, and even one woman who said she was that missing nursing student, Maura Murray. Chris did some checking and found out 'she' was actually some weird guy living with his parents in eastern Texas. This is the only story Lora is ever mentioned in, but Grace wanted to talk to her. She found her living up in Niles somewhere."

"Did she meet or talk to her?"

"I don't know. I wish I did." He rolled back to the living room area, so Annalisa and Nick followed. "Like I said before, Grace had no compunction about confronting people. She and Chris were alike that way. Most of us in the group, we sit around at our computers, analyzing databases or blowing up old pictures to try to find new clues. Grace and Chris would actually go out into the world to track a lead if they thought it would help. This guy, it's possible he saw her piece on Channel Seven, but it's also possible he looked out his kitchen window and saw her walking down the street. She liked to go to the scene of the crime."

"Did you ever go with her?" Nick asked.

"I don't get around as easy," he replied, gesturing at the chair. "The perps, they don't have to follow the rules laid down by the Americans with Disabilities Act. I never wanted to hold Grace back from wherever she needed to go."

"What happened?" Annalisa's gaze raked over his chair. "If you don't mind me asking."

"Not a bit, but I wish it were a better story. Wouldn't you know it, I served three tours overseas and came back fine, only to have some idiot door me on Clark Street when I was riding my bike." He pantomimed opening a car door and then arced his hand high in the air. "I went ass over teakettle and landed half over the curb. Broke my back in two places, and then I didn't heal right after the surgery."

"I'm sorry."

He shrugged. "Life is a kick in the nuts sometimes. Or a door to the handlebars, I guess. At least I didn't break my head." He rapped his knuckles against his temple. "Still hard as ever. Plus, it doesn't matter for my current job, or my fun. Everyone lives their lives online now, and on the net, we're all the same."

Annalisa thought of an old cartoon, a schnauzer with a computer. *On the internet, no one knows you're a dog.* The memory gave her a new idea. "You mentioned that the Grave Diggers always have new people wanting to join."

"Sure. Cold crime is hot, hot, hot. I follow four different podcasts and watch three channels of it. Seems like everyone wants to be a detective these days." He smiled at the pair of them, the genuine articles, apparently figuring they'd appreciate this admiration.

"I'm wondering if it's possible to get a list of people who joined after Grace's story ran on Channel Seven."

"Well, sure, any of us can see the new members. Except . . ."

"Except what?"

"You can see for yourself." He returned to the computer, where he called up the dedicated Grave Diggers website. The landing page was one Annalisa had seen before. It displayed a slick banner with the group's name and a stylized cemetery beneath a full moon. Underneath, cartoon case folders marked SOLVED in red letters across the front linked to brief descriptions of some of the successes that the group had accomplished. Barnes went past the front door of the site to a password-protected section that included interactive forums. "See, if you search by join date, you can get the full list here." He tapped a few keys and the list of user names came up on the screen. Each one had an avatar, some of which were tiny squares depicting people's faces, but others had no human form at all: a magnifying glass, a Mardi Gras mask, or simply the blank blue face that the software generated if the user failed to select a personalized option. "Not everyone uses a real name," Barnes explained.

Annalisa could see the problem as she scanned down the list. They had names such as Mermaid Life and The Real Slim Shady or even just numbers like 44202. Interspersed with these were recognizable names like Latrice Matheson, Joe Kelly, and Kendall Sommers, but that didn't mean the names were real. "Did these people have to register to join? Give their real names?"

"There's a form, yeah." He paused. "But you can just lie. It's not like anyone checks. Also, it's run by Integra, the company that powers the software. We wouldn't have access to that information. Not even Chris."

Annalisa sighed. "Can you please print me out a list of the people who joined the Grave Diggers since April 28th in any case?"

He did as she asked, and Annalisa accepted the two sheets of paper, which had two columns of user names apiece. "There must be a hundred people here at least."

"The Lovelorn Killer is very popular."

She gave him a pointed look, and he held up his hands in defense.

"I don't mean likable. I mean that people are curious about these guys. Men who are born to hunt humans for sport. There are groupies and collectors and people who send them love letters on death row. If you start looking around the internet, you can find some truly sick stuff."

"What's the attraction, do you think?"

"You tell me." Barnes surprised her by calling up a picture from his archives. It showed a bunch of cops milling around the outside of Denise Marklund's apartment building while her body passed by, zipped up in the coroner's bag. "Everyone turns out for the big cases," he murmured as he watched the screen. "It must be exciting, no?" He turned to look up at her. She kept her expression neutral.

"Someone has to stop them. That's our job."

"Of course. But you chose the job." She tried to figure out an answer to this, but he didn't seem to require one. He'd returned his attention to the screen. "I suppose everyone has a different reason for their interest, but at the core, it's transgressive, right? Here is a line no human being is supposed to cross, but these men do so repeatedly and without remorse. Maybe you make yourself look because you want to understand, to find a reason for the sickness, or maybe you want to learn all the killer's secrets so you can convince yourself it could never happen to you."

"Oh yeah? So, what's your reason?" Nick asked, his tone confrontational.

"The same as yours. To catch him. I saw an interview once with a cold case detective, and he said that when he sat down with a case file, the killer would almost always be in there already, usually in the first hundred pages. What if the cops have already seen this guy? What if they interviewed him and let him go?"

Nick shook off this possibility. "No. No way. A guy like this, he'd ping your radar."

Barnes sat back in his chair. "Well, then. Happy tracking."

They returned to Nick's car, where a smattering of fresh raindrops covered the windshield. "Is it me, or do all the yahoos want to rub it in our faces how inept the cops have been?" he asked her as he started the engine.

"They're not wrong," Annalisa returned without looking at him. She had the printout in her hands and was scanning through the long list of names. "I refuse to take it personally at this point. Whoever the killer is, he's been walking around free for decades now without attracting any attention. If the cops didn't see him, we're hardly alone."

"What do you think about this Lora Fitz story?"

"I want to ask Don Harrigan about it to see if they followed up at the time. Wait a sec." Annalisa brought the paper closer to her face, squinting to make sure she hadn't invented the name she'd found on the page.

Nick glanced over, impatient when she didn't continue. "What?"

"Rod Brewster is one of the names who recently joined Grave Diggers. Assuming it's the same guy, he's a neighbor of mine. I mean he was, at the time Katie Duffy was murdered. He still lives down the street from my parents." She had a flash of him on that long-ago Halloween night—a hulking guy with broad shoulders, dressed as Frankenstein, carving jack-o'-lanterns with a large knife.

"Yeah, so?"

"So, he's also a cop."

CHAPTER SIXTEEN

....

NEWS TRUCKS CAMPED OUT ON MICHIGAN AVENUE WITH SATELLITE DISHES SO BIG THEY LOOKED LIKE THEY WERE TRYING TO MAKE CONTACT WITH LIFE-FORMS ON ANOTHER PLANET. Annalisa watched out the window as Nick edged his car around back to the restricted-access area. One would think that with a potential serial killer on the loose, the public would want every officer out patrolling the streets. Instead, three or four uniforms were dedicated to crowd control, holding back the sea of humanity that threatened to wash over Chicago Public Safety Headquarters.

Inside, they found another scene of barely controlled chaos. The chief, Zimmer, and the special agent FBI guys each held court in a different corner of the room, four different conversations happening at once. Someone had rolled in a giant whiteboard and put up the names and photos of the known victims. Boxes of binders sat stacked three high against the wall, narrowing the cramped space even further. There were twice as many bodies on the premises as usual, but the phones were ringing faster than people could answer them.

Nick and Annalisa had turned sideways to make it down the hallway to the last interrogation room. "I heard they ran down more than 30,000 leads on this case," she said as she turned the door handle.

"More than 40,000, actually, and we ran down every one of them." She halted at the sight of Don Harrigan, who had already taken possession of the room she wanted. He'd rolled up his shirtsleeves and put on his reading glasses to study the stack of files in front of him. On the wall, he'd tacked up a map of the greater Chicago area with red sticker dots marking the location of each murder, along with several photographs showing the presumed entry point of the killer into the homes and a close-up of the interconnected knots binding one victim's hands. "You like it?" he asked her as she studied his work. "I have one just like it at home."

Annalisa was reminded of Grace Harper's wall. "Forty thousand leads," she repeated as she entered the room with Nick and shut the door behind them. "And yet everyone's still looking at the same few pictures."

Harrigan leaned back in his chair and rewarded her with a grin. "You're Vega, right? I remember when you used to run around in little pigtails." His phone beeped, and he fished out a prescription pill bottle from the pocket of the jacket hanging on the back of his seat. He uncapped a water bottle and downed a pale yellow pill. "Never get old, Vega," he told her as he set the bottle down. He frowned in Nick's direction. "Don't believe I know you."

"Nick Carelli. I'm new. Or old, depending on how you look at it."

Harrigan grunted. "New. That's what they told me they needed when they pulled me off this case twelve years ago. 'We want to give it fresh blood, see if new eyes can find a different angle.' But there's no angles here. Just a quagmire that will suck you in waist-deep if you're not careful." He gave the closest stack of folders a slight shove. "I retired with three hundred and eight collars, did you know that? I hauled in God-only-knows how many bangers and pimps and thieves. I even nailed that dentist who was drugging and raping his patients. Remember him? Of course not. No one ever wants to talk about him." He looked at the wall. "It was my face on the TV back then, and those mics felt like hot pokers when I was standing in front of them. Even today, I'll be out to dinner with my daughter and her kids, and someone will come right up to the table and wave their finger at me. 'You're that cop, the one who went after the Lovelorn Killer. How come you didn't get him?'"

"It wasn't just you." All those leads would've required a small army.

He waved her off. "I don't want your sympathy. I don't have regrets. I went balls to the wall for this case the same way I did all the others.

The people of the city, they paid my salary for thirty-three years. If they want to come up and ask me questions while I'm eating my pasta primavera, I guess I can't blame them. The truth is, I keep thinking . . . one day it might be him standing in front of me, a damn smirk on his face. I like to think I'd recognize him, but maybe I'm just kidding myself."

Annalisa exchanged a look with Nick. "You really think he'd make contact with you?"

"Why the hell not? He did it before."

Her heart quivered, and she took a step closer. "When?"

Harrigan looked shrewdly from her to Nick and back again, as if weighing whether they could be trusted. "This ain't exactly public knowledge."

"We're not exactly the public," Nick pointed out, drawing up a chair. He turned it around backward and took a seat in front of Harrigan's makeshift desk.

Harrigan licked his lips and regarded the ceiling for a long moment, his eye on the camera lens hidden there. "It was July of 1996, about a month after we found Maureen O'Donnell. The press hadn't let up an inch. The mayor wanted daily reports. Maureen lived three blocks from a new high-rise going up, so we had a couple hundred names of guys to track down from all the crews working there, and some of them proved hard to find. Then someone blew up Olympic Park down in Atlanta, and our case took a back seat in the papers. We worked it just as hard, but for once, we didn't have a pack of reporters following our every move. It was a nice change of pace for me, but for the Lovelorn guy, I guess he missed the attention. One afternoon, me and a few other guys were looking over the different pictures from the crime scenes. We each had a bunch on our desk, passing them back and forth. At lunchtime, we went down the street for subs and sodas. When I came back, this photo of Maureen O'Donnell was sitting on my desk with the rest of her pictures. I didn't even notice it at first."

He pulled out a folder and removed a printed photograph from a plastic bag. It showed a nude woman with dark hair lying facedown on a wooden floor, her hands tied behind her back and yoked to her neck and feet in the usual series of knots. Her mouth was frozen in a silent scream. The picture appeared the same as any of the others Annalisa had seen. "And?" she said.

"Look in the background, under the chair."

Annalisa and Nick leaned in together to study the photo. She saw twin glints of light peering out from the dark void under the chair. "A cat," she guessed.

"Lulu. The first officers on the scene found her yowling under the sofa, at which point they called animal control and had her removed for her own safety."

"Under the sofa. Not the chair."

He folded his arms across his chest. "That's right. We didn't take this picture. The cat was gone by the time our photographers showed up. No, Mr. Lovelorn himself snapped this shot. Then he waltzed in here, free as can be, and left it on my desk—just like Lulu there might have done with a headless mouse. We analyzed it, of course. No prints. No DNA. Just a little 'fuck you, pay attention to me' from the city's most murderous prima donna."

Nick let out a low whistle. "No video? No witnesses?"

"Nope, nothing we could find. This asshole is freakin' invisible."

Annalisa ignored the cold, clammy feeling starting to spread across her neck and torso. "He stopped for years," she said to Harrigan. "Why?"

He scratched the back of his head with one hand. "I've asked myself that question almost every day for the past twenty years. Something must've spooked him about the Duffy killing. Maybe the husband, Owen, nearly caught him. Maybe it took longer than usual to subdue her. She had bruises on her arms that we didn't find on the other victims." He indicated his forearms. "That's always been my only theory, that he was losing the physical strength to pull this kind of thing off. He's getting older like the rest of us." He rattled his pill bottle for emphasis.

"Except now he's back," Annalisa murmured.

"Goes to show what I know," Harrigan replied with a snort.

"Does the name Lora Fitz mean anything to you?"

"No. Should it?"

"She was a waitress at O'Malley's around the time that Katie Duffy was killed. She says she had an encounter with the Lovelorn Killer."

"Oh, yeah. Now that you mention it, I do remember her. A dope fiend who liked to trade sex for drugs. She might as well have said she saw E.T. and the queen of England tap-dancing in the street."

"Except she didn't say that," Annalisa replied.

"Hey, we checked it out. She was interviewed the same as everyone else who saw the bogeyman standing in their shadows."

"Do you have her original statement?" Annalisa wanted to read it before reinterviewing the woman all these years later, to make sure the details matched.

Harrigan let out a peevish sigh. "Let me check the index binder," he said, his knees creaking as he rose to his feet. They followed him back down the hall to the main squad room, where he lifted a large blue binder from the end of the main table by the whiteboard. "Binder 214," he said. He proceeded to the stack of boxes, shifting them around until he found the one marked 208–215. He dug out the binder labeled 214 and handed it to Annalisa. "She's in there somewhere. Knock yourself out."

Annalisa found a free square foot of space by the copier and wedged herself in to read through the witness statements. A hardware clerk in Pilsen reported a man buying lots of rope. A woman jogging through Grant Park said a man had yelled obscenities at her. Annalisa paged through all of them once, and then again, but she did not find anything from or about Lora Fitz. She hunted down Harrigan in his windowless room. "It's not here."

"What do you mean, it's not there?" He reached for the binder with a scowl.

"I went through it twice. There's nothing about Lora Fitz."

He didn't take her word and flipped through it, page by page, from front to back. He came up as empty as she had and sat back in his seat with a perplexed expression. "Must've been misfiled."

Annalisa rubbed the tension knot forming at the base of her neck. "I don't suppose you remember who took her original statement?"

"Sure, I do." He eyed her. "He practically begged for the assignment. It was your old man."

"Pops talked to her?"

"It was Vega, definitely. Him and his buddy Brewster."

CHAPTER SEVENTEEN

············

THEY LOCATED LORA FITZ'S HOME ADDRESS IN NILES, AS WELL AS HER CURRENT PLACE OF EMPLOYMENT, A FAMILY RESTAURANT OVER BY THE NORTH SHORE. Being hungry, they decided to try her work first. If they struck out, at least they got lunch. Nick drove so Annalisa had a chance to admire the view. Normally she loved the lakeside drive, the winding road along the shore with the city's shining skyscrapers on one side and the vast expanse of Lake Michigan on the other. The water, usually a source of recreation and relaxation, had a predatory appearance today. The lake mirrored the sky, gray and choppy, and wind whipped high waves along the concrete barriers. "Take the next left," she said turning her gaze toward the land.

Nick turned on the blinker. "I didn't get down to the shore much when I lived here last," he remarked.

"That's how it goes around here. You stick to your own neighborhood."

"I remember," he said with a curve of a smile. "You brought me home to meet your family and they were mystified. 'He's from Florida?' Like it was outer space."

"You have to admit, it kind of is."

He grinned. "Point taken."

She rolled her neck until it cracked. "My parents grew up two blocks from each other, which was three streets over from where they live now.

Pops used to say there were two single girls on his street, and he decided to start with the prettiest one. When she said no, he asked Ma to the homecoming dance. The pretty one got caught shoplifting bras from Marshall Field's a couple of months later. Supposedly there's a lesson in there somewhere."

"He must've picked the right girl, if they've been married all these years."

"Forty-four years this summer. Ma used to get red-in-the-face angry at him when he failed to show up on time for yet another dinner, the table set and four hungry kids whining at her by the time he strolled through the door well after dark. He'd just pour her a glass of wine, put on some Sinatra tune, and dance her around the kitchen to her place at the table." They had made it look easy, this math where one couple somehow added up to a happy family, but Annalisa failed the test no matter how she tried. Colin had fled. Nick was a decent cook, but he'd never once danced with her in the kitchen.

She took a surreptitious glance at her cell phone, but it showed no new calls. Nick caught her looking. "Hoping Mr. Lovelorn will give you another buzz?" he asked.

She shoved the phone back in her pocket. "Have you considered what an awful nickname that is for this guy? Lovelorn makes him sound like a moony teenager with a crush, not a sadistic asshole with a bunch of nylon rope."

"You're not allowed to put 'Sadistic Asshole' on the front page of the papers."

She pursed her lips and looked out at the leaden sky. "Maybe they should. Maybe then he wouldn't be so pleased with all his awe-filled news coverage."

His phone rang then, trilling over the speakers of the car. "Maybe he's calling me now," he said, trying for levity but failing. He pushed the button to take the call. "Carelli here."

"Nick?" A young female voice, almost a purr, came over the line. "It's Kelsey."

"Speaking of moony teenagers," Annalisa muttered, and Nick made a face at her.

"Hey, Kelsey," he said easily. "What's up?"

"Oh, nothing much. I just got back from a trip to the gym, and I'm so gross and sweaty." Annalisa rolled her eyes dramatically and Nick swatted her. Kelsey continued, "I'm free this afternoon if you're available to look at my bike. I'd be happy to repay you with a drink or whatever."

"Or whatever," Annalisa mouthed at Nick. He ignored her.

"I'd love to, but I'm at work at the moment. There's a place on Everett Avenue that can help you if you need it fixed right away."

"No rush. If you get off early, just come by. I'm just going to shower and then lounge around."

Nick said goodbye and clicked off. "It's not what you think."

"Oh, it's exactly what I think," Annalisa replied with a dark laugh.

"She's my neighbor. Her bike isn't shifting gears smoothly, and I told her I'd take a look at it."

"Look at her bike. Right."

"You think I'm making it up? You heard the woman."

"No, I think you really believe you're going over to help her with her bike. It's the 'or whatever' that comes afterward that's always a surprise, right? Just like that time you wanted to help that waitress in the coffee shop down the street with her broken window. Or how you met that girl in the park with the lost dog. So many damsels in distress, and only one Nick Carelli to go around." He said nothing, just stared ahead out the windshield. She felt a prick of conscience, then a burning curiosity. She knew she shouldn't ask, but she couldn't stop the words coming out of her mouth. "What about me, Nick? What were you going to help me with?"

He gave her a long look. "I don't know," he said finally. "Whatever it was, I never found it." He turned his attention to the road, nodding at a squat brick building with a faded sign, once red and now a mottled pink, declaring it to be Monty's Restaurant. "This looks like the place. Think Lora's here today?"

"She didn't answer her home phone. Either way, we're getting something to eat." Her empty stomach gave a painful rumble, disgruntled by her sense memories of Ma's dinners and determined to make her pay. Her brothers would be over there now, probably enjoying a roast and mashed potatoes.

They entered through a heavy glass door and found a college-age brunette woman wearing way too much eyeliner manning the hostess station. She looked up from her cell phone as they walked in. "Two for brunch?" she asked, already grabbing the plastic menus, eager to move them through as fast as possible.

Annalisa didn't follow her. "Is Lora Fitz working today?"

"Lora? Yes, she's here."

"We'd like to sit in her section if possible." Annalisa smiled. "She's an old friend."

The girl shrugged and returned to check off a different box on her seating chart. "Right this way." She led them to a brown pleather booth with a white Formica table, chipped on one edge. "Enjoy!" she said brightly and took out her cell phone for the thirty-foot walk back to the front of the restaurant. A young man flitted by to drop off waters, paper placemats, and tableware. "Lora will be right with you," he muttered, like it was all one word.

Nick examined his reflection in the butter knife and brushed a lock of hair back from his forehead. "So, your father interviewed this woman originally?"

"Him and his partner." She craned her head around, looking for any waitress who might fit the mental picture she had for Lora—an aging, washed-out blonde with a thickening waist. "And yes, I know what you're thinking. If they gave Pops this part of the case, it probably means nothing." Such a piece of nothing that no one even filed it correctly in the tomes of evidence reports.

"It'd be wild, though, if it were true." He leaned across the table. "Imagine she got a look at him. We'd have the first real lead in this case in decades."

Annalisa drummed her fingers on the table but didn't reply. If it was a lead, it was an old one, not new. Chicago PD would look like fools for not following up when it was hot, with Pops and Brewster maybe getting the worst of it. They had talked to this woman and dismissed her story. "She may not even remember anything after all this time."

"I disagree. I met a woman once in Florida who had been a member of the Chi Omega sorority house when Ted Bundy came through and attacked all those girls. She wasn't at the house the night it happened because she'd gone to stay a couple of days with her aunt over in Pensacola.

She came back to find the whole place roped off and a couple of her girlfriends dead. Eventually when they were let back inside, the walls and ceilings of the bedrooms were coated in blood. That was more than forty years ago now, but this lady talked about it like it was yesterday. You could see it in her face, how it changed her. I don't think you come that close to evil and forget it."

"I think we're about to find out." Annalisa had noticed an older woman in an apron approaching, a redhead not a blonde, although the brassy color was straight from a bottle. She walked with purpose, nimbly dodging the angled tables and small children running around.

"Hi, welcome to Monty's," she said, her voice low and gravelly. "What can I get you?" Her nametag said LORA so they had found the correct woman. She didn't look like the wild child Harrigan had described. She wore a demure gray cardigan, the barest hint of makeup, and sensibly flat sandals on her feet.

Annalisa ordered the ham and cheese omelet with a side of fruit. Nick selected the burger and fries. "What we'd really like is the chance to talk to you, Lora," Annalisa said, and Lora looked up from where she was scribbling their orders on her pad of paper.

"Me? What'd you want with me?" Her eyes narrowed with the skepticism of a woman who hadn't been asked for anything more meaningful than a ketchup bottle in quite some time.

"We read your story about your encounter with the Lovelorn Killer."

She stiffened visibly. "That was decades ago."

"If you've seen the news, then you know why it's important now." Annalisa withdrew her police shield from the inside of her coat and showed it to Lora.

"Now." Lora huffed the word with scorn. "That's rich. I tell you guys all about this animal twenty years ago, and now you think it's important. That woman who died? Grace Harper? She's on you." She pointed from Annalisa to Nick. "My conscience is clear."

"We're here because we want to listen," Annalisa replied.

Lora pursed her thin lips, clearly not believing them. "Fine," she said at last. "I take my break out back in half an hour. You can talk to me then if you don't mind the smoke."

She pivoted on her heel and returned to the kitchen to put in their orders. Later, she dropped off their food without a word. At the appointed hour, they laid their money on the table and went around to the back of the restaurant in search of Lora. They found her up against the brick wall near a dumpster, smoking and trying to keep out of the path of the fierce wind. It plastered her red hair against her pale face, and she clawed it back with one wrinkled hand. "What'd you want to know?"

"Everything," Annalisa replied.

Lora squinted and took a drag. "You know I was on pills back then, right? I started taking them when my back went out. I needed them for work. Then I couldn't work without 'em. The doc was the one who kept writing me scrips, but somehow it was all my fault anyway."

"We're not here to judge," Nick told her. "And we're not here to bust you."

"Bust me for what? I'm clean." She clutched her sweater closed and shivered. "I've got a good job here, a steady paycheck. I don't need trouble."

"If you saw him," Annalisa said, "then he saw you. He's still out there, and he's still got those ropes."

"Okay, okay." She held up her palms in surrender and then crushed out her cigarette butt on the ground. "This guy, I hadn't seen him before the night he came into O'Malley's. It was a Tuesday, so business was slow. He had dark hair and a scar that cut across his eyebrow right here." She indicated a slash in her left brow. "I asked him how he got it, and he said running with the bulls in Spain. I told him it was a bull story, all right." She smiled at her own wit. "Anyways, we got to talking and he seemed nice, funny. He said he had some pot out in his truck, and would I like to smoke with him when I finished my shift? I said sure. So, we go out there after closing to his red pickup truck, passing this joint back and forth, and soon we were the only people left in the lot. It was a new truck—shiny, no rips in the seats. I thought he seemed normal. Nice, you know?"

"Yeah, I know the type. Then what happened?" Annalisa prompted.

"We started fooling around, and right away, he changed. He started slapping me, light at first, but then harder. He liked it when I yelped. I tried to call it off, but he'd locked me in. That's when he pulled the rope out of his glove box. He tied my hands behind my back and bent me over the seat. Called me names that would make a sailor blush while he did me from behind. After, I was a mess, all shaking, my mascara running. He turned back into Mr. Nice Guy. He offered me tissues and a bottle of water. He said he would drive me home but I didn't want him knowing where I lived. I had him drop me at the L and then I walked back from there."

"Can you describe what he looked like?" Nick asked.

"Big, over six feet. Strong. Black hair, dark eyes. Scar like I mentioned. Kind of olive-colored skin—sort of like she has." She gestured at Annalisa and pulled out her pack of smokes to light up another. Her hand trembled slightly as she took the first drag. "I didn't say nothing at first about what happened in the truck. I figured it was my fault, going out there with him. We were both high. I knew what the cops would say if I tried to report it."

Annalisa wished Lora was wrong, but she knew better. Back when Pops was on the job, there'd been a scandal because a woman called to report she'd been raped, and the officers not only didn't believe her, they crank called her back, mocking her story. "What happened later?" she said. "Did you see him again?"

"I was scared he was going to come back to the bar, but he didn't. After a couple of weeks, I started to relax again. My shoulders came down off my ears, you know? Didn't jump a mile every time someone touched me. But then I was walking home after closing one night, over on Myrtle Street, and I heard this rustling in the bushes behind one of the houses. It was past two in the morning, and those streets are usually dead quiet by then. I looked over and I saw a man standing in the shadows right by the house. He wasn't doing anything, just standing there, but I got the creeps. I booked it down the street and got the hell out of there. As I was running, I saw a red truck parked down the block, and that's when I knew it had to be him. Ace, the same guy from the bar."

"Did you see his face? The man in the shadows?"

"No, it was too dark. But he was the same size and shape. Then later, I saw that woman who got killed, Katherine Duffy, and her house was right next door to the one where I seen that guy. I read in the papers how he stalked the women before killing them. That must have been what I saw." She shuddered and took a deep drag. "I could just tell by the way he was standing there so close to the house that he was up to no good. So that's when I reported what happened with Ace."

"Can you tell us anything else about the man?" Annalisa pressed. "Was he white? Black? Thin? Fat?"

"Big guy. Dressed in dark clothes. I didn't see his face, thank God. What if he came after me?"

"If it's the same guy, you did see his face," Nick pointed out. "Do you think you could describe him for a sketch artist?"

Lora blinked rapidly, her lips parting in fresh horror. "You mean it really was him? You think I'm right?"

Annalisa's cell phone buzzed in her pocket, making her jump. "Excuse me a moment," she said, moving to the side. She dug it out and saw a text from Zimmer: *The Tribune has a new letter.*

CHAPTER EIGHTEEN

....

A DIRECT MISSIVE FROM THE LOVELORN KILLER WAS WAY ABOVE ANNALISA'S PAY GRADE. Even Zimmer didn't get to eyeball it in person before the FBI whisked the original off to the lab to have it analyzed down to the pulp of the paper it was printed on. If it was the real deal, and no one had reason to suspect it wasn't, the letter would yield no identifiable marks. Ordinary paper and plain black ink, a reminder that murderers shop at the same places as everyone else. Still, they had to check. An irregularity in the paper, a hair caught in the envelope—cases this big still turned on the tiniest bit of evidence.

Annalisa had to make do with a copy of the letter, which was neatly block printed in the style of the others. It was addressed to Grace, but of course it wasn't ever meant for her. For all anyone knew, he'd written it after her death.

> *Dearest Grace,*
>
> *I've looked a long time to find a woman such as you, one who is a seeker like me. A watcher. I see the way you observe the people in your store, the employees and the patrons. You move the bodies around seamlessly so that the whole operation flows smoothly. Produce needs a little attention? You pull in someone from baked goods. You pat employees on the back when they deserve it, but you've always got your eye out in case they take advantage. No*

free snacking, eh? But you can understand why a minimum wage checker swipes an extra chocolate bar or two. It's the rich guys in suits who try to slip out with a $1.00 piece of candy in their pocket that make you wonder about this world. I know you see them because I see you watching them. It kills you, doesn't it, to let it go. But you can't prosecute for such petty ante so they just get away with it. It's enough to drive one 4011! ☺

You have nice hands. Neat and capable, smooth and well-maintained. I'm so glad you don't have a nasty habit like biting your nails. I can't stand women who do that. Think of all the dirt they must eat—such otherwise pretty mouths sucking down bacteria and viruses, not to mention all those nail shards carving up your intestines on the inside. You clearly take care of yourself, which is good because it doesn't seem like there is anyone there to do it for you. I've seen you alone at night eating salad in front of the computer, the blue screen glowing in your eyeglasses. What are you looking for so intently in that piece of machinery? Is it me? I've been looking too, you see, for someone just like you. Someone who understands what it's like to be the smartest one in any room, how tiresome it can be. Dare I even say it's lonely? Let's not be lonely any longer, Grace. You and me, we can be each other's forever.

—Mr. Lovelorn

Annalisa put the printout down and looked to Nick, who had his own copy. "What's 4011? Some kind of code?"

"You mean you never had a job in a grocery store? It's bananas."

"I'm sorry?"

"4011 is the produce code for bananas."

Annalisa looked down at the letter. "Well, maybe that means something. Maybe he's worked in a grocery."

"Sure," Nick agreed. "Add that to the list of maybes."

The *Tribune* didn't wait for the morning paper to run their scoop. The headline took over the web page in seventy-two-point font, and ten minutes later, every news organization had some version of the story.

In an era when it still took several days for an actual letter to reach its intended recipient, this one traveled the earth in less than an hour. The *Tribune* spared no detail, including the fact that the letter had been postmarked in Elgin. TVs in the police station were tuned to different channels, set on mute with closed-captioning engaged. They showed the networks angling for a fresh take. One of them interviewed a mail carrier in Elgin. The mail didn't run on Sunday, but they dressed him up in his blue uniform anyway, conducting the interview on the street near a postbox. "It's crazy to think about," he said. "That you might be touching something this guy touched. That he's using you as part of his sick game."

"What do you make of the fact that he sent the letter in Elgin?" The female reporter asked from off camera.

What is this world now, Annalisa wondered, *where mailmen are asked to comment on the behavior of the serial murderer?*

He didn't shy away from his moment in the spotlight. "You like to think that he drove in from somewhere else just to mail it—you know, to disguise his identity and where he lives. But this is a big city, with more than a hundred thousand people in it. So, you've got to wonder now if maybe he's been living here this whole time."

....

Annalisa returned to her condo late in the evening, under a dark sky pregnant with clouds. She breathed a sigh of relief when she saw that her block was ablaze with light. The crews had restored the power for now, but Mother Nature was gearing up for another punch. Fierce winds bent the trees' branches and battered the windows. Annalisa stopped short in the street when she saw her neighbor next door, Amy Yakamoto, struggling to bring in several bags of groceries as the wind kept slapping her front door back and forth. "Wait, let me help you," she called out her window, pulling to the side so she could get out of her car. She jogged up the steps and took two bags from Mrs. Yakamoto, who braced the door so that Annalisa could safely transport the groceries across the threshold.

"My goodness, thank you," Mrs. Yakamoto said, a bit breathless as Annalisa set the bags on the kitchen table. "I thought I could get out and back before the latest storm hit but I misjudged the timing." Thunder rumbled in the distance, as if to show up her folly.

"I bet Aldi was a mess." The slightest hint of a major storm, and Midwesterners bought out all the milk and bread.

"Oh, it wasn't too bad." She pulled out her half gallon of milk with a mischievous glint in her eyes. "I got the last one."

They shared a laugh, and Annalisa moved to admire the lush indoor garden her neighbor kept in her bay window. She had violets in three colors, a pink-edged leafy green potted plant, and a blooming lavender. A fern hung down with its spidery tendrils. "This is wild-looking," Annalisa remarked of a strange succulent that reminded her of an armadillo.

"That's a donkey's tail. Very easy to maintain."

"Maybe for you. I have a black thumb." Annalisa held it up to demonstrate. "And, oh my, these are beautiful." A tall potted plant with enormous pink blossoms stood near the back door. Annalisa fingered one delicate edge that called to mind crepe flowers she used to make in grade school.

"Those are peonies, and they are so cheerful, aren't they? Unfortunately, I had to drag all the bigger plants from the back deck before the storm hit yesterday. I'm afraid it's rather crowded in here at the moment."

"I think it's amazing. Like living in a greenhouse."

Mrs. Yakamoto's eyes crinkled with her smile. "I'm glad you appreciate it. Harry didn't mind the first few plants I brought home, but when the place started to resemble a jungle, he'd start speaking to me like Tarzan." Annalisa knew Harry Yakamoto had passed away from cancer last year.

"I'm sure he secretly loved the jungle," Annalisa assured her.

"Oh, I expect not. But he definitely loved me." She looped her arm through Annalisa's as they walked back to the main part of the kitchen. "Can I make you some tea as thanks for helping me with my groceries?"

"Another time," Annalisa said. "I have a box full of files to read through tonight." She'd taken home more of the witness statements from around the time of Katie Duffy's murder to see if there were any reports that matched Lora Fitz's description of "Ace" or any other mentions of a red pickup truck.

Mrs. Yakamoto's expression turned melancholy. "Yes, I saw the news. How terrible it must be for all of you right now, having to confront such evil."

"It's the job," Annalisa replied, shrugging off the weight of the other woman's words.

"It's a hard job." She reached out and squeezed Annalisa's hand. "But I thank you for doing it. I'm sure I speak for all of us on the street when I say how much safer we feel with a police officer living nearby."

Annalisa demurred and bid the woman a pleasant evening. She thought again of Katie Duffy, who'd been married to a cop for so long, who'd been at a party full of them the very night she'd died. She remembered the nights she'd lain in bed, listening to Pops and his buddies from the job—Owen, Rod, and Gene—sitting around Ma's kitchen table, eating her cookies and laughing as they swapped crazy stories. "This lady called in a noise complaint at two in the morning, so I go out to her place to check out the problem. Turns out, it's the cicadas. You know, those god-awful bugs that come around every seventeen years? Her backyard trees were chock-full of them, making a terrible racket, and she's crying at me about how she can't sleep. I felt bad for her, but what was I gonna do? Break out a thousand tiny handcuffs?" Annalisa had loved those nights when the house filled up with good men. She had drifted off to sleep to the sound of their strong voices, imagining herself a part of it.

She hefted the box of binders from the car and battled the wind to her front door just as the rain began in earnest. The house was already full of light since she'd never turned them off the night before. She set the box in the front room and went to the large window at the back. It was so dark outside that she couldn't even see the trees thirty feet beyond her door. She put her palm to the cold glass and peered out at the rain. A large man appeared out of nowhere, right up in her face. She gasped in horror and wheeled back, groping fruitlessly for the gun she'd already unholstered.

"Anna!" He hollered her name through the glass. "It's me!"

She halted and turned around again for a better look. He pressed his face against the window, and she recognized him at last. "Colin?" He was wet, his hair plastered to his head, but the long nose and dimpled chin were just as she remembered. She unlocked the rear door and slid it back to admit him. He brought a compact black carry-on with him into the flat, both of them sopping with rain. "Sorry, I didn't mean to scare you," he said. "That's a nice deck chair you've got out there. Of course, it's probably more enjoyable when it's not pouring buckets."

"How long have you been out there?"

"The Uber guy dropped me off at six. I figured you'd be off work by then. Forgot you don't work a usual desk job." He looked sheepish and gave her a weak wave. "Hi."

"Hi." She looked him over in wonder. In her head, he'd remained seventeen years old, lean and full of mettle, with hair as black as smoke and just as curly. He'd smelled like sweaty cotton and male hormones, tasted like cherry cola. The man before her had broad shoulders, a nine-o'clock shadow, and the remnants of alcohol on his breath. He smelled like the rain, earthy and raw, like the moment a spade first strikes the dirt.

He spread his arms. "I'd hug you but I'm all wet."

She did not care. "You're here," she said, launching herself at him. He had to take a step back, steadying himself, but then his arms closed around her, tight like he used to do. He stroked the back of her head while she buried her face in his neck.

"Anna," he murmured, and the word vibrated through to her skin.

She took a deep breath and released him. "You look just the same."

He grinned, showing off a line of white teeth. "You were always such a shitty liar," he said, poking at her while she squirmed away. "You don't look the same, though. You went and got badass on me. Check out that power suit you're rocking."

"I can't wait to take it off," she replied, and then realized how suggestive it sounded. "I mean, it's been a long day. You probably want to get changed, too. The washroom is right around the corner over there."

She slipped into jeans and a sweatshirt while he changed into what appeared to be a carbon copy of what he'd already had on—a black T-shirt and dark-wash jeans. "I hung my stuff up to dry in your shower. I hope that's okay."

"It's fine."

"I did book a hotel. I'm not just crashing."

"Oh." She stood up from where she'd been peering into her refrigerator, hoping to find dinner among the takeout containers. "You can stay if you want, but all I have to offer is the couch. I use the second bedroom as an office."

He shook his head, bemused. "You have an office. I remember the desk in your bedroom at home. It was covered in stickers, CDs, and stacks of romance novels."

"I only read the good parts." She'd had to find out if she was doing it right.

"Is that so?" The way his eyes darkened told her she'd done enough right to be memorable.

She folded her arms over her chest. "All I've got here is pasta and sauce from a jar. Maybe a meager salad. The wine isn't half bad, though."

"Then let's eat."

Over dinner, they deliberately avoided talking about the reason for his visit. Instead, she plied him with wine in return for more stories from his travel adventures. "One night, I took this super sketchy bus from Hanoi to Laos. There wasn't one driver but a team of men in charge of the bus. It made these random stops by the side of the road, and they'd get out to shift things around in the storage area under the bus. That was when I realized I was riding with a bunch of smugglers."

"Get out."

"After four stops, I finally got a look at the illicit cargo." He paused for effect. "It was pallets of Coca-Cola."

"How much does it go for? I've got an unopened twelve-pack in the laundry room."

"I decided not to ask."

"Mmm, probably smart." She swirled the last of her wine around in her glass. "What's your favorite place you've traveled?"

He considered a moment. "Probably Cuba. The writer in me always wanted to pilgrimage to Papa Hemingway's house, and I finally got to go in 2013. It's changing now with the more open visa policies, poised to become just like anyplace else with Starbucks and the Gap, and soon it'll be caramel macchiatos instead of café Cubanos. But right now, it's completely its own style, its own flavor. You can see a ruby red Chevy Bel Air or a '59 Thunderbird cruising the street, postcard perfect. The fishing communities look just like they did when Hemingway wrote about them. But down by the seawall, there are buildings with incredible facades that are literally crumbling into the street. Uncovered manholes. It's like you can see right through to the guts of the city."

She leaned in with a sigh. "It sounds amazing."

"Don't even get me started on the food. I had a plate of costillitas that were so sweet and tangy, it was like eating a symphony of flavor."

She eyed the remainder of the simple spaghetti in front of them, food she ate every day without ever questioning it. "Remember when we planned to go to India?"

"Yes. You were determined to hug an elephant."

She had drawn temporary henna tattoos on her hands. Ma had made her wash it off immediately even though it was summer and there wasn't anyone in charge to care. "Have you been?" she asked, toying with her fork, trying to sound casual.

"Several times. I can show you some pictures on my laptop if you like."

She nodded and cleared away the dinner dishes to the sink while he booted up his computer. They sat shoulder-to-shoulder on the couch, and he showed her a series of breathtaking images: girls at night, lighting tiny lanterns around a peacock created by a mosaic of flowers; piles of colorful fruit lined up at the open-air marketplace; a goofy close-up of a camel draped in braided yarn. The pictures made India feel both closer and farther away than her dreams. "How many places have you been?" she asked, touching the edge of the computer screen lightly.

"I've been to fifty-three different countries."

She couldn't fathom it. She'd been to Florida on vacation once with Nick, but besides that, she'd barely set foot out of Chicago. The city had so much to offer that she'd convinced herself she wasn't missing anything. Colin's photos put paid to her delusion, made her miss their old dreams. They were supposed to have conquered the world together. He'd made good while she'd stayed put. Never had her cozy condo felt so small. "That's astonishing," she murmured. "But . . . where is home?"

He sat forward, withdrawing from her, and put the computer down on the old trunk she used as a coffee table. "I keep an apartment in Texas, outside of Dallas. The rent is comparably cheap and it's a major airline hub. It's quick to get in and out."

"Easy come, easy go?"

"Hey, now." He glanced back over his shoulder at her. "I didn't mean it like that."

She folded her legs up under her, not touching him at all anymore. "I wrote you letters," she said in a low voice. "Back when you left to live with your dad's cousin in Ohio."

"I know. I read them, I swear I did."

"You didn't answer me."

He looked away, his mouth set in a firm line. "I—I didn't know what to say."

But you're the writer. She somehow held this back. They never even officially broke up, she realized. He'd kissed her goodbye, promised he'd keep in touch, and then boarded a plane. It had taken her months to get the message. She blinked rapidly as the hot flash of humiliation washed over her like it was yesterday. "You could have said anything," she said. "Even if it was 'Sorry, I don't want to be with you anymore.'"

"I did," he said, his voice tight. He balled his hand into a fist and hit his knee lightly. "I wanted to be with you more than anything."

"Right. That's why you left and never looked back. Fifty-three countries traveled. Wow. How many thousands of miles is that? Somehow you never managed to make it back here."

He let out a shaky breath and picked up his computer again. "I can't excuse it, but maybe I can explain. I can show you."

"I've seen enough of your travelogue for one night." She curled into the corner of the sofa.

"No," he said gently. "Look."

She glanced at the screen in spite of herself and saw he'd called up a picture taken years ago, when they were children. He must have scanned it because these were the days before the rise of digital photography. It showed her at perhaps age four, in a ridiculous red-and-white bathing suit, complete with a ruffle on the butt, her hair in pigtails. Alex stood next to her with a pail and shovel, and Colin was on the other side with a watering can. The lopsided sandcastle they were constructing sat in the foreground. "I don't get it," she said petulantly. "What am I supposed to be looking at here?"

"There's more." He took her through a series of old photos. Pops at the grill wearing an apron designed to look like a bulletproof vest. Ma and Katie making Christmas cookies. The four kids playing soccer in the backyard. Tony being held aloft by his Little League team when they won their playoff game. The adults with cocktails in hand, gathered around the firepit. They all grew older as the photos progressed. Vincent's graduation from high school. Alex with his first car, the rest of them crowded around for a joyride. Ma with a broken arm from when they went ice-skating. She and Colin at a picnic table, their arms around each other. Annalisa crept closer again as he clicked through the images. When he got to one of her grinning at the camera in a devil costume, she held her breath. This was the night of the Halloween party when it all went to hell. "Do you see it now?" he asked hoarsely. "We were all mixed up together. After it happened, after my dad died too . . . I just couldn't stay here anymore. I could barely stand to walk around in my same skin, let alone be in the house where it happened. Everywhere I looked, there they were, but only in my memories, and that just made it worse. I had to get out or I felt like I would die too."

She reached over and grabbed his hand, tight. Tears blurred her vision. "I'm sorry," she said, and he reached over to enfold her in his arms.

"No, I'm sorry. Mona Lisa, don't cry. I never, ever wanted to make you cry." He kissed her head and she gave a teary sniff at his use of her old nickname. She sat up and wiped at her eyes with the hem of her T-shirt.

"No, I get it. You did what you had to do to survive." She thought of Alex and his drinking. Pops begging for scraps of the case. Ma, going silent for what felt like months. "I guess we all did."

Her cell phone buzzed across the room from inside her jacket pocket. She rose from the couch and fished it out, instantly on high alert when she recognized the burner phone's number. She cursed inwardly and swiped around until she found the recording app that the IT department had loaded onto her phone. She opened it while the phone continued to ring, unsure if she was doing it right. Finally, she had to answer or risk losing the call. "Hello."

"Detective Vega," said the whispery voice. "How are you tonight?"

"Fine. Yourself?" Across the room, Colin stood up with a confused look on his face at the tension in her voice. She shook her head vehemently at him and he stopped moving.

"I'm very well, thank you for asking. Terrible weather we're having right now, isn't it?"

The storm had died down, actually. Rain pattered on the roof and windows but the howling winds and thunder had moved on. "Do you like storms?" she asked him.

"They're beautiful but so destructive," he said, disdain in his voice. "Afterward, we see the damage on the news—the trees torn up, houses destroyed, people dead. They like to lead with that, don't they? They know they're supposed to be sad but somehow it makes the story all that more exciting. People died."

"Dead people," she said. "Is that something that excites you?"

He gave a dry chuckle and then tsk-tsked her. "Such a forward question, Detective. We barely know each other."

"We could fix that," she blurted out, her stomach rising at the thought. "We—we could meet."

A long pause on the other end. She heard only the blood rushing in her ears. "No, I don't think so. Not tonight. It's late and tomorrow's a workday, yes? Rest on Sunday, work on Monday. Did you go to Mass today, Annalisa?"

She stammered, unsure of what answer would keep him talking. "I, uh, I'm afraid I'm a lapsed Catholic. What about you?"

"I enjoyed the morning service at St. Thecla's."

Her heart, thundering in her chest, lurched to a halt as he named her family's church. "Oh? What—what did you like about it?"

"The lesson on giving. How the best gifts are unexpected. Don't you agree?"

"What gifts?"

"I like personal gifts the best, don't you? The ones from the heart."

"Yes, I like gifts."

"Then you'll really like this one."

He clicked off and she stopped the recording with a shaking finger. Colin rushed forward. "That was tense and incredibly weird," he said. "Who the hell was that?"

"It was him," she said, and Colin went rigid, veins bulging in his neck.

"Him? *The* him? He has your number? Jesus, Anna."

She barely heard him. "I've got to go," she said, reaching for her holster and her jacket. "I've got to get over there."

"What? Where are you going?"

"St. Thecla's."

"Our old church? Now? Why?"

She fastened the holster in place and slung her shield around her neck. "Because he said he was there this morning, and I'm pretty sure he's left me a gift."

CHAPTER NINETEEN

···········

Annalisa dashed out the front door in such a hurry that she failed to notice that Colin was right behind her until he climbed into her car. "What the hell are you doing?" she demanded as she started the engine.

"What the hell are you doing? Some guy who's maybe a serial killer called you up and you take off by yourself after him? I don't think so."

"I never said I was going by myself."

"Then you won't mind me tagging along." He buckled himself in and she held back a frustrated scream. There was no way to drag him physically from the vehicle. She could drive him to the nearest station and have him arrested for interference, but then she would have to explain where she was going and why. *Don't tell anyone but me what you find,* Zimmer had said. And Nick's warning: *What if it's a cop?* Maybe Lora Fitz's statement had simply been misfiled amid the reams of paper generated on this case, but until she knew for sure who was foe and who was friend, she wasn't going to broadcast her actions over the open police radio.

"Fine," she said to Colin through a clenched jaw as she jammed the stick into gear. "But you do exactly what I tell you."

He held up his palms. "Yes, ma'am."

She roared down the street and hit the button on the wheel to call the one cop she knew she could trust with this latest development. He sounded sleepy when he answered. "Yeah?"

"Nick, it's Annalisa. I need you to meet me right away at St. Thecla's Church in Norwood Park. I'm en route now."

"Why? What's going on?" She could hear him pulling on jeans.

She told him briefly about her latest mysterious phone conversation and the caller's mention of the specific church. "All that talk about the importance of the unexpected gifts," she said. "I'm thinking he may have left something there."

"Maybe. Seems a little thin to me."

"Carelli. It's my church, the one I went to when I was a kid. My parents still attend."

"I'm on my way," he replied, plainly convinced. "Do not get out of the car until you see me pull up. Understand? For all we know, this is a trap to lure you out there alone."

"Not really his style. Besides, I'm not alone." She looked sideways at Colin, who was openly eavesdropping on the conversation. "See you when we get there."

Colin sat with his fingers clenched around his legs. "When you said there were new developments in the case, you didn't tell me this guy was calling you to chat."

"We don't know for sure it's him. We can't trace the calls to a specific person." She hesitated a beat. "But he has made contact with detectives on the case in the past, so it wouldn't be shocking if he decided to do it again." Someone had walked right up to Don Harrigan's desk in the middle of the day to plant the crime scene photo, someone who drew absolutely no attention to himself. Who better to blend in at a cop shop than one wearing a badge? It would be easy to know when to tweak the detectives if you had a front-row seat to the investigation.

Colin looked out at the passing scenery, his face blank. "The old neighborhoods look just the same. The houses, the trees. Jimmy's Pizza is still back there on the corner with the same neon orange sign. I used to ride my bike down here. Hey, it's the Superdawg. Remember that was our first date?"

Of course she remembered. How could she forget? She'd driven past the drive-in hot dog stand a thousand times since he'd gone away. "Colin."

"Hmm?" He didn't look at her. He remained fixated on the parks, the buildings, and the old storefronts, scrutinizing them as if they were an alien landscape.

"I thought you should know—I can see all the files now from your mom's case, and they fill a whole room. They went after this guy with everything they had." It had surprised her, how touching it was to see the boxes and binders and piles of paper, all of which translated to thousands of hours spent in Katie's defense. Annalisa hadn't realized how much her perceptions of the mishandling had been colored by Pops and his friends, grieving and angry at how they were sidelined from the investigation. Just because the cops in her life hadn't been working the case didn't mean that others hadn't sweated every detail. Only now she did have to wonder if they'd missed the devil walking beside them the whole time.

"Yeah? That's nice, I guess." He finally looked at her again, shifting restlessly in his seat. "I used to fantasize that I could catch him. I'd make him beg for his life while I held a gun on him, and then just when he thought it was over, I'd shoot him twice. Once in the head for Dad and once in the heart for Mom. It got so I'd dream about it, and I'd wake up shaking from the fury."

He turned his face to the window again.

"The thing is," he continued eventually, "I never knew what he looked like. He was just some faceless guy dressed in black, and no matter how much I would scream at him to look at me, he would never come into focus. I had the gun in my hand but I still felt totally helpless. It didn't matter how many times I killed him off because I never got what I wanted."

She tightened her grip on the wheel. *Maybe we'll get him now,* she wanted to say, but she knew how hollow the promise would sound after twenty years. "I know other details now that I've seen the files," she said. "Stuff held back from the press."

He didn't have to guess. "She was pregnant when she died."

"Did you know?"

He shook his head slowly. "No, my father told me after. They hadn't been trying. In fact, they didn't think they could have any other kids since it'd been years since they had me. He told me how happy they were, but I think it was just him. I don't think she wanted the baby."

"Why do you say that?"

"A couple of weeks before her death, I heard her crying in the bath-room. I should've knocked, I should've asked what was wrong, but I just felt all awkward and ran back out of the house like I was never there. I know she was thinking of going to design school. She got the bug when I started looking at colleges, and she started looking too. Dad wasn't thrilled about paying for it, but he didn't tell her no, either. A baby would've definitely messed with that plan. If you look at the pic-tures from the party that night, you can see it in her eyes, how sad she was about everything. I just . . . looked the other way, I guess."

Annalisa gunned the car through a red light. Late Sunday night after a big storm, they had the wet roads mostly to themselves. She knew she should make sympathetic noises at Colin, but the defeat in his voice made her skin hot and itchy. *No,* she wanted to say, *it wasn't like that.* Katie would never have stayed unhappy. A new baby was a bless-ing, and their tight-knit families would have found a way to make it work. It was the killer who came and tore everything apart.

The square tower of St. Thecla's came into view, its spire stretching into the sky like an antenna. The church itself sat mostly dark and silent. Annalisa glided her car to a stop out front and peered at the shadowed grounds surrounding the old church. The trees, fresh from the storm, quivered their wet leaves in the remaining breeze, glinting from the harsh white light of the lone streetlamp. There was a faint glow through the giant stained glass windows that took up most of the front wall, suggesting perhaps someone was inside. She did not see any sign of Nick.

"Well?" Colin asked as she twisted first one way and then the other in her seat. "What are we looking for?"

"I'm not sure yet. Maybe nothing. Wait, hold on." She detected move-ment close to the building. She leaned across his body for a better look and saw it again—a shadow that could be a man creeping along behind the hedge. "Stay here."

"Anna, don't—"

She clicked the car door shut on the rest of his protest and took out her gun, staying low as she hustled across the manicured lawn toward the trees and hedges on the side of the building. She heard him before she saw him when a twig snapped under his feet. Her heart pounded erratically as she raised her arms. She'd never had to pull a gun on anyone.

Stealthily, she crept in the direction of the sound, her visibility still hampered by the vegetation around the church. She stepped out around a tree trunk and saw him, huge and dressed in dark clothing. He was bent over in the bushes as if planting something, his face obscured. "Stop right there!" She held the gun steady and pointed at his torso. "Police. Raise your arms above your head."

He jerked in surprise at the sound of her voice and drew himself up to his full height. In the dark, she still couldn't make out his face. He twitched and her finger started to press on the trigger. "I said don't move!" she commanded, and the man obeyed. She licked her lips, preparing to tell him to come out and lie down on the pavement where she could cuff and search him. But just then, behind her, a woman started to scream.

"Don't shoot! Don't shoot!" The hysterical woman came running up behind her.

"Ma'am, step back!" Annalisa ordered, her gun and her eyes still trained on the suspect.

"But Detective Vega, that's my boyfriend," the woman said as she ran in front of the gun. "Please don't hurt him. Don't hurt Travis."

The use of her name penetrated the adrenaline buzz humming in Annalisa's ears. She recognized this woman, she realized. "Molly?"

"Yes, Molly Lipinski. Don't shoot Travis. He wasn't hurting anything, I swear."

"Come out of there," Annalisa instructed the man sharply. She lowered her weapon but didn't put it away. He stepped forward into the light, and she saw that Molly was correct. The prowler was her boyfriend, Travis. "What are you doing trespassing on private property?"

"I got an email a few hours ago from someone calling himself Alexander Pichushkin. He said if the Grave Diggers wanted to know who killed Grace, we should come to this church tonight and God would reveal the answer."

Travis nodded in agreement. "That's what the email said. I read it when Molly showed me, but of course I wasn't going to let her come out here by herself."

"Barnes and Oliver and Chris all got the email too. We argued about whether to come."

"You didn't call the police?"

Molly put a hand on her hip. "The email said God was going to tell us who killed Grace. You think the police would take that seriously?"

"But you did."

Molly and Travis traded a significant look, and Molly shoved her hands inside her windbreaker. "Alexander Pichushkin is the name of a Russian serial killer. We figured we had to at least check it out. If we found anything of value, then we would have called the police."

"Well, did you find anything?" Annalisa couldn't hold back her impatience.

"Nothing," Travis said. "Just a bunch of wet flowers."

Annalisa turned her head and saw Nick had appeared, and he wasn't alone. He walked with a lean African American man, and Barnes rolled alongside in his wheelchair. Colin had joined the parade, bringing up the rear. "I found these two poking around on the west side of the building," Nick said, indicating Barnes and the other man. "Meet Oliver Benton."

He inclined his head. "Pleased to meet you, Detective."

"I assume they told you the same story about the email," Annalisa said to Nick.

"Barnes was kind enough to show me on his phone," Nick replied as Barnes waved his Android. "It checks out."

"Great," Annalisa muttered. "The gang's all here."

"Everyone except Chris," Nick answered.

"He thought it was a hoax," Oliver explained.

Molly cleared her throat. "He thought it was Doug being a dick again."

"Doug?" asked Annalisa.

"My ex. He was in the group for a while, but he got kicked out when we broke up."

"No one was sorry to see him go," Barnes told her. "The guy's a pompous a-hole." He looked up at Molly. "No offense."

"Hey, I've called him worse," she said, and Travis put an arm around her.

Annalisa gestured at Nick and stepped to the side with him. He nudged her and glanced back to where Colin stood around awkwardly with the Grave Diggers. "You brought a date with you?"

"He's not my date. That's Colin Duffy, Katie's son. He just got into town a few hours ago and happened to be with me when my secret admirer phoned. I don't know what this little stunt is all about, but I don't like it."

Nick kept his voice low and his back to their audience. "It's got to be the same guy, right? The one who called you and the one who sent that email. Otherwise, how would we all end up in the same place?"

"The question is why. What's the point of this?"

"If it was an ambush, we'd be dead by now." He looked around at the shadowed grounds. A fine mist hung over everything, and the breeze stirred the trees. "Maybe he just wanted to get us all wet."

"It would be great if it were that simple, but I think we should search the place just to be sure. I'll check inside."

He grabbed her arm when she started to move. "Not alone."

"C'mon, Carelli. I'm hardly alone." She waved an arm in the direction of their impromptu search party. "And someone needs to stay with them."

"Whoever this guy is, he's not phoning me up for a heart-to-heart." He shook his head, resolute. "You're not leaving my sight, Vega. For all we know, this is still a trap."

"Fine." She heaved a sigh. "Then let's all go." If by some remote chance the killer was lurking inside, he couldn't possibly grab them all. "Listen up," she said to the group. "We're going to take a look around inside the church. You'll come with us, but stay behind me and Detective Carelli and don't enter the building until we say so. Are we clear?"

"I can help if you need it," Travis said, and pulled back his jacket to reveal a semiautomatic handgun strapped to his belt.

"Whoa, what's that?" Annalisa said.

"It's legal, and I know how to use it. I was in the army for four years."

"I don't care if you're Secret Service or God's own body man. Give it here." She held out a hand for the gun, but Travis bristled.

"I don't have to give it to you."

"If you want to see the inside of the church, you hand it over. Otherwise, you can wait out here with my partner while we check it out."

"I'm going with Molly," he insisted.

She waggled the fingers of her outstretched hand. "Then that makes your decision real easy, now, doesn't it?" She wasn't about to have him freaking out over a shadow and then shooting up a hundred-year-old stained glass window. Reluctantly, he took the gun out from his belt and handed it to her. She slipped it into her holster. "You can have it back when we're done. Now, let's go."

The group went to the front of the building and up the concrete steps. Oliver pushed Barnes up the ramp at the side. Annalisa tried the heavy door and it opened with a loud creak. "I'll go first," she told them. Her weapon drawn, she slipped inside, keeping her back against the stone wall. When she saw no one immediately apparent in the giant sanctuary, she whispered back to Nick. "Clear."

He entered with his weapon at the ready, and the rest of the group trailed in behind him. Annalisa regarded the rows of long wooden pews that ran the length of the room. How many Sundays had she sat here, itching in her frilly dress, being shushed and reminded not to kick the pew in front of her while the priest droned on and on? She felt the eyes of the saints on her, their faces watching from the rafters as she walked down the main aisle toward the altar. It was lit by recessed lamps, beamed as though from the heavens.

"This is creepy," someone murmured behind her.

"Shh!" Annalisa halted and held up her arm. "Do you hear that?" Faint music played from somewhere, but the direction was difficult to place in the cavernous hall.

"It's Brahms's 'Lullaby,'" Oliver offered after a few moments.

Annalisa took another step, paused to listen, then walked a bit more. The group shuffled behind her as she hunted the source of the music. She reached the marble steps leading up to the broad altar and mounted them slowly, one by one. "There," she murmured, pointing. The group closed in around her, and they all inspected her find: an ornate silver music box with its lid propped open.

"Oh my God," Molly said, covering her mouth with her hands. "That's Grace's. Her grandma left it to her."

"Look," whispered Barnes, pointing overhead, and Annalisa tilted her head back to see. In the shadows among the rafters, hanging down and swaying gently back and forth, was a noose.

"What's that hanging from it?" Nick asked, shining his flashlight up to see. The beam caught one bulging white eye peering back down at them. "Is it . . . ? Is that a frog?"

"It's Filmore," Annalisa replied as she stared at it in horror. "He's my frog. This guy has been to my house."

CHAPTER TWENTY

....

GRACE NOTES

Journal Entry #428

THE GRAVE DIGGERS GOT INTO AN ARGUMENT TONIGHT, AND IT STARTED BECAUSE CHRIS WAS PATTING HIMSELF ON THE BACK AGAIN. I'm just going to cut and paste the chat transcript because I think everyone misunderstood what I was trying to say and maybe if I read it again later I might see things differently. But probably not.

Chris: Did u see that special last night on the woman who died in a fire but it wasn't the fire that killed her, it was her husband? I knew it was him since before the opening credits. I knew the minute they showed his face.

Molly: Yeah, because it's always the husband or bf.

Chris: She had a boyfriend and it wasn't him. It was the ex. Totally guilty, and I knew it.

Grace: Congrats, genius, you've cracked the super-secret code! If the producers interview the guy for his story but don't show his clothes, that's because he's wearing prison garb. 2+2=4 He was convicted. Irl, the suspects don't wear orange jumpsuits to make it so easy for you.

Chris: Y do you bust my balls all the time?

Grace: Because you're always telling us how big they are.

Barnes: Can we please change the subject to something other than Chris's balls?

Molly: Yes, plz. Ew. I saw the special and I almost couldn't watch because of the thing with the kids. He's choking her and she's begging him, "What about our kids? Think of our kids!" Horrible.

Grace: Horrible, yes, but she married him.

Molly: Are you saying she asked for it?

Grace: No, of course she didn't ask to be murdered. But victims and abusers always seem to find each other. Think about it—this guy was asking random people at his work if they knew anyone who could help him kill his wife. You think a dude like this kept his inner monster a secret? Not freakin' likely. He flew his flag and she saw it waving, and something in her said, yep, he's the one for me.

Oliver: You're not being fair. She was divorcing him.

Molly: Doug slapped me once & I stayed with him for 3 more months. He was so nice half the time, I thought if a sweet guy like that hit me, I must've deserved it. U just don't understand what it's like 2 be in a relationship like that. It messes with ur head.

Chris: Yeah, Grace, way to blame the victim. . . .

Grace: I'm not blaming the victim. Many of these women grow up in families that didn't love them like they should. Maybe Daddy was an abuser too. Maybe Step-daddy was. Whatever the background, it creates a cyclone of chaos around the victim that allows the abuser to sneak in. But then something changes. The victim gets tired of the storm and they want out. When the abuser realizes they don't have the tornado to help control their victim anymore, that's when they are most dangerous.

Barnes: So, what about the Lovelorn case? Those women were attacked by a stranger in their own homes. Are you saying the killer peeps in their windows and sees a tornado?

Grace: No, the Lovelorn guy is different. I think this kind of killer makes his own tornado. Big enough to encircle all of us.

Chris: Cripes, not this crap again. The people with access to the actual case files say he's dead or in jail somewhere.

Grace: They said that about the Golden State Killer, too. Look what happened to him.

Barnes: I want to hear more about this citywide tornado.

Grace: Ok, we know he likes to torture his victims, that he strangles and revives them over and over until finally snuffing them out. That's an intimate one-on-one act, but he's not content to let it end there. He sends his letters to the news media to frighten the whole city. Maybe the whole state. He kills just a handful of women but he makes everyone afraid.

Molly: I was only 10 when he killed Katherine Duffy but I remember my dad installed an extra lock on the front door that weekend. I wasn't allowed to ride my bike to school anymore either.

Oliver: Sandra had to take two buses home from work at the time, and then she walked three blocks in the dark. I worried about her, especially on nights I had to work late. I'd call her up just to hear her voice and she'd laugh and say, "Honey, this is one time it's better to be black. He's not gonna come for me." Then he killed Karen Lovell and none of us was laughing anymore. Almost like he knew we'd been counting ourselves safe.

Grace: That's what I'm saying. He fed off of everyone's fear.

Molly: Ok, he wins then. I was terrified.

Grace: I'm not. He's probably a shriveled old man now. How awful it must be for him to have terrorized a whole state for years and not be able to tell anyone about it. How small he must feel now that everyone's forgotten to be afraid of him. The kids on my street go whizzing by on their bikes without a care in the world.

Chris: You think because you don't see him, he's not there. That he's impotent now. Remember, he chose to go silent. It's not like anyone could touch him. Evil like that doesn't shrivel up and go away.

Grace: He's not the devil, Chris. He's just a man.

Barnes: Don't be so quick to denounce the devil. In Baghdad, our part of the war was supposed to be over, but that meant diddly-squat to the Shiites and the Sunnis, who continued to kill each other every chance they got. Then they'd dump the bodies around the city and it fell on us to clean them up. We'd find them DRT in a pool of blood or shoved out of a moving car by the side of the road.

Grace: DRT?

Barnes: Dead Right There. Anyway, one day, we get a call from the Iraqi police that there are four bodies that need retrieval. It was hot like Hades, indescribable if you haven't lived through it. Temperatures were routinely 120, and we were wearing metal jackets. I got volunteered with these two other guys, Eddie Mack and Bob McGuinness, to go out and get the bodies. Eddie and Bob were opposite personalities. Bob was quiet, stern, all business. He never used more words than necessary to communicate. Eddie was like a golden retriever, blond and big-eyed, always clapping guys on the back and cracking jokes. On the ride out to get the bodies, Bob said nothing while Eddie went on about how he could construct the perfect woman out of every girl he'd been with—he'd take the tits from one, the ass from another, etc. It was stupid but it was just easier to let him run his mouth than use up energy telling him to shut up.

Chris: Cool story, bro. Is there a point to this?

Barnes: We picked up the first two bodies, no problem. Then we got to the third one, which had been dragged behind a couple of trees. He had blood coming from his mouth and his hands were bound with wire. It was obvious he'd been severely beaten. I bent down to pick him up, but suddenly he moved. His eyes opened and he groaned. Scared the shit out of all of us. He started babbling in Arabic. I only caught a few words but one of them was *musaeada*. Help. He said it over and over—help, help—looking right up at us. Literally begging for his life. Bob said, "We need to get him to a medic." I was about to radio it in when Eddie stopped me. He said to wait a second. He went over to the man, bent down, and touched his face. He said, "We will help you." Then he stood up and shot him right between the eyes.

Molly: OMG!

Oliver: That's barbaric.

Grace: What did you do?

Barnes: We loaded him in with the others. Eddie said he did the guy a favor by ending his suffering. I just remember looking at Bob's face after the rifle shot rang out. He looked like he'd seen the devil.

Molly: What happened to Eddie?

Barnes: Last I heard he's got a wife and two kids out in Ohio. I'm sure he's got his rifle with him too.

Molly: That's comforting.

Chris: War is different. It does stuff to people, makes them do things they wouldn't dream of doing in regular life.

Chris likes to think he's a genius, but he can be dumb as a sack of hair. Unlike him, Barnes has actually seen a dead body. I know what he was trying to tell us: most people need a reason to pull the trigger; others just need an excuse. If you're one of those who needs an excuse, then you will always find one.

CHAPTER TWENTY-ONE

....

A NNALISA CALLED ZIMMER FROM ST. THECLA'S, AND ZIMMER HAD NO CHOICE BUT TO CALL THE CHIEF OF POLICE, AND HE, OF COURSE, CALLED IN THE FBI. She had no idea who'd alerted Don Harrigan, but he, too, showed up outside the church. The normally quiet street looked like a club scene with all the flashing blue and red lights casting frantic shadows against the high stone walls. Colin stood with the Grave Diggers, all of them guarded by uniformed officers, while the forensic techs went to work on the church. Annalisa knew they were all going to be questioned thoroughly before the night was over, just as she already knew that none of their answers would prove satisfactory. The Lovelorn killer had orchestrated this show well in advance, and if he was watching at all, it would be from a safe distance.

She strolled over to Colin, trying to look casual, and touched his arm. "Some welcome home party, huh?"

"I have dreams that look like this," he said as he surveyed the controlled chaos. "Our house roped off with yellow tape, cop cars all over the street."

"I'm sorry." She gave him a sympathetic squeeze. "After they interview you, you'll be free to take off again for Budapest or wherever. . . ."

He turned to her with horror. "And leave you here alone? With this?"

"It's my job, Colin. I can handle it." Zimmer motioned to her, and she touched Colin's arm again, this time in apology. "I'll be back."

She stood facing Zimmer, which gave her a prime view of St. Thecla's. The techs had turned the lights on inside the sanctuary, illuminating the stained glass windows from within. Their glow was muted, nothing like the view she remembered from the pews, when the strong sun poured in through the red, yellow, and blue glass, casting beams of color through the enormous hall. Even as an adult, whenever Annalisa tried to picture God, this was the image she saw in her mind: the saints lit like fire in the Sunday sun.

"You've positively identified the music box as belonging to Grace Harper?" Zimmer was asking, and Annalisa jerked her attention back to her boss.

"Her friend Molly Lipinski has identified it, yes."

"And the frog is definitely yours."

"My grandmother made it. There isn't a second one in the world, as far as I know."

"Then that's it. Lovelorn has to be the guy who's calling you." Zimmer sounded grim, not excited, by this lead.

"I recorded the conversation."

Zimmer turned dark eyes to Colin and the Grave Diggers. "What about the rest of them? Who are they?"

"The guy on the end is Colin Duffy, Katherine's son. The others are members of the same amateur sleuth group that Grace Harper belonged to." Annalisa recapped their story about the email, and Zimmer's frown deepened.

"So, he wanted all of you out here to witness this? To find the music box?"

Annalisa regarded the church again as a Bible verse from her childhood came back to her. "And he said unto them, go ye into all the world, and preach the gospel to every creature."

"I beg your pardon?"

"We're his disciples, the ones who help him spread fear. He dragged us out here to make sure we got his latest message. The Grave Diggers were necessary to authenticate Grace's music box. I'm here to herald in all of this." She waved her arm at the cars, the lights, and the line of people trooping in and out of the church.

"Yeah, well, he's not getting his headlines this time. The FBI wants to play this as a false alarm, a bomb scare that turned out to be nothing. The idea is that it may prompt this guy to make contact again."

"Terrific," Annalisa muttered. "I so enjoy our chats."

"Yeah." Zimmer chuffed a humorless laugh. "We'll be parking an undercover unit in front of your house just in case he decides to discuss matters in person. Although it wouldn't be the worst idea in the world if you decided to stay with a friend or family member for a few days."

"No," Annalisa replied immediately. No way would she make a target out of someone else. "He doesn't want to kill me. He wants to rub it in that we can't catch him. I can't be impressed with him if I'm dead."

"All the same, we'll be discussing your new security detail before you go home tonight."

As the hours stretched on toward morning, the party moved back to headquarters, where Annalisa lost sight of the others as she took turns explaining the phone calls and the events of the evening to various people higher up in the food chain than she was. "I don't understand," one gray-haired suit said to her in a peeved tone. "Why did he decide to call you?"

They're all jealous, she realized as they surrounded her and hurled repeated questions until she was emotionally and physically exhausted. They played and replayed the recorded conversation, nitpicking her every response. "Why didn't you press him more? Ask him about the case?"

"I let him lead the conversation to keep him talking as long as possible. The longer he talks, the more material we have to work with." She slumped in her chair. They'd been cooped in the windowless room for three hours, and the men had their shirtsleeves rolled up like they were ready to go another round. She'd drained the one water bottle they'd given her and then peeled off the label. It lay curled up on the table in front of her, and she found herself wishing she could do the same.

"He mentioned a service at St. Thecla's and you took that as a cue to go over there. Why?"

"There was no other point to bringing up the church unless he wanted me to check it out."

"Why didn't you alert the task force?"

"Because at the time, I had no proof it was actually him."

A sharp rap on the door made the men turn their heads, and Zimmer poked into the room. "Let's give it a rest now, gentleman. She's not skipping town on bail. You'll get to talk to her tomorrow."

The FBI guy in charge, Agent Grayson, stepped between Zimmer and Annalisa. "With all due respect, ma'am, there's a human predator on the loose. We can all sleep when he's caught."

Zimmer made a show of checking her watch. "You Washington boys have been on this case for twenty years now. You're telling me you haven't had so much as forty winks in that time span?" She leaned around him and beckoned to Annalisa. "Detective Vega answers to me, not to you."

"And you'll answer to the chief."

"Great, have him call my office. I'll be at home, sleeping. That's no doubt where your killer is right now, and we have to be fresh enough to face him for another round."

Annalisa followed Zimmer out, and they strode down the hall while the men sputtered behind them. "Thanks, Commander," she said under her breath.

"Don't thank me. You should have called me the moment he phoned you." She halted and pinned Annalisa in place with a piercing look. "I can't protect you if you keep me in the dark."

"Yes, of course. I'm sorry."

"I don't want you to be sorry. I want you to be smart." She pointed at her own head. "Think. When a serial murderer says he's got a gift for you, you don't go running down there by yourself to find out what it is."

"I took Carelli with me."

"Yes, I've heard his narrative, and I don't find it reassuring. By the time he arrived, you could have been dead at the scene."

"Sorry," Annalisa said, more petulantly this time as fatigue took over. "I don't usually get calls from a serial killer. I'm unfamiliar with the protocol."

Zimmer wasn't amused. "Protocol is that you go home and stay there until you hear from me. If he so much as sends you a smoke signal, you let me know immediately. The FBI has set up a trace on the number. If he turns the phone on, we can locate it and finally nail this bastard. The best thing you can do is stay home, and if he calls, try to keep the line open as long as possible."

"Stay home," Annalisa echoed. "I can't just stay home and wait for his call. I'm still working this case."

"Not if I say you aren't."

It isn't up to you, Annalisa almost blurted out. All of a sudden, she understood why the men in the room had been so frustrated with her: on this case, the killer outranked them all, and for some reason, he'd picked Annalisa for a lieutenant. "Fine," she told Zimmer with a sigh, holding up her hands in defeat. "I'll go home."

"I'll drive her." Carelli had materialized from nowhere to appear behind her.

"Good." Zimmer nodded her approval. "The UC unit is already in place. Be careful out there."

Nick jerked a nod in Annalisa's direction. "C'mon, let's get out of here."

She didn't have the energy to argue with him. The bags under her eyes had bags of their own. She checked her personal phone on the way out and found a text from Colin. *Went to my hotel to crash. I'll call tomorrow about picking up my bag from your place. Xx* She tucked the phone back in her pocket, too exhausted to parse what the sign-off might mean. Back in the early days of their courtship, she had hung on every word he said or wrote, sifting through them as if panning for gold. *He said he'd love to date a girl like me. Does that mean he wants me or just someone similar?*

At her place, Nick parked the car and unbuckled his belt. She blinked tired eyes at him. "You're coming in?"

"Hell, yes, I'm coming in. I'm doing a complete sweep of the place before you set foot in there."

She didn't even care anymore. "Knock yourself out," she said, holding up the keys for him. He exited the car, unlocked the door, and then withdrew his gun before entering her home. She watched the lights go on in the windows one by one until he reappeared and waved to her from the door.

"All clear."

She smothered a yawn with her arm and followed him inside. Despite her exhaustion, she had to go look at the backyard. She flicked on the outside light, and sure enough, there was a circle of dirt where the frog had sat. The guy had been eight feet from her door, and she hadn't known a thing. A shudder went through her and she jerked the door to check the lock.

Back in the living room, Nick stood amid the remains of her earlier evening—the wine glasses and candles and dented pillows on the couch. "I thought you said he wasn't your date."

"Don't start with me."

"Who's starting?" He watched her begin to rinse the dishes. "I am getting the distinct feeling that I entered in the middle of the second act."

She halted with a soapy plate in hand to gape at him. "Meaning what? That I dated someone before I met you? You'd bedded half the North Side."

"How come you never told me about this guy?"

"I did tell you."

"Right. You had a high school boyfriend who lived on the same block as you. Just your ordinary puppy love that didn't work out once you went to different schools. You never mentioned that his mother was murdered by the Lovelorn Killer. You never told me . . ."

"Told you what?" she challenged.

His shoulders sagged, and he waved vaguely at the table where she'd eaten dinner with Colin. "Why did you break up?"

She went back to the dishes. "We didn't. He just moved away after his dad died and then he never talked to me again."

"Ah." Nick nodded as if to himself.

"What's that supposed to mean?" She put the plates in the rack and dried her hands on her jeans. "You think you have some sudden insight now? You think you glimpse my high school boyfriend, see a couple of wine glasses, and now you understand me?"

"No. I would never think that."

His words held no fight in them, so she felt the anger evaporate from her as well. "You can go now. I don't think there's anyone hiding in my closets."

"If it's okay, I'd like to stay on your couch."

"Nick, there's a car parked outside watching my front door."

"Yeah, and I'd like to be watching you." He regarded her soberly. "Look it, this is not a knock on you and how tough you are. This guy has eluded like seven different law enforcement agencies for almost a quarter century. Now he's set his sights on you, and I just don't want to take any chances."

Her mouth twitched in a near smile. "Seven different agencies, but you'll be my guard dog, huh?"

He did smile. "Grrr," he replied, snapping at her for emphasis.

"Fine, for one night only. I'll go get you a blanket and a pillow for the couch."

"Just like the old days," he quipped, and she shot him a dark look.

"Don't push your luck, Carelli."

She brought him the bedding and went to her room, where she closed the door and changed into her nightshirt. As she was brushing her teeth, she heard him getting a drink of water from the kitchen. It surprised her, how she recognized his footsteps so easily even after all these years. She took her toothbrush and went to the living room, where he had turned out the lights and taken to his bed on the sofa. "Nick?"

"Hmm?" He sat up and she could just make out his face in the shadows.

"Why did you ask me to marry you? I mean, we could've just had a fling like you did with all the other girls."

He thought about his answer for a long time. "It seemed like that's what you wanted," he replied finally, and the words hit her like a punch to the gut. She had wanted to get married, all right. To Colin. No wonder she'd never mentioned him to Nick.

"But what about what you wanted?"

Again, he made her wait while he considered his reply. "I wanted to make you happy."

She remembered their wedding day, the tiny, perfect ceremony in her parents' backyard. The cherry tree had rained blossoms like a blessing from above, and she'd felt so safe inside his arms. She hadn't known then that the vows meant nothing to him, that Nick Carelli would use whatever words he needed to make someone like him, even signing his future away in the process.

"Zimmer would love us right now," she said. "Some instincts we've got, huh?" Cops were supposed to be good at reading people; somehow, they'd each married a stranger.

Nick hummed a non-reply and thumped his pillow with his fist. "What we've got," he said finally, "is another chance."

CHAPTER TWENTY-TWO

··············

A NNALISA AWOKE FACEDOWN ON HER MATTRESS, HAIR PLASTERED AGAINST HER CHEEK. She jerked upright, immediately on threat alert because of a shadowy presence in her room. "Relax." Nick's voice penetrated the adrenaline rush in her brain. He stood by her door wearing a pair of snug jeans and a smirk. "It's just me. I made coffee and I thought you might like some."

"Be there in a minute," she mumbled, yanking her nightshirt down over her bare thighs. When he left, she staggered into the bathroom and took the world's hottest shower. She hoped the stinging water would revive her enervated skin and wash out the vague nausea rippling in her stomach. She felt hungover and strung out, whirled backward by a sinister time machine that left Nick Carelli once again shirtless in her kitchen and the monster from her childhood prowling the streets. She stood under the shower spray for a long time and felt almost human when she emerged. She pulled on some clothes, and thankfully, Nick had done the same. He wore a crisp white shirt, rolled up at the sleeves, which somehow failed to show a single wrinkle despite the fact that he'd slept on her couch. He held a coffee mug in one hand and the framed picture of her family and the Duffys in the other.

"I remember you had this back at our old apartment," he said. "I didn't know then what it meant."

You never asked, she thought, but she couldn't blame him. They had been careful not to ask each other anything that mattered. She took the other steaming mug from the counter and tried a small sip. Milk with a hint of sugar, just the way she liked it. She hid a smile in the rim of the cup and went around the island to stand next to him so she could see the picture too. "After she died, I stared at this photo for hours. I wanted to crawl inside it."

"I know what you mean."

She regarded him curiously. He took a breath and set the photo gently in front of them. "My father shot my mother to death when I was eight years old."

Her jaw fell open in horror. "What? And you never told me?"

He gave her a pointed look. "I guess that makes us even."

"You said your mother died in an auto accident and that you never knew your dad."

"That's the story I told everyone." He took a deep breath. "She was leaving him. We'd moved out into a new apartment. My bedroom had pink walls and I hated it. She told me I could pick out any new color I wanted, but I never got that chance. One night, I woke up to hear him shouting at her, and her crying. She was begging him. Don't hurt Nicky. Don't hurt Nicky. Then the gunshots. They were the loudest sound I'd ever heard in my life. The neighbors called 911, but it was too late."

She shook her head as she tried to absorb the story. "What happened to him?"

"The cops went on the hunt. They found him in his car outside an abandoned Burger King. He'd shot himself in the head."

"Nick . . . I'm so sorry."

He nodded. "I went to live with my grandma, my mom's mom. She was nice, but every morning for a year I'd wake up thinking maybe it was all a dream. But then I'd see the blue walls, not pink, and I'd remember the truth."

"You never told me."

"You have to understand," he said. "I didn't want it to be true. I spent my whole childhood as the kid whose mom got shot by his dad. First thing I did when I hit eighteen was to leave Jacksonville as far behind me as possible."

"You came up here," she said, piecing the story together.

"Yeah. I got real good at convincing myself it was over, that I was happy. Got my own place with my own white walls. Got a job and some friends who had no idea what happened when I was a kid. I ignored the part where if I was alone for two minutes, I felt like I was coming out of my skin."

For her, it had been a depression, a lead weight on her chest. She'd lain in bed, staring at the cracks in the ceiling and listening to the silence in the house—Vinny and Tony were gone away at school, Alex was off drinking, Pops was out driving the streets, hunting a faceless killer. Ma cooked so many dinners that no one ever ate.

"When I met you," Nick continued, "I had a sense of recognition, but I didn't understand why." He gave her a ghost of a smile. "I think I see it now. We have the same holes, you and me."

At that moment, she felt like Swiss cheese. "You may be right."

He looked down at the picture of her and Colin with their arms around each other. "I guess there are a lot of things we kept from each other."

Her phone started ringing on the far end of the counter, and they shared a look of instant panic. "It's my personal cell," she said, reaching for it. The caller ID said it was Alex. "Hello?"

"Hey, sorry to bother you so early, but we have a situation. Pops fell and broke his hip. He's in the hospital being prepped for surgery now."

"What hospital? When did this happen?"

"Northwestern. Mom found him at the bottom of the ladder to the attic early this morning. From her description, he took quite the crash."

"What the hell was he doing upstairs, let alone trying to get into the attic?"

"You know Pops. He refuses to believe he's disabled. I'm here with Ma and Tony. Vin's on his way, too."

"I'll be right there." As she hung up, she remembered that her car was still parked downtown at the station. Nick already had his keys at the ready.

"Your dad?"

"He fell and broke his hip. They're going to operate to fix it."

He drained the last of his coffee and nodded to the door. "Let's get over there, then."

Annalisa fidgeted in her seat, her anxiety rising as they hit the

Monday-morning traffic. Chicago streets became gridlocked, entire light cycles passing with no forward progress or movement as cars crammed the intersections. "I should get out and walk. It'd be faster."

Nick remained loose and calm even as people started laying on their horns around them. "Your dad is as tough as a Bears lineman. He'll be all right."

Annalisa snorted. "The toughest part of him is his thick skull. He knows better than to be climbing around in the attic." At last, traffic inched forward half a block. Annalisa bit back a groan as they halted again. Nick used the wait to bring up a sore spot from the night before.

"St. Thecla's church," he said. "You said it's the one you go to?"

"Used to go to," she corrected. "My parents are still active there." She should say a prayer for Pops now, she realized with a sudden shame. She might be lapsed, but Pops still attended Mass every Sunday. The least she could do was to put in a good word on his behalf. She closed her eyes and prayed for his health and safety. As if her silent hopes were granted, traffic opened up after the light and cars moved more freely down the street. Relief flowed through her, and she leaned her body forward in the seat, urging them on.

"You need to tell them, then," Nick said.

"Tell who what?"

"Your caller last night didn't pick that church at random. There's got to be a thousand to choose from, and yet he hangs a noose in the one you attended as a kid. How's he supposed to have guessed that if you don't go to Mass anymore?"

"He was watching my parents," she said as she followed his logic. She cursed softly and balled her hands in her lap. "Can't you go any faster?"

At the hospital, she discovered all three of her older brothers managed to beat her to the waiting room, as usual. She was always the last to know, the last to get a say. The Vega family had run just fine for years before she'd joined it already in progress, and they had never granted her a seat on the family council even as a legal, voting adult. Her elders still treated her like she was five years old and wanted to name the family schnauzer Mr. Stinky Feet. Vinny engulfed her in a big hug. "You made it," he said, as though she had been missing for days. She reached up and rubbed his bald head.

"How's Pops?"

"Ma's back there with him. The nurses are doing something with him now, and we're waiting on the surgeon to get scrubbed in or something. We're hoping to see him again before they slice and dice him." He looked past her for the first time and saw Nick hovering by the water cooler. "What's he doing here?"

"He gave me a ride."

"I didn't know he was back in town," Vinny said, making a face like he'd just learned of a disease outbreak.

Alex came over to join the party. "Is that Nick Carelli?"

Nick waved and edged toward the group. "Hey, Alex. Sorry to hear about your dad."

Alex wasn't having it. He stepped forward, his chest puffed out. "If I remember right, I still owe you a punch in the face."

"Alex, please. Not now." Annalisa laid a hand on his arm.

"What'd you bring him for? He's not family."

"It's about work. We're working together."

"Work? You dragged the job in here with you now? When Pops is about to go under the knife?"

His agitation brought Tony over to the conversation. "What's going on?" he asked as he put a large, gentle hand on the back of Annalisa's neck. He rubbed the tension there and she slipped an arm around him in thanks. His black curly hair was thinning on top, but the bottom curls just brushed his shirt collar. Annalisa would bet a year's salary that Ma had already nagged him to get a haircut, hospital or no hospital.

"Look what trash Annalisa's brought with her," Alex said, thrusting his chin in Nick's direction. "Better hide the candy stripers."

"Nick." Tony the peacekeeper stepped forward to offer his hand. "It's been a long time, man. You look good."

Nick gave him a quick, embarrassed handshake before hanging back. "I'm not here to intrude. If you want, I can step outside and you guys can take turns hitting me in the gut."

"I'd go first," Annalisa said mildly, leading Alex away by the arm. Tony chatted up Nick while Vinny joined them by the magazine rack. "Look, I can't go into a lot of details, but if you've seen the news, you know why work is a major priority right now." Alex's gaze went to the

TV mounted in the corner. It was tuned to a twenty-four-hour news channel and set to closed-captioning. The image showed footage from St. Thecla's church last night, while the voice-over text read, "Chicago Police deny connection between late-night church raid and the Lovelorn Killer."

Alex grew pale as he watched the cops encircle St. Thecla's. "That's Mom and Dad's church. They had some sort of bomb scare there? Jesus."

"Yes. I need to talk to Ma and Pops about that."

He looked at her aghast. "Now? Jesus, Anna, they need you to be a daughter for two seconds here, not Nancy Drew."

Her hackles rose. "I'm not playing dress-up in our backyard, Alex. It's my honest-to-God job to investigate these things now."

"Let him go do it." He shot a venomous look at Nick. "You have more important stuff to worry about. Like family."

"All right," Vinny interrupted them. "Alex, why don't you go get everyone a soda? Take a walk. Clear your head."

"No, I want to be here for Pops."

"We'll text you if anything changes." He nudged Alex on his way. "Go. Call Sassy. Talk to your kids. We'll be here when you get back." When Alex reluctantly left the room, Vinny glanced at the TV and back to Annalisa. "It's true, then? He's back?"

"It's more probable that he never left," she replied in a low voice. "But he's above ground for the first time in years, so now we have a real chance to nail him."

"Yeah? No offense, but I'm glad I moved out of his radius. I've got Carrie and Quinn to worry about," he said, naming his wife and young teenage daughter. "So, Nick is working the case too? Shouldn't he be out beating the bushes or questioning witnesses? I highly doubt the killer's in this waiting room." He scanned the other anxious people sitting in the nearby chairs.

"Nick is on the job." Annalisa rubbed her tired eyes. "He's watching me."

"I can see that. The dude's barely taken his eyes off you. Maybe if he'd kept that kind of focus while you were married—"

"He's watching me because the killer is watching me too."

Vinny's long jaw snapped shut. He looked again at the horror movie playing out on the morning news. "What did you say?"

"The killer has my phone number," Annalisa murmured. "He saw me on television and called me up."

"Called you to say what?" Vinny demanded, and the heads around them swiveled at his burst of noise.

Annalisa made a motion for him to calm down. "It's fine. He just wants to brag about how smart he is."

"Yeah? He is smart! Look how many women he's killed and gotten away with it. Now he's calling you?"

"I'm fine." She held out her arms and turned around to prove it. "See? Not a scratch on me. Nick is staying at my place, and my commander has parked an undercover unit on the street in front of my door. Nothing is going to happen to me. I just . . ." She broke off and ran a hand through her hair. "I need to tell Ma and Pops to be careful. This guy tracks his news coverage super closely. I'm sure he knows that we were friends with the Duffys and that Pops was a cop who worked with Owen. I don't think he'd hurt Ma or Pops at this late date, but I wouldn't be surprised if he wanted to taunt them or scare them, just for his own sick amusement."

"That's the last thing they need right now." He cast a worried look in the direction that Alex had gone. "Do me a favor and don't tell Alex any of this, okay?"

"Why?"

"He's been stressed out lately."

She put her hands on her hips. "Stressed out how?" Sassy hadn't said anything to her about trouble with Alex.

"Keep it down, will you?" He looked around before continuing. "A couple of weeks ago, he was chaperoning the school dance, and he caught a couple of boys with a bottle of vodka. Naturally, he took it from them and sent them home. Unfortunately, he didn't toss the vodka."

"Oh, no." She leaned against the nearest wall, a sinking feeling in her gut.

"It's fine," Vinny said, a desperate tinge in his voice, the way they'd reassured each other a hundred times in the past. This time, Alex would get clean. He'd hit bottom. He'd stop. But there was always a lower level, and Alex kept rolling right downhill. "It's just one slipup. But some busybody history teacher saw him drinking and she's threatened to tell the principal. Alex says it's like walking around with a bomb strapped to his chest. He's never sure when or if she's going to go off."

"What would happen if she told?"

"I don't know. Worst case, maybe he gets fired. But it might be okay. She chewed him out and he apologized. He says he wasn't falling down drunk or anything . . ."

They'd all heard that one before, too. She tilted her head back against the wall and stared at the particleboard squares on the ceiling until they blurred in front of her. "Do you ever blame him?" she whispered to Vinny. "Not Alex, but the man who murdered Katie. It's like he broke in and stole everything at once—Katie, Owen, Alex, Pops. He created this . . . this hole that everyone kept falling into, and sometimes it feels like we'll just keep falling until they catch him."

"Catch who?" Alex reappeared and handed her a can of Coke that was slippery with condensation.

"Uh, no one. Nothing." Her personal cell rang, saving her from further stammering. She checked the caller ID, but she didn't recognize the number. "Hello?"

"Anna, it's Colin. How are you? Was everything okay at your place last night?"

"Yes, fine," she said, relaxing at the sound of his voice. "How are you doing?"

"Jittery. I've been up for an hour and I'm on my third cup of coffee. I'm wondering if it would be all right if I came by for my suitcase."

"Oh," she said regretfully, turning to face the waiting room full of people. "I'm not home. I'm at the hospital, actually. Northwestern. My father fell and broke his hip."

"George is in the hospital? That's terrible."

She wondered if he knew Pops had been sick. The Parkinson's symptoms hadn't begun until years after Colin left town, but in her mind, the whole downward spiral started at the same time. She'd read theories about a relationship between stress and Parkinson's disease. The damage occurred in brain areas responsible for movement, when neurons producing a certain chemical called dopamine all died off. Why did they die? She had pored over inscrutable medical journals, looking for answers, and that's where she found stress cited over and over. The brain cells, when stressed, didn't clean up their proteins correctly. Too many junk proteins accumulated inside the cells like overflowing trash and caused the cells to die. Near as she could tell, the doctors weren't claiming that mental stress literally caused the protein pileup, but they couldn't say it didn't. No one knew the cause. All Annalisa knew for sure was that Pops had been healthy and strong before Katie Duffy died, and that he was never the same afterward. She'd seen the stress piling up in the way he lost his hair, lost weight, lost the spring in his step and the cheery whistle he gave to announce he'd come home.

"I'm not sure yet when I'll be back," she said to Colin, her voice watery. "They're going to operate on Pops at any minute."

"Don't worry about it. I'll come to the hospital. Maybe I can take your keys and hop over to your place while you wait."

"Sure."

"I'll see you soon. Give my love to Pops."

"I will." She hung up and went back to the waiting area. Her brothers sat together against one wall while Nick sat by himself some distance away. She saw he had one eye on the TV. After a moment of internal debate, she took a careful seat next to Nick and cracked the lid on her Coke. "Any developments?"

"None in the news. I don't think they're buying the bomb scare story, though. The cameras caught Don Harrigan at the scene, and he's only known for one case."

"Great." The PR angle was at least someone else's headache, not hers. She took a cold swallow of soda and leaned back in her seat. "You don't need to stick around. I have no idea how long this will take, and I think we can be sure this guy won't make any moves in a crowded hospital. The security cameras alone make it high-risk even to set foot in here."

"If it's all the same to you, I think I'll stay." He stretched out his long legs, settling in.

"Suit yourself." She eyed her brothers across the room, all of whom were watching her and Nick with varying degrees of bemusement and fury. "Right now, I can't tell if you're protecting me or I'm protecting you."

"If they want to take a swing at me, I can't blame them."

"Fifteen years ago, maybe. I think they have bigger concerns now."

"How's your dad?"

She shrugged one shoulder. "Still waiting to hear."

"Your dad always told the best stories. I remember after dinner, he'd take his drink in one hand, a cigar in the other, and he'd say, 'So I was rolling Code 3,' like it was his version of 'Once upon a time,' and you knew you were in for some crazy tale. I think my favorite was the time some guy called 911 because his neighbor stole his pizza."

She smiled, remembering. "Pops showed up to investigate and found out there was no theft. The neighbor had just ordered the same pizza."

"Oh, and remember that time someone was out on the street yelling 'Help! Help!' and your dad rushed over to find out the emergency. Only it turned out the idiot had named his cat 'Help.'"

She laughed. "That's nothing. I got called out once because a preschool teacher reported a strange man staring at them for hours in the window across the street, scaring the children. I rolled up thinking I was going to bust a disgusting pedophile, only it was a life-size cardboard cutout of Arnold Schwarzenegger."

"You're freakin' kidding me. Well, I got one even better. Down in Florida, I answered a call from a woman who reported that two boys were in her yard cutting down her marijuana plants."

"Oh my. Did you bust her?"

"I told her to think really hard before making an official report. After some consideration, she declined to go on the record."

She chuffed. "Imagine that." The merriment faded, but she felt lighter than she had in several days. Shyly, she nudged his knee with hers. "Thanks for staying."

"Hey, he was my Pops too. For at least a little bit there." He measured the time by separating his thumb and forefinger.

"Yeah, well, if you're lucky, he still likes you that much," she replied, making the same gesture with her hand. Nick laughed, but he shut up quick when her mother emerged from the swinging doors. Annalisa got up and went to her.

"Ma, how's Pops?"

"Anna, you're here." Her mother held Annalisa's face between her hands and kissed her on both cheeks. "He was just asking for you."

"Can I see him?"

"If you hurry, maybe for a second. The surgeon is here so they've just paged the anesthesiologist. He's in room 322."

Annalisa pushed through the doors and jogged down the hall until she reached Pops's room, where she slowed and tiptoed over the threshold. He lay in bed with his eyes closed, looking thin and gray next to the white sheets. She went to take his hand, which was rough but reassuringly warm. His eyelids fluttered open as she squeezed him. "Hey, Pops, it's me."

"Annalisa?"

"Yes. The doctors say they're about to fix you up."

His speech came out garbled and soft, difficult to understand, but she thought she heard him say, "Too late for that." He gave her hand a clumsy pat. "I tried to be a good dad to you."

"You are. You're the best father we could've had."

He shook his head against the pillow. "Mistakes. Too many."

"Shh. Everyone makes mistakes. That's not what we remember. Nick's outside right now, telling some of your greatest hits. Vinny, Tony, Alex—we're all here because we love you. The only mistake you made is thinking you should be rooting around in that dusty old attic."

His eyes, dark and dazed from the painKillers, bore into hers. "I didn't listen. I didn't see."

"See what?" He dozed off and she shook his hand. "Pops, what didn't you see?"

He licked his chapped lips. She saw the grizzle on his chin as his mouth worked, but no sound came out through his lips. "Should've . . . should've stopped him."

She didn't have to guess which him. "No, Pops. It's not on you."

"It is," he said, sinking back into unconsciousness. "It was."

She couldn't press him any further because the nurses showed up to shoo her outside. On her way back to the waiting room, her work phone started buzzing in the back of her jeans, sending a shockwave up her spine. She dug it out and the number was not the one the Lovelorn Killer had been using, nor was it identified. She ducked into a nearby alcove for privacy and answered the call. "This is Vega."

"Detective Vega, it's Barnes from the Grave Diggers. Do you remember me?"

"Of course," she said, breathing easier when she recognized his voice. "What's up?"

"I don't like to bother you, but you seemed like the best person to call. After the interview last night, I was completely exhausted. The L wasn't running as often at three in the morning, and I had no immediate way to get home, so I called a friend and crashed at her place on the couch. We had a late breakfast this morning and she's just taken me home now."

"Uh-huh," Annalisa said, wondering what the point of this story was.

"Someone broke into my apartment last night while I was at the church."

"What?"

"My computer is gone. In its place is a noose."

"Get out of the apartment and don't touch anything," she said, already in motion. "I will be right there."

CHAPTER TWENTY-THREE

....

GRACE NOTES

Journal Entry #431

TODAY, MOLLY AND I WENT TO THE GAS STATION WHERE JANEESA WAS WORK-ING THE NIGHT SHE DISAPPEARED. I brought my recorder as usual, even though it wasn't about the Lovelorn case. You never know what might make it into the book. Besides, if I go help Molly with this case, she might come with me to some Lovelorn locations. We went late, past midnight, to get a sense of the area like it might have been that night. Molly fibbed to Travis that we were going to dinner and the movies, and then she'd spend the night at my place. He doesn't like her out late on her own, which she thinks is sweet but I find kind of controlling. This tendency to see the man's monitoring as care or concern is how Molly got stuck with Doug for so long, and after what happened tonight, I wonder if Travis is just another Doug, only smoother and with a better line.

The first thing we noticed is that the gas station does a good business even late at night. It must be one of the few still open because cars and trucks just kept pulling in. Most people got their gas and maybe a drink before going on their way. Only a couple of cars used the parking lot where Janeesa's car would've been. We went inside the tiny convenience store, and that security camera is still in the same place in the corner. Across the street, there's a nail salon, a sandwich joint, and a pawnshop. All three were closed, but we looked through the door in the pawnshop and it appears like they have cameras too. The one aimed at the front door would definitely capture the gas station in the background, maybe even including the convenience store. I made a note to look up whether the place had been in business six years ago. There's no way they'd still have the tape, but I still want to talk to the owners if possible.

Molly and I sat with Slurpees in my car, right where Janeesa had parked. There were no lights on this side of the building, and it felt strange to be parked in her spot. I kept looking toward the station, like maybe I would see her coming around the corner with her keys in hand. "Why do you want to talk to the pawnshop people?" Molly asked me. She said the cameras would be useless for anything that happened when Janeesa was working here.

"Whoever took her knew exactly where the cameras were," I reminded her. He grabbed her in that thirty-foot area between the convenience store and the parking lot. Maybe he just got lucky, but I don't think so. That means he would've known about the pawn-store cameras, too. Why wasn't he worried about them?

Molly she caught on. "Maybe because he worked around here."

If he'd worked nearby, he would've seen Janeesa every day. He would've known her schedule as well as she did. If there's one thing you learn from watching true crime, it's that work can be as dangerous as your marriage sometimes. I still remember the story about the guy who showed up with a samurai sword at the grocery store in California and just started whacking people. I think about it every time I set foot in my store. These thoughts about workplace connections to crime made me confide in Molly about one of my theories on the Lovelorn case. "I've been thinking that the Lovelorn Killer might have hung out at O'Malley's Bar," I told her.

"You believe that waitress's story about getting raped by the killer?"

I said I definitely want to talk to her. Even if her attacker wasn't the guy, that doesn't mean he wasn't there. The Lovelorn Killer had almost a sixth sense about what the cops were up to. He knew exactly how to needle them and how to avoid the extra patrols they had set up to catch him. Maybe he was bellied up to the bar with them, listening when they had their beers and talked shop. One thing is clear, the guy can get close to them and they still don't see him.

"I think I read somewhere Katie Duffy's husband drank at O'Malley's," Molly said.

"Him and a bunch of others."

The recording sounded like a wind turbine as Molly suctioned out the last of her blue raspberry. When she was done slurping, though, she had an interesting theory: "You know, that would've made a tidy way for Owen Duffy to get rid of his wife if they were having problems. He had to know the killer's MO."

"Yeah, everybody did. It was all over the front page of the papers."

"But Owen Duffy would've known even the hidden details, right? The stuff the cops hold back from the press."

"Maybe. I know he was questioned, and he had an alibi for that night—he was at the Halloween party, remember? Also, he dropped dead of a heart attack about a month later, he was so grief-stricken."

"Or guilt-ridden. I'm just saying it's a theory. And then maybe the real Lovelorn Killer stops because he's got a copycat now. Someone's messing on his turf, freaking him out. Ooh, or maybe he was the Lovelorn Killer! His wife found out, so he did her, too."

"Whoa, hold on. Now you're in Geraldo Rivera territory." I didn't think Owen Duffy could be the killer. I remember watching the broadcast of her funeral on local TV. That man was completely broken up over his wife's death. Could a true psychopath fake that kind of emotion?

We were about to get going, when a pickup truck came screeching into the parking lot and blocked our exit. "That's Travis," Molly said, but she needn't have bothered to tell me because he was already out of the truck and heading our way—all six and a half feet of him. You can hear him screaming on the recording. "What the hell are you doing?" he yelled at Molly through the window. "Are you trying to get yourself killed?"

He looked so big and mean right then that I locked the doors and windows, but Molly begged me to open them again. She swore he wasn't going to hurt us. I've seen enough of those cheap reenactments on crime shows to know how that goes. I left the doors locked.

"We're just checking out the scene of the crime," she hollered at him through the glass. "It's perfectly safe."

"Safe? Some guy got shot three blocks from here last week!" He was waving his arms like a psychotic windmill. "I picked up my phone to

text you good night and I saw the app said you were on the move toward this part of town. I didn't have to guess real hard where you'd be."

"The app?" I asked her.

"He put an app on my phone that shows him where my phone is so
he doesn't have to worry. I didn't think he actually checked it."

Travis's angry face took up half my windshield. "He's a regular hall
monitor," I replied.

"I'll get him to calm down. Let me out." She jiggled the door handle
again, and I had no choice but to let her go or keep her prisoner in
my Subaru. She practically fell out the door and into his arms. "Travis,
honey, we're fine. See? You don't have to worry."

His voice got all tender, like he hadn't been screaming in our faces
thirty seconds ago. "Baby, it's not safe down here, especially at night. I
know you want to play cops and robbers, but real bad guys live in this
part of town."

"I'm not playing. The Grave Diggers solve actual crimes, you know.
Crimes the cops couldn't solve on their own."

"Yeah, but the cops carry actual guns. What are you going to do if
you find the guy who grabbed Janeesa? Hit him with your notebook?"

He shifted his weight so I could see his hip for the first time, and
that's when I realized he was armed. I beeped the horn and they both
jumped. I leaned out my window. "Molly, you want to get going? We
can still have that sleepover."

Travis glowered at me over his stupid sheep-farmer beard. "She can
ride back with me." His truck was still running.

Molly looked cowed. "Uh, yeah. I guess so. Just let me get my purse."
He stood there and watched her as she opened my car door and bent
down inside again.

"You don't have to go with him," I said, moving my lips as little as
possible. "He's not the boss of you."

"I should go. He doesn't sleep well when I'm not there."

"And how do you sleep?"

"Grace, don't do this."

"Don't do what? Point out that your boyfriend is being a belligerent,
controlling jerk?" I didn't take my eyes off him, nor him me.

"You can't go around thinking every guy is a homicidal maniac. Not if you ever want to be in a relationship. It's my fault. I shouldn't have lied to him."

She grabbed her purse to leave, but I shot out my hand to stop her. I whispered but you can still hear it on the recording. "You've said it yourself, Moll. It's always the boyfriend."

She pulled away from my grasp without a word. Outside, Travis tucked her under his enormous arm and made a show of helping her inside the cab. He even kissed her and said something in her ear that made her giggle. She took one look back in the mirror at me as they drove away, and I thought I saw regret there. Or maybe it was pity for poor, boyfriend-less me.

I drove home thinking it might be time to check into Travis's background a little more. I can't tell Molly who to date, but I can say who gets to come to our meetings.

CHAPTER TWENTY-FOUR

....

I SAW THAT THE LOCK HAD BEEN PRIED OPEN," BARNES SAID AS HE WHEELED FOR-
WARD THROUGH HIS BROKEN FRONT DOOR. Annalisa and Nick followed behind him, inspecting the doorjamb as they passed through it. "Looks
like maybe a crowbar, but it wouldn't take much to defeat the lock. It's a
cheap POS. Then I came in here and saw what he was really after."

He led them to his living room, and Annalisa saw that the computer
corner had been ransacked. The monitors were overturned and broken,
the cables cut, and the computer itself was missing. The flat-screen TV,
stereo, and speakers all remained in place. "Did you find anything else
amiss?" Annalisa asked as she eyed the rope hanging from the ceiling
over the computer desk.

"I haven't checked," Barnes admitted. "I saw that rope and got the hell
out of here to call you guys."

"Smart move," replied Annalisa. "A place like this probably has security cameras, right? Maybe we get lucky."

Barnes grimaced. "There's one in the lobby and by the front door,
but none at the back by the parking lot. You're not supposed to prop
that door open, but everyone does it anyway."

"We'll check it out," Annalisa said. "Right now, we'll just take a quick
look around. You sit tight." She and Nick both snapped on gloves as
they went to inspect the remainder of Barnes's apartment. She poked
her head into the kitchen, which showed smooth countertops with only

a coffee maker to disrupt the clean lines. The sink held no trace of dirty dishes. She flipped open a top cabinet and found it full of neatly lined cans and boxes of food, their labels pointed outward. She furrowed her brow as she studied the distance between the floor and the tall cabinets. Barnes rolled up behind her.

"Everything okay?"

"Yeah. I'm just wondering how you reach all the stuff up here."

He smiled and picked up a metal rod with a kind of rubber claw on the end. When he squeezed, the claw contracted. "Can I offer you a cookie?" he asked as he took down a box of Nilla wafers.

"Thanks, I'm good. Let me know if you see anything out of place here, okay? It seems fine to me." She checked the windows and found them locked. Their intruder had probably exited the same way he came in, through the front door. She went to the bedroom, where Nick had the closet door open. It revealed shirts and pants hung neatly on a bar that had been lowered from standard height.

"Anything of value?" she asked him.

He picked up a pair of beat-up sneakers, wrinkled his nose at them, and dropped them in the closet again. "No. The place looks like the maid just got here. The bathroom shines so bright you could use it in a toothpaste commercial. No footprints, no obvious fibers. If the intruder set foot in here, you can't prove it by me."

"We're going to have to call in forensics anyway."

"Waste of time. But yeah, I'll make the call." He took out his cell phone and went back out to the living room.

Barnes appeared in the doorway, watching as she peered into his bathroom. "I hope I remembered to put the seat down," he quipped.

"Sorry," she said as she exited. "I know it's invasive."

"No, having a serial killer come in and hang a noose in your living room—that's invasive."

"I'm just glad you weren't here to meet him."

He blinked rapidly behind his glasses, his mouth growing pinched. "Do you think he was here when we were at the church? That it was a lure to get us down there so he could break in?"

"It's a distinct possibility, yeah." She scanned the room again, taking in the blank walls and his tidy bed, complete with hospital corners.

You can quit the military, but the military never quits you, she thought. She turned to Barnes. "Any guesses about why he wanted your computer?"

"Not especially. He took the external drives too, but these days, I back everything up to the cloud."

"What about any correspondence you had with Grace Harper?"

"That's over chat, mostly. Some emails. But again, those would live on the server, not on my hard drives. I can still access them." He pulled out his phone and tapped it a few times. "Huh, that's funny. I can't seem to get into my email account."

"He locked you out?"

"Maybe." His frown deepened as he tried again to get into his email. "That's so strange. Grace and I had a few conversations about the Lovelorn case, but nothing that stands out as particularly incendiary."

"Maybe not to you. What did you talk about?"

He put the phone in his lap and ran both hands through his hair. "I'm trying to think. We talked about his psychology, mostly. Grace thought he probably had obsessive-compulsive disorder in addition to his psychopathy, given the precision of each murder. I think the narcissism is the more dominant trait. He wants to own these women, and he's sure no one can stop him."

"So far, he's right," Annalisa pointed out. "What else? Maybe something related to her theory about the storms?"

He narrowed his eyes at her. "What theory? She didn't mention storms to me."

"There must be something." Annalisa's frustration ticked up a notch. "He didn't break in here to take your computer just for the challenge of it all."

"I wish I could help you. I really do." He rubbed his palms on his jeans and screwed up his face in concentration. "We disagreed also about O'Malley's Bar. She made a lot out of that waitress's story, the one who said she'd had an encounter with the Lovelorn Killer. Grace thought maybe the killer was hanging around the bar, listening in on what the cops had to say about the case. I said no way. Back in my drinking days, I spent way too much time in one of those neighborhood bars like O'Malley's. You know the kind—far from anything else, draws mostly the local crowd. My hangout offered military discounts, and so any given night, you'd find a lot of us Army guys drinking cheap beers and playing pool till closing time. We knew everyone who walked through the door. If a stranger showed up, which happened from time to time, practically the whole place would turn to stare. I just can't imagine the Lovelorn guy taking that kind of chance in a bar full of cops."

He looked to her as if seeking her agreement or approval of his logic. She could think of one way the Lovelorn Killer wouldn't have to worry about everyone staring him down at a cop bar, which was that he already belonged there. "Anything else? Anything she shared with you but not the others?"

"No, I don't think so . . . wait. There was one odd incident a couple of weeks before Grace was killed. You know she, ah, borrowed some files from Chris's collection?"

"I've heard, yes."

"One of the items he had was a photo of Katie Duffy on the night she died. It was taken at the Halloween party, and it showed Katie with some guy's arm around her. Probably the husband, but we can't see his face. Over her shoulder, you can see someone walking around wearing that mask from *Scream*. The ghost face? Anyway, Grace couldn't show the picture to the group or Chris would've blown a gasket, but she showed it to me and said, 'Wouldn't it be crazy if the Lovelorn Killer had crashed the party? Think about it—everyone's in costume, so who would notice?'"

Annalisa's stomach seized up at the thought, and she struggled to keep her expression neutral. "Do you have a copy of this picture?"

"I don't think so. Chris would, though. He scanned everything." He picked up his phone again and began tapping away. "Grace didn't share the picture with the whole Grave Diggers group, but she did share her idea about the killer crashing the Halloween party. It generated a lively discussion about what kind of costume he might have picked. I don't think anyone took it too seriously until this one member totally went off on us for discussing the idea. He said we were sick to joke about it, and that he was at the party and there was no way people wouldn't have picked up on some stranger stalking Katie."

"Do you recall this member's name?"

"I can look it up. The whole thread is still up on the message board."

He logged on to the Grave Diggers site and called up the discussion for Annalisa to see. "Here you go."

She scrolled through the thread until she found the angry poster. "You people spew this crap without any thought about who might see it and no idea what the hell you're talking about! It was a neighborhood party filled with people who've known each other for years. No way some psycho puts on a mask to stalk Katie Duffy and none of us knows about it. Real cops would laugh their asses off over your little 'theories.' You're a bunch of sickos, using real people's deaths for entertainment!" Annalisa's gaze slid over to the user's name: RBrewster. "Okay, thanks. We'll check it out."

If R. Brewster was at the party, then her earlier hypothesis had to be true: this was Rod Brewster, Pop's partner at the time and his neighbor down the street. She remembered his big barrel chest and the way his booming voice bounced off the porcelain stove in Ma's kitchen. Rod and his wife, Carol, had been a fixture at the Vega family cookouts and Super Bowl parties, but they had no kids of their own, so Annalisa had confined them to her parents' orbit. Rod had tossed the football around with her brothers on occasion, but he'd mostly ignored her. She recalled him rubbing her head and asking if she'd broken any boy's heart yet. She had been about eight years old at the time.

Nick rejoined them in the room. "The forensics team is on the way."

Barnes looked pale and stricken. "I didn't believe her," he murmured.

"Believe who?" Annalisa asked.

"Grace. When she said we could find this guy, I thought it would be an interesting intellectual challenge, a fun discussion. I never thought . . ." He shook his head. "I never thought we'd summon him."

"Do you have somewhere else you can stay for a while? Maybe with friends? Or family?"

"Sure, but how could I even ask that right now? How can I be sure I wouldn't be bringing all this along with me? He's got to be watching us. I can't risk dragging one of my other friends into this mess. I can take care of myself, anyway. I have my gun, and I'll put in better locks."

"We'll speak to patrol," she told him. "See about getting you some extra drive-bys."

Annalisa and Nick waited long enough for the forensics team to show up, at which point they returned to his car. "You want to go back to the hospital?" he asked her.

She checked her phone and found a text from Vinny: *Pops is in the OR. Should take 1-2hrs.* "Not yet," she said. "First I want to go rattle Chris Colburn's cage."

"Colburn? Why?"

"He was the only local Grave Digger not at the church last night. Also, he has a photo of Katie Duffy from the Halloween party that is among the evidence Grace Harper took from his place."

"Haven't you seen the files? We have a hundred pictures from that party."

"Yeah, but it's possible our suspect wants this one. I'd like to know why."

They located Chris Colburn on a computer-repair job at a dentist's office, and he wasn't excited to see them again. "I'm kind of in the middle of things here," he said. He stood over a computer that had its plastic casing removed, exposing the inner chips and wires like the guts of an autopsy victim. Meanwhile, the persistent whine of the dentist's drill in the background made Annalisa's teeth start to ache.

"We won't take up much of your time," she said. "We're interested in a picture you have of Katie Duffy taken at the Halloween party the night she died."

"You mean the picture Grace stole from me," he said as he bent over his work again. "Check her place. I don't have it."

"We were told you have a scanned copy."

"Oh, yeah? Who told you that? Barnes? He's such a little know-it-all. He probably has a copy himself. Everything Grace did, she went running to him with it."

"If he had a copy, it's possible the killer took it."

At this, Chris's head snapped up. "What are you talking about?"

Annalisa explained about the break-in at Barnes's apartment. She deliberately didn't mention anything about the church scare from the previous night. "Where were you last night, say between nine and midnight?"

"Me? You think I broke into Barnes's place?"

"You said it yourself. He probably has a copy. You wanted it back."

"Hell yeah, I wanted it back, but I'm not going around breaking into anyone's place for it, especially if it's just a copy. Last night, I was online playing Original Sin with like six other people. I wasn't anywhere near Barnes's apartment."

"We're going to need names," Nick said.

"Yeah, let's see . . . there was Starfighter69, JugHead, Lucy in the Sky with Diamonds. . . . no one uses a real name. But if you check my ISP, you can see I was on." He dug out his cell phone and played around with it for a moment. "As for the picture, is this the one you wanted? Doesn't seem like much to me."

Annalisa took the phone and saw the picture was just as Barnes had described. Katie Duffy, her dark hair in loose curls under her purple headscarf, looked directly at the camera, but her smile appeared strained, her mascara smudged. The person in the ghost-face costume was visible over her left shoulder. To her right stood a man out-of-frame, his hairy arm snugly around Katie's shoulders. Annalisa enlarged the photo with her fingers so she could see the silver watch around the man's wrist. "Where did you get this?" she asked Chris as Nick crowded in for a closer look at the photo.

"eBay. I picked it up maybe five years ago. Why?"

Annalisa returned his cell phone to him. "We're going to need a copy of this picture and anything else that Grace Harper took from you that might be related to the Lovelorn case."

He gave a smile that was somewhere between a smirk and a nervous twitch. "It's a little late to file a stolen-property report, isn't it?"

"Lucky for you."

"What's that supposed to mean?"

"The killer seems intent on tracking down whatever the Grave Diggers were working on that could be related to the case. You opted out of pursuing the investigation, and then Grace liberated your files. No reason for him to come looking for you."

His chin dropped to his chest. "I'll send you copies of whatever Grace took."

"Thanks. If we run across the originals, we'll make sure they're documented as your property so that they eventually get back to you."

He held up his palms. "You know what? Keep them. Keep it all. I don't think I'll need that stuff anymore."

CHAPTER TWENTY-FIVE

....

GRACE NOTES

Journal Entry #435

I'VE BEEN READING ALL THE NEWS ARTICLES I CAN FIND ABOUT THE ORIGINAL Lovelorn Killer investigation, and what I love are the man-on-the-street interviews. People talk about keeping their shades drawn and their kids locked up at night, or sleeping with a baseball bat next to their bed. These people flooded the tip lines with their fear. By the third murder, the cops got thousands of calls per day from people reporting a suspicious car rolling down the street at low speed (always the paper carrier, as it turned out) or gunshots in the neighborhood (usually thunder, firecrackers, or in one spectacular boom, an electrical generator explosion). One lady turned in her landlord because he'd hung a rope out back. The cops came to check it out and found he'd put up a clothesline. Another guy reported his clergyman half brother for a bunch of BDSM paraphernalia he'd uncovered in the closet. Bet that made for a fun Thanksgiving dinner a few weeks later.

The thing is, you can hardly blame people for being so paranoid. The cops carped in the media about all the false leads coming in, but they gave people nothing to work with. The killer could be anyone, so everyone had to be a suspect. Your neighbor. Your dog walker. The guy on the corner who keeps a tarp over his shed at all times—what's he really hiding in there? The killer lives in our neighborhoods, shops at our grocery stores, buys his gas at the same station, and drives down the same streets. The whole time you're squeezing cantaloupes or trying to figure out if $2.73 is the lowest price per gallon for unleaded, he's right behind you, imagining you with a rope around your neck. No wonder the city was on edge.

The Grave Diggers read the profile the FBI put together, and there's one thing we agree on: the guy is white. Oliver put it best when he said that the killer had to move undetected in predominately white neighborhoods, so bland and unassuming that no one would ever remember seeing him even if they passed right by him on the sidewalk. That makes him white as Wonder Bread. Not that it mattered back twenty years ago. Oliver pointed out that people were still turning in nonwhite suspects by the truckload even after the profilers had stressed that they were looking for a white dude. "He's so white he's invisible," Oliver said.

"Like Casper the ghost," Molly agreed.

I decided to go ghost hunting. I went down to O'Malley's Bar last Thursday night, me and my digital recorder. I didn't tell anyone else about my little expedition because Oliver has enough to worry about right now, Molly would just drag Travis along, and Barnes doesn't agree with me that there's anything to be learned there, especially after all this time. He might be right, but I wanted to check it out for myself. My gut tells me the Lovelorn Killer has been in that bar, and since I can't see him yet, the closest I can get is to look through his eyes.

I discovered that Barnes was right about how a stranger sticks out in a neighborhood bar. I walked in and everyone turned to look at me, like I was personally interrupting their conversation or baseball watching. I felt a flush go up the back of my neck, but I just acted like I belonged there anyway and went up to the bar to order a beer. The place wasn't crowded, maybe half full, mostly older guys but also a few couples and a pair of middle-aged women with tattoos playing pool in the back. I'd been a little concerned that I might get hit on, being a woman out in the bar alone, but I needn't have worried. After they gawked at me for daring to cross the threshold, the clientele of O'Malley's ignored me like I was just part of the decor—old, faded, and creaky. The bar itself was clean, but it needed refinishing because the varnish had rubbed off in front of every stool.

The only guy to chat me up was the bartender, a short, round white guy with thinning gray hair. He wore a vintage Walter Payton jersey and an apron with stains on it, but he was friendly enough, talking about the spring storms that had been through lately and the hot start for the Cubs. Turns out, he was the owner. I had to order a second beer and a plate of nachos before I got the courage to bring up the Lovelorn Killer. Hoo boy, he had some words about Lora Fitz! "What a waste, eh? Pretty little thing, a decent brain in her head, but high as a kite half the time. It's the pupils. You can always tell by the pupils."

He peered in to give mine a good look-see, and I guess I passed muster because he kept talking. I asked if maybe Lora's story about how she'd served the killer in his bar could be true. "Utter bullshit," he said. "I did twenty years on the job before taking over this place back in 1984. You see that guy over there? He's a former captain. Them two at the table watching the game, they were on the job for thirty-five years between them. Probably still packing heat right now."

"What about you?" I asked him.

He took out a revolver from behind the bar. "No one's going to hold me up, I can tell you that. As for that Lovelorn guy, he's a coward, going after women who are home alone and then writing prissy letters to the papers for attention. Why? Because his mommy didn't love him enough? Gimme a break."

"It could be exciting for him, coming in here where all the cops are."

"I'd like to see him try it. I really would." He stroked that gun with more affection than I've seen since my high school boyfriend. I decided to try out my big theory as long as I had his attention.

"Maybe it would be a way for him to keep tabs on the case—you know, find out what the cops were talking about after a few beers."

He scowled at me like I'd just come out as a Cardinals fan. "You must think we're a bunch of idiots if you imagine we sit around telling tales out of school where anyone might hear 'em. Besides, the big boys on that case didn't come 'round these parts. Don Harrigan probably drank at some chichi place downtown. The FBI? Those pricks are wound so tight they probably don't drink at all."

"They didn't come to check out Lora's story?" I found this hard to believe. The papers made it sound like the cops had chased every lead.

"Sure, they sent the local boys, Vega and Brewster. Vega had to retire when he got sick, but Brewster's still on the job. He's sitting over there right now, as a matter of fact." He pointed to a burly guy with a '70s mustache and glasses to match. "Hey, Brewster, this lady's interested in the Lovelorn case. You wanna impress her with your fifteen minutes of fame?"

I'd rather he didn't, not from the way he was looking at me, like I was a punk from the street he'd like to pound into dust on the pavement. He took his draft beer and came to sit on the stool next to mine, his elbow practically in my ribs. "Who's asking?"

"This lady's part of some wannabe crime-solving group on the 'World Wide Web.' What'd you say your name was again, honey?"

"Grace," I said, declining to offer my last name.

"She's after the Lovelorn Killer," the bar owner said with exaggerated condescension, as though I was a kindergartner who'd announced her desire to fly to the moon.

"That's serious business," the cop, Brewster, told me. "He killed a half-dozen women just like you."

"And then he disappeared," I said. Neither one liked that fact very much, I could tell. "Mr. . . ." I looked to the bar owner to fill in the blanks on his name.

"Stan. Stan McGuinty."

"Mr. McGuinty said you'd interviewed Lora Fitz about her encounter with the Lovelorn Killer."

Brewster snorted derisively. "She had an encounter, all right. With a pocket full of Vicodin and a little weed on the side. She might as well've said she'd seen a pink elephant in a tutu doing a hula on the bar here." He rapped it with his knuckles for emphasis.

"But she didn't say that. She said she was raped in a red pickup truck and then saw it on the street near Katie Duffy's house right before she was murdered."

"You know how many red pickup trucks there are on the streets? We looked into her story. No one in here remembered that guy she called Ace. No one else remembered any red truck. Maybe she was telling the truth that some guy passing through got rough with her, but we didn't find anything to suggest he was the Lovelorn Killer. And believe me, we looked. We interviewed everyone in a six-block radius of the Duffy house. That's real, serious police work—not a bunch of guessing games on the internet. You think you can do better? Go ahead, I say. Bring it on." He waggled his fingers at me in aggressive fashion.

"We aren't out to criticize."

"Ha! You'd be the first, then." He tapped the bar in front of him. "Another one, please, Stan."

McGuinty complied, but he also said something interesting. "I was always surprised that the interviews on Katie Duffy never made it down this way."

Brewster froze with his hand around the beer glass. "What do you mean?"

"I mean Katie herself was in here on and off that summer, and not with Owen. You remember. I know you took her home at least once."

"I don't know what you're talking about."

"Mmm. It was a long time ago, but I remember. She seemed restless to me. I don't want to say looking for trouble, but . . ."

"She wouldn't find it in here," Brewster shot back. "No one would go messing around with Owen's wife. Come on, Stan. What the hell are you saying?"

"Not saying anything, other than Katie seemed lonely. Maybe bored. Her kid would've been all but grown-up by then. Owen was on the job, then fiddling around with his computers. What's she got to do all day?"

"You're saying she came in during the daytime?" I asked. I regretted butting in because both men seemed to clam up when reminded there was an outsider listening.

"Stan, if you've got something you want to report, you can go down to the station and say so on the record. Otherwise, this is just nasty gossip."

McGuinty had a challenging look in his eye, one that suggested cases sometimes got solved with nasty gossip, but he shrugged and didn't argue. "Maybe you ought to settle up," he said, and Brewster pulled out a twenty.

He slapped it down and got off his stool. Standing up over me, he seemed eight feet tall. I could smell the beer on his breath. "And you better leave the investigating to us. Amateurs don't know what the hell they're dealing with, and criminals are unpredictable. You don't want to end up hurt."

The funny thing is, when he said it, it sounded like a threat.

CHAPTER TWENTY-SIX

....

By the time Annalisa and Nick had checked in with Zimmer about the break-in at Barnes's place and answered another round of grilling from the lead detectives about that particular development, the hour was late and she wanted to get back to the hospital to see Pops. Nick tried to argue to stay with her. "No," she said as they sat idling in his car outside of the hospital. "You're already wearing yesterday's clothes. Let's not go for day three, hmm? The Board of Health might start tailing you."

He had rings under his eyes and beard growth that was threatening to move from "rolled out of bed sexy" to "homeless person." Nick ran his hands fretfully over the steering wheel. "I don't feel right leaving you alone."

She gave him a tired smile. "I'm not alone. I have the entirety of the Vega clan inside waiting to cross-examine me about where I've been all day. I'll call you later, okay?"

He got weirdly quiet and agreed to let her leave with a simple nod. Only in the elevator did she realize that maybe he was the one who hadn't wanted to go home alone. She had to ask three different people to find Pop's new location, and, just as she'd imagined, the nearest waiting room was packed with Vegas, young and old. Tony and Vinny sat across the way with Colin, who gave her an embarrassed half-wave as she entered. Had he really been sitting here the whole day? His slouch was so familiar, the same one she'd admired years ago in American Lit, and it made her stomach seize up with memories. She detoured past the empty seat next to him and instead opted for the controlled chaos of Alex's family.

"The prodigal daughter returns," Sassy said wryly, and Annalisa took the open seat next to her.

"Auntie Anna, look what I can do." Carla, Alex and Sassy's dark-eyed four-year-old, scrambled off his lap to demonstrate a backbend on the waiting room floor.

"Impressive," Annalisa said, reaching over to tickle the sliver of bare belly that Carla had exposed in the process. "You're a regular Mary Lou Retton."

"Who?" Still upside-down, Carla wrinkled her nose in confusion.

"Baby, there's all kinds of germs down there. Get up here." Alex scooped his older girl up from the floor and hoisted her high in his arms. Annalisa smiled, remembering when Pops used to do the same for her. Carla giggled and clutched her father's head.

"How's Pops?" Annalisa asked him.

"He came through the operation just fine, according to the doc. Ma's with him now."

"Daddy, I'm hungry," Carla said, drawing out the word to signify the intensity of her need.

"Me, too," Alex said, and pretended to bite her tummy. She shrieked with delight and wriggled in his arms. "I'm going to take this monkey home for dinner," he said to Sassy. "You want to come with?"

Sassy had the baby, Gigi, asleep on her shoulder. "No, she's finally out, so I'll stay here for now. Plus, this way I get to see my so-called best friend for two seconds." She stretched out her free hand and patted Annalisa's knee.

"Call me if there's any change with Pops."

"I will," Annalisa promised. She watched him slide Carla up to his broad shoulders, bouncing the girl along as they went toward the elevators. "Sometimes I still can't believe my grouchy slob of an older brother turned out to be a lovable goofball dad," she said to Sassy.

"He says the girls are his reward. You know, for everything he went through before."

Annalisa recalled what Vinny had said about Alex's drinking on school property. "Hey, I don't want to pry, but Vinny mentioned Alex might be in some trouble. Are you guys okay? I want to help if I can."

Sassy shifted the baby on her shoulder and avoided Annalisa's eyes. "Yeah, thanks, we're all right. It was just one slipup, and the teacher who caught him hasn't ratted yet. But the school budget got cut last year, and there's talk about consolidating the two middle schools into one, which would mean layoffs. Everyone's a little on edge."

"But Alex has worked there for more than five years."

"Yeah, and there are other teachers who have worked triple that." She patted Gigi's back absently. "We'll just have to see how it shakes out with the voting this fall. The parents are plenty mad about the idea, and they're mobilizing against it."

"Just let me know where and when I can picket," Annalisa said with a smile. She reached over to stroke the baby's tiny hand. "She looks so peaceful."

"They always do when they're sleeping. It's their secret weapon that allows them to make it out of infancy." Sassy nodded across the room to Colin. "Speaking of out of infancy . . . he grew up fine, didn't he?"

"Stop. He's your cousin."

"Third cousin. Our grandparents were barely related."

"I think if you have to quantify it at all, it's a no-go. Plus, you're married to my brother, which, given that we all grew up together . . ."

"That feels incestuous enough," Sassy agreed with a grin. She elbowed Annalisa. "The way he's looking at you, he definitely doesn't see you as a sister."

"Oh, stop it." Annalisa nudged her in return. "He's here for the case, not for me."

"Yeah? Don't look now, but he's headed your way."

Colin crossed the room and came to sit on Annalisa's other side. "Hi," he said, the single word soft and layered with emotion. She almost teared up, overwhelmed by the day and by his familiar kind blue eyes. She'd almost given up hope of ever seeing them again, and yet here he was in front of her like no time had passed at all. He tucked a lock of her hair behind her ear. "How are you holding up?"

"I'm all right. Sorry to run off on you earlier."

"I know. Duty calls."

"Your clothes are still at my place."

Sassy made a small choked noise of delight, and Annalisa shot her a dirty look. Colin laughed gently. "I left my suitcase at Annalisa's yesterday. Or was it today? My days and nights are all mixed up."

"That must be a hazard of your job," Annalisa said, feeling a stab of envy again at all the roads he must have traveled.

"Mostly it's not too bad. There was that one time I flew to India, but the plane was held over in Turkey for ten hours, and by the time I landed I was five hours from deadline for three articles. I took a handful of caffeine pills and wrote in this internet café until I couldn't see straight anymore. I went looking for a bathroom and somehow ended up in an argument with a goat."

"What were you arguing about?" Annalisa asked, amused.

"I believe I accused him of stealing my wallet. Turns out I was looking in the wrong pocket."

"I hope you apologized for impugning his honor," she said solemnly.

"If I recall correctly, he bit a hole in my trousers for revenge. I stumbled to my hotel and slept for eighteen hours, after which I had to redo all of the articles because my first drafts were not in anything resembling the English language."

"Ouch." Gigi stirred, rubbing her fist in her mouth and blinking huge dark eyes at Annalisa. Annalisa cooed at the baby and tickled her chin until she smiled and gurgled. "I don't know how Alex makes children this beautiful," she said to Sassy. "Your genes must have a lot of heavy lifting to do."

"I definitely do a lot of heavy lifting," Sassy replied with a sigh as she stood to gather her things. "Like now, when I have to lug this one back to the car."

"Do you need a hand?"

"No, I got it," Sassy said as she waved her off. "You stay and chat. Give us a call if anything changes with Pops, okay?"

"Will do." She turned to Colin. "I just want to see how Pops is doing, and then we can go pick up your stuff, okay?"

He laid a hand on her knee. "No hurry. Really."

She went down the hall to Pops's room. The door stood partway open, and when she pushed it in, she saw Ma sitting in the chair by the bed. The second bed beyond him was empty for the moment, so at least he had some privacy. "Ma," she whispered as she moved into the room. "How is he?"

"Sleeping still. I guess that's good."

"The operation went well?"

"They fixed his hip, yes." Annalisa heard what her mother did not say: the doctors couldn't fix the rest of him. The Parkinson's disease would only get worse. Her mother reached out and smoothed the blanket by her father's leg.

Annalisa went to squeeze his hand. "It's me, Pops. We're all here rooting for you."

He did not reply. His face looked gray and drawn, his thin hair matted against his head. The arms that used to swing her high in the air had wasted away to brittle sticks. She adjusted the blanket higher over his chest to keep him warm.

"Vinny said you wanted to talk to us about something important," her mother said as Annalisa blinked back tears. Even Ma seemed old and tired sitting here in the low light. She didn't want to burden them further. They would be safe in the hospital for now.

"Not now. What's important is that Pops gets better. You should go home with Sassy or Vinny. Get something to eat, get some rest."

"Tony and Vinny brought me dinner. I don't want to go home just yet."

"Mom . . ."

"I'm not sleeping in that house without him. Not . . . not tonight."

Annalisa snapped her mouth shut. She went to the nightstand and poured her mother a glass of water. As she did so, she saw Ma had brought a small family picture and placed it by Pops's bed. There was also a flower arrangement from somebody. Next to the flowers, she saw his watch. She handed her mother the glass and picked up the watch to study it. "Ma, why was Pops climbing around in the attic in the first place?"

"Because he's a pigheaded fool," Ma said, loud enough to wake Pops, if he'd been amenable to waking. "There's nothing up there but old furniture, some dishes, and holiday decorations."

"And his work files. Right?" Annalisa turned and held the watch to her middle. She closed her eyes because she'd known it was true from the moment she saw the picture: the male arm around Katie Duffy at the Halloween party belonged to her father.

"He doesn't work anymore," Ma scoffed. "You know that. That part of his life is finished now." She smoothed the blanket again, her repetitive strokes removing even the smallest wrinkle.

CHAPTER TWENTY-SEVEN

....

A NNALISA AND COLIN TOOK A CAB TO HER CONDO, WHERE SHE PRETENDED NOT TO NOTICE THE UNDERCOVER CAR PARKED ACROSS THE STREET. Her home felt like a zoo display. She checked her phone three times while Colin located his suitcase and toiletries. She was both relieved and disappointed to see no texts or missed calls. She didn't want to hear the killer's whispery voice, but his silence was somehow worse. At least if he called again with the same number, they could use it to track his location. To keep busy, she cleared away the cold remnants of coffee from that morning, where Nick's mug and hers had been left sitting on the counter as they'd dashed out the door. She debated calling him to check in as she stood in the living room and stared at the blanket and pillow he'd left folded and stacked on the end of her couch.

Behind her, Colin made a clearing noise in his throat, and she nearly jumped out of her skin. "All set," he said, his tone apologetic for startling her. "I can catch another cab or—"

"No, I'll drive you. It's not far."

He tilted his head. "Better yet, why don't you join me?"

She blinked at him. "What?"

"You look dead on your feet. Come stay the night with me. I've got two giant beds, a Jacuzzi tub, and a room service menu that reads like a novel. We can order food and catch up some more." He gave her the same crooked smile that had melted her heart in high school, the same one she'd seen on Katie's face in the missing Halloween photo. How had she never noticed the similarity before?

"Okay," she surprised herself by saying. "Yes." Better than sitting here alone in her apartment like a stuffed goose on Christmas morning.

His grin widened as he held her gaze. "Yes."

She threw a few things together in a small tote bag and then drove them both to his swanky downtown hotel. "Travel writing pays better than I would have guessed," she said to him as they rode up in a shimmering gold elevator.

"Oh, don't be fooled. I have stayed in some luxurious places, but more often, it's an Airbnb or a fly-by-night hotel. Once, I even slept on the beach."

"Sounds romantic."

"Not really," he said as he swiped his key at the door. "There were sand fleas."

She hid her smile and followed him into the giant room. As he'd advertised, there were two large beds with fluffy white comforters and an ocean of pillows. Her body ached just looking at them. Gingerly, she perched on one cushy edge while he consulted the room service menu.

"What do you feel like?" he asked. "Pasta? Steak? Seafood?" He put the menu down and rolled his eyes. "Listen to me, I sound like a flight attendant asking for your dinner selection."

"Do they still serve you dinner on planes?" She'd only traveled by airplane once, a three-hour flight to Florida that had netted her a single can of ginger ale and an impossibly small package of pretzels.

"Sometimes." He took the menu and sat next to her on the bed, close enough that their shoulders touched. "But here you can have anything you want."

"Mmm," she said, springing up from the bed. "I'll have a burger, and I'd love to use your shower if that's okay."

"Of course, it's fine. I'll order the food."

She fled to the other room and spent longer than usual standing under the hot spray. Colin's hotel room was gorgeous with its thick carpets, damask drapes, and giant porcelain tub, but it was paid for by the night. No one actually lived in a room like this, and she had no idea how long he planned to stay. Best not to let herself get too comfortable.

She floated out of the stall on a steam cloud, refreshed from the shower, and towel dried her hair before wrapping herself in a giant white robe.

Outside, Colin was setting up their dinner along the desk. "I don't have a table," he said, rueful. He'd dragged over the high-backed armchair for himself while she took the rolling desk chair. They ate burgers and drank cold beer from tall glasses. "Tell me about Nick," he said eventually.

"What about him?"

He looked suddenly uncomfortable. "Well, from what your brothers said, he didn't treat you very well."

"Let's just say his wedding vows were more aspirational than inspirational."

"Sorry."

She shrugged. "We were young and stupid."

"And now?"

"Now? Definitely less young. Maybe less stupid. Time will tell on that one, I suppose."

"But you work together. That could get awkward."

"It isn't," she said, surprised it was the truth. "He was a lousy husband, but Nick's a great cop. A great partner."

"Partner." Colin looked at the floor as he tested out the word.

She waited but he didn't say anything further. "I wanted someone to notice me," she said finally. "I wanted someone who listened when I talked." She remembered those early days when she had rattled on to Nick about her family, her college classes, her girlfriends and their boy troubles. She'd tried to give him a crash course in Annalisa Vega, to catch him up to where Colin had been when he'd skipped town.

Colin raised his gaze to hers. "I'm listening."

"Yeah," she said softly. "But for how long?" He had no good answer for that so they stared at each other in silence for a long moment. "Is it really terrible?" she asked. "Being back?"

He let out a slow breath. "It's weird. I've spent so many years deliberately not being here, you know? I'd take any assignment, anywhere, as long as it was far away from Chicago. I built this place up in my memory to the point where I felt like I might shatter if I came back here. But . . ."

"But?"

"It looks so much the same. Every so often, there's a strange build-ing, wham, out of nowhere, but mostly it's just as I remember . . . and I'm finding that I . . . like it? I thought I'd left this place for good, but seeing it again makes me realize how much I've carried it with me this whole time. When the plane came down, I was legitimately excited to see the skyline and the lake beside it. I love the bridges and the food trucks and the jaywalkers and all the seagulls everywhere. When I saw the river today, it felt like it was running through me." He shook his head. "I believe you can live anywhere and be happy. But maybe only one place can ever be home. It's the place you recognize with your heart as much as your eyes."

She smiled through her tears. "I've missed you."

He stretched out a foot and hooked it around the base of her rolling chair. "And I missed you," he said, dragging her closer. He cupped the side of her face. "My Mona Lisa. The girl with the prettiest smile."

She thought he might kiss her then, but he merely ran his thumb over her cheek and then dropped his hand back to his lap. "I realized today when your brothers were sharing their feelings about Nick that I, too, would like to punch his mouth. Then I realized he could probably punch mine. I haven't treated you very well either."

She reached for his hand and squeezed it. "You had to get out. I un-derstand."

He regarded her with an intense look. "And you had to stay." She'd been sixteen with no distant relative for escape. All those nights sleep-ing with her light on, terrified that a man might come in with his ropes. Colin gripped her hand tightly, and she resisted the temptation to look away, to refuse to show him how much she'd hurt. "I think I'm only re-alizing now how hard that must have been," he murmured. He brought their joined hands up to his lips and kissed her knuckles.

She felt an answering flutter in her belly. "Colin . . ."

"It's my turn for the shower," he said, breaking contact. "Feel free to order dessert if you like."

"No thanks, I'm stuffed." She wiped her hands and mouth one last time on the linen napkin and then amused herself with the TV remote while Colin took his shower. The Cubs were losing to the Pirates, eight to three. She flipped over to the travel channel, which was featuring the top ten most stunning beaches or some such mindless countdown. Colin reappeared dressed in a robe that was a twin to hers. She realized she should probably put on pajamas, naked as she was under the terry cloth, but she was too comfortable to move, sprawled atop the downy comforter.

She flinched, surprised when he stretched out next to her instead of taking the other bed. He left a foot of space between them. "Have you been there?" she asked, waving the remote at the white, sandy Turks and Caicos beach that shimmered on the TV.

His gaze flicked to the screen. "Yes."

She gave an envious sigh. "Is it that blue in real life?"

"Crystal. Like a summer dream."

"You're not making this any easier, you know," she said, rolling to face him.

He gave her a tender smile and tucked a lock of her unruly hair behind her ear. "You could go. You could go anywhere you want."

"I don't even have a passport."

"So, get one. Get one and I'll show you the world."

Her insides jolted at his words. She said nothing.

"Colin . . ."

"Hmm?" He'd picked up his phone, his attention elsewhere.

"Did you ever make it to Salar de Uyuni?" She held her breath after the question, which she knew was foolish to care about. What did it matter whether he remembered their plans from twenty years ago?

He looked up from his phone to meet her eyes. "No. Not yet."

A flush went through her as he held her gaze. She saw that he felt it, too, that their relationship still existed in a place of improbability, like a prehistoric dry lake set high in the Andes Mountains.

He flashed a grin and snapped off the TV. "Hey, check this out." He fiddled with his phone until a song began to play from it.

She smiled as she recognized the tune, "More Than a Feeling," by Boston.

"You remember?" he asked as he lay down facing her again.

"Yes." Their first dance, their first kiss. "I remember." She felt overcome again, exhausted and yet giddy with memory. For years, she'd thought she carried all these moments alone. Her eyes filled with fresh tears, and she couldn't blink them away.

"Shh, don't cry." His face crumpled too and he pulled her into a full body hug. He stroked her spine and rubbed the back of her head while she burrowed against him. She listened to the familiar thrumming of his heart and smiled when she realized he was still so excited to hold her. Her fingers wandered up his back to play in his damp hair.

"It feels funny to be in a hotel with you," she confessed into the fragrant hollow of his neck. "Back then, we were lucky to get ten minutes in a room with a locked door."

"But we made the most of them, as I recall." He traced one fingertip down her collarbone and into the shadowed V of her robe.

"You certainly were Johnny-on-the-spot."

"Hey, now, I think I'm being maligned."

"You were sixteen. Sixteen-year-old boys are known for their enthusiasm, not their stamina." She grinned and pressed a quick kiss to the underside of his chin, which made him growl in the back of his throat and flip her under him. Their bare legs rubbed together and his mouth settled on hers. She opened for him right away, as hungry as he was. Her skin warmed in all the old places. The robe sagged open as they moved together and his hand slipped inside.

"Anna," he said, his voice aching as his palm found her naked breast.

"Colin." She forced herself to think. "I—I didn't come prepared for this. I don't have anything. . . ."

"Oh." He shifted off her and leaned over the side of the bed for his pants. From his wallet, he withdrew a condom like a magician with a black hat. "Ta-da."

She decided not to linger on the issue of why he had one so handy. "Ever hopeful, hmm?" she asked, gently teasing as he settled over her again.

"Yeah, I remember you made me carry one around for the better part of a year before I finally got to use it." He puffed up, pretending to be affronted.

"Poor baby." She touched a finger to the dent in his chin. "I had to be sure you really meant it."

"Anna." His expression softened, and he held her face between his hands. "I always meant it."

They kissed some more, robes falling away completely, and she discovered he'd learned some new tricks in the years they'd been apart. But then again, so had she. Their bodies still spoke the same language, as eager to be joined as they'd been during their early fumblings in his twin bed, ears cocked for the creak of parental footsteps on the wooden stairs. She didn't have to hold back her groan of satisfaction when he finally slid inside.

After, he cuddled her like a long-lost teddy bear, tighter than she really enjoyed, but she didn't want to leave the shelter of his arms. She kissed the smooth flesh of his bicep and closed her eyes for sleep.

She awoke an unknown number of hours later. The drapes held back most of the light, but she could see a corona of sun burning around them. *Phone,* she realized with a start. Hers was ringing on the desk across the room. Colin stirred as she scrambled naked from the bed and checked the number. Him. She pressed opened the app to record the call and hit the answer button with a shaking finger. "Yes?"

"Detective Vega. I hope I haven't woken you."

"It's fine." Her heart pounded so fast it made her dizzy. She gripped the back of the chair for strength. "I'm—I'm awake."

Colin sat up bare-chested and watched her intently.

"I take it you retrieved the gift I left for you," said the man on the phone.

"You mean the music box? It's beautiful." She licked her lips. "Maybe you could tell me where you got it."

"Oh, I think you already know."

"Why did you pick that one? I mean, Grace had a large collection."

"It was the one she and I listened to together," he replied, and her flesh rippled with goose bumps. She struggled to focus, to keep him talking.

"It was kind of you to think of me. I was less charmed by the rope, though. And that you took my frog."

"But I gave him back," he said, putting on a pout. "He can return to his place next to the azalea bush."

Her stomach lurched at the reminder of how close he'd been. "You went to my house."

"And you weren't home." He sighed. "It's a pity we keep missing each other."

Bile rose in her throat but she swallowed it back down. "We could meet." On the nightstand, her personal phone started to ring. Colin snatched it up.

"Meet you? I've been trying, but you're not cooperating." He sounded peeved now. "I've had to improvise."

"Just name the place."

Colin climbed off the bed with her other phone. She tried to wave him off but he kept coming. "It's Zimmer," he whispered, holding it up for her.

"Who's that?" the man on the phone demanded at the sound of Colin's voice. "Is someone there with you, Annalisa? Someone in your bed?"

"No one," she said desperately, feeling him slipping away. She shushed Colin even as he took the other call.

"I'll let you get back to him, then. We can talk some other time when I have your full attention."

He clicked off and she tossed the phone down with a curse. Colin stretched out her other phone to her. "I think you'd better take this."

"What now?" she snapped, a hand to her head.

"They traced his phone. They got a location." His eyes were huge and terrified.

"What? Where?"

"He's calling from your house."

CHAPTER TWENTY-EIGHT

....

ANNALISA YANKED ON HER CLOTHES, HOPPING ON ONE LEG AS SHE GATHERED HER PHONES, HER BADGE, AND HER GUN. Everything else she was prepared to leave behind. This included Colin, who was furiously dressing alongside her. "You can't come with me," she told him as she moved for the door.

He ran after her. "The hell I can't."

"Colin, I mean it," she said, striding down the hall to the elevator. "Stay here. Stay out of it."

She didn't want to look at him, but he shoved his face in hers, his expression twisted in incredulity. "Stay out of it? How can you even say that? He killed my mother, Anna. My mother."

She couldn't argue with this, and she didn't have time to grapple with him as he followed her into the elevator. She paced her side of the car, watching the numbers count down and willing them to go faster. When they hit the parking level, she burst forth, her keys already in hand as she stalked her car in the lot. Colin kept pace and scrambled into her passenger seat the second the beep signaled the unlocked doors. She blew her bangs out of her face and ignored him. The tires screeched as she pulled out of the space and headed for the street.

"C'mon, c'mon," she muttered, swerving around a family in a minivan that was slowing to a stop. The traffic light turned red just as she reached the intersection, but she barreled through it anyway.

Colin clutched the passenger side door as she invented an imaginary lane between the traffic and the sidewalk, her wheels practically up on the curb. *Faster, faster.* The one word pulsed in her brain in time with her heartbeat, and she put the pedal to the floor. "Do you think we'll get him?" Colin asked.

"Not we. You stay in the car."

"But—"

"No!" She glared at him. "You're a travel writer, not a cop."

"This is my fight as much as anyone's."

"It's not. You left. I stayed. Me, not you." Her heart pounded as she imagined the killer from her own nightmares, huge and dressed in black, standing in her house. Touching her things. Hanging a noose from her ceiling.

She rounded the corner to her street, and all she saw was a crush of squad cars in front of her house, their blue lights blazing. She jerked her car to a halt next to them and ran up the steps to her front door, just in time to meet Zimmer coming out. "What happened?" Annalisa demanded. "Where is he?"

"Here and gone. Looks like he left the burner phone on the kitchen island."

Annalisa tried to push past her. "Let me in. I have to see."

Zimmer restrained her by putting her hands on Annalisa's shoulders. "He left rope, Vega. You might not want to see it."

Annalisa wrenched free. "I'm going in."

She charged into her house, barely registering Zimmer's commandment not to touch anything. The living room appeared the same. No noose swinging from the ceiling. But the place already smelled different, filled with men and their leather boots. She went to her bedroom, passing a uniformed cop in the hall. He flashed her a sympathetic look before avoiding her gaze, and she steeled herself for what she'd find on the other side of the bedroom door.

Ropes. Laid out on her bed and tied in intricate fashion. He'd placed a pair of her panties where her pelvis might have been.

Annalisa's chest froze of its own accord, the breath evaporating from her lungs even as her heart beat out a silent, horrified alarm. She looked around wildly, half expecting to see him standing there to admire his work. With a trembling hand, she pulled open the closet door.

"The place is clear," Zimmer said, materializing behind her. "Obviously, we'll have the forensics team go through it. We'll also need you to do a thorough inventory to make sure he hasn't taken anything with him. The back door was jimmied open, so that appears to be the point of entry."

Annalisa wandered her house, slowly this time. "What about the team stationed out front? Didn't they see anything?"

Zimmer looked chagrined. "About that. They, uh, there was a miscommunication. They thought they should be positioned here only when you were home. When you didn't come home last night, they answered a call for an armed robbery and never returned."

"Terrific." She half wondered if their killer could be the armed robber too. He was a phantom, all-powerful, able to be everywhere at once.

Annalisa looked at her blue couch, at the pillow and blanket that Nick had used. They appeared undisturbed, but that didn't mean he hadn't touched them. She swallowed her revulsion and moved to the kitchen. Dirty dishes. Same old pile of junk mail. "Nothing looks amiss in here," Zimmer said from behind her.

Annalisa froze as she saw the kitchen window. On the narrow ledge sat a small vase filled with pink flowers. She knew their name because her talented gardener neighbor had taught it to her. "Peonies," she breathed.

"Beg your pardon?"

Annalisa had already started to run. "I didn't put those flowers there," she called back. The killer's whispery words rang in her ears. *We keep missing each other. I've had to improvise. . . .*

"No, no, no," she muttered as she ran. She said a silent, fervent prayer that Amy Yakamoto would be okay as she raced to the building next door and pounded on the front door of the lower unit. "Mrs. Yakamoto? It's Annalisa. Are you in there?" She looked over her shoulder and saw Zimmer coming up the walk behind her. She also saw the rest of the neighbors, those who were home, had spilled out of their homes into the street to watch the show. Annalisa banged louder and tried the door. It was locked. "Mrs. Yakamoto? Amy?"

"What is it?" Zimmer asked.

"Those flowers are from my neighbor's house. I'm worried about her."

"Let's try around back."

Both women ran around the side of the condo, through the wet grass until they reached the back door. Annalisa banged loudly. "Mrs. Yakamoto?" She cupped her hands around her eyes and peered through the glass doors. What she saw made her recoil in horror. "Oh my God."

Amy Yakamoto lay bound and unmoving on the floor of her living room.

"She's in there! We have to do something!"

Zimmer stepped forward for a look, and she immediately took out her radio. "We need a medic in the third unit. Now."

"We have to get in there now." Annalisa looked around frantically for anything she could use to defeat the door. She found a painted white rock Mrs. Yakamoto used for decoration in her gardens. "Step back," she told Zimmer and then hurled the rock at the glass window at the top half of the door. It shattered, and Annalisa reached through the jagged edge to unlock the door from the other side. The glass scraped a cut through her forearm but she didn't care. "Mrs. Yakamoto?"

She ran to kneel at her neighbor's side, but she could see from the color of her face that the older woman had died. Her body was stiff and cold to the touch. Annalisa began tugging at the ropes, trying to free her. Zimmer pulled her back.

"Let me help her!"

"You can't help her. Not like this."

Annalisa struggled, but Zimmer held firm as the EMTs banged at the front door. "Let's go let in the medics, okay? They will help her."

Annalisa stared at her. "He wanted me. Don't you see that? It was supposed to me."

"Come on," Zimmer said, her voice full of sympathy. "Let's open the door."

Annalisa allowed herself to be propelled through the living room to the front door, where Zimmer let in the EMTs and pushed Annalisa outside into the sunshine. "I should've been here. I should've stopped him."

"This is not your fault. This is on him, not you."

Annalisa's eyes filled with tears. She shook her head and stared at the chaos mobbing her street. "I didn't warn her. I should've warned her."

"We didn't know she was a target."

"Why did the undercover unit leave? What the hell were they thinking?

Didn't they know how dangerous this guy is?" Annalisa gestured wildly at the parked cars.

"I will speak to them. Right now, I have to call the ME. Why don't you come with me?"

"No . . . no, I should stay here." Annalisa hugged herself and cast a look back inside Mrs. Yakamoto's house. Zimmer hesitated a fraction of an instant but then left with a short nod. The hot sun beat down from overhead, but Annalisa felt cold and clammy. Colin was out there somewhere, she realized, her gaze sliding over to the cars and the crowd. She didn't have the strength to deal with him at that moment.

She looked away, down the other side of the street. Wait. There was something familiar in her sight line. A red coupe parked about half a block down. *Nick.* Her head whipped around, searching him out, but she did not see him anywhere. Dread creeped up inside her as she began to run.

No, no, no. Please no. She fled down the street, yelling his name. The sun glinted off his windshield, making it impossible to see inside the car. She skidded to a stop by the passenger door and yanked it open. The overwhelming smell of blood made her cough. "Oh, God. Nick . . ." She climbed inside and found him slumped in the seat. His shirt was soaked with blood. "Nick, no . . ." She felt for a pulse at his wrist and found none. Her fingers came away wet with his blood. She held them to his neck, pressing in and holding her breath. She detected a faint beat and adrenaline surged through her.

She bolted from the car and waved frantically at the EMTs down the street. "Help! I need help! Officer down! Help!"

When she saw them mobilizing, she got back in the car with Nick. "I told you to go home," she chided him in a desperate voice. "I told you not to be here." She tried to determine the cause of his injury, but his black shirt concealed the wounds. A knife, she guessed, since she did not smell gunpowder. The EMTs came and asserted control, pushing her out of the way. She watched helplessly from the sidelines as they laid him on a stretcher, started an IV, and carted him toward an ambulance.

"What the hell happened?" Zimmer asked as she joined the scene. "He got to Carelli?"

"Nick wanted to keep watch outside my place," Annalisa replied woodenly. "I told him it wasn't necessary. He must've driven over here anyway."

"Jesus, Mary, and Joseph," Zimmer breathed, her face going pale.

"I have to go with him." Annalisa moved to get her car to follow the ambulance, and Zimmer jogged alongside her.

"Wait, we need you to inventory the condo. We can call Nick's next of kin."

"That's me. I'm it." Annalisa's tone said not to bother fighting her on this. "Everything else can wait."

Wordless, Zimmer let her go. Annalisa found Colin, ashen-faced, waiting by the driver's side of her car. "I need to go to the hospital," she said.

"Is it Nick? It looked like Nick on the stretcher."

"It's Nick. Please move."

He did as she asked, moving to get in the shotgun seat. She didn't bother to fight him. When the ambulance pulled out, lights and sirens blaring, Annalisa gunned the engine and followed. When she glanced down at her hands on the wheel, she saw the right one still had Nick's blood all over it. "He was watching the house," she said to Colin. "He was trying to protect me."

"This isn't your fault."

"I wish people would stop saying that to me," she snapped as she floored it through a red light, using the ambulance for cover.

Colin said nothing for a moment. "I get it," he said finally, his head bowed. "You can't help but feel responsible."

"Don't tell me how I feel."

"I'm telling you how I feel," he replied, a sudden edge to his voice. "You and I were making out in the basement and sneaking drinks while this guy strangled my mother. I knew she went home sick. I knew she wasn't feeling good. You know what I thought? Great, now she's out of my hair. I don't have to worry about her watching my every move all night. If I'd gone home, if I'd gone to check on her . . ."

"Don't," she blurted, feeling sick. "Don't even say it."

He stared out the window at the scenery racing past. "Now you know," he said without looking at her. "Why I had to get away."

CHAPTER TWENTY-NINE

··········

THEY RUSHED NICK TO NORTHWESTERN, THE SAME PLACE POPS WAS STAYING, AND SO FOR THE SECOND TIME THAT WEEK, ANNALISA WAITED HELPLESSLY IN THE HARD CHAIRS OUTSIDE OF THE SURGICAL SUITE. Colin fetched them coffee, which she drank without tasting. She chewed her thumbnail and kept her eyes focused on the swinging doors, waiting for the moment that some doctor in scrubs would come through it and determine Nick's fate. Eventually, Zimmer showed up, along with Don Harrigan, and Bob Grayson from the FBI. They pulled her aside from Colin for questioning. "What's the latest on Carelli?" Zimmer wanted to know.

"No news yet." She still didn't know for certain if he had been stabbed or shot, let alone the details of his wounds.

Harrigan pounded his fist into his palm. "This damn bastard. It's not enough for him to leave notes and pictures anymore. He's gunning straight for us now."

Annalisa narrowed her eyes at him. "You mean me, right? He's after me. Nick was watching my back."

"Who could've gotten to him?" Zimmer asked in a low voice.

Annalisa had been asking herself the same question. In a way, it was a variant of the problem that had vexed them from the beginning: How did the Lovelorn Killer move through crowded neighborhoods without ever sounding an alarm? Nick's attacker had been in the car with him, yet Nick's weapon remained holstered at his hip. "Someone he didn't see as a threat," she said to Zimmer. "Maybe . . ." She licked her dry lips, hesitating to admit the next part. "Maybe even someone he knew."

The group sat with this heavy news for a long moment. "We have to hope he pulls through," Harrigan said. "The killer got sloppy. He left a beating heart."

"We're going to need you to go over everything that happened from the moment you got the phone call," Grayson told Annalisa.

She cast an anxious look at the blue doors that led to the operating rooms. "Sure, fine. Whatever. But we'll have to do it here because I'm not leaving until Nick wakes up." She stuck out her chin, daring them to contradict her. Grayson pursed his lips and appeared ready to object, but Zimmer didn't give him the space.

"I'll get coffee for everyone, and we can set up camp over there," she said, indicating a shadowed, unused portion of the waiting room that had a partition between it and the main area. Annalisa figured if she positioned herself by the opening she could still see the doors.

"Lead the way."

They went over her story several times from different angles, but it didn't matter how hard they shook her, no answers fell out. All the grilling accomplished was to underscore her lack of insight into a killer who was now stalking her. "He said we keep missing each other so he had to improvise." Her chest tightened as she remembered Amy Yakamoto lying bound and gagged on the living room floor. "I wasn't home so he went next door."

Her head throbbed but rubbing it did nothing to ease the pain. Grayson consulted his notes. "She wasn't naked. There was no scent of bleach at the scene. He, ah, he didn't kill her for sexual gratification as he did the others."

Harrigan wasn't impressed with this insight. "No kidding. She doesn't fit the Lovelorn victim profile. Vega, here, on the other hand . . . she ticks all his boxes, yeah? Young, dark hair, lives in a nice neighborhood. As a bonus, she's carrying a badge as well. No wonder he's got such a hard-on for her."

"Harrigan," Zimmer broke in, fatigued. "Not every metaphor requires mention of the male genitalia. Especially when you're referring to a fellow officer, hmm?"

"You want to bust my chops for language now?" he asked, incredulous. "There's a psycho out there who wants to hog-tie your detective and choke her to death."

"A fact of which I'm sure she's aware."

"I think we're getting off track," Grayson said.

"There is no track," Annalisa replied dully. "We just pile up reports, enough to fill a storeroom, a whole forest's worth of paper devoted to this guy, and we're no closer to catching him than you were twenty years ago."

The rest of them exchanged a look, significant enough to make Annalisa's antennae twitch. "What?"

"There is something new," Grayson said carefully.

Excitement flickered in Harrigan's eyes. "We got DNA," he said. "He finally fucked up."

"Where? How?" Annalisa asked.

"From Grace Harper's body," Grayson told her. "A saliva sample."

"He—he bit her?"

"We're keeping the nature of the sample confidential at the moment. Unfortunately, the DNA did not return any hits from the usual databases."

"What about unusual ones? He's got to be in the system somewhere."

"We're looking into it. For now, let's keep this bit of information to ourselves, okay?"

Annalisa saw a tall doctor in green scrubs come through the doors and look around the waiting room. She bolted for him, leaving the others in her wake. "Are you here about Nick Carelli?" she asked when she reached the doctor.

"You are his wife?" he asked kindly, with a hint of a South Indian accent.

"Ex-wife. How is he?" She tried to read his face but all she saw was lines of exhaustion.

"Mr. Carelli sustained a deep laceration to the right thoracic cavity. It ruptured the pleural membranes and collapsed one lung, as well as puncturing his liver. We have repaired the lung and cleaned up the damage to his liver, but he remains in a fragile state."

"But he'll be okay, right? He's going to get better?"

"We are certainly doing all we can to ensure a good outcome. Mr. Carelli was lucky in some respects. The location of the wound is such that it did not impact any major arteries. Moreover, gravity worked in his favor. His position, seated in the car, kept the wound mostly closed until help could be summoned, which minimized the blood loss. Even still, he lost more than two units, and his kidneys are registering that shock. We have placed him on dialysis for the moment to ease the stress while his body recovers."

"Recovers," Annalisa said with relief, seizing on the word. "That's good."

"I don't want to mislead you. Your friend is still critically injured. But he's stabilized, and he's healthy and strong. I am optimistic he'll pull through."

"Thank you." Annalisa grabbed his hand and pumped it. "Thank you so much. Can I see him?"

"He's not conscious."

"I don't care." She just wanted to lay eyes on him. A welfare check, as they called it in her business. Always see for yourself.

"Give him an hour or two, okay? Then check with the nurses. They'll let you know if it's all right to pop in for a minute."

"An hour. Okay. Thank you."

She jogged over to Colin, who had been sagged in his seat, systematically unrolling the edge of his empty coffee cup. "Nick came through surgery all right. The doctor thinks he'll make it."

Colin stood up and enfolded her in his arms. "That's great," he said, hugging her tightly. "Finally, some good news for a change."

"Yeah." She wiped her eyes with her hands. "I have to go tell Zimmer."

Annalisa went to deliver the cautionary good report on Nick, and Zimmer looked equally relieved. Harrigan clapped her on the back in celebration. Even Grayson managed a smile. "I'm going to go check on my father upstairs," Annalisa said. "I'll be back."

"Vega, wait." Zimmer frowned and pulled her aside.

"What is it?"

"The three of us were just talking. You need more protection."

"Commander, I'm . . ."

Zimmer held up a hand. "Don't even start with it. We've already got one detective in the hospital, and your neighbor is down at the morgue awaiting autopsy."

The words landed like a punch to the gut. Annalisa swallowed back her protests. "What kind of protection?"

"Well, you can't go home tonight, that's for damn sure."

Annalisa glanced back at Colin. "I can stay at a hotel, with a friend."

"Is that where you were last night?"

Annalisa nodded.

"Who else knows you were there?"

"Just you, me, and Colin so far, and he knows to keep his mouth shut."

Zimmer eyed him critically from across the room. "That's Katherine Duffy's boy, right? I remember him from before."

Annalisa's heart ached. *So do I,* she thought. "Amy Yakamoto has a son too," she said. Annalisa had seen the framed picture of the young man sitting on Mrs. Yakamoto's piano. "Jason. He lives in Seattle. Does something with computers." She imagined him out there far away, going about his day, unaware of the tsunami that was already sweeping in his direction.

"I'll make the call to him myself," Zimmer said. "I'll also post officers in the hotel lobby, and one outside your room if you want."

"I don't think that will be necessary. It's got a million security cameras. He'd have to be on a suicide mission to try something there."

Zimmer fixed her with a hard look. "We don't know his endgame. You need to be extremely careful."

"I will. Right now, I think I'll run upstairs to see my dad for a few minutes."

"Give him my best. And let me know when you're leaving for the hotel. I'll arrange an escort for you."

Annalisa told Colin her plan, including the part where she'd invited herself to stay at his hotel again. "Of course, it's fine," he said, rubbing the back of her neck with one hand. "I wouldn't want you anywhere else. Why don't I grab us some sandwiches while you go see your dad? You haven't eaten all day."

Her stomach had clenched itself into such a tight ball that she wasn't sure she could force any food into it, but she was glad to give him something to do. "That would be great, thank you." She squeezed his arm and went to the elevator, where she was alone in the car. The stainless steel wall reflected a blurred image of her, and she leaned against it wearily. She roused at the soft ding that signaled her arrival and forced herself to stand up straight as she went in search of her father.

She found Ma instead, coming down the hall. "Anna," her mother said, reaching to embrace her. "How are you?"

"Fine," Annalisa said automatically. "How's Pops?"

"He's good. The nurses just kicked me out so he can use the bathroom and get changed. We can go back in a few minutes." Her mother took her arm and walked her to the nearest waiting area. "You look tired, sweetheart. You've been working too hard. When is the last time you had something to eat?"

"Colin is getting sandwiches." Annalisa sank into the chair next to her mother. She had to tell her what happened before she saw it on the news, but she couldn't find the right words. Her mother would be terrified, and she'd already been through so much.

"Colin," Ma repeated with faint disapproval. "There is a name I wasn't sure I would ever hear again."

"He was an orphan, Ma. It wasn't his choice to leave."

"No, but he chose to stay away." Her mother reached out to smooth Annalisa's hair. "Don't think I didn't notice how much it hurt you. How you wrote letters but received none in return."

"It was a long time ago." Annalisa ducked her head. "He'd just lost his mother, then his father. I think we can cut him a break, hmm?"

Ma yanked back her hand and pursed her lips. "I'm not saying he did wrong. I just don't want to see you break your heart again. That boy is a born wanderer. He's got a restless soul, just like his mother had."

"What are you talking about? Katie barely left the neighborhood. We went camping in the UP that one summer, and it was like an event—just to cross the border into Michigan."

"Physically, yes, she never left."

And she never would. Katie Duffy was buried in a cemetery mere blocks from the house where she'd lived. Annalisa wondered if this was part of the reason Colin traveled the world, to see all the places his mother had not. She looked sideways at her own mother, saw how the years had softened her cheeks and left lines around her eyes. Her black hair was streaked with gray, her hands slowed by arthritis. "Ma," Annalisa said softly. "What about you?"

Her mother made a soft harrumphing noise. "What about me?"

"Did you want to travel? Or . . . I don't know. Do something else with your life."

"I have a great life. I have your father and I have you four kids. You're all I ever wanted."

"Katie Duffy had a family too."

"Yes. She also wanted more."

"Did you know she was pregnant when she died?"

Her mother's frown deepened, and she picked up her giant purse to start rooting through it.

"Ma? Did you know?"

"She didn't tell me," her mother said, her head practically in the purse. "She didn't tell me lots of things. Maybe . . . maybe she didn't have the words to say it. Maybe she knew she shouldn't say it."

"Say what?"

Her mother gave a deep sigh and reemerged from her purse. "She knew she made a choice. She knew there were some things she couldn't have."

Annalisa was about to press further, but she halted when she noticed her mother snap to attention, her gaze fixed across the room. "Him again," she muttered, and Annalisa saw Rod Brewster striding toward them.

"Maria! I figured I'd find you still here. And Annalisa, too. I heard the news about Nick Carelli. I hope he knows we're all pulling for him."

Ma turned to Annalisa. "What's this about Nick?"

"She didn't tell you? Someone stabbed him outside of Annalisa's place last night."

Her mother gasped in horror as Annalisa shot Brewster a warning glare. "We've been discussing other things. Ma, it's okay. The doctors say Nick should be fine." Probably. Maybe. If she said it enough times, then it would be true.

"Someone stabbed him? Outside your house? Anna, what's going on?"

"I wasn't home," Annalisa said soothingly. "Everything's all right."

"He's back," Brewster said, almost with a grim satisfaction. "George and I, we warned them not to put away the files. A monster like this doesn't just go hide in his cave."

"The monster is after you?" Ma asked her.

"He's not a monster. He's just a man." If you expected the devil to show his horns, you would never notice him falling into step beside you. "I have protection, and I'm going to see to it that someone watches your house, too. Just in case."

Ma's face crumpled. "Why can't he just leave us alone?"

"He won't hurt us, I promise." Annalisa rubbed her mother's shoulders and scowled at Brewster. "I heard you knew Grace Harper."

"Grace Harper? Never met her."

"Online. Through the Grave Diggers site? You're a member there."

He rubbed one hand over his considerable belly, like he had sudden indigestion. "Oh, yeah. The online thing. Yeah, I checked it out to see if they had any real insights into the case. No stone unturned and all that. But they're just a bunch of wannabes with cracked-up theories. All talk, no substance."

"Someone must've thought differently, if Grace got killed."

He met her stare and held it. "Nothing these yahoos had on the Lovelorn case was worth killing for. I did my due diligence and had a look. Best they could figure, it was some lowlife skulking around O'Malley's Bar. George and I already checked into that story, and it was ridiculous. What did it matter if Katie Duffy had a few beers there once in a while? So did I, so did the lot of us from the neighborhood. Big whoop. I don't know why this guy went after Grace Harper. Maybe the killer didn't realize what a big fat zero these computer geeks had come up with, or maybe he just thought he'd show 'em."

"Show them what, exactly?"

"That this isn't some puzzle on the internet. That real people died. That they ought to be afraid." His expression darkened for a second, but he shook it off, and he slapped the sports magazines in his hand against the nearest empty chair. "Hey, I brought these for George to amuse himself during his recuperation. Okay if I go on back?"

Ma didn't get a chance to answer because Colin came rushing up to them. He had a pair of wrapped sandwiches in his hands and his blue eyes were fever bright. "Nick is awake," he told Annalisa.

Annalisa didn't wait for further information. She raced to the elevator and mashed the button with a hard jab, willing the doors to open. When she reached the ICU, she pestered the nurses until she was allowed to see Nick. She held her breath, bracing for the worst, so by comparison he didn't look too awful. His face had no color except for the odd bruising under his eyes. He had a bunch of wires taped to him and a vitals monitor stood next to the bed. An IV extended from his left hand, and he had an oxygen tube fixed under his nose. His eyes were closed. Tentatively, she crept closer to the bed. "Nick?" He didn't stir. She took his right hand and squeezed it gently. "Nick, it's me. Annalisa."

His lids twitched and he slowly opened them, as if dragging them up was a Herculean task. His lips moved but no sound came out.

"You're going to be all right," she said, hoping she sounded sure.

"Sh— Shoes."

She looked at the black sneakers on her feet. "Yes, I'm wearing shoes."

His dark eyes looked sunken and hollow. Anger flared in them. "Shoes," he repeated. "Him." He pointed weakly at himself and she looked around. He wore only a thin hospital gown, and she had no idea what they'd done with his clothes. Probably cut them off him, if she had to guess.

"I'm sorry, I don't know where your shoes are. I'll try to find out."

His eyes fell closed again.

"Nick. Who did this to you? Did you see him?"

His eyelids fluttered but he didn't reawaken. She shook his arm gently.

"Nick, help me here. Did you see the guy?"

A nurse came over to check the machines. "Honey, he's not going to be any use to you until the drugs wear off. Give him a few more hours. Maybe tomorrow."

Annalisa stroked Nick's hand and stared hard into his sleeping face, as if she could somehow see into his brain. He didn't move and eventually she had to give up. "Hang in there," she murmured to him. "I'll be back." She looked around at the mauve walls and remembered his story from childhood, about waking up in the wrong-colored room. She chose to look at the pink walls as a positive sign from Nick's mother. He would be okay. He simply had to be. She stretched across him carefully and kissed his forehead before tiptoeing from the room.

She found Colin had already wolfed down his sandwich. She took a few halfhearted bites of hers and drank down the Coke he had provided. "Zimmer can have a squad car take you back to the hotel," she said.

His brows dipped in concern. "What about you?"

"I'll be there when I can. There's something I want to talk to Harrigan about." Brewster's comments niggled at her.

"You're not seriously still working on this case."

"I am until someone tells me I can't."

He gaped at her and grabbed for her hands. "I'm the one telling you. Me. Come back to the hotel and we can leave again when they've caught this guy. Better yet, let's get that passport for you and go to Paris. Or Crete. Or Cape Town. Anywhere that's not here."

She pulled one hand free and pressed it against the side of his face. "I can't," she said. "I'm the one who stayed, remember?" She kissed him swiftly and then stalked off in search of Harrigan. She found him in the lobby, barking orders into his cell phone.

". . . swab the whole damn house if you have to. I don't care." He hung up when he saw her standing there. "How's Carelli? Did he give us anything on the doer?"

"Nothing yet. I think we should post a guard outside his room. This guy probably won't chance to come in here, but better to be safe than sorry, you know?"

"Zimmer's already on it."

"Great. I want someone to take Colin Duffy back to his hotel, too."

Harrigan scratched behind his ear. "You know, Vega, we're going to run out of cops here."

"Then call in more. They got your ass off the bench, they can find others like you." She waited, her eyes boring into his, until he nodded.

"Okay. You have a point. I'll chauffeur Mr. Duffy myself if I have to."

"No, I need you for something else."

He gave her a ghost of a smile. "You? Need me? For what?"

"I need you to help me go through the Lovelorn files to see if anything else is missing."

His jaw dropped slightly. "Vega, those boxes of files fill an entire storeroom."

"Yeah." She clapped a hand on his shoulder. "And you told me no one knows them like you do."

CHAPTER THIRTY

....

GRACE NOTES

Journal Entry #439

Barnes and I had an interesting instant message chat about the psychology of the Lovelorn Killer. I saved it . . . because I have it on the record that he's finally agreed to go out with me!

Grace: On YouTube, I found an old unsolved-cases show about the Lovelorn Killer from about fifteen years ago. I'll send you the link so you can check it out, because parts of it are hilarious. It has super cheesy reenactments with big-haired models scream- ing and clutching their faces like that *Home Alone* kid while someone off-screen waves a piece of rope at them. But they interviewed a real FBI profiler about the case. She said the usual stuff about how he probably had a fractured family with either an absent or domineering father and a weak-willed mother whom he blamed for the father's misdeeds. I just can't believe these people get paid to say this crap. Okay, so he had shitty parents. So did a lot of people, and they didn't become murderers. This guy, if he ever gets caught, he's going to end up in books with BTK and Bundy and Dahmer. A rarefied crowd. Don't try to make him seem like the ordinary victim of a boo-hoo sad divorce.

Barnes: I agree with you. It's like studying Einstein and trying to use his brain to explain how the rest of humanity understands physics.

Still, it's irresistible to imagine, isn't it? What makes one human hunt and kill another just for the sport of it?

Grace: They say they have to try to think like him to be able to catch him. It hasn't worked out great so far.

Barnes: Maybe we should give it a whirl.

Grace: Think like the killer?

Barnes: We're trying to find him, aren't we?

Grace: Sure, but if you think like him you'll only see what he sees. The point is to find his mistakes.

Barnes: Okay, so start there. Name one of his mistakes.

Grace: Jeez, I don't know. Katie Duffy, I guess. Something went wrong there because he never sent the letter after he killed her.

Barnes: Never sent it or never wrote it?

Grace: We can't answer that because we don't know one way or the other. Maybe he sent it and it just wasn't received.

Barnes: Wouldn't he just send another?

Grace: Huh. That's a good point. There's definitely a reason why no letter surfaced after Katie Duffy's murder. So . . . what? He didn't love her like the others?

Barnes: Or he didn't pick her. At least not for the same reasons.

Grace: She was a cop's wife at one time, living in a neighborhood full of them. Maybe she was a message victim.

Barnes: Ah, who the hell knows? Maybe his domineering father tore up the letter.

Grace: LOL! See, the profilers were right all along!

Barnes: They could be on to something. Maybe the killer's father hit his mother and hit the boy when he was a child. It made him feel . . . what? Humiliated? Powerless?

Grace: Sure. Who wouldn't be?

Barnes: But then one day the boy takes his humiliation and pain outside the house. Maybe the most recent whipping is still stinging on his body when he finds some creature in the yard. A chipmunk or maybe a frog. He catches the thing and watches it struggle in his grasp. He sees its frantic beating heart, which is just like his own racing heart when his father took the switch to him. He takes a rock and crushes the creature. All the life goes out of it, and now he's got just a dead thing he can split open and examine. He forgets his pain.

Grace: Animal abuse is common among serial offenders. A lot of them start there.

Barnes: Until one day it isn't enough. Killing a cat or a squirrel doesn't take the edge off anymore. He starts having fantasies about snuffing the life out of humans. A girl with long dark hair catches his eye in the school hallways.

Grace: She won't talk to him. Doesn't pay him any attention.

Barnes: No, I don't think that's right. She sees him but dismisses him. He's a nobody. He's the guy she'll ask to borrow a pencil when she forgets hers, the guy she asks to pass on her love note—the one she wrote to the guy she really likes. She trusts he'll do it because he seems so nice. She can't see the thoughts in his head when he takes the note or gives her the pencil. She thinks he's harmless.

Grace: That's part of his power. He likes that he's standing in front of her and she has no idea what he is. He thinks about the moment he'll reveal himself and how sorry she will be. How humiliated and ashamed that she should've seen it coming.

Barnes: Yes, yes. Exactly. He wants to transfer all his rage and embarrassment onto these girls and then choke it out of them. He wants to love them but they won't let him. They disappoint him every time.

Grace: I hope they spit in his face. That's what I'd do. I hope they let him know he's still nothing but a loser outside in the real world, where you can't rope a woman like cattle. All this theorizing is fun, but we still have the same problem as the profilers. We can sit around and pontificate about how he probably wet the bed as a teenager and feels insecure about the size of his penis. The cops can't go checking everybody's pants. We need something that we can use.

Barnes: I agree. But what?

Grace: I'm working on a theory. I've been to the places he's been and I've read all the stories. I have an idea about how he's choosing the women, how he was present at all these scenes and nobody saw him or noticed anyone unusual. The newspapers had the answer all along, only it wasn't on page one with the big headlines. You have to go back a couple of days beforehand to see it.

Barnes: What? Don't hold back, woman. Reveal your mysteries!

Grace: I will. Say, over dinner at Sacco's on Saturday night? I'm buying.

Barnes: Grace, we've been over this. I like you, but . . .

Grace: It's just a dinner. I won't jump your bones in the alley afterward. Not unless you want me to.

Barnes: Okay, we'll have dinner. But can I at least get a hint about your theory?

Grace: I'll say this much: You'd better go close your windows. There's a storm rolling in.

CHAPTER THIRTY-ONE

....

"Y OU WANT TO TELL ME WHAT EXACTLY IT IS WE'RE LOOKING FOR?" HARRIGAN ASKED AS HE LIFTED THE LID OFF OF ANOTHER DUSTY CARDBOARD BOX.

"Whatever isn't here." Annalisa paused over her own box and used the back of her hand to wipe the sweat from under her nose. It was so hot in the storage room that she wished she could put her boobs in a ponytail.

"So we're looking for something that ain't here. That makes sense." He flipped open a binder and let the pages fall open at the center. "You realize they took thousands of tip calls, right? And they're all recorded in here?"

Annalisa looked into her box and checked the numbered binders. They all appeared to be in order. She shoved it aside and moved onto another box marked DUFFY, K. with an accompanying case number. She pulled off the lid and immediately stepped back.

Harrigan noticed her reaction. "Whatcha got over there? A rattlesnake?"

She shook her head, mute, and he ambled over to take a look for himself. "Oof," he said when he saw the ropes and the bags that held Katie Duffy's fortune teller costume from the night she died. He pulled out a pair of gloves from a nearby box and picked out a white nylon rope. There was a bloodstain visible partway down. "You knew her, huh?"

"Yes." Annalisa stared at the rope. "Our families were friends."

"That's right, her old man was a cop there for a while. Owen Duffy. He and your dad used to ride together back in the day."

"You really do remember everything."

"About this case? Yeah." He dropped the rope back in the box, his mouth twisted in disgust. "I remember the night I walked into the house. The stench of bleach about knocked me out. My eyes were red for two days afterward. Everyone was standing around, teary-eyed like we'd been gassed, but we were freakin' grateful for the cover. We knew it was one of our own lying there. They all eat at you, but Katie Duffy . . . she was family."

Annalisa put on gloves and forced herself to wade through the rest of the evidence in the box. There wasn't much. Lengths of rope, Katie's peasant blouse and patchwork skirt with the colored scarves attached to it. "No underwear?" she asked, and Harrigan shook his head tightly.

"We think he took it with him."

Annalisa got to the bottom of the box and peered inside as though the dark, empty cardboard might hold an answer. The bright scarves caught her eye from inside their clear plastic bag, and she picked up the package for inspection. Purple, blue, green, yellow. Katie had ordered a whole set. Annalisa frowned as she recalled the original crime scene photos, the ones Grace Harper had put up on her wall. She opened the plastic bag and dumped out the contents onto the table, pawing through them.

"What is it?" Harrigan asked her.

"It's not here," she replied as she searched through the meager contents once more. She turned the box upside down and shook it. "The red one isn't here."

"Wait. Are you sure?"

"Look for yourself." The red scarf was the one the killer used for his improvisation. It had been the one around Katie's neck when she was found dead on the floor.

Harrigan joined her in the search. "Maybe it's in another box."

Together, they pulled the lids off each of the fifty boxes and rifled the contents. No scarf. "Could it have been misplaced? Maybe some of the boxes are still back in deep storage."

"Maybe," he said, but he didn't sound convinced.

"It should have been in here, right? Box seven."

"Let me check the master index." He hunted down the main binder for the Duffy case and tapped his finger on the page. "It's listed here with the rope and other clothes, bagged separately. At one point, it was tested for DNA, but only Katie Duffy's came back."

"Could it have been left at the lab? Lost in transit?"

"Says here it was returned. Let me check the log for the signature of who received it." He picked up yet another binder and flipped it open. After locating the correct page, he ran his finger down until he hit the correct entry. He froze and looked up at her.

"What?" she asked when he didn't say anything.

He held the logbook out to her so she could see for herself. She accepted it wordlessly and looked down to where he had pointed. Her heart sank when she saw the heavy, left-slanted scrawl. It was a signature she had known all her life: George Vega.

"He wasn't supposed to be working this case in any major capacity," Harrigan said. "He definitely wasn't supposed to be anywhere near the evidence. He socialized with the victim, for cripes' sake."

"He wanted to avenge her," Annalisa murmured. All those nights she spent listening to him pacing in his study. Then the roar of the car engine as he left to roam the streets, looking for a faceless killer. She'd been terrified the man would come to the house to get them while Pops was gone.

Her cell phone buzzed. A second later, so did Harrigan's. They both found a text from Zimmer: *My office. Now.* They hastily stowed the evidence back in the correct boxes and signed off that they had been in the locked room. Annalisa's feeble lunch curdled in her stomach as she imagined the worst, that something had happened to Nick. She broke into a jog on the way to Zimmer's office, and Harrigan had to huff to keep up with her.

Zimmer stood behind her desk, her face grim and her eyes apologetic as Annalisa came through the door. "What is it? Is it Nick?"

"The *Tribune* called. They've received another letter."

Her heart lurched in confusion. "Wha-what? Another victim?"

"No," Zimmer said. "It's addressed to you."

CHAPTER THIRTY-TWO

....

"WE SENT SOMEONE TO RETRIEVE THE LETTER FROM THE *TRIB*," ZIMMER SAID. "It should be here any minute."

Annalisa gripped the back of the chair so hard her fingers turned white. "What does it say? Do you know?"

"Based on what was relayed to me, the content is similar to the other letters."

"So, he really did mean to kill her," Harrigan said. "He must've been confident he'd do it, too. The letter had to have been mailed before he went to Vega's place."

"That is our best guess right now." She looked Annalisa over critically. "You want to take a seat, Vega? You're looking a little pale. Harrigan, get her a glass of water, will you?"

"No, no. I'm fine." Annalisa slid into the chair before her knees could buckle. "It's not like this is brand-new information. We knew he was there to get me. Maybe the letter will offer a new direction."

A sharp knock on the door got Zimmer's attention. "Come in," she called, and a uniformed officer entered with a manila envelope in his hands. "Is that the parcel from the *Tribune*?"

"Yes ma'am. The mail attendant wanted me to relay to you that he has been wearing gloves to process the mail, as instructed."

"Thank you. Keep this errand to yourself, okay?" Zimmer dismissed him and then rooted around in her desk until she found her own box of gloves. Annalisa wanted to grab the envelope and rip it open, but she made herself wait. She sat on the very edge of the chair, her gaze trained on Zimmer as she carefully opened the standard envelope inside the larger one. Harrigan practically breathed down her neck from behind.

"We're supposed to defer to the FBI on this," Zimmer said. "But the *Tribune* called us. It's addressed to one of my people."

"Let's see it," Annalisa said, her voice tight.

Zimmer read the contents silently. Harrigan couldn't take it. "Well?" he blurted.

"Dear Annalisa," Zimmer read, distaste dripping from her words. "I couldn't believe my luck when they sent you to me. For years, it's been all hairy-armed, flat-footed men with ten-dollar haircuts and cheap suits. You are a breath of fresh air, my darling, a rose among the thorns! I saw you on TV and immediately had to look you up. Your story is so intriguing. Daughter of a cop. I didn't know George Vega personally, but he must be a fine man to have his daughter want to follow in his footsteps. Your footsteps are light, aren't they? Light on your feet, like a cat in the night. But I hear them close now. You trail behind me so delicately, I have to remind myself that you are actually very dangerous.

"You aren't married, and I have to wonder if you've been waiting for me. If you knew that one day I'd come. I've had many women now, but none as determined and watchful as you. You're a hunter, like me. We both go out in the night when other people are asleep, dreaming away their insipid lives. I see you clearly now. We've missed one another by moments, you and I. Others have tried to come between us, but I've dispensed with them as needed. I think it's fated that we should meet, that our stories become bound. We'll be tied together for all eternity."

Zimmer set the letter back on top of its envelope. "It's got the same signature. Mr. Lovelorn."

"Can I see it?" Annalisa stood up, and Zimmer turned the letter around so she could read it. The neat block printing was identical to the previous letters. "He gives nothing away," she said in frustration. "There are no new clues here."

"We'll have lab guys go over it for trace evidence, but I think we have to assume it's a bust like the others. This stuff is for show, to puff him up. It's his gilding of the lily. I think he'd love it if we spent our time parsing his word choice for hidden meanings. But it does underscore one important matter, which is your safety, Annalisa. He meant for us to be reading this when you were dead. There is no assurance that he won't try again."

"I'm being careful."

"I want you more than careful. I want an officer with eyes on you at all times."

Heat rose up the back of Annalisa's neck. "Will he be accompanying me to the shower?"

Zimmer wasn't amused as she picked up her phone. "That's up to you."

"Fine." Annalisa tried to find a way to spin this to her advantage. "Can I at least pick the detail?"

Zimmer paused with her phone in hand, her expression curious. "Within limits. Who are you thinking?"

"I'd like Rod Brewster for now."

"Brewster? He's not in uniform anymore. He does special investigations, assists with the DA's office. This isn't his kind of assignment."

"He's a family friend from way back. I think he'll do it." When Zimmer hesitated, Annalisa played the only card she had left: sympathy. "Please," she said. "It would mean a lot to me to have a friendly face around now."

Zimmer gave in with a curt nod. "I'll see if he's amenable."

Annalisa was not surprised to learn Brewster was available and eager for the chance to align himself with the Lovelorn case in any capacity. He joined her at her desk, his big shoulders straining against his suit jacket. Annalisa saw it gape open near his hip to reveal his police-issue 9 mm. "Hey, kid," he said with a forced grin. He reached for her, like he'd ruffled her hair in the old days, but dropped his hand before he made contact. "Looks like it's you and me, huh?"

"Don't get comfortable," she said as she stood from her chair. "I want to take a drive over to my parents' place. Mom needs some stuff for Pops at the hospital."

"Now?" He checked his watch, his frown registering the fact that it was past nine at night. "I figured you'd want to pack it in for the day. You must be running on fumes by now."

"No, I'm good." She raised her eyebrows at him. "Unless you're too tired . . . ?"

He puffed out his chest. "Me? I'm rarin' to go."

"Great. I'm driving."

In her car, he adjusted the passenger seat as far back as it would go, but his knees still bumped up against the dash. The weather had turned wet again, the dark sky packed with heavy clouds. Her wipers set a lazy beat, and she turned on the dehumidifier to try to clear the fog from her windshield. Streetlamps cast a watery glow on the slick roads, but Annalisa knew the way home by heart.

"I just want you to know," Brewster said, "this asshole isn't going to win. Nick, he's going to pull through. You're going to be safe. This time, we nail his ass."

Annalisa thought of Grace Harper, dead on her floor, and Amy Yakamoto, who wouldn't be there to see her summer flowers bloom. "He's taken more than enough already," she said, striving to keep her tone neutral. She glanced in her rearview mirror to make sure they weren't being followed, but there was no one behind them. "You and Pops went after this guy hard," she said.

"Hard as they would let us." His tone was bitter, all these years later.

"It must have been frustrating to be kept on a leash."

"A case like this, you want to use everybody you can. George and I knew that neighborhood better than anyone. We knew the Duffys. Somehow, that knowledge was deemed a liability by the powers that be."

"You mean Don Harrigan."

He shifted in his seat. "Let me tell you something about Harrigan. He's a good cop, but he lives in Glencoe with his Richie Rich wife but uses some cousin's address to pretend like he's following regulations. You priced a house up in Glencoe lately? They start at a million bucks and go up from there. He doesn't live here, didn't know the people like we did. How's he supposed to find a guy who blends in like he belongs?"

"Maybe the outsider perspective gives him an edge," Annalisa countered lightly as she turned the wheel.

Brewster answered with a derisive snort. "Some edge. It's twenty years later and he still ain't got the guy."

"Why do you think he's resurfaced?" She genuinely wanted to know his answer. "He got away with it, like you said. Why come back now?"

Brewster shrugged. "Guess he got that old itch."

"Still. Twenty years."

He looked sideways at her. "You've been on the job awhile. You should know why he's back. It's got to be the same reason they all do it. They can't help themselves. Not just the crime. The talking about it afterward. Imagine you're this guy. You've pulled off some of the most heinous unsolved murders in history, and where's your glory? Who can you tell? No one."

"You're saying he wanted an audience again."

He looked out at the rain. "Wouldn't you?"

She sat with that for a moment as they drove in silence. "You and Pops, did you come up with any leads? Any angle on the case you thought Harrigan was missing?"

His posture stiffened. He gave her a curious look. "Nothing that panned out. Why do you ask?"

"I just wondered. I thought maybe you did your own review of the evidence." She paused. "Pops's name is on the logbook. He definitely took a look."

She'd kept her questions casual but he didn't buy her tone. His whole body tensed. "You've been studying the old logbook? What for?"

She decided to lay one of her cards on the table. "Some of the material from the Duffy case is missing."

"Oh, yeah? What's missing?"

She gave him a pointed look that said she wasn't about to answer. He made a face like he'd tasted something foul.

"I don't like what you're suggesting here, Annalisa."

"I'm not suggesting. I'm asking."

He went quiet, and she thought he was going to ignore her in perpetuity. Finally, he said, "You ever do something you're not proud of? Or that you wouldn't want getting out?" Her skin tightened all over, as if she'd been put to a flame. What was he going to confess? She wondered if she could reach her phone to record this, but decided any movement might scare him off.

"Of course you have," he continued, staring out the window. "I remember you as a kid, sneaking out at night to run around with the Duffy boy. About broke your mother's heart."

"I was a stupid kid," she replied. Headlights flared in the mirror, a car rushing up from behind. She held her breath as it passed her and disappeared down the road.

"Right," he said. "Stupid. We all do stupid stuff. The thing is, when you're dead, it all comes pouring out. The secret journal you kept about how you loved one of your kids more than the other. The office supplies you filched from your job. Maybe you had a lover or a hidden kid or you trashed your ex's place when he broke up with you. Whatever. All the secrets, suddenly they ain't secret anymore. Part of our job is to turn over all those rocks and see what crawls out because probably one of them is the reason you got killed."

"Sure. I see what you're saying."

He hesitated, seeming to choose his next words extra carefully. "It's not the same with this case. The killer is a stranger. He didn't know these women, so it didn't matter what their secrets were."

He couldn't possibly know that, but she didn't want to argue with him. "Who cares if they cheated on their taxes," she said. "Right?"

He visibly relaxed. "Right. There you go. It doesn't matter. It would only confuse the investigation and slow it down."

She drove without speaking as her mind raced to connect the dots. Secrets that would confuse the investigation. Pops messing around with evidence. "You and Pops knew Katie Duffy's secrets," she guessed. "You wanted to keep them from Harrigan and the others."

"You make it sound dirty. We were helping keep the focus where it belonged."

"What did you do?" she pressed.

He glared at her. "It ain't any of your business. Like I just got done telling you, these details don't matter."

"It's Pops's name on the book, and evidence has gone missing. Harrigan has already noticed, so if you want my help in talking him off the ledge, you'd better tell me everything right now."

"Aw, hell." He scowled at her and turned away to face the passenger-side window. She just waited him out in silence until he turned around again with a heavy sigh. "Your dad and Owen Duffy used to ride together. You know how it is with partners. The squad car is like a confessional—say whatever you want, and it goes no further. You get absolution, understanding." He appealed to her for the same. "Right?"

"Sure, yeah." She moved restless hands over the wheel. Get to the point.

He took a deep breath. "Duffy told George some stuff about his private life with Katie. Uh, bedroom stuff. I guess they liked to role-play and do other stuff that some folks might find . . . surprising."

She was going to make him say it. "Like what?"

"Like blindfolds, handcuffs. Silk scarves and that sort of thing." He looked at his lap.

"Ropes?" she guessed.

"I don't know. Maybe. George wasn't sure. But he was damn sure that Owen didn't kill Katie, and he didn't want anyone getting confused by what they found in the Duffy's bedroom closet."

"So he tampered with evidence." What about the red scarf? She wondered. Maybe the colorful scarves had been used other places than just for Katie's Halloween costume.

"It wasn't evidence," Brewster growled at her. "Haven't you heard a damn word I said? He was helping his buddy, his partner. You were sweet on the Duffy kid. Colin, right? How do think he'd have felt if it came out that his dead mother liked to get tied up and take it in the ass? He would've been disgusted, that's what. Ashamed. And for no good reason, since whatever the Duffys did in their bedroom had no bearing on this case."

She tightened her hold on the wheel and brought the car to a stop at a red light. He'd given her an image she wouldn't soon forget. She thought of her own bedside drawer at home and the goodies hidden inside. The thought of her fellow officers going through them made her skin crawl. It made sense to her that Pops would want to protect the Duffys from any lurid details during their vulnerable time after Katie's death. But outright tampering with evidence . . . she couldn't yet see her way clear to that.

"You understand, right?" Brewster was saying. "George was trying to help."

Annalisa didn't answer. She was looking down the side street to where a bright light illuminated a utility crew as they worked to repair lines after the recent storm. She'd seen dozens of crews around town in the past few days, she realized. They were everywhere. The white spotlight caught the mist and made it look like an electric cloud. STORMS. SEVERE WEATHER. Grace's tacked-up headlines came back to her in a rush. Annalisa jerked the car to the left, turning down the road toward the crew.

"Hey, you just ran that light." Brewster looked backward at the empty road.

"I want to see this." All the deaths had been preceded by a recent storm, Grace had noted. Annalisa glided to a halt by the crew and craned her neck to look up at the guy on the pole.

"What are we doing here?" Brewster asked, but she shushed him.

Her heart rate picked up as she got out of the car. No one ever noticed the killer, a stranger to these neighborhoods. It was like he belonged everywhere at once. Invisible.

"Can I help you?" the guy on the ground asked as Annalisa approached him.

She flashed her badge and introduced herself. "You guys doing the whole neighborhood?"

"Hey, yeah, usually we have one of Chicago's finest doing traffic duty for us, but I guess you guys are kind of all busy right now." He gestured at the dark, quiet street. "It's not like anyone's really out and about tonight anyway."

"You mind if I go up there?" She nodded to the man working the pole.

"Huh? What do you want to go up for?"

"I'm checking out a lead." He didn't seem moved by this, so she doubled down. "It's for the Lovelorn case."

"Oh. Oh, well, that's different. Frank!" He yelled up to his buddy. "This lady is a cop, and she wants to take a look up on the pole. Can you give her a hand?"

Brewster got out of the car to watch as the utility guys armed her with climbing gear and let her up on the pole. She felt her excitement rising as she gained height. This had to be it. She got to the top and looked around—right into the top floor of the neighboring houses. She saw a guy watching the news. A woman in a bra walking around her bedroom. She was up in the trees, an eye in the sky. The storms came in, and the crews came after to clear away the debris and make repairs. The cops, the tree trimmers, and the utility workers were everywhere after a major weather event. She turned first one way and then the other, marveling at how much she could see of other people's lives.

He must have felt like God.

CHAPTER THIRTY-THREE

....

YOU WANT TO EXPLAIN TO ME WHAT THAT STUNT BACK THERE WAS ALL ABOUT?"
BREWSTER ASKED HER AS SHE TURNED OFF THE MAIN ROAD AND ONTO HER
PARENTS' STREET. His street too, she remembered. Brewster lived just three
doors away from the Vegas.

"Not right now," she said. She parked the car in her parents' driveway
and sifted through her keys for the one that worked the house. Brewster
unbuckled his seat belt. "You can wait here," she informed him.

"Like hell. My orders are to keep you in sight."

"I'm just going inside. No one followed us here. You honestly think
he's hiding in my parents' bushes, just hoping I drop by?"

"I'm not chancing it," he replied as he opened his door. "You're going
in, then so am I."

She didn't want him trailing her up to the attic, but she acquiesced
to having him follow her into the house. They went in through the back
door, into the kitchen. The house sat dark and silent but smelled like
home, of cooking spices and old wood. She flicked on a light. "Wait
here," she said, indicating the large table.

He shrugged out of his coat and tugged at his collar. "Your folks have
a soda or cold bottle of water in there?" he asked, nodding at the refrigerator. "This place is like an oven."

The house had been locked up tight since Pops went into the hospital. The air was close and warm. Annalisa opened the fridge and handed

him a diet cola. "Enjoy." She heard him pop the top and settle his hefty frame into one of the wooden chairs as she went up to the second floor. She found the drop-down door to the attic and jumped to reach the string. The door opened with a noisy creak, and she pulled out the folding ladder. Heat emanated from the attic, hitting her like a brick wall. She pressed onward and hoisted herself into the dingy room. Using her cell phone as a flashlight, she located the single bulb overhead and switched it on. A nearby spider scuttled away and Annalisa buried a sneeze in her arm.

She found boxes upon boxes, most of them labeled in Ma's handwriting. *Vinny high school,* read one. *Mother's tea set,* read another. There were boxes of old books and family papers going back twenty years. At last she discovered the one she sought: a box marked *George's study.* She ripped off the tape and opened it, praying she didn't find a red scarf.

No scarf. Folders of papers from old investigations. She flipped through several before coming to one marked *Katie.* She held her breath as she sat back and prepared to dive in. The folder felt surprisingly thin in her hands, and when she opened it, she felt a stab of disappointment. There was a sketch of the crime scene, a tentative timeline, and some interview notes with neighbors, many of whom had been at the party. From the questions, Pops seemed fixated on when Katie had left, who had seen her leave, what they had talked to her about, if anything, and if they noticed anything else unusual about the party. She scanned the answers, but no one seemed to have any revelatory information. It matched what she had seen in the official files. There was also a small packet of developed photos.

She took them out and saw they were from the Halloween party, maybe even taken by Pops himself. There was Ma in her witch regalia. Brewster carving pumpkins with the butcher knife. Her heart skipped a beat when she found one of her and Colin. Colin grinned obligingly, but she glowered at the person behind the camera. Lame old Dad, interrupting the fun to snap photos. Her smile faded as she ran a finger over the old image. It would have been taken an hour or two at most before everything changed forever. She kept flipping through the photos and saw Tony dressed with a bunch of cut-out little chickens taped to his gray T-shirt. Chick magnet, she remembered. Alex was in there too, dressed in his pirate costume. It looked like an ordinary, fun party.

She set the photos aside and pawed through the rest of the box, but it held no further clues. She had the distinct feeling of chasing her tail, that there was a truth in all of this that she somehow had missed, but maybe she just wished it were true. She was Pops, revving up the engine on the Chevy to go in search of a killer she'd never find. She was in the process of putting the files back in the box when she heard a loud thump directly below her. She froze. Brewster was supposed to be at the kitchen table, and she hadn't heard his footsteps on the stairs. Silently, she rose and used her light footsteps to creep to the open hatch in the floor, where she listened intently for any noise below. After a moment, she heard someone move, heard a desk drawer open and close. She took out her weapon and began her descent from the attic.

As she climbed down, she heard Brewster in the kitchen, rooting through the fridge. It definitely wasn't him in Alex's old bedroom. Annalisa swallowed hard and inched along the hallway toward the closed door of Alex's room. As she got closer, the sounds got louder. Whoever it was, they were searching for something. Slowly, she reached for the knob. She braced herself and pushed the door open all at once. "Stop, police!"

She trained her gun at the man, who turned around from the closet.

"Holy shit, Anna. It's me!"

Alex took a stumbling step forward. He was drunk, she realized when she got a whiff of him. "What the hell are you doing here?" she asked, her heart still going like a runaway train.

"Looking for my old baseball mitt. I want Carla to have it. You know where it is?" He returned to the closet and resumed going through its contents.

Brewster materialized in the doorway. "I heard voices. What's going on?"

Annalisa waved weakly at Alex. "You remember my brother."

"Oh, hey, Mr. Brewster." He smelled like a distillery. She spied an open bottle of Jack Daniel's sitting on the bed.

"Alex, what's going on?"

"Nothing," he said obstinately. "I jus' told you I'm looking for my mitt."

"It's almost ten on a Tuesday night, and Carla's four years old. She doesn't need your Little League mitt right this very minute. Does Sassy know you're here?"

"Sassy," he repeated sadly. "She's gonna kill me."

"No, but she's probably worried about you."

He shook his head and went to the bed, where he took up the bottle again. "She's too good for me. Better off alone."

"Don't talk like that. She loves you. She's loved you since you were kids." She tried to smile as she approached him. "All my life, I've tried to find a relationship like Ma and Pops have, someone who'll be there for you, no matter what. You have that."

He looked at her with glassy eyes. "You don't know what the hell you're talking about."

"I know you should put down that bottle." She made to grab it from him but he held it back. "Alex . . ."

"What're you doing here? And what's he here for? Did Sassy send you to look for me?"

"I wanted to look at Dad's old papers."

She felt Brewster's eyes on her neck. Alex looked confused. "What kind of papers?"

"The Lovelorn case. You know it's back in the news." She didn't want to bother him with the specific threats against her at this precise moment. "Dad had some notes in the attic from back when he worked Katherine Duffy's murder."

Alex's mouth hung open for a moment. He wiped it with his bare arm. "Did you find them?"

"Yes. There's nothing of value. Come on, let's get you home."

She reached for him again, but he shook off her hand. "He was screwing her, you know."

She halted and drew back. "I'm sorry. What?"

"Pops. He was screwing Katie Duffy when she got killed."

"Why on earth would you say such a thing?"

"'Cause it's true." He uncapped the bottle and took another drink. "What'd you think we were yelling about the night of the party? I caught them together."

"I don't believe it." Her gut, though, knew immediately it was true. Ma's tears. Pops's fury. There had been something more beneath the surface in the weeks after Katie Duffy died. "Whatever you think you saw, you're wrong."

"You just don't want it to be true. Think for two seconds, you'll see I'm right."

Her brain dragged out an old memory from the summer before Katie died. Annalisa had been out with Colin at the movies, but then they had parked his car at Crescent Ridge and missed her midnight curfew by an hour. She'd taken off her sandals and crept barefoot over the grass to her back door, only to find Pops in the yard waiting for her. He'd lit into her like he'd been standing there in the dark all night to give her the tongue-lashing, and she'd been grounded for two miserable weeks. Only now did she remember the scent from that night, mixed in with the roses and lilies from Ma's garden: Pops's aftershave. Maybe he hadn't been waiting for her after all.

Alex pointed a wavering finger at her. "I know what I saw."

"I think we'd better get him home," Brewster said quietly, stepping up from behind her.

She whirled on him. "Is it true?" If Pops had told anyone, it would've been his partner.

He held her gaze for a long moment. "I don't know," he admitted at length. "I'd heard rumors that maybe she played around. I didn't know who with."

"She was pregnant," Alex said from the bed. He fell backward and looked at the ceiling. "Everything was going to hell."

Brewster moved to take Alex by the arm. "Let's go. You live around here, right?"

"About three blocks away," Annalisa supplied. "Forty-two Gardner Street." She hadn't seen his car out front. She hoped that meant he'd walked here, but Alex disabused her of that notion.

"My car. It's over there." He pointed west. "No, there." He turned around wildly and pointed east instead. "Sassy needs it to take Carla to school. I'm okay. I can drive it."

"No, you don't," Brewster said as Alex produced his keys from his jeans pocket. He took the keys away and pushed Alex toward the door. "We'll find your car and take it home together."

"Not me," Annalisa said quickly. She wanted to get another look in the attic. She needed to see those pictures again. "I'll be fine here."

Brewster narrowed his eyes at her. "You're supposed to stick with me."

"I'll be right here. We've established there's no one else in the place. It'll take ten minutes to run him home. I still need to close up everything upstairs. By the time you get back, I'll be ready to go."

"Ten minutes," he said. "You don't move from this house."

She crossed her heart. "Where would I go?"

He grunted and nudged Alex to the door. "Come on, buddy. Let's go play 'Where's my car?'"

When they left, Annalisa climbed back into the attic. She got out the photos and flipped through them until she found one she'd passed right over the first time. In the foreground, Tony posed with a friend, holding a jack-o'-lantern where the friend's head was. In the background, Katie Duffy was watching the camera with an intense look on her face. Pops had been behind the lens. Annalisa noted the odd framing, the way Tony and his buddy were off to the far-right side, not centered, as if the camera had been drifting in Katie's direction at the time of the shot.

Her cell phone rang in her jeans and she fished it out. The number was unrecognizable, but by now she knew what it meant. Her fingers, slippery from the heat in the attic, struggled to hold the phone. "Yes," she said, her eyes shut as she waited to hear his voice.

"Annalisa. You've been a busy girl."

The whispery voice sent a cold shiver down her spine, making her damp skin go clammy. "No busier than you. You were at my house."

"And you weren't there. Where were you, hmm? Out somewhere all night long, warming someone's bed? Was it that son of Katherine's? I know you had a thing for him once upon a time. Personally, I think you can do better."

"Like you?" She bit out the words, harsher than she intended. "You think somehow I'll want you after what you've done?"

He clucked at her. "I'm sorry about your neighbor. She seemed like a nice woman. It's too bad she had to pay for your mistakes."

"What mistakes?"

"You weren't home when I called. I was forced to go elsewhere."

"And Nick? What about him?"

"He was just in the way. Speaking of, I recognize your escort—that large fellow. I think I've met him before, one time when the police were investigating my early ladies."

Her heart skittered. She gripped the phone tight to her ear. This was new knowledge, a way to get him. The cops had interviewed him before. "You know Rod Brewster?"

"Oh, yes. We've met. I've met a lot of your friends. In fact, I'm meeting another one very soon now."

"What? Who?" He clicked off. "No!" She shouted into the phone and then shook it. She did what she'd been told not to do: she called him back. The phone rang and rang, but there was no answer. She cursed and climbed out of the attic, already on the phone again, this time to Zimmer. "We have a real problem," she said when the commander picked up. "He just called again, and he's got a new victim in his sights. He says he's meeting a friend of mine."

"Who?"

"He didn't say. He's also got a new phone, presumably another burner." Annalisa strode through the house and burst out the back door into the misty night. Where the hell was Brewster? "There's a guard on Nick, right? And someone at the hotel with Colin?"

"Nick Carelli is under guard, yes. There's no one at the hotel if you're not there."

"Then get someone over there—now!"

"I'm on it. Who else? Where else might he go?"

"I don't know. I can't think." She walked in circles in the yard, tearing at her hair with her free hand. Sassy, her brothers. He could be anywhere.

"I'll get a team in motion. Then I'll call you back."

Annalisa clicked off and jogged to the end of the driveway and peered down the dark street in the direction Brewster would be walking back from Alex's place. She had her car keys. She could just leave him here. But go where? The hotel seemed like the best option, as he'd mentioned Colin on the phone. Wait. She froze and looked at the phone in her hand. *I recognize your escort.* Brewster had only been with her for a few hours.

Annalisa called Sassy. Voicemail picked up, so she dialed her again. This time, Sassy answered, sounding tired. "Hey," she said. "This isn't a great time."

"Alex got home?"

"Yeah, he's passed out in our bed. Thanks for sending him back."

"What about Brewster? The guy who dropped him off?"

"He left. Maybe five minutes ago."

Annalisa strained to see down the block. The trees blocked out the streetlamps, limiting her visibility. "Okay, thanks." She thought maybe she could see him now at the end of the street, and she bounced on her heels, eager to make progress. Yes, it was him. A large shadowy figure headed her way.

A sharp gunshot split the night, like lightning from the sky. The figure disappeared.

Annalisa began to run.

CHAPTER THIRTY-FOUR

....

ANNALISA RACED IN THE DIRECTION OF THE GUNSHOT. The mist had co-alesced to outright rain, and it slashed at her face as she ran down the empty sidewalk. Trees quivered around her from the wind. Her sneakers hit the wet pavement in rhythm with her pounding heart. She slowed as a body came into view on the sidewalk up ahead. The pale blue shirt matched the one Brewster had been wearing when she saw him last. She drew her weapon and approached with caution, hiding herself behind a large oak tree. She could still smell the gunpowder in the air.

"Brewster?" She called loudly from where she was sequestered. No reply.

She eyed the surrounding yards, which were cloaked in shadow. Rain poured down through the trees. It dripped from her nose, from her eyelashes. The gunman could be hiding behind any nearby fence or tree, and she would be an open target if she approached the victim. *Screw it*, she thought, and went to kneel by her fallen comrade.

"Brewster, it's Annalisa. Can you hear me?" Blood seeped out from a wound in his back. She felt for a pulse in his neck and her hand came away red. "Hold on, okay?" she told him, fumbling for her phone. "I'm going to get you some help. Just hold on."

Like magic, the nearest house turned its porch light on. A man in a UIC sweatshirt stepped out onto the porch. "Everything okay?" he called out.

"No," she hollered back. "This man's been shot. He's a police officer. Call 911!"

He ran back into the house as Annalisa tried again for a pulse. She couldn't tell if she was feeling his heartbeat or hers. She knelt there with him in terrible silence, waiting for the sirens, but the only sound was the rain battering the trees. Her wet clothes stuck to her skin. Her hair plastered to her face. For once, she didn't mind the water because it covered up her tears.

The man came back with a blanket and an umbrella. "I don't know if this will help. The ambulance is on its way."

She covered up Brewster. "Did you see anyone out here on the street?"

He shook his head. "I was watching TV when I heard the shot. Scared the bejesus out of me."

Finally, approaching sirens wailed in the distance. The ambulance arrived first, followed by two squad cars. Annalisa watched long enough to see that the EMTs had control of the scene, and then she took off running again. She went down the middle of the street, her head spinning in all directions as she searched for any sign of the shooter. Every tremble of the trees, every rustle from the bushes made her heart jump. "I know you're here!" She shouted into the rain. "You want me so bad, why don't you come out and get me?"

She went through people's backyards, smacking at the bushes with her gun. She ran through side streets and alleys and a little park where the empty swings swayed alone in the wind. She ran until her lungs burned, until her shoes squished and the water ran a river down her back. "You're such a coward!" She halted and yelled at the sky. "You shoot a man in the back and run away with your tail between your legs! Who's the frightened one now? Huh?"

Blue lights rippled in the puddles at her feet. She turned and saw a squad car slowing to a stop behind her. Zimmer got out from the passenger side. "Vega! What the hell do you think you're doing?"

"I'm the one he wants. Let him come out and get me!"

Zimmer came around the car and grabbed Annalisa's weapon from her. "Stop it. This isn't the way to solve anything."

Annalisa's nostrils flared with her anger and adrenaline. "He's here.

He's got to be." She raised her voice and shouted again. "Who wouldn't want to see this show?"

"We'll look for him. You're coming with me." Zimmer strong-armed Annalisa into the back of the car and then climbed in after her. "Back to base," she ordered their driver as she looked Annalisa over with a critical eye. "That was really stupid. I could have two cops with a bullet in the back instead of just one."

Annalisa wiped at her face in vain. There was no part of her that wasn't soaked. "How is Brewster?"

"I don't know. They've taken him to the hospital."

Annalisa shook her head and looked out the window. "If he dies because of me . . ."

"It's not you that shot him."

"I asked for him to be there!"

"And if it wasn't him, it'd be someone else. Brewster knew the risks when he signed up, just like the rest of us. But we can't lose focus. We need to find this guy and stop him before anyone else gets hurt."

"Did you send a team to the hotel?"

"Yes, and we'll take you there later. I think, under the circumstances, the smartest move is for you and Mr. Duffy to switch to another room under an assumed name. We can keep a second team in place on the old room in case this guy makes a play for it."

Annalisa rubbed her head. "He said he knows my friends," she murmured. "We can't possibly protect them all."

"Let's start with just you."

Annalisa closed her eyes and leaned her head back against the leather seat. "He said he'd met Brewster. He's been interviewed at some point in the past, possibly during the original investigation."

"Good, that's something we can use."

Annalisa sat forward, remembering her earlier insight. "There's something else." She described Grace Harper's clue about the storm and what she saw from climbing the utility poles. "He may have worked for the power company at one point, or the department of public works. Any service involved in cleanup after a major storm."

"We'll get on it. Meanwhile, you'll sit your ass down in a chair for a full debriefing. Then you're in protective custody at the hotel for the near future. No more work on this case."

"Commander—"

Zimmer held up her hand. "It's not your fault this guy has fixated on you, but it's plain to see he has. I'm not going to let you make a target of yourself and those around you. You'll stay out of sight until we nail this guy."

Annalisa's dark mood couldn't resist a jab. "So far, that's twenty-five years and counting. Am I supposed to stay locked up forever?"

Zimmer's brows lowered, displaying her lack of amusement. "Let's try it for at least one night and then go from there."

It was past one in the morning before they finished with her, the FBI and Chicago PD taking turns grilling her for information, going over the latest phone call word by word. They took down his new number and would obviously try to trace it, but it was clear by now that he had a variety of disposable phones. Annalisa drank burned coffee and sat through the interrogation in wet underwear, replying to all the questions but providing no useful answers. Before they sent her off with a fresh police escort, she had a question of her own: "How's Brewster doing?"

The FBI guy, Stanton, averted his gaze. Harrigan cleared his throat and gave a gruff reply. "He, uh, he didn't make it."

Annalisa went cold inside at the news. She said nothing on the drive to the hotel and let the armed escort show her to Colin's new room. Despite the late hour, he was up and dressed with the lights still on. "Oh, thank God," he said, taking her in his arms as she came through the door. Over his shoulder, she saw he'd moved her bag along with his. She felt his strong arms, his fingers in her riotous hair that frizzed out in all directions from the rain, but the embrace did nothing to warm her. She extricated herself and pulled away. "They won't tell me what happened," he said. "Just that we had to move rooms."

"He's been watching me," she said as she lowered herself to sit on the end of the bed. "He knows who you are."

Colin blinked rapidly, looking frozen now himself. He moved stiffly to sit next to her on the bed. "I guess I've always figured that he did—know my name, that is. He had to have read the news stories after Mom's murder."

She rubbed her face with both hands. "You should probably go," she said behind her fingers. "They can give you an escort to the airport, and then you can be out of here."

"No." He tugged her hand away from her face and held it in his lap. "I'm not leaving you alone with this."

"I'm off the case. We're trapped here until they catch him."

She saw his jaw tighten. He knew the abysmal math on this case as much as anyone did. "I got you something earlier today," he said, dropping her hand and rising from the bed. He went to the desk and picked up a piece of paper. "It's a passport application."

He gave it to her and she looked it over without really seeing it. "Thanks," she said as she tried to set it aside. He pushed it back into her hand and rejoined her on the bed.

"I know it seems impossible now. But this whole mess will have to end sometime."

"Your optimism is . . . well, it's a nice try, but—"

"After my mom died, I felt like I'd been gutted. I felt like I had an open wound that would not stop bleeding. I couldn't even look at normal people anymore. They went to school and work and cooked dinner in their normal kitchens. My kitchen went silent. Dad didn't turn on the stove or put food in the refrigerator. We ate the food that the neighborhood ladies brought over after the funeral, and when that ran out, we had frozen pizzas. Then Dad died too, and I figured that was it for me. I started thinking up ways to join them."

She looked at him with horror. "Colin . . ."

"I'm not after your pity. I'm just telling you how it was. I went from being a regular college-bound kid in a nice family to being an orphan in the space of a couple of months. I didn't have the vocabulary to exist in this new world, so I went to a new one. At the time, it felt like the only way to survive."

Her gaze fell to the floor. "I get it. You can't stay here."

He took her hand again and squeezed it. "That's not what I'm trying to say now," he said, his voice low and urgent. "I'm saying it did eventually get better. I couldn't see it back then but it did happen. I went on. I learned to cook some of my mother's food, and then I went out into the world and ate foods she'd never dreamed of. I made good friends and danced at their weddings. I heard the whisper of the sun when it hits the Pacific Ocean at night. I can say this with certainty because I've felt stuck and hopeless before: this room is not a prison and you don't have a life sentence here."

"Okay." She looked down at the application on her lap. "I'll fill it out."

"Good." He squeezed her again. "Now what do you say we get some sleep?"

She let him convince her to change into sleep clothes, brush her teeth, and crawl beneath the covers. When the lights went out, all she heard was the gunshot. She screwed her eyes shut, tense beneath the crisp white sheets. Colin slid across to her. Only when he reached for her, when he murmured in her hair, "Of everyone I left behind, you're the one I missed the most," did she remember what Alex had said about their parents' extramarital affair.

"Don't," she said, dodging when he moved to kiss her.

His face hovered over hers in the darkness. "What is it?"

She swallowed the lump her throat. His mother had been gone for twenty years. Was Annalisa really supposed to dig her back up now and run her memory through the shredder? Maybe Brewster was right—some details belonged only to the dead. She stroked his prickly cheek and he leaned into her touch. "I just don't want to lose you again," she said, her voice breaking.

He wrapped her in his arms. "You don't lose me," he replied. "You can't."

She closed her eyes and held on tight, but she wasn't sure she believed him. Somehow, she managed to remain still long enough for her body to unclench and find its way to sleep. She awoke hours later with a gasp, like rising from underwater. Colin slid his palm across her stomach. "Easy," he said. "We're safe here."

She patted him rather than open her mouth and disabuse him of his innocent trust in the guards in the hall. The Lovelorn Killer had proved already that he could take down any obstacle in his path. It was sweet, really, the way Zimmer was determined to protect her, but Annalisa knew eventually he'd come for her again. She went through the day on autopilot, responding to Colin when he spoke but otherwise spending time alone with her thoughts. Brewster had met the killer at one point; maybe Harrigan had too, if the guy had the guts to step into headquarters. Had she seen him? Spoken to him face-to-face? The voice on the phone felt familiar, but perhaps that was because she'd talked to him multiple times now.

They ordered sandwiches for lunch and sat through a rom-com on pay-per-view. At Colin's urging, she filled out the passport application. Here was one solution in front of her. If she stayed alive long enough to get the passport, she could leave like Colin and not look back. But that meant leaving Ma alone with Pops. Leaving Sassy with Alex, who was now apparently well off the wagon. She wouldn't see her nieces or nephews grow up. They would be family in name only. Still, she felt the pull of it when Colin showed her more of his photos from his laptop— arches of the Roman ruins, the vivid gold of the African plains, the cobalt blue of the Mediterranean Sea. She stared at the watery landscape until it blurred her vision, until she felt she could disappear within it.

She called Ma for an update on Pops. "He's doing good," her mother said, sounding more chipper than she had in days. "They're going to move him to rehab tomorrow, and then he'll be able to come home."

The news on Nick wasn't as rosy. He'd developed a blood clot that traveled to his lungs and required a second surgery. It was once again touch-and-go. She curled into a ball at the news, fetal on the bed. She remembered what he'd said about death being all around, just waiting for an opportunity. Not everyone gets to run the full race. "Not Nick," she muttered. "You don't get Nick."

Only when Colin answered from the other side of the bed did she realize she'd spoken out loud. "You still care about him a lot," he observed.

She sat up and looked at him. "I certainly don't want him to die," she replied, a hint of accusation in her voice.

Colin held up his palms. "Nor do I. I just mean . . . I don't know. Most people I know who are divorced aren't that friendly with their exes. Especially when one of them cheated."

He didn't understand her forgiveness. She saw that now. "I wanted him to be you," she said, holding his gaze. "I can't blame him if he failed." If he was forgiven, then maybe she could be too.

They splurged for dinner—salmon for him, herb-roasted chicken with red bliss potatoes for her—but the starched napkins and fancy silverware did nothing for the growing sense of claustrophobia. Colin checked the windows about a dozen times, pulling back the curtain and looking at the street below. The scenery never changed, so she didn't bother to look. By nine, it was dark and there was nothing to see. The TV played on mute. Annalisa texted Sassy to see how Alex was doing while Colin paced the room. "I think I'm going to take a shower," he announced.

"Knock yourself out." They'd been cooped up for less than twenty-four hours, and already she felt like her brain was on fire. She welcomed the sound of a door closing between them. She relaxed as the shower came on. *Looking into an intensive counseling program,* Sassy texted back. *He may have to take a leave of absence.*

Before Annalisa could answer, her other phone buzzed. She grabbed for it, dreading the news, whatever it was. She did not recognize the number. Maybe it was Zimmer with an update on Nick. Maybe it was him. "Vega," she said into the phone.

Him. "I watched the news for hours, flipping through the channels. I didn't see you once. Annalisa, did they take you off the case?"

She wasn't terrified this time, only angry. "You know very well why they did. You stabbed one cop and shot another. You've signed your own death warrant. Even if you live like a monk from here on out, they'll never stop hunting you."

"How flattering," he replied. "To be so wanted. It's such a pity they took you out of the game."

"They didn't," she said. "You did. Your threats and actions put me here."

"Here? Where's here? The same hotel, perhaps? Or maybe they moved you to a different one."

She didn't answer. He chuckled.

"Hidden you away, have they? How . . . quaint."

"Go down to any police station and ask for me by name. I guarantee you'll get a quick response."

"Why should I? I've got your full attention now."

She wanted to scream but she kept her voice even. "What do you want?" she said, biting out each word.

"Oh, it's not what I want. I have someone else here who wants to say hello to you."

Her throat seized up. *Ma*, she thought. *Pops*. But it was Jared Barnes's voice that came on the line, thin and frightened. "Detective Vega?"

"Barnes. Where are you?"

"He grabbed me outside my place and shoved me in a van. I don't know where we are, but it's very dark. He has a gun. He wants you to come get me but I don't think you should—"

She heard the phone grabbed away. The raspy voice was back. "You can come find us, Annalisa, or you can have another body on your hands. I'll go through as many as it takes to get to you. The FBI can't protect them all."

"Okay, I'll come. Where?"

He barked a laugh. "Like I would seriously be that stupid. No. You get on I-57 and drive south until you get to Paxton. There's an old gas station off the exit with a pay phone where you can wait for my call. Be there by midnight or the ropes start tightening. Call in the cavalry and he's dead immediately. And I will know if you call them."

She heard a whimper in the background. The drive alone would take two hours at top speed, and she still had the pit bulls waiting for her outside in the hallway. She weighed her scant options. She could bluff him and call Zimmer to scramble the FBI, which might work, but also had a high probability of killing Barnes in the process. Or she could try to slip her guard detail and go it alone. Suicide, maybe. But nothing else had worked, and she didn't trust that her distress call to Zimmer would remain confidential. The guy always seemed to be one step ahead of them.

"Annalisa? We're waiting."

"Midnight," she repeated as she holstered her weapon. "I'll be there." One way or another, she was finally going to see his face.

CHAPTER THIRTY-FIVE

....

S HE SCRIBBLED A NOTE TO COLIN: *HAD TO GET OUT AND BREATHE FOR A MINUTE. WENT TO THE BAR TO HAVE A DRINK AND WILL BE BACK SOON.* She hesitated just a beat before adding *Love, A.* The uniformed cop she found waiting for her in the hall was a baby-faced guy with a tight, faded Afro and a thin mustache. He sat in a chair by the elevator and stood up at the sight of her. "Is there a problem, ma'am?"

"No problem. I'm just going to go downstairs for a drink."

"Ma'am?"

"At the bar. One beer. Right downstairs in this hotel."

He looked uncomfortable. "I don't think that's a very good idea. You and Mr. Duffy are supposed to stay in the room. I can arrange to have a beer brought up to you."

"I don't want a beer brought up to me. I want to go have it at the bar. I'm not staging a rebellion here . . . what's your name?"

"Derek Sylvestry, ma'am."

"Sylvestry, I just want to stretch my legs. Get a change of scenery. Surely you get that."

"Yes, ma'am," he replied with the enthusiasm of a man who had been watching the hotel's pale green walls for the past few hours. "But it's not safe, is the thing. We haven't cleared the bar."

"So clear it." She put her hands on her hips. He looked pained.

"Ma'am—"

"Quit calling me ma'am. It's Detective Vega to you."

"Yes, ma'am. Detective. I'm just following orders from the commander here."

"And what are those orders? That I'm a prisoner in that room for as long as she says so?" She reached around him to hit the call button on the elevator.

"No, nothing like that. It's just—"

"Just what?"

"I'm not supposed to leave this spot."

"Who's asking you to?"

He took a deep breath. "Let me call downstairs, okay? Kwan is in the lobby."

"Great, tell him I'm on my way." The doors slid open and she ducked inside before Sylvestry could register further complaint. Her heart hammered in her chest, and she looked at her phone. It read 9:16. When the doors dinged open, she was met by a frowning man about her age. He wore plain clothes, blue jeans, and a windbreaker that she knew obscured the gun at his back. "You must be Kwan," she said, striding purposefully across the lobby toward the bar.

"Detective Vega, please understand, we're trying to keep you safe."

She didn't slow down. "I understand. And I need you to understand that if I stay locked up in that room another minute, I will eat my gun and then you won't have to worry about it. You feel me?"

"I hear you," he replied, dismayed. "But it's just me down here. Sylvestry has to stay with your— With Mr. Duffy upstairs. I'm supposed to be keeping a watch on the front door."

They reached the bar and she looked around for the best-positioned stool. "What are you watching for, exactly?" They had no idea what the killer looked like.

"Anything suspicious."

"Great. Right now, you can watch me drink a beer. But not too close, okay? You'll ruin my vibe."

His frown deepened. "I don't like this. Anyone could come in here."

She turned and met his eyes, stared hard at him for a long moment. "Kwan. You know why you're on duty here tonight, yeah?"

"Yes. The Lovelorn Killer has made direct threats against you."

"He's said he's coming for me, and I gotta tell you, based on my day so far, I think he means it. You want to catch him? Sit there and watch my back. It's far more likely to pay off than watching the bellhops run around the lobby." She stalked across the bar to take a seat close to the restrooms. Kwan took a seat at the other end of the bar and kept her directly in his sight line. She ordered a beer from the female bartender, an older woman with a dark ponytail, Italian-looking, who could have been her sister from another mister. Kwan had a seltzer with lemon.

She felt his eyes on her as she sipped her beer. She pretended to be interested in the basketball game playing on the TV, but inwardly, her racing heart beat out the precious passing seconds. There was a red-lit EXIT sign back by the restrooms, but she knew Kwan would follow her back there if she just got up and tried it. The bartender sauntered over. "How you doing, honey? Need anything else?"

Annalisa played the only card she could summon. "There's a guy at the other end of the bar."

The woman didn't have to turn around to look. Her lips jerked up in a smile. "The one who won't take his eyes off you? Yeah, I saw him. You want an introduction or what?"

"No, he's my ex. He followed me in here."

The bartender grew concerned. "He's dangerous?"

"No, I don't think so. Just persistent. I broke up with him last week and he's not taking the hint."

"You want me to call the cops?" The bartender reached in her pocket for her cell phone.

"No, no. I was hoping you could maybe talk to him, create a diversion. I'll just slip out the back when he's not looking." Annalisa surreptitiously slid a twenty toward her. "Would you help me?"

The bartender eyed the money and waved it off. "Keep it. I got two ex-husbands who won't mind their own damn business. Just leave him to me."

Annalisa had to give it to her—the woman played it cool, talking first to a pair of young men in ball caps, giving one a second beer. Then she headed casually in Kwan's direction. Annalisa held her breath, waiting for the slightest opportunity. Kwan could easily see around the woman, as she wasn't that big. Suddenly, she cried out and went down, disappearing under the bar. "Ah, my ankle! Jesus, who left this trash can down here?"

Kwan came around the bar to help her, and Annalisa slapped her money on the bar and disappeared out the back. She retrieved her car and gunned it out of the garage into the night, heading south as fast as she dared. She had mere minutes before Kwan and Sylvestry discovered she'd flown the coop and called in the authorities. She needed to put enough distance between them that they couldn't easily follow. She switched off her cell phones and left them sitting on the passenger seat.

With the late hour, traffic was light and she barreled toward the highway, cutting around the intermittent cars like she was in a teenage boy's video game. She escaped the city, its skyscrapers becoming smaller in her rearview mirror. As she drove farther, the exits came spaced farther apart, and the terrain became more rural. Her surroundings grew darker. She kept one eye on the mirrors for any signs of blue lights on her tail, but none appeared. She drove it like she stole it, her tires practically levitating from the asphalt, until she found the exit and the gas station with three minutes to spare. The place was small and quiet—just a tiny convenience store that was closed up tight and only four pumps. She pulled around to the side and located the lone pay phone by the air pump. It had ugly weeds to the left and a crude bit of graffiti sprayed on the side. Annalisa waited in her car until the phone began to ring.

The loud trill jangled her taut nerves, and she jerked the receiver from the hook. She didn't say anything, so he spoke first. "I knew you would make it. You want me as much as I want you."

"I want your head on my wall."

He laughed. "All in good time. First, I have to make sure you're not wearing a wire."

"I'm not."

"You wouldn't lie to me, I'm sure. All the same, I'd like to see for myself. Lift up that blue T-shirt you have on and let's take a look."

Her skin broke out in a hot prickle as she realized he could see her. She whirled around but the place appeared deserted. There was a chain-link fence bounding the parking lot behind her, and trees on the other side of it from which frogs and bugs sang a buzzing, chirping night song.

"That's right," he said with satisfaction as she scrutinized the branches. "I can see you. Look up under the overhang."

She did as he asked and saw the eye of a tiny camera nestled by the roof.

"Wave hello," he told her. She scowled instead. "Now to business," he continued. "Show me what you've got."

She hesitated before lifting up her shirt to show him she had no wire. "Happy now?"

"I will be when I see the other side."

She turned around and showed him her back.

"Excellent," he said. "We can go on now."

"No, I want to speak to Barnes."

"That isn't possible."

She tightened her hold on the phone, her breathing unsteady. "Then I'm getting back in my car and going home." Proof of life or she wasn't going to play this game.

She heard some footsteps, the sound of tape tearing, and then a soft moan. "Say hello," the voice ordered.

"Hello," Barnes repeated weakly.

"Barnes. Are you hurt? What's happening?"

The kidnapper took over again. "You can ask him when you get here."

"Where is 'here'?"

"Bellmore Hospital. Do you know it?"

"Bullshit. That place has been closed for years." Bellmore Hospital for the Incurably Insane had housed patients until the early 1970s, at which point the grounds had been shuttered for good. Now it only showed up in headlines around Halloween when journalists needed a good spook story.

"I've found a way in. If you want to see Barnes alive again, then you'll do the same."

"Tell me how to get there," she said, and he gave her a few directions, indicating a road to the north.

"Remember," he said, "I can see for miles. I have other cameras. If you aren't alone, then our little friend here gets a knife to the ribs. I have an escape hatch, Annalisa, but Barnes does not." She gritted her teeth but said nothing. He took her silence for agreement. She could almost hear his smile when he signed off. "See you soon."

She got back in her car and turned on her personal cell to use the GPS. The small town was pitch-dark once you got past the few buildings on the main roads, and she didn't trust that any of the turns would be marked. There was a text message from Colin: *Went to the bar but you're not here. Police are looking for you. Where are you??* She did not answer.

She eased back out onto the road and tried to think through a plan. The Lovelorn Killer was practically a one-man executioner. They knew he had a knife, a gun, and of course, a varied collection of ropes. *All he needs is the candlestick in the conservatory to round out his collection,* she thought darkly.

He had tried to get to her twice but kept running into her protection detail, so he'd devised a different plan: lure her to him. He didn't want anything to do with Barnes. Barnes was just bait. She could hear Nick's admonition in her head, crying out that she was giving the Lovelorn killer exactly what he wanted, but she didn't see another option. Multiple law enforcement agencies had tried valiantly to pin this guy down for decades now, and he was volunteering to meet with her. He had a hostage and had already made clear he'd dispense with interference quickly if he didn't get his way. She didn't believe he'd just shoot her in the back like Brewster or shiv her in the ribs like Nick. He'd had those ropes laid out for her, and she bet her life that he still intended to use them. The fantasy wouldn't be fulfilled any other way. This meant he would have to come in close.

The road grew dark, then darker still as she left the main drag and turned down the deserted access road to the old psychiatric asylum. Tall weeds and young trees blocked her line of vision on either side while her headlights illuminated the gravel road in front of her. The *ping, ping* of the tiny stones against her car rapped out a warning and gave away any hope she had of approaching quietly. The hulking shadow of the abandoned hospital came into sight ahead of her, and she stopped her car outside the main entrance. It was a massive brick building, bigger than a castle and Gothic in appearance with its many arches and peaks.

It stood six stories high with a square tower in the center and multiple gabled peaks on each side. The iron spikes on the roof glinted in the moonlight.

Annalisa left her headlights on, their beams slicing through the darkness and providing a detailed look at the bright-red brick and the contrasting ivy climbing up the side of the hospital. The ground was muddy under her feet from all the recent rain. She took her flashlight in one hand and her gun in the other as she searched for a way in. All the windows and doors had been boarded up for years. She inspected a few doors at the front of the building, but none of them seemed accessible. Reluctantly, she abandoned the light from her car and went around to the side of the hospital. The weeds were knee-high and filled with night critters. She pressed onward past one door and then another. The third one had a board loose. She pulled it aside and squeezed in, keeping her back close to the wall and her gun at the ready.

She halted immediately for a look around. Part of her doubted her own logic and wondered if he could be waiting to shoot her dead between the eyes. She paired the gun with the flashlight, pointing them first in one direction down the hallway and then the other. She saw only peeling paint, fallen ceiling tiles, and abandoned and rusting medical equipment not valuable enough to sell. The hallway was pitch-dark except for her flashlight, with all outside illumination having been blocked by the boards. She listened and heard nothing but her own breathing. Cautiously, she stepped deeper into the building.

She passed the remains of an office, with a rotting desk and overturned file cabinets. A hand-lettered sign on the wall displayed the visiting hours. She searched over the rubble with her flashlight beam and gasped when she saw a skull looking back at her. Animal, she told her pounding heart as she flickered the light over the other nearby bones. A cat or dog. A coyote that came here to die. Or died trapped in here. Cobwebs on the wall tangled in her hair, and she fought the urge to scrape them off.

She crept farther down the hallway, passing other signs of long-ago life. Lumpy couches pointed at a boxy TV with its screen shattered. Multiple twin-size beds with rusted springs. A dentist's chair made gooseflesh rise up on her skin. She saw no trace of Barnes or anyone else. The hospital looked like no one had been inside for years.

She reached an intersection in the hall, hesitated, and then turned left, going deeper into the belly of the beast. She passed what looked like a broken-down laboratory, with shattered glassware and a rusted sink. Exam rooms. She heard water dripping from someplace above her and cold drops splashed down onto her cheek. She made another few turns and marveled at how the place kept going. The hallway smelled like animal feces, decaying leaves, and rust. She was no longer sure how to find the exit.

A creaking noise from far ahead made her stop short and listen. She waited but heard only the skittering of rodent feet above her head. Swallowing hard, she advanced in the direction she'd heard the noise. It came from beyond the double doors at the end of the hall. She trained her flashlight and gun at them as she grew closer. At the threshold, she paused to listen. She heard the creak again, almost like a porch swing in the summer, and she pushed through one of the doors.

She found herself in a large room, a gymnasium or auditorium, with a dilapidated wooden stage at one end and a circle of perhaps twenty chairs at the other, like a group therapy session for ghosts was just about to begin. Hanging upside down over the circle, bound and gagged, was Barnes.

CHAPTER THIRTY-SIX

....

S HE DID A CURSORY CHECK OF THE ROOM WITH HER FLASHLIGHT BUT SAW NO OTHER PERSON NEARBY. Picking her way around the folded chairs on the floor, she went to where Barnes had been strung up from a wooden rafter with ropes and a metal hook. "Barnes," she said in a loud whisper. "It's Annalisa Vega. Are you okay?"

His eyelids fluttered open, and she saw his pupils were huge and dark, unfocused. She dragged one of the chairs over and stood on it next to him. She had to temporarily holster her gun and put aside the flashlight to fish out the army knife she carried in her pocket. She used it to cut through the rope hanging Barnes, at which point he crashed to the floor. Quickly swapping the knife for the gun again, she knelt next to him as he began to stir. She pulled the tape from his mouth and felt his breath on her hand. "Wake up," she urged, keeping one eye on the double doors as she tugged loose the rest of his binding. "We've got to get out of here."

"Detective Vega." He gave her a weak smile. "You came."

"We're getting out of here," she said with grim determination.

"I can't. I don't have my chair. You go."

"I'm not leaving you." She shifted so he could grab hold of her shoulders. "Get up. Quick."

He looped his arms around her neck and she used all of her strength to pull herself and his deadweight up from the floor. "You're a hero," he murmured from behind her.

"Not unless we make it." She started for the door. "Do you know where he is?"

"I heard him upstairs a while ago. Then I passed out."

A fierce wind came through the towers, making the building shudder. Annalisa halted to listen at the double doors. He could be hiding anywhere, ready to ambush them. She pushed through the doors and cast the flashlight beam on ahead of them. Debris littered the floor. The doorways provided ample places to lie in wait, if he should choose. She pressed onward gingerly, trying to retrace the path she'd taken to find Barnes. Barnes lay heavy on her back, his breathing unsteady. "Can you find the exit?" he asked.

"I think it's this way," she whispered to him, but she wasn't sure. Had she passed the green-tiled bathroom with the broken toilet?

"It feels so far."

"We're going to make it." She picked her way through the fallen tiles and the piles of rotting paper. Periodically, she had to pause to adjust her weight so Barnes didn't slide off.

"You're very strong," he said admiringly. "But also light on your feet. Like a cat."

"Mmm," she replied, trying to concentrate on the next turn. She didn't know whether to go right or left. *Light on your feet like a cat.* His words penetrated her fog and gave her a chilled, eerie feeling. She remembered them from the killer's letter, the one to her that had not been made public yet. She halted, breathing hard, and the flashlight beam slipped down, catching his feet at her sides and pooling on the floor in front of them. "What did you just say?"

"You're strong," he repeated. "Stronger than you look."

She glanced at his sneakers. The sides had the same mud on them that hers did, from the muck outside. The tips were worn smooth from use. *Shoes,* Nick had said. She recalled him in Barnes's apartment, dropping an old worn-out pair of sneakers to the floor of the closet. A man who couldn't walk would not wear out his shoes. Horror shot through her as she realized she wasn't looking for the killer; she was carrying him on her back.

He must have felt the tension in her spine. "Are we not getting out of here?"

"Just—a minute. I need a rest." She would set him down and go for the gun at her back. Just as she prepared to let go, his hold tightened around her neck.

"Ah," he said, his voice tinged with regret. "The game is over, then." His voice turned into a familiar rasp as she started to choke. "I knew you would come."

The pressure on her windpipe took her breath away, and her head started to swim. She'd be unconscious in seconds if she didn't get him off of her. She crouched lower and used his unbalanced weight to flip him over her head. He dragged her with him and they landed with a painful crash on the floor. Her flashlight skittered away down the hall and hit the wall with a *thunk,* winking out as it did so and plunging them into total darkness. His hold on her loosened enough for her to wrest free. She kicked at him with her feet as he tried to grab her again and connected with his ribs. Frantically, she scrambled away and reached around for her gun.

He got up and ran. She fired several shots in the direction of his footsteps. The flash illuminated his retreating figure, but she missed hitting him. He disappeared down one of the hallways and out of sight. Annalisa rose shakily to her feet and patted her pockets. He'd lifted her car keys and her cell phone. She felt around until she found the flashlight, which turned on again when she twisted it back together. She shone it all around, looking for an exit. She tried kicking at the nearest door, but it was locked and of course nailed shut with boards from the other side.

Cautiously, she moved against the wall, her ears cocked for any sound from Barnes. He had ropes and other weapons hidden somewhere. He'd bragged of an escape hatch, and at that moment, she prayed he took it. Now he had a name and face, so he wouldn't get far if she got the chance to report him. If. She turned the corner and found a staircase. She heard shuffling farther down the hall in the direction she'd been headed and decided the stairs looked like a better option. The higher-level windows were not all boarded, she recalled, and some of them connected with fire escapes. He would not be looking for her up there.

She turned with her shoulder against the wall and crept up the stairs.

Paint chips fell like rain around her. The gun was sweaty in her hand. *Just find an exit,* she told herself. *Find an exit and get the hell out of here.* The asylum sat just three-quarters of a mile from the main road; she could reach it easily on foot if she could just get out of the building. She went up to the top floor to put as much distance between herself and Barnes as possible. The stifling heat had collected at the top, but the few un-boarded windows provided slanting moonlight to the hall. She passed bird skeletons, empty bedrooms with wire frames left for beds. Ghosts of humans past hung on the walls in magazine clippings and personal photographs. She tried several of the windows but couldn't make them budge. Peering out, she saw no sign of a fire escape from this vantage point, so she continued down a different hall.

She didn't hear him coming. She heard only the gunshot as the bullet blew by her. She ducked into the nearest doorway and returned fire twice. Heart pounding, she listened for his footsteps. Nothing. She turned off her flashlight and ran down the hall toward a room that had a comparatively large amount of moonlight spilling out of it. Lots of light meant a large window.

She turned the corner into the room and gasped. A noose hung from the ceiling. She saw more rope on the floor. She heard footsteps coming down the hall and didn't have time to search further. She shot out the window panes, taking the rotted wood frame with them. As Barnes entered the room, she fired at him, forcing his retreat. She scrambled out the window, slicing her arm on the broken glass as she did so but not slowing down. She found herself six stories high, on a narrow ledge that connected with one of the high peaks. With no choice, she edged along it and climbed over the pointed tower. There was a relatively flat section in the middle part dominated by skylights. She had no alternative but to walk over them and pray they held. She carefully hurried over them and checked the roofline. She was on the other side of the steep towers now, which offered some protection, but she could no longer see the sides of the hospital to know where the fire escapes were located.

"There's nowhere for you to go," Barnes called to her from a distant part of the roof. She saw him standing back at the point where she had emerged from the windows. He had a gun in one hand and a coil of rope in the other.

She braced herself behind one of the towers. Blood dripped from her right arm and landed on her shoes. "You're under arrest, you son of a bitch!"

He laughed. His voice sounded closer. "By whose order? Yours?"

She came around and fired almost blindly in the direction of his voice before ducking back into hiding. When she peeked again, she saw he was still standing. She eased backward, out of his line of sight, putting more space between them. "Come out, come out, wherever you are," he called.

She edged as far as she dared to peer down off the side of the building. The fire escape was fifty yards still behind her. She had a large pointed tower between there and here, and she'd be exposed to him if she tried to climb around it. She had no choice but to confront him.

"My dear Annalisa," he said, his voice carrying on the wind. He sounded very close now. "Come out and fulfill your destiny."

She waited, counted to three. "You first," she said, whipping around the edge and firing at him multiple times. He yelled and she saw him collapse into the shadows on the rooftop. She went back into hiding, her heart thundering in her chest. She listened in vain for any noise from him. Maybe he was dead. Maybe it was over. She waited as long as possible before coming around the corner with her weapon at the ready.

He was there. Standing upright again, this time on the same skylights she had crossed.

She had hit him. She could see blood shining on his left shoulder. He trained a gun on her even as she aimed hers at him. They were separated by about thirty yards, just outside of her range of accuracy. She knew the clip, and she didn't have many shots left. From the way he was looking at her, like she was captive prey, she knew he'd done the same math. "Ready to give up?" he asked her.

Just come a little closer, she thought. Her finger trembled on the trigger.

"You'll have to shoot me first," she replied.

"You know I can."

She knew. She also knew he didn't want to. He was still dragging those damn ropes. "Do it, then." She inched forward. He eased back.

"Aren't you curious?" he asked. "Don't you want to know what it's like?"

"No," she said, her voice steady. "I thought you were going to shoot me."

He scowled. "Don't tell me what to do. I'm not your sniveling boy-friend or inept partner. Your choice in men is pathetic, Annalisa."

She took a step forward. Almost in range. Almost. "You want to talk about pathetic? Where have you been for the last twenty years?"

"Right here," he hollered back, crowing now. "Right fucking here, and no one had a goddamned clue. How's that for pathetic?" The gun wavered on her.

"Grace found you though, didn't she? She figured out the weather connection. It was only a matter of time before she pieced everything together. You were working for a utility crew."

He jerked at the sound of Grace's name. "She had nothing. That whole group of imbeciles just circle-jerked each other, imagining what it was like to be me. It was laughable how far off they were."

"Sure," Annalisa said, sounding bored. "That's why you had to kill her."

"She said she'd spit in my face! Well, I spat in hers."

The DNA on the body, Annalisa realized. He'd made a mistake. She took another half-step forward. Another step or two and she'd be in range. She wouldn't miss. "She found you," she repeated. "She forced you out from your hidey-hole, the place you went when things got too hot. Maybe you were getting rusty? Maybe the cops were closing in."

He snorted with derision. "The cops. The cops only know as much as I give them. Look at you. You're here because of a private invitation. Otherwise, you'd be as lost as the rest of them."

"Lost." She licked her lips. "Yes, you have."

His eyes went wide at the first shot. She took out the skylight under him in rapid fire with her last three bullets. Glass shattered. He screamed her name on the way down. She heard a *whack* and then a distant crash. Her calculations had been correct—he was standing over a six-story stairwell, and she'd sent him plunging down the center of it. She started shaking uncontrollably as the enormity of the situation hit her. No phone. No keys. She'd have to leave him while she hiked on foot. Just then, she saw over the trees, in the distance—a line of blue lights heading toward her in the darkness. They must have traced her cell.

She cradled her injured arm against her body and walked to the roof's edge so she could watch the parade of cars growing closer. A chopper appeared in the sky over her head, its spotlight searching the ground for any sign of life. Annalisa felt tears stream down her face. "Here," she called hoarsely, although she knew they couldn't hear her over the spinning blades. She waved her uninjured arm in the air and the spotlight veered in her direction. Finally, it captured her and she fell to her knees in the circle of bright white light.

CHAPTER THIRTY-SEVEN

············

W HEN IT WAS OVER, WHEN THE BIG DOGS CAME IN TO SOMEHOW MAKE IT
LOOK LIKE THEY HAD ENGINEERED IT ALL THIS WAY—THAT IT WAS THEIR
CUNNING PLAN TO HAVE A SHOWDOWN AND NOT JARED BARNES'S—ANNALISA HAD
NOWHERE LEFT TO GO. They'd bandaged her arm in the ambulance and
taken her back to base, where she spent the next twenty-four hours
answering questions and sleeping in one of the bunks behind the break
room. Now she was free, and she didn't want cameras or kudos. She had
seen Barnes's face at the moment of his defeat, and this would sustain
her through whatever hard questions were left to come. She couldn't
imagine returning to her condo, where he had laid out the ropes for
her and then moved on to Amy Yakamoto. She didn't want to go to
the hotel and face Colin and whatever emotions he would be having at
the moment. She could barely hold in her own feelings right now. She
sat in her car outside the precinct and considered going home to her
childhood bed. Even this seemed impossible, given what she now knew
about Pops and Katie Duffy.

Her phone buzzed, and she about jumped out of her skin. When she
saw the text was from Nick, she smiled, although her face cracked with
fatigue. *CNN tells me you are a hero,* he wrote. *MSNBC says the governor
wants to host you for dinner. You are blowing up on Twitter. I hope you're going
to remember the little people, Vega.*

She wrote back: *New phone. Who dis?*

Stop that, he wrote. *It hurts when I laugh.*

You going to be okay?

I'm a miracle of modern medicine. But I'm laid up here for a week more, at least. Missing all the action. The little dots danced for a long time as he composed his next message. *I'll be here if you want to talk.*

Tears stung her eyes as she read the words. Finally, somewhere she could go where she wouldn't have to play pretend for anyone. *I'll be right over.*

She found he had been moved from the ICU to a regular room, one with white walls—a blank slate. He was sitting propped up in bed while a health aide gave him a shave. "Aw, hell," he said when he saw her. "I was trying to look all pretty for you."

"You look great to me," she told him truthfully. He was pale, his hair lank, and he'd dropped weight, but he was alive. As far as she was concerned, he'd never looked better.

"I'm wearing the blue gown," he said, smoothing a hand over it. "Lauren here says it brings out my hematomas."

Lauren rolled her eyes and wiped the last of the shaving cream from his face. "You've gotta watch this one. He's a charmer."

"I've seen his bag of tricks."

Lauren gathered her things and left the room. Nick extended his arm to Annalisa and waggled his fingers at her. "You look like hell," he said. "Come over here."

"I'm not the one in the hospital bed," she answered, but she did as he asked. She put her hand in his and he squeezed her with surprising strength. She squeezed back. "I'm so glad you're okay," she whispered.

"Same," he said. "You want to pull up a chair and tell me about it?"

She drew a shuddering breath as emotion threatened to overtake her again. "I don't even know where to begin."

Nick patted the bed next to him. "Start right here."

She perched on the edge of the bed and in a halting voice told him about the killer's phone calls, about finding Amy Yakamoto dead on her floor, and about finding him almost dead inside his car. "You nearly got killed trying to keep me safe," she said, looking down at her hands.

"You're my partner." He nudged her. "I was doing my job. I'm just sorry I couldn't clue you in sooner."

"You said shoes. I realized eventually what you meant."

"I couldn't make my brain come up with his name. I only remembered the odd thing that stuck in my head when we searched his place. Why were all his shoes so worn out and dirty?"

"Because he'd been running around killing people," she said dryly.

"The wheelchair sure made a nice cover. Did he ever really need it?"

"It seems so. The medical records back up his story that he got into a bike accident about six months after Katie Duffy's murder. I guess we know now why he took such a long break."

"Yeah, but why did he start in the first place?"

She bowed her head. "We can't very well ask him that now, can we?" Jared Barnes had been dead on the scene with a fractured skull and shattered spine. "It would've been better to take him alive."

"Screw that. It was him or you, and that's no choice at all. Besides, the guy had been lying to everyone for years about who and what he was. I don't believe he'd suddenly open up and explain why he'd decided to murder a bunch of people. Go look at interviews with other serial offenders. I have. You know what the honest ones say? They just like watching people die. It gets them off, that life-or-death control over another human being. I'm not sure there's ever going to be a satisfying answer for that."

She tried to smile for him. "You always were such a sweet talker."

He took her hand again. "He finally messed with the wrong woman."

"Not me," she said, withdrawing from him. "Grace Harper. Ten to one they're going to find Jared Barnes's name among the old utility crews. Grace knew it, and he killed her before she could say anything."

"I keep thinking about her wall with all those gruesome pictures on it. He could have taken them too, and then we'd never have known about her theory. He stole the laptop. Why not take the murder room with him? He had all the time in the world."

She could visualize the room as he'd left it—all his victims laid out, the map of the murders, the large-font headlines screaming his nickname. "Because it was a monument to him."

"Ego," he said with a chuff. "I guess it gets us all in the end."

"Not you." She said, finding a smile for real. She poked him gently at the hip. "At least not yet."

He caught her hand and held it. "When I get out of here, maybe you'll let me take you to dinner."

Her phone buzzed in her pocket. "Hold that thought," she said, squeezing him before taking out the phone to look at the text. It was Colin. *When are you coming home?* He meant the hotel, and her heart swelled, looking at the words. He'd been home to her once, and maybe could be again. She had enough hope that she texted back. *Soon.*

"About that dinner," she said as she put her phone away. "If it's a partnership celebration, I'm all in."

"Oh." His face fell and he cleared his throat. "Just for work, then."

"We tried the other kind of dinner before," she said gently. "Seems I recall it didn't work out so well in the end."

"I guess it depends," he countered.

"Depends on what?"

His smile returned. "On whether or not you consider this the end."

....

When she returned to the hotel, the guards were gone, and she lingered in the silent hallway for a few moments before knocking softly on the door. Colin whipped it open immediately and grabbed her in his arms. "Anna. Thank God." They held each other and he cradled her head with his hand. She relaxed for the first time in forever. "That was an unbelievably foolish and dangerous thing you did, running off by yourself after a murderer." He paused, emotional. "Thank you."

After all these years, they still fit together like interlocking pieces, the top of her head just under his chin. "I need a shower. And food. And sleep." She wasn't sure what order.

"Anything. Anything you want."

She opted for the shower first, and then her body decided on sleep, conking out dramatically the minute she lay down on the bed. When she woke, they ordered a mountain of food from room service, and she devoured it all. Eventually, she had a different hunger, one only he could assuage, and Colin proved an eager lover. He kissed her everywhere, marveling in her physical form like she was a goddess brought to life, and she drank from the forgiveness that she tasted on his lips.

In the dark, his fingers trailed down her shoulder and across her arm as she listened to the steady thrum of his heart beneath her ear. "I have so many questions," he murmured.

She tensed up and shifted away, thinking of the answers she didn't want to give. "Can they wait?"

"Of course." He gathered her closer. "Of course, they can wait. We have all the time in the world."

The world. She wanted to see all of it now, with him. She hugged him around the middle. "Let's plan a trip somewhere."

"Yes, let's. First, I have to go on a whirlwind tour through Scandinavia, during which I have to file about a dozen pieces. That would be no fun for you. After, though, we can go anywhere you want. Just name the place."

"Italy? No, Brazil. Or maybe Egypt."

He laughed and rolled her under him. "Tell you what. Let's do them all."

....

Eventually, she had to go home. She drove down her familiar street but it looked different to her now. The front yards were empty, doors and windows locked up tight. They had caught the killer, but the wounds he left had not yet healed. She wondered if they ever would. Annalisa almost turned around and fled again when she saw Jason Yakamoto carrying a box out of his mother's home and loading it into an SUV. Instead, she forced herself to go and offer her condolences. His smile, his naked relief at seeing another human being, intensified her guilt. "I saw on the news that you got him. The guy who killed her. I don't know how I can ever thank you."

"Please don't." She swallowed with effort and looked down the bare street. "If your mom hadn't lived so close to me—"

He cut her off. "Mom loved it here. She said the neighborhood was friendly, full of kids and dogs. She loved the light that came through the bay windows in the back. Perfect for her plants." His voice took on a note of regret. "I'm shipping some of her stuff back with me to Seattle, but I can't take the plants."

"I'll take them." She blurted out the offer, surprising herself. "I mean, I would love to have them. I don't know that much about gardening, but I'd like to learn."

He tried to smile. "I think she would like that." He helped her carry the larger pots from Amy's condo to hers, and soon her windows overflowed with greenery. They looked out of place and misarranged, but she was determined to make them a home.

Jason handed her a misting bottle and gave her a small salute. "Good luck."

He left and she squirted the nearest plant a few times. The leaves shivered and so she stopped. She curled up on her sofa and looked at the family photos on her bookshelf. Sassy had offered to have Annalisa stay with them, but she had two small children and Alex's relapse to manage. Annalisa didn't want to crash her own issues into their otherwise delicate atmosphere. No, she'd stay here with the bewildered plants. Together they would find a way to adjust to the new view.

Over the next few days, she escaped to work whenever she could. The shooting investigational board cleared her promptly, but Zimmer kept her chained to the desk anyway. "Wait for the media to cool down," she said. "How are you supposed to work a case with six news trucks following you everywhere?" But Annalisa discovered she was still the officer of record in Grace Harper's murder, and she remembered the people who had first reported her missing. The Grave Diggers deserved some answers.

She met the remainder of the local team at Oliver Benton's home in Lakeview. It was a Queen Anne–style worker's cottage, built in brick, which meant it had been constructed after the Great Fire of 1871. His wife, Sandra, answered the door, and the colorful headscarf she wore reminded Annalisa that Sandra was battling cancer. "The hero of the hour," she said warmly as she widened the door to admit Annalisa. "Welcome."

"I'm no hero. I was as shocked as you must have been."

"I'm furious. There is no part of this that does not make me see red. Those poor women. And Grace! He pretended to be her friend, to be a friend to all of us, when in reality he was just this horrible monster. I've been thinking about him in that wheelchair that he apparently didn't need. He wouldn't come out here, you know, on account of the stairs we have inside the house. I'm glad now, but I felt bad then that we couldn't accommodate him. I also felt scared. What if I ended up like him in a chair and Oliver and I had to leave our home? I know it sounds pitiful, given all the heinous acts he committed, but it just shows you how low he would stoop—using a disability to hide his true self."

She walked Annalisa into the wood-paneled den where Oliver was bringing out a tray of cheese and crackers. Chris hovered by the window, drinking a Coke. Travis and Molly sat on the sofa, dressed for Sunday church. "Detective Vega," Oliver said with a broad smile. "Thank you for coming."

"Of course. I wanted to tell you what I can about the case, about what we've learned so far about Jared Barnes." They all sat and gave her their undivided attention as she recited what little she could: Barnes had grown up with a violent drunk for a father while his mother was a secretary in a doctor's office. She also cleaned houses to make ends meet and was often not at home to shield Barnes from his father's rages. Barnes enrolled in the Army at age eighteen and had a distinguished but brief career as an MP. After, he'd worked various jobs, including three years at the power company during the time of the original murders. He had probably joined the Grave Diggers to keep tabs on what they knew about his case.

"That story he told us about his friend who killed the man in Iraq," Oliver said. "Was it true?"

"Eddie Mack," Molly added with a shudder. "I had nightmares after that story."

They'd been conducting interviews with every known contact of Jared Barnes. "Our people interviewed an Edward Mack in Ohio," she said. "He mentioned Barnes had killed a man for sport while they were serving together in the Middle East."

"So he was talking about himself," Oliver said as though he'd suspected it.

"Bragging is more like it," said Molly. "Everyone wants his story now. We've been flooded with people wanting to join the Grave Diggers since the news broke. A thousand people at least, from all over the country."

"Doesn't matter," Chris replied grimly. He crushed the Coke can with one enormous hand. "I'm shutting it down."

"What?" Oliver asked. His confused expression said this was news to him.

"Gracie got killed. Don't you get that? It's not worth it."

"But the bodies we've identified," Oliver said quietly. "The missing people who aren't missing anymore. Surely that counts for something."

"Grace is dead." He ground out the words between his teeth. "And we're responsible. All of us. We didn't even see the guy when he was sitting in our own living rooms. How's that for amateur sleuthing?"

"Grace found him," Annalisa said, and they all turned to look at her. "She just didn't know it yet. I think—no, I know—if Grace had pursued her theory about the storms and the utility workers to the end, she would have uncovered his secret. I've seen the storeroom of evidence on this case, with all the boxes stacked up to the ceiling. The cops had all of that but came up empty. It was one of you who figured out the solution based on a simple idea no one had considered yet."

Molly smiled and dug out a tissue to dab at her eyes. "Gracie's brain was like my mama's nacho dip—seven layers deep. She had notes on other cases, too. Did you recover her laptop?"

"I don't know," Annalisa replied. Teams of cops had torn Barnes's apartment practically down to the studs, and they'd found a rented storage locker in his name. She wasn't sure what all they'd found. "I promise you this, though—I will find out."

....

It took her several days to track down the answer, which was yes, they had recovered Grace Harper's laptop from Barnes's storage unit. Computer forensics would eventually go through it, but it was not a high priority since the case was closed and would not be going to trial. Annalisa tried to wheedle a mirror copy of the hard drive out of the tech department, but they weren't interested in making the time to help her out. She took her case to Zimmer.

"What do you want with it, anyway?"

"Does it matter? I'm the lead on the case. Technically, it's my call."

"Technically, I'm your boss. I believe that makes it *my* call." Zimmer peered over the rims of her glasses. "You did good, Vega. You got justice for her. There's nothing more you can do to help Grace Harper."

Annalisa read the concern on her commander's face. Zimmer wasn't about to foster what she viewed as a possible growing obsession, so

Annalisa needed to think fast to come up with a compelling reason she needed the laptop. "Grace Harper was working other cases," she said. "She almost beat us on this one. I don't think we want the Grave Diggers making any more headlines right now, do you? Let me see what other notes she had."

Zimmer bought the line, and Annalisa got her mirrored hard drive. She found various cases, all neatly bundled with notes and pictures. Grace Harper had added to the Lovelorn Killer file just hours before she'd been killed: *Molly's uncle may be able to help us access power company records.* Annalisa wondered if she'd mentioned this to Barnes, if he'd known how truly close she was. She closed out of that file and clicked on a folder labeled *Grace Notes.* It appeared to be an electronic journal. Intrigued, Annalisa made herself a cup of strong coffee and took the laptop to a small private room where she could meet her victim in peace.

CHAPTER THIRTY-EIGHT

....

Annalisa read the journal until her neck ached and her eyes dried from staring too long at the screen. Grace Harper was by turns insightful, petty, generous, funny, and pedantic. Plenty fearless, Annalisa noticed. No wonder Barnes had fixated on her. He'd seen himself as important and powerful. She saw him as impotent and afraid. Still, she'd been romantically interested in the man he'd presented himself to be, the mask hiding the monster within. Grace had included a bit of a chat transcript she had with Barnes, which Annalisa thought might be the closest they'd ever get to a look inside the killer's head.

Grace: I can't imagine what it must be like for him to walk around among people and act like he's normal.

Barnes: Part of him is normal. He just puts that face out front. Like dressing up for work.

Grace: He's not normal. This isn't like putting on a suit to work an office job. He ties up women and tortures them to death.

Barnes: We all do things in private we won't admit to others. This is just more extreme. He knows he's different. He's probably known it from childhood.

Grace: So you think he was born this way?

Barnes: Born with the devil inside, yes. The devil is patient. He can
wait a long time to come out and play, but after a time, he will not
be denied.

The whole journal made for fascinating reading, but the part that
caught Annalisa's attention concerned a second case Grace was working on at the time of her death: the disappearance of a young woman
named Janeesa Bryant. Janeesa had been working alone at a gas station
convenience store one Tuesday night and had apparently closed up as
usual but never made it to her car in the parking lot. Her volatile relationship with a reprobate named Hector Sanchez made him the prime
suspect. Annalisa looked up the case in the record books and found it
was open but inactive. The detectives had interviewed Sanchez multiple times, but he had consistently denied harming Janeesa, and they
could not shake his alibi. One note she found in the file, which Grace
Harper could not have known, was a detail deliberately held back from
the public: Janeesa's rear left tire had been slashed at some point while
she was working in the store that day. Her abductor had grabbed her
before she'd reached the parking lot, but he'd planned ahead and disabled her vehicle so she couldn't have escaped him.

Annalisa returned with interest to Grace's notes, especially the part
about the closed-circuit security footage. A search of Grace's computer
turned up the video in question. Annalisa's hair stood on end when she
saw what Grace had seen: the heavyset man with a bomber jacket looking right into the convenience store camera.

She closed up the laptop, locked it in her desk, and then took out
a faded Chicago Cubs cap from her drawer. She kept it in hand as she
walked casually past Zimmer's office toward the back doors, at which
point she put the cap on and prepared to dodge the press. She borrowed
an unmarked department vehicle rather than take her own car, which
helped her to make an escape.

At the gas station, she stopped her car where Janeesa had once parked
and surveyed the scene. Grace had planned on checking the pawnshop
across the street to see if they'd had cameras up six years ago when
Janeesa had disappeared. Annalisa took up the trail and jaywalked across
the busy street to inspect the pawnshop. It had an outside camera now,

just above the door, but she didn't know how long it had been there. A bell tinkled her entrance, and a slim Korean man, perhaps sixty years old, emerged from the back with a remote-controlled Ferrari in his hands. "Yes, hello," he said with a smile. "May I help you?"

"I hope so." She showed him her badge, and his smile faded.

"Is there a problem?"

"No, nothing like that. I just had some questions about your security cameras. How long have you had them?"

"I have been the owner just one year." He held up an index finger to illustrate. "But the cameras were already here when I came."

"I see. Do you know the owners before you?"

"Kathleen and Ronald Dunlop, yes. They were here many years. Retired now."

"Do you have contact information for them?"

He brightened. "Yes. They sometimes still get mail here, and I send it to them. Would you like the address?"

"Yes, please." She eyed a toy rocking chair, currently occupied by a floppy-eared stuffed rabbit wearing a tiara. Her niece Carla would love it, and Sassy and Alex sure needed a reason to smile. "I'd like the rocking chair too, please."

"With rabbit?"

"Sure, why not. Throw in the rabbit."

"Tiara is perfect for the rabbit. Very sparkly."

She hid a smile as he showed off the snazzy rabbit. "The tiara too, of course." She managed to get out of the store before she agreed to buy the whole place. The address he'd given her was way out in Campton Hills. She bought an apple, a chocolate bar, and a water from the gas station convenience store before making the trip. The camera in the corner that had captured the guy in the bomber jacket still watched over all the patrons from its spot on high.

When she reached Campton, she located the cottage marked 212 Rose Hill Way and stopped her car in front of it. She tossed her apple core in the nearest garbage and wiped her hands on her jeans before ringing the doorbell. She heard uneven footsteps on the other side, and a woman with a shock of white hair opened. "Yes?" she said, her voice hard with suspicion.

"Kathleen Dunlop?"

"Yes, that's me. What do you want?"

Annalisa showed off her shield and introduced herself. "I'm looking into an old case in Chicago," she explained. "A young woman was abducted from the gas station across the street from your pawnshop six years ago. Her name is Janeesa Bryant."

The woman's expression softened, her liver-spotted hand curling around the door. "Ah, that poor girl. I remember when it happened, her family hanging up those posters around the neighborhood. We put one in our window, of course."

"Do you mind if I come inside to ask you a few questions?"

"No, yeah. I don't see how I can help you," Mrs. Dunlop said, but she widened the door to admit Annalisa, who readied her speech about the security cameras. She followed Mrs. Dunlop to a small, sunny kitchen, where she drew up short because there he was—the heavyset man from the gas station security camera. He sat with the local paper, drinking coffee at the table.

Surprised, she blinked at him. "Ronald Dunlop?"

"Depends on who's asking."

"This young lady is a Chicago detective," his wife explained. "She's here about that poor girl who disappeared from the gas station downtown. Remember?"

"'Course I do," he said, narrowing his eyes at Annalisa. "Terrible thing to happen."

"Did you know Janeesa?" Annalisa asked, sliding closer to him.

"No. Saw her working from time to time, but it's not like we were friendly."

"I noticed your shop has security cameras set up, and one had a view of the gas station."

"We wouldn't have any of that footage now," Mrs. Dunlop said. "It's been years."

"The cops came looking for it back then," he told her. "Didn't matter. The cameras were on the fritz that week."

"Is that so?" Her heart rate picked up as she closed in on her new suspect. Ronald Dunlop, the man who could watch Janeesa every day as she came and went from her job at the gas station. The man who would know the location of every camera on the block. The man who could be sure that the pawnshop's unblinking eye would record nothing of consequence the night she disappeared. "Were you working that day, either of you?"

"I was home with a bum ankle," Mrs. Dunlop said.

"I was there," Mr. Dunlop allowed. "Working behind the counter, though, you don't see much outside."

"Maybe you went outside . . . perhaps to get a snack from the convenience store across the street?"

"I mighta. Don't recall. I did go in there sometimes for a bag of chips and a soda or what have you."

"Then you might have seen Janeesa the day she disappeared."

"I told you I don't remember. You know who I did see a bunch of times—that no-good boyfriend of hers. The detective from six years ago asked me lots of questions about him." He wagged a finger at her for going off script.

"You saw Hector Sanchez? What did you see?"

He licked his lips and leaned back in his chair, considering his answer. "Well now, seems to me I saw him and his buddy hanging around the parking lot. That's where she kept her little car when she was in the store, you know."

"Hmm," Annalisa said, taking notes. "What kind of car did she drive . . . if you remember?"

"A blue Kia," he answered without hesitation. He grinned to himself. "Piece of shit, if you ask me. I always buy American."

"You say you saw Hector and a friend in the parking lot. Are you sure it was the day she disappeared?"

"Pretty sure. Can't swear to it. He had a knife, you know. Like a switchblade? I saw him with it once, slicing up a piece of fruit while he was waiting for Janeesa to get off work."

"Seems like you saw a lot." Annalisa made sure to inject a note of admiration into her voice. "Who needs surveillance cameras when we have you, right?"

"Right, right." He leaned forward, warming to her. He cupped his hands around the coffee. "What I'm trying to say is, that boyfriend could've used his knife to slash her tire. You should ask him about that."

Annalisa froze with her pen on the pad. In that moment, she understood the Grave Diggers and their obsessive quest to hunt down cold cases. This guy had no idea what was about to hit him. "Her tire," she repeated, looking up at Ronald Dunlop.

"He punctured it, right? So, she couldn't run off on him. I remember reading about that in the papers."

Dunlop didn't realize he'd been made. He wore the self-satisfied grin of a man who'd gotten away with it. "Is that any help to you?" Mrs. Dunlop asked as she poured herself another mug.

Annalisa would need to return with a warrant. At that moment, she said a silent thank-you to Grace Harper and her eagle eyes. After six years, Janeesa Bryant might finally be coming home. "Yes," she said to the Dunlops, a slow smile spreading over her face as she closed up her notebook. "Yes, I believe you've helped me a lot."

CHAPTER THIRTY-NINE

....

I T WAS AN ORDINARY SATURDAY, THE LAST SHE HAD PLANNED FOR SOME TIME. Annalisa did laundry and studied the gardening book she'd checked out from the library. She liked to read it out loud to the plants, as if maybe they could chime in with their own advice. The house sitter she had booked for the next two weeks would no doubt do a better job, but she didn't even care. Tomorrow Colin would swing into town, and they would embark on a tour of six European countries, starting with Paris, France. If they still liked each other at the end, then maybe there would be other trips in the future—the future she'd originally planned back when they had daydreamed together under the old oak tree in her backyard.

Her cell phone rang and she didn't even jump. "Hey, Ma," she said, flopping backward on the couch. "Before you ask, yes, I packed my toothbrush. And my underwear. And an umbrella."

"What about toilet paper?"

"They have toilet paper in France, Ma."

"I just worry about you."

"I know you do," she replied, feeling tender. "I'll be okay. I promise."

"I need you to do me a favor. I have a bunch of old clothes I need to drop off for the church rummage sale. Can you come sit with Pops for an hour? Alone, he'll probably get hungry and climb the pantry cabinets for the cookies I hid on the top shelf. We'd find him on the floor with his thick skull split open like a melon."

Annalisa sat up, suddenly uneasy. She hadn't been alone with her father since Alex's disclosure about the affair. "I don't know. . . ."

"It's just one hour. Then you're gone for an entire month!"

"Two and a half weeks, Ma." She bit her lip, deciding. "Okay, I'll do it. I'll see you in a few." She rehearsed her words on the drive over to her parents' place. She would tell Pops she knew, say how foolish he'd been. A part of her still held out hope that he'd deny it all and somehow she could believe him. Alex had been roaring drunk the night of the Halloween party. He might have misconstrued an innocent exchange.

Her mother met her at the door. "There's meatballs in the fridge," she said, bussing Annalisa on the cheek. "Oh, and tuna salad. Plus, some pasta and a bowl of fruit."

"Ma, you said you'd only be gone an hour."

Her mother grabbed her large tote and went to the door. "He needs his medication at four P.M. Directions are on the kitchen table."

"I've got it. Go." Annalisa shooed her mother out the door. She found Pops sitting in the den watching golf from his special chair, the one where the seat rose up with the touch of a button to help him to his feet. He muted the TV when she came in.

"It's my beautiful daughter," he said, reaching for her with unsteady hands. "Come give Pops a k-kiss."

"Hi, Pops." She brushed his grizzled cheek with her lips and took a seat on a floral sofa that was at least as old as she was. "How's your hip?"

"Titanium," he said, patting it. "I'm bionic now." He leaned over toward her. "Seeing how the guard is off duty, how about you and me have some ice cream?"

"Her car probably isn't even out of sight yet."

Pops grinned. "She is a good woman, but sh-she makes a lousy nurse."

"She loves you," Annalisa said with more bite than she'd intended. "She's trying to take care of you."

"Oh, I know. She thinks if I eat the right magic foods, I'll live forever." He shrugged. "Kale and spinach and all kinds of beans. I try to be good and eat what she puts in front of me, but I wonder if it really makes you live longer—or if it just seems that way."

"I will get you some ice cream." Annalisa fetched him a small dish of fudge swirl and then watched as he worked hard to eat it. His arm trembled as he held the spoon, and she could hardly believe this was the same man who'd once split firewood in the backyard. "Pops, I've got to ask you something."

"What's that?"

"It's about Katie Duffy."

He grunted. "C-case is closed now, thanks to you. May she rest in peace."

"I'm asking about the time when she was alive. Rumor had it she was seeing someone."

He stopped eating and wiped his mouth on a napkin. "That so?"

"Maybe a cop."

"Who's to say? Water under the bridge now."

"Pops." She waited until he looked at her, until she would be able to read the truth on his face. "Was it you?"

He opened his mouth and closed it again. The pain in his dark eyes told her everything. Her stomach dropped to her knees, and she couldn't say anything for a long minute.

"Oh, Pops," she murmured, full of disappointment.

He could feel it, she saw. His shoulders sagged and he pushed aside the ice cream. "It was a mistake. The worst one I ever made."

"How could you?"

"I didn't plan it. Y-you have to understand, your ma and me got together when we were just kids. By that time, our lives were half over. You and your brothers were grown up. We'd spent years focused all on you and getting you ready for the world."

"So now it's our fault?"

"No. No, I don't mean it like that. I just mean, we had our roles, her and me. Then you didn't need us so much, but we didn't know how to talk to each other like husband and wife anymore. Just Ma and Pops. It was routine."

She sat forward, her head in her hands. Her face burned at his words. The very marriage she'd idolized all these years, the one she thought was built on love and devotion, he talked like it had been a shackle. A sham. "I thought you loved each other," she whispered.

"We did. I do." He clawed for her but she moved out of his reach. "I would die for your mother. She and you kids mean ev-everything to me."

"Except when you were screwing Katie Duffy." She looked up, glaring at him. "That was you who Lora Fitz saw that night, creeping around the Duffy house. Wasn't it? That's why you had to make her statement disappear, in case anyone ever tried to follow up with a sketch artist. God, Pops. You're lucky they didn't haul you in as the Lovelorn Killer."

"I know that! Don't you think I know that? It was stupid. Reckless. I've been sorry ever since."

"Katie was pregnant when she died," Annalisa said steadily. "Tell me it wasn't yours."

He looked even more miserable. "I . . . I don't know. She couldn't be sure."

"I can't believe you did this. What about Ma? Does she know?"

"No," he said swiftly. "It would break her heart."

"Nice of you to think of that now."

He rubbed his eyes with one hand. "You're angry. I don't blame you. But it was a long time ago—a bad mistake that's in the past. I ask you to forgive me. You've got to know how sorry I am and that I would do anything for you, for your mother, for any of your brothers. We are still a fa-family, and family is what really matters."

"Convenient of you to say that now."

"Now is when it's finally over," he said, leaning back and closing his eyes.

She wasn't as sure. "Pops, what about your stash in the attic?"

He looked at her. "What about it?"

"You can't get up there anymore, but Ma can. Is there anything up there that could, you know, hurt her? Pictures? Letters?"

He frowned deeply. "There is one box."

Her stomach lurched, but she made herself stand up and speak normally. "Tell me where it is. I'll get rid of it."

Relief colored his features, tears in his eyes. "You would do that for me?"

"I would do it for Ma. Like you say, it's over now."

"The box is in the back, behind the left gable. It is labeled TAXES, 1998."

Annalisa left him to go up to the attic, disgust in her mouth. She considered burning the box without ever looking inside it. Summer heat greeted her like a crematorium as she opened the hatch and climbed into the stuffy attic. She picked her way through the boxes and old furniture until she found the one Pops had mentioned. Curiosity got the best of her, and she ripped off the tape holding it shut. Inside, she found several shoeboxes. The first held a letter in Katie's handwriting, receipts from the Edgebrook Motel, and a Valentine's Day card with a big red heart on the front. *Darling, be mine.* Her father's signature was on the inside. Tears of fury rose up inside her and she choked back a sob. She wiped at her face with her bare arm but only succeeded in sliding dirt and grime across her cheek. She would have to wash or Ma would know she'd been up here.

She pulled out the second shoebox, and she froze when she saw the contents. The missing pages with Lora's statement sat folded neatly on top. Underneath was the missing red silk scarf, the one used to strangle Katie. Her heart split open like it had been shot. She felt like she was dying inside. "Pops, no. No, no, no." She bent over, a desperate groan escaping from her lips. She sat curled like that for a long time.

Eventually, she rose on unsteady legs and took the box with her back down to the den. Pops had the golf game turned up like usual. She stood in the doorway and let him see her streaked, dirty face. Let him see the horror in her eyes. "Pops," she whispered. "What have you done?"

"Did you find it?" He clicked off the TV. "Hurry and get rid of it before your mother gets back."

"Pops, what is this?" She fisted the scarf and held it up for him.

He stiffened as if struck. "Put that away."

"This is what killed her. The scarf from her costume. Isn't it? You took it from evidence."

"You don't know what you're asking," he said, his hands moving fretfully on the arms of the chair. "Just leave it be. She's gone. Nothing will bring her back now."

"Did you kill her?" She took a step into the room. "Did you use the

Lovelorn Killer as a cover to get rid of your mistake? Your pregnant neighbor? The wife of your best friend?"

"Stop this right now! You have no right to question me."

She drew back, looking down on him with disgust. "Pops, I'm on the job now, remember? I have every right."

"You going to turn me in? You'd do that to your own father? Over what? A red scarf that could've come from anywhere."

"It didn't, though. It came from Katie Duffy's body. I bet the DNA evidence that you conveniently managed to circumvent will prove that's true."

"Anna, I'm begging you . . . let this go. For the family's sake."

"Hey, Pops!" She whirled as Alex entered the room wearing a Blackhawks shirt and a red bandana. He held a hammer in his hand. "Oh, hi, Annalisa. I thought that was your car outside. Pops, I came over to fix that broken step. Finally, huh?"

"Alex, this isn't a great time," Annalisa muttered.

"She's right," Pops said sharply. "Go home, Alex."

He looked from one to the other, confused by the weird energy in the room. "What's going on?" When they didn't answer, his gaze drifted to the scarf in Annalisa's hands. "Uh, Pops? Is that what I think it is?"

"I told you to go home."

The color drained from Alex's face. He pulled the bandana from his head. "What are you doing with that scarf, Anna?"

"She's doing nothing with it," Pops said. "Right, Anna?"

"I—" She looked down at the box in her hands. The missing report lay flat against one side, and she had removed the scarf, revealing a small packet of photos at the bottom. She took them out and saw they were from the Halloween party. There was one very similar to the shot she'd seen before, Katie Duffy smiling with Pop's arm around her. Only this time you could see his face. She felt loathing now, looking at it, but she also realized something as she stood there holding the scarf: it wasn't in the shot. Katie's costume included purple, green, yellow, and blue scarves. Not red.

Her memory jarred loose. She'd seen a red scarf that night. Frantically, she flipped through the pictures to confirm, and there he was:

Alex the pirate, with the red scarf around his neck. She looked up aghast. "It was you."

He twitched. "What?"

"You wore the red scarf." She turned the photo around so he could see it. "Pops didn't kill Katie Duffy. You did. He just helped you cover it up."

"I don't know what you're talking about."

She sank onto the sofa, clutching the evidence in her lap. Her head spun. "You found out about the affair and you took it out on Katie," she said, unable to look at him. "You must have followed her home from the party and strangled her. Pops probably showed up. He'd have been worried about her when she went home sick. He knew how to fake the murder scene—somehow he even knew about the bleach."

"Just got lucky," Pops said, his head wobbling as he trembled. "I didn't know the killer used bleach. I just wanted to erase any evidence of your brother."

"Pops," Alex said, a desperate edge in his voice. "What are you doing, telling Anna this stuff?"

Pops waved a hand. "She knows enough. She may as well know it all."

"She can't know." Alex waved the hammer wildly. "She's a cop!"

"So was I," Pops shot back. Then he added softly, "Once."

"You gotta understand. I didn't mean to do it." Alex turned to her, his expression pleading. "I didn't mean to kill her. I just went there to confront her, to get her to leave our family alone. She called me a child. Told me to mind my own business. Like my family wasn't my business!"

"Alex," Annalisa said, her eyes on the hammer. "Put down the hammer."

He looked at it as though seeing it for the first time. "You think I would hit you with it? Huh, is that what you think? That I'm some monster who would kill his own sister?"

"I don't think that. I just want you to put it down."

"What are you gonna do, Anna? Huh? You've got to throw that shit away for good. You have to." His throat bobbed as he swallowed. There were tears in his eyes. "I've got a family, Anna. Think of Sassy, and Gigi and Carla. They need me."

She wanted to die, thinking of it. How many lives were about to be exploded? "I can't," she said tightly. She couldn't carry their sins with her. She wouldn't.

"Anna . . ." Pops tried cajoling her. "What good would it do now?"

Tears streamed down her face. "Your secret got one woman killed, Pops. It almost destroyed your son." It made sense now, how Alex's drinking had intensified after Katie's death. "You want it to take me, too? Because that's what will happen. I can't go the rest of my life pretending I don't know."

Pops's face turned hard. "You will kill this family, then. All of us."

Alex sobbed, the hammer dropping to the floor with a thud. He leaned his back against the paneled wall and slid to the floor, burying his face in his hands. Her phone buzzed and she looked at it out of habit. It was a text from Colin. *Epic vacation countdown is at ten hours. Can't wait to see you.* She swiped angrily at her face and turned the phone against her leg so she couldn't see his words. Another relationship, shattered. There would be no vacation from this, not ever. Her new passport sat on her kitchen table, pristine and unused. She could go anywhere in the world that she wanted, but she could never come home again.

She trembled as she raised the phone again. She dialed a familiar number, heard Zimmer's terse reply on the other end. Zimmer would know what to do. Her commander would be able to arrange as soft a landing as possible for Pops and Alex. Still, Annalisa had to swallow twice before she could make any sound come out. With Alex weeping in the background, she forced herself to say the words. "Commander, it's Vega. I—I need to report a murder."

EPILOGUE

....

T HE BRILLIANCE OF THE SUNNY DAY GAVE HER AN EXCUSE TO HIDE BEHIND
DARK GLASSES AS THE JEEP MADE ITS WAY THROUGH THE MOUNTAIN ROADS.
Annalisa's guide, a trim, chatty man named Emilio, more than kept
up his end of the conversation by pointing out geological oddities in
the craggy rocks, regaling her with stories about his four kids. He gave
her credit for being brave enough to travel to Bolivia on her own. She
smiled wanly and turned her face to the passing scenery. She had re-
searched the trip for months but booked it on impulse, at the tail end
of the rainy season, in the space between Pops's and Alex's arrests and
their upcoming trials.

Pops could probably get a plea deal, but only if he agreed to testify
against his son. "I'd rather die in prison," he'd replied from his wheelchair. Annalisa was forbidden from the legal meetings, but she heard
the details from Ma, who was determined to tell Annalisa every last
awful development. Maybe she wanted to rub her daughter's nose in it.
Maybe she just didn't want to carry the horror alone. Annalisa would
take it, would keep taking whatever anguish her mother cared to un-
load. "I'll tell them everything I've done," Pops said. "I'll cop to every
last bit of it, but I'm not getting on the stand and running my mouth
against my boy."

So far, his standoff with the prosecutor had earned Pops a house arrest with an ankle monitor. "Like I was going anywhere anyways," Pops

had scoffed, but Annalisa knew it had to eat at him. All those years running down bad guys, and now Pops had a shackle around his leg, a constant reminder of which side he'd ended up on. *The side he'd chosen,* Annalisa had to remind herself whenever she lay awake at night.

Alex had dropped twenty pounds. The system had no mercy left for him, and he would be tried as an adult for Katie Duffy's murder. With the photos from the Halloween party and the red scarf returned to evidence, the state would likely have an easy win. He remained locked up with dangerous men—the real killers, as Annalisa had once thought of them. Jared Barnes would have been among them if he had lived. To think of her beloved older brother in the same breath as a serial murderer, as a man born to hunt women for sport, seemed unbelievable and preposterous. "It was a terrible mistake," Alex had insisted to her on her visit to see him. "I never meant to kill her. I just wanted her to leave us alone. . . . I wanted her gone." Looking into his teary eyes, Annalisa had believed his sincerity and felt his remorse. But she'd also read the autopsy reports on the victims and learned how long it took to strangle a healthy adult woman to death. Two minutes, sometimes more, of relentless pressure. Holding them down as they struggled and tightening the binds around their necks. Her brother and the Lovelorn Killer were not so different after all.

At least Sassy still spoke to her, even if she didn't always meet her eyes. But then again, Sassy needed her. She had legal bills and two kids to manage on a part-time librarian's salary. Her other friends had fallen away when Alex's crime had been revealed. What kind of woman lies down with a murderer? Annalisa took groceries over to her and watched her nieces so Sassy could escape to the gym at the YMCA for an hour. They never talked about Alex. In fact, they never talked about anything important anymore. The weight of holding back the dread of Alex and what he'd done left no room for anything but the barest conversational necessities. *Hold the baby, will you? Let me pick up a gallon of milk.* A few weeks ago, after an especially large glass of wine, Annalisa had texted her. *I miss you.*

Sassy had answered: *I miss you, too.*

Let's go get dinner. I'll pay. Ma will be glad to watch the kids.

Can't. I can't eat anywhere in this town. Not with everyone staring.

So we'll drive to Peoria, Annalisa countered. She felt it, too, the desperate need for air. Her fellow officers looked at her funny now. She was related to a murderer. Daughter of a dirty cop. And now, on top of it all, she'd ratted them out. Annalisa didn't know which of her crimes was the worst in the eyes of the boys in blue.

Another time, Sassy had written back after a while.

Ok, when? Annalisa asked her.

Sassy had yet to reply.

"Here it is," Emilio said with pride as the salt flats came into sight. "Earth's largest mirror."

Salar de Uyuni stretched farther than her eyes could see. The lake had once covered much of southwestern Bolivia, and the flat crater left by its absence was larger even than some countries. The dry sections were hard going, the Jeep struggling through white sand and salt. At last, they reached a shimmering pool of shallow water. Emilio stopped the Jeep and allowed her to exit. Suddenly hesitant, she slowly touched her waterproof boots down on the ground. The endless blue of the sky and its cotton candy clouds seemed to be everywhere at once, over her head and beneath her feet. She felt like she might fall into space. "It's something to see, no?" Emilio grinned and spread his arms wide.

"Yes. Amazing." She inhaled a deep breath. The air was cold and briny.

She explored the terrain like a moonwalker, with cautious steps at first and then gleeful bounds. Other tourists nearby mirrored her awe. A bunch of college-age kids took crazy pictures of themselves in a human pyramid. A couple who could have been on their honeymoon held hands and laughed together in a language Annalisa didn't recognize. She took their picture surreptitiously, hoarding their joy.

She looked at the men wandering around the pool, searching for the particular curve of Colin's face or the easy grace of his long limbs. They hadn't spoken since she'd met him at the airport with tears on her cheeks and agony in her heart. The way his happiness had evaporated at the sight of her was seared in her memory. Her brother had committed the atrocity. Her father had covered it up. But it fell to Annalisa to relay the painful truth about his mother's death and, in doing so, become the person who dug up Katie and murdered her all over again. "No, I don't believe it," he had said at first. "You're wrong."

She'd caught the killer she'd dreamed about in her childhood bed. Back then, when the earth was still wet and loose over Katie's grave, she'd thought that solving her death would put things right. Instead, it became the end of everything.

Of course, Colin couldn't bear to look at her now. Most days, she couldn't bear to look at herself. She'd created a social media account using his nickname for her, Mona Lisa, and followed him to see his ongoing journeys around the world. He'd been to Tibet, to Anchorage, Alaska, and was currently in Sardinia, if his account could be believed. She never really expected to find him here. He would have had to have wheedled her plans out of Sassy or his aunt, and Annalisa couldn't imagine he bothered to ask about her.

Annalisa picked up her fancy new camera, purchased for this occasion, and took some shots of the surrounding scenery. Nick would like to see them, if no one else did. He was back on duty now, fully healed, but they were still careful with one another. He'd broken her trust once, if not her heart. He'd had no way to break her heart, she realized now, because she'd never fully given it to him. But he'd almost died for her. She'd had his literal blood on her hands. This was stronger than any marriage vow.

"You want me to take one of you?" Emilio called to her, indicating the camera in her hands.

She looked down at it, considering. "Sure, thanks." She gave him the camera and took off her sunglasses. When he took the snap of her, she made sure to look directly into the lens.

Later, when she had returned home to her lone condo and greeted Amy's plants, she downloaded the photographs onto her computer and looked through them one by one. She planned to choose the best of the lot to replace the missing family photo on her bookshelf. She halted when she saw the single shot that contained her image. Emilio had captured the dizzying expanse of sky around her and her slim figure mirrored in the water beneath her feet. In the frame, Annalisa looked right back at the viewer, her gaze unyielding. On her face was a ghost of a smile, like a weak sun breaking through the January clouds. *Almost,* she thought, *like the* Mona Lisa.

On a whim, she uploaded the picture to her photo-sharing account.

Enter a caption, it suggested to her. She thought for a minute and wrote: *I never thought I'd see myself here without you.*

She sat back on the sofa and regarded the photo on her laptop. She would use this one for her bookshelf, she decided. A moment later, her computer dinged. Despite the fact that she had zero followers, someone noticed her picture. A little heart appeared, and next to it, a name: Colin Duffy. She hurriedly clicked over to his account. The latest post, dated two hours ago, said he was still in Italy, more than three thousand miles away. Gone, yes. But maybe not for good.

ACKNOWLEDGMENTS

Books have one name on the front but dozens who make it happen, and I am fortunate to have the best people on my team. I am ever grateful for the fabulous folks at Minotaur Books, especially my terrific and supportive editor, Daniela Rapp, but also Kelley Ragland, Cassidy Graham, Kayla Janas, and Danielle Prielipp.

Thanks also to my agent, Jill Marsal, who provides quick answers and steady guidance whenever I need it.

Writing can be a lonely pursuit where you have to give birth to an entire universe, but I am lucky enough to have a crackerjack beta squad to share the experience. They offer advice, encouragement, criticism, and daily hilarity. Thank you to Katie Bradley, Stacie Brooks, Rony Camille, Ethan Cusick, Rayshell Reddick Daniels, Jason Grenier, Suzanne Holliday, Shannon Howl, Robbie McGraw, Michelle Kiefer, Rebecca Gullotti LeBlanc, Jill Svihovec, Dawn Volkart, Amanda Wilde, and Paula Woolman. Special thanks to Suzanne Magnuson for Chicago beta assistance this time around.

I am blessed to have the kind of parents who will carry my book around in a bookstore and show it off to customers. I think it's resulted in exactly one sale, but it's the cutest darn thing. Love you, Brian and Stephanie Schaffhausen. As a bonus, I got the kind of in-laws who show up to my book launches even in terrible New England winter weather, and they even bring friends. Love you, too, Larry and Cherry Rooney.

As ever, my deep thanks to the family that lives with me and supports me through all things, my husband, Garrett Rooney, and daughter, Eleanor. Most people would not love a summer vacation to Chicago that featured photographing police headquarters and walking the streets near O'Hare, but you endured it with good humor. Love you to the moon and back.

Finally, thanks to my basset hound, Winston, who got off my lap long enough for me to complete this book. If you happen to find any stray hairs in your copy, he's the reason why.